Jessica Matthews gr... where reading was ... romances and adve... textbooks and resear... technologist, but her love for microscopes and test tubes didn't diminish her passion for storytelling. Having her first book accepted for publication was a dream come true and now, she has written thirty books for Mills & Boon.

Jennie Lucas's parents owned a bookstore and she grew up surrounded by books, dreaming about faraway lands. At twenty-two she met her future husband and after their marriage, she graduated from university with a degree in English. She started writing books a year later. Jennie won the Romance Writers of America's Golden Heart contest in 2005 and hasn't looked back since. Visit Jennie's website at: jennielucas.com

Previously a teacher, pig farmer, and builder (among other things), **Meredith Webber** turned to writing medical romances when she decided she needed a new challenge. Once committed to giving it a 'real' go she joined writers' groups, attended conferences and read every book on writing she could find. Teaching a romance writing course helped her to analyse what she does, and she believes it has made her a better writer. Readers can email Meredith at: mem@onthenet.com.au

Passion in Paradise

June 2022
Stolen Moments

September 2022
Sunset Proposals

July 2022
Second Chances

October 2022
Holiday Fling

August 2022
Stranded and Seduced

November 2022
Caribbean Escapes

Passion in Paradise:
Second
Chances

JESSICA MATTHEWS

JENNIE LUCAS

MEREDITH WEBBER

MILLS & BOON

First Published in Great Britain 2022
By Mills & Boon, an imprint of HarperCollins*Publishers,* Ltd
1 London Bridge Street, London, SE1 9GF

www.harpercollins.co.uk

HarperCollins*Publishers*
1st Floor, Watermarque Building,
Ringsend Road, Dublin 4, Ireland

ISBN 978-0-263-30561-6

SIX-WEEK
MARRIAGE MIRACLE

JESSICA MATTHEWS

To Judi Fennell for her Spanish-language expertise.
Any errors are my own.

To adoptive and foster parents across the world.
Your generous spirit is truly an inspiration to
all of us.

CHAPTER ONE

"ANOTHER ambulance is coming."

Leah Montgomery didn't spare her nursing colleague a glance as she stripped the used hospital sheets from the bed. "Tell me something I don't already know," she said wryly. "The moon was full when we came to work this morning."

Although it wasn't a scientific fact, hospital staff the world over recognized and accepted that full-moon shifts were the proverbial shifts from hell. So far, this was shaping up to be one of them. Everything from car wrecks, heart attacks, lawn mower accidents, and simple sore throats had flooded the Spring Valley ER on this hot August day.

While many of her staff bemoaned the extra workload, she didn't mind the increased pace at all. Being busy kept her mind off things she didn't want to think about—things like her husband's plane crashing in the Mexican jungle a month ago today. Or the report stating that there were no survivors, which meant Gabe was dead.

Dead!

After four painfully long weeks, it still seemed surreal, as if she might wake up some morning and discover she'd simply had a horrible nightmare. To her disappointment, each day was like the one before—the facts hadn't changed overnight. Neither did they change when she worked until she was too exhausted to reflect on the losses in her life.

If her boss would allow it, she'd cover more shifts than her PRN status allowed in order to keep her demons at bay. She was willing to do *anything* to stay busy until time took away the anguish over her last conversation with Gabe—the one where she'd asked to make their separation permanent with a divorce.

Some might call her crazy, others might say she was being silly and sentimental, but the truth was, she was mourning for Gabe on so many levels. Grieving that his vibrant life had been cut short at age thirty-eight; grieving that their marriage had reached an impasse; grieving for the loss of their dreams and missed opportunities. Was it any wonder she needed the fast pace of the hospital, the steady stream of new patients and drama as a life raft she could climb aboard?

"I hear Maternity is swamped," Jane rattled on, blithely unaware of Leah's inattention. "They're so packed with new moms, they're overflowing into the med-surg unit." She unfolded a fresh sheet and began tucking the corners under the mattress.

Leah pictured a nursery filled with bassinets of sleeping babies wearing pink or blue stocking hats, the hallway crowded with beaming fathers and proud grandparents while new mothers, some having already forgotten the pain of childbirth, looked on benevolently. She didn't begrudge the new families their happiness, but a familiar pang of disappointment shot through her chest.

At one time, she'd imagined herself in similar circumstances, with her parents waiting for their first peek at her child while Gabe passed out the bubblegum cigars and strutted as only a new father could. She'd fallen pregnant almost immediately after they'd decided it was time to start their family, making that dream seem like a sure thing and easily within her grasp. In her mind, and Gabe's, the future couldn't have been brighter.

Life, however, had rewritten her beautifully scripted scene.

Instead of joining the ranks of other new mothers, she'd become one of a small percentage of women who became a gynecological emergency. Shortly after entering her last trimester of an unremarkable pregnancy, her placenta had separated without warning. She'd lost the baby as well as her hopes for future children when profuse and unstoppable bleeding had necessitated a hysterectomy. Afterwards, she'd been whisked away to the surgical floor where babies weren't seen or heard.

Her parents had been there for her, of course, but pity, not pride, had shown on their faces. As for Gabe…he'd been on one of his occasional trips for the Montgomery family's medical foundation. He'd come as soon as her parents had called him, but time zones and flight schedules had prevented his return until the day she was ready to be released.

"I just love to stop and peek at the newborns," Jane gushed. "They have such cute little wrinkled faces." Suddenly, she stopped short. "Oh, Leah. Here I am, babbling on so insensitively about babies after everything you've been through. First a miscarriage, then the adoption fiasco—"

Leah cut off her friend's reminder of their failed foray into the world of adoption. After her surgery, still hazy from the grief of her loss, Gabe had convinced her to think about adoption and then so many things had fallen into place with amazing speed—Gabe's lawyer had known a young woman who'd wanted to relinquish her baby. They'd hurriedly filled out the necessary paperwork and completed the required governmental home studies and background checks. The entire time the birth mother had been adamant about her choice— she was making the right decision for both her and her unborn child. Yet when the hour arrived for Leah and Gabe to pick up the baby from the hospital, the young woman had changed her mind and Leah had once again driven home empty-handed.

Leah couldn't fault the girl for her change of heart—it had to be difficult to relinquish one's child, especially after seeing that tiny person for the first time—but understanding didn't take away her gut-wrenching disappointment.

"It's okay," she lied. "I don't fall apart just because someone talks about babies or mentions how cute they are."

Admittedly, they were, but seeing those adorable little faces was tough, which was why she never, *ever*, entered the secured area to stare at them through the plate-glass window. Why add insult to injury? she'd rationalized.

"I know, but—"

"It's okay," Leah repeated, as much for her own benefit as Jane's. "Honestly."

Jane nodded, but the worried wrinkle between her eyes suggested her good-mood bubble had burst. Determined to regain their easy footing, Leah thought it best to gently steer the conversation in another direction, for both their sakes.

"OB isn't the only busy department in this place," she commented as she tucked a fitted sheet around a corner of the mattress. "Our daily patient census is above average across the entire hospital and we both know our ED visit numbers are up, too. The extra business should make the bean counters happy."

"Maybe this year we'll get a Christmas bonus for a job well done," Jane responded hopefully.

Word from the last supervisors' meeting was that the possibility was remote, but Leah wasn't going to rain on Jane's picnic. "Maybe, but, bonus or not, more patients means more nursing staff are necessary, which means I work more often."

Jane paused from working on her own two bed corners. "Look, hon," she said kindly. "I know you're probably feeling guilty because you'd never resolved your differences with Gabe, but killing yourself now that he's gone, working sixty-plus hours a week, isn't the way to cope."

"I'm not killing myself," Leah protested mildly, pointedly ignoring Jane's opinion about her reasons for the pace she'd set for herself. "I'm merely keeping busy. Just like I have for the past year."

"Keeping busy is one thing. Doubling your hours is another."

"Okay, so I am working a few more hours," Leah conceded reluctantly, "but I was off duty yesterday and I spent the day puttering around the house. And then I treated myself to dinner and a movie."

"Dinner *and* a movie?" Jane's eyes brimmed with curiosity. "Did you *finally* put Jeff out of his misery and go on a *date*?"

About six months ago, Dr. Jeff Warren, one of Spring Valley's ED physicians, had invited her to a concert, then a community theater play. Both times she'd declined, not because she didn't enjoy his company or didn't want to attend those particular events. No, she'd gently refused his invitation because in spite of being separated from her husband of ten years, going out with another man while she was still officially married made her feel as if she was cheating.

Which was why she'd wanted Gabe's signature on those divorce papers. It was past time to stop expecting a miracle and start thinking about the future—*her* future—instead of the past. As it had turned out, she didn't need his signature after all.

Leah shot her friend a spare-me look. "Are you kidding?" she asked. "I haven't even buried Gabe and you're asking if I'm seeing Jeff?"

"Buried or not, you've been separated for over a year," Jane reminded her. "It's time to move on."

"I will," Leah promised. "But I can't until I've dotted all my 'i's and crossed all the 't's."

Jane rolled her eyes. "What's left to dot and cross? From what you've said, his body may never come home."

How well she knew that. The Mexican authorities had reported the discovery of the airplane's charred remains in a ravine. They lacked the resources to recover the bodies and in their bureaucratic minds the burned-out shell of the aircraft made it pointless to do so. Undaunted, and after greasing palms for several weeks, Gabe's second-in-command Sheldon Redfern had received permission to send in a private recovery team. As of yesterday, they hadn't reported any more encouraging news than what the authorities had already shared.

Their success, however, wasn't the reason she was dragging her feet...

"The annual foundation fund-raiser is coming up in a few months," she pointed out. "It seems tacky to plan a tribute to my deceased husband while I'm dating someone else." Their relationship may have been rocky the last two years and she might be finally ready to look for male companionship and find romance again, but in honor of the good times and the love they'd once shared, she owed it to Gabe to wait.

"Did you tell that to Jeff?"

She nodded, remembering their conversation. He'd been so understanding, which not only came as a relief but also endeared him to her all the more. "He's agreed to give me time," she said, deciding not to mention that she'd set their first official date for the Saturday night after the fundraiser. If Jane knew that, she'd be bouncing off the walls with excitement and Leah didn't want to see her sly smiles and winks in the meantime.

Jane stared at her thoughtfully. "Personally, I think you're worried too much about what other people think, but another month or two won't make much difference. Just be sure your decision to stay out of the dating game is based on the right reasons."

"What other reason could I have?"

Jane shrugged. "Oh, I don't know. Maybe that you still love Gabe and are waiting for the ultimate proof that he won't be coming back."

"Don't be ridiculous." She avoided her friend's gaze because she didn't want Jane to recognize what she herself refused to dwell on or admit. "If I loved him, why would I have moved out?"

"You tell me. I just don't want you to be stuck on hold for the rest of your life."

"I'm not," Leah insisted. "I'm merely being cautious. There's no sense rushing into something I might come to regret." She grabbed a fresh cotton blanket and shook it out of its folds with a decisive snap, effectively signaling an end to their conversation. "Do you know what's coming in next?"

Jane shook her head. "All I heard was that they were bringing in three from the airport."

"The airport?" She considered for a moment. "Bigwigs, no doubt."

"What makes you say that?"

"It's probably food related and the only folks who get food on a plane are seated in first class. And who usually can afford to sit in first class?"

"Ah." Jane's eyes gleamed. "Bigwigs."

"Exactly."

"You're stereotyping, you know. Regular people buy first-class tickets, too."

Leah flashed her a wide smile. "Okay, so I'm generalizing but, mark my words, it won't be three average Joes who roll into our ambulance bay. They'll be fellows wearing suits and ties, carrying briefcases and BlackBerrys, and wanting a magic pill to fix whatever ails them. Oh, and can we hurry because they're already late for a meeting."

Jane laughed, probably because Leah's scenario had actually taken place often enough to become a legend in the ER. "We'll find out if you're right in about three minutes. Marge wants us to be on the dock, ready to go."

As the emergency department's nurse manager, Marge Pennington was a person who believed in keeping busy every minute, so it seemed odd she would ask them to waste time waiting. Her request only seemed to substantiate Leah's prediction of several Very Important People arriving on this transport.

"Far be it from me to argue," she said, although it bothered her to think Marge was willing to discard her normal habits in order to impress people with money. Having married into a family with the Midas touch, Leah had always been leery of people who didn't treat her as they would anyone else.

"According to her, the person radioing in specifically asked for you."

Leah's eyes widened. "Me? Why me?"

Jane shrugged. "Maybe it's someone you know from Gabe's trust organization."

Leah mentally ran through her list of regularly generous contributors to the Montgomery Medical Charitable Foundation. As chairwoman of the annual fund-raising ball, which would take place in six weeks, she was acquainted with nearly all of the supporters, but none knew she worked in the Spring Valley Hospital Emergency Department.

"Impossible," she said.

Jane shrugged. "Who knows? In any case, I'm only following Marge's orders and if you know what's good for you, you will, too."

Marge wasn't the easiest charge nurse to work for, but she was a model of efficiency and a brilliant nurse. No one, not even the hospital's CEO, crossed her when she was in battle mode.

Leah gave the bed a final pat, pleased with their results. "Okay, then. Let's go. I can use a few minutes of fresh air while we're waiting." She grinned. "Just think, we might even get to sit and rest our weary feet."

Outside, Leah did exactly as she'd hoped to. Ignoring Jane and the two extra staff who'd joined them with wheelchairs and an extra stretcher, she sat on the concrete loading dock and dangled her legs over the edge as she breathed in the fresh air and soaked up the heat.

If only the summer sun would chase away the coldness inside her—the same coldness that had settled into every cell, the same coldness that had taken hold ever since she'd realized Gabe's plane had gone down with her request for a divorce ringing in his ears.

She'd agonized for weeks over taking their separation to its logical conclusion before she'd contacted a lawyer, but they'd lived apart for nearly a year. After the adoption had fallen through, they'd simply shut down. It was understandable, she supposed. They'd been obsessed with the baby when she'd been pregnant, and then they'd focused exclusively on adopting a child. Their marriage had been so driven toward that end goal that their sudden failure had simply sidelined their relationship.

Consequently they'd drifted apart until the only solution had been to ask for a change of scenery. She'd wanted time and space to redefine what she wanted out of life and, more importantly, she wanted Gabe to have the same.

A year later, she'd finally faced the facts. Remaining in their legal limbo wasn't doing either of them any favors. They both needed the freedom to pursue their dreams—she wanted companionship and Gabe wanted a family. Although she hated the idea of Gabe finding a woman who could give him what she couldn't, it had seemed silly, selfish and almost spiteful to keep him from his heart's desire. With the stroke of a judge's pen, they would end their estranged state and could move on with their lives. To start over, as it were.

In the end, her altruistic decision had been wasted. Fate had stepped in and had the last laugh at their expense before he could sign the papers dissolving their marriage. Before he'd created the family he'd always wanted.

Since then, she'd told herself on a daily basis to stop beating herself over everything from procrastinating to her bad timing. After all, divorced or widowed, she was still alone.

Alone or not, though, it pained her to imagine what final thoughts had run through Gabe's head. No doubt his last one of her had involved the unpleasant scene when she'd asked for a divorce. Some would say she was being too hard on herself. Others would say she was worrying over nothing. After all, if she wanted to completely sever their matrimonial ties, why did she care what his last thoughts of her had been?

In one corner of her heart, she'd wanted Gabe to realize their marriage needed as much attention as he gave his family's charitable foundation, but if he'd entertained any regrets during his final moments, she'd never know. Chances were, she repeated to herself for the millionth time, he hadn't thought of her at all…

Jane straightened, her gaze riveted in the distance. "Looks

like they're about two blocks away." She glanced at her watch. "Right on time, too."

Leah slowly got to her feet then brushed the seat of her scrub pants. "I wish we knew what we were getting," she fretted.

"We'll find out soon enough."

A black Lexus squealed to an abrupt stop in the aisle of the parking lot. Apparently the driver didn't care about the traffic snarl he'd created.

"Security is going to eat him alive," Leah commented.

"Maybe you should tell him."

The ambulance pulled in and began backing up to the dock, its warning beeps intermingling with the other city noises. "He'll have to take his chances," Leah said. "We have things to do and people to see."

As the ambulance inched backwards, Leah heard someone call her name. A familiar figure, Sheldon Redfern had jumped out of the Lexus and was running toward her.

"Leah," he panted. "Wait!"

"Sheldon, what are you doing here?" she asked, amazed to see him.

"I have to tell you—"

The ambulance braked. "Save it for later," she ordered. "I'm busy right now."

"This can't wait."

He grabbed her arm at the same time she saw Jane twisting the handle to open the back door. "Sheldon," she protested. "I have work to do."

"Leah," he urged. "It's about Gabe and the search team we sent."

Instinctively, her heart sank. Sheldon's eagerness to contact her only meant one thing.

"They finally located his remains," she said dully, feeling her chest tighten and a painful knot clog her throat as her eyes dimmed with sudden tears. For all the problems they'd had, she hadn't wanted anything so drastic and so *final* to happen to him. Yes, a divorce was like a death—the death of a marriage—but part of her consolation had been that they each would carry on and eventually find the happiness they couldn't find with each other.

Unfortunately, Sheldon's announcement had irrevocably destroyed that thin hope. Why had he felt compelled to deliver the news now, *at this very moment*, with patients breathing down her neck, when she wasn't mentally prepared to deal with the finality of the situation?

"No," Sheldon corrected in her ear.

"No?" She stared at him in surprise.

"What he's trying to say unsuccessfully is that they found *us*." Sheldon's voice suddenly sounded closer…and deeper… and more like…Gabe's.

And it was coming from inside the ambulance.

She focused in that direction, ignoring the paramedic to glance at the human cargo—two men and a woman. They looked tired and dirty in clothing that was tattered and torn, but broad smiles shone on their faces. An uncanny sense of familiarity struck her.

In spite of their gaunt and disreputable appearance, she *knew* all three. Yet her brain couldn't reconcile what she was seeing with what she'd been told.

She homed in on the man who'd spoken. He was just as dirty as the other two and equally as disheveled. His right pants leg had been cut open at some point but in spite of being tied closed with strips of gauze, she glimpsed a white bandage circling his shin. A splint encased his left forearm and another bandage was visible above the open neck of his torn shirt. But there was no denying that this man was Gabe.

"I tried calling you all morning," Sheldon babbled in the background as the identities of Gabe's colleagues— Jack Kasold and Theresa Hernandez—registered before they stepped onto the concrete. "You never answered my messages."

The pink scraps of paper tucked in her tunic pocket suddenly weighed like the proverbial ton of bricks. She'd ignored them when she'd seen who'd phoned because she'd assumed he simply wanted to hash out more details for the foundation's upcoming charity ball. Apparently, she'd been wrong.

"I was going to call you during my break," she said numbly as she looked past all the people to study her husband once again.

Tape bisected his forehead, his beard was scruffy, his hair shaggy, and lines of apparent pain bracketed his full mouth, but his midnight-black eyes were so familiar.

Could it be true? Really *true*? Her heart skipped a beat as she feared she might be hallucinating and hoped she was not.

"Gabe?" she finally asked, aware of how thin and reedy her voice sounded.

He stepped out of the ambulance, balancing himself on one crutch. His reassuring smile was one she'd seen before—the same one that belonged to the man she'd married when their future had been bright and it had seemed as if nothing could stop them from living their dreams.

"Hi, honey. I'm home."

CHAPTER TWO

UNCERTAIN of the reception he'd receive when he finally saw Leah again, Gabriel's tension had escalated with each mile closer to his destination. Considering how Sheldon hadn't been able to reach her all morning, Gabe had expected her to be surprised and shocked by his astonishing return and she didn't disappoint him.

"Gabe?" she whispered in that soft voice he remembered so vividly. "Is it really *you*?"

He met her gaze and offered a rueful smile. "A little the worse for wear but, yes, it is."

"Oh, my." She covered her mouth with both hands. Suddenly, she turned pale and a dazed look came to her eyes.

She was going to faint. Cursing because he wasn't in a position to catch her himself, he roared, "Sheldon!"

Fortunately, his second-in-command was beside her and grabbed her arm. At the same time the paramedic did the same. For an instant she sagged, then straightened and shrugged off the two men's hold.

"I'm okay," she insisted, losing a bit of her deer-caught-in-the-headlights look.

"Are you sure?" The paramedic didn't sound convinced as he eyed her closely.

"I'm fine. Really."

Of course she was, Gabe thought wryly. Leah thrived on her ability to handle anything and everything by herself, without help from anyone. In fact, at times he'd felt rather superfluous in their marriage, but he intended to change all that.

"Truly," she insisted, tentatively reaching toward him.

Eager to touch her and prove just how wrong the reports of his death had been, as well as to reassure himself that he was truly home, Gabe grabbed her hand.

Her skin was soft and warm and soothingly familiar. Oh, how he'd missed her!

Before he could say a word, before he could do anything but entwine his fingers with hers, she flung herself against him and buried her face in his shoulder.

His crutch clattered to the concrete and his ribs protested, but having her in his arms where she belonged was worth the pain. When his plane had landed and Leah hadn't been standing with Jack's and Theresa's elated families on the tarmac, he'd been so afraid...but this was the response he'd dreamed of and hoped for every night they'd been lost in the jungle.

The coldness of despair, the survivor's guilt, and the soul-racking regret that he'd labored under for weeks now began to diminish until he slowly felt warm from the inside out.

His wife's fresh, clean scent filled his nostrils and reminded him of how desperately he needed soap and water. If he'd been thinking properly, he might have asked Sheldon to detour to his corporate offices where he could have made use of the executive washroom, but he'd been too eager to see Leah to consider it. Quite frankly, though, with his stiff shoulder and the slow-healing gash on his leg, he wasn't sure he could manage the feat on his own, anyway.

He gripped her with his good arm, feeling her slight frame shake beneath his hand. As her tears soaked his shirt, his throat tightened and his eyes burned with more emotion than he could begin to describe.

"Oh, honey. Don't cry," he said hoarsely, relieved by her reception and grateful the paramedics and ER staff were giving them a few minutes before they whisked him away.

"I'm not," she sniffed, swiping at the moisture on her cheeks as she stared at him. "Oh, Gabe. I can't believe it."

As he gazed at her, one thought ran through his mind. She was beautiful—more beautiful than the picture he'd slipped out of his wallet and stuck in his shirt pocket shortly after they'd crashed. The photo was now dog-eared and a little dirty, but her image had given him the incentive to keep going when he'd sworn he couldn't hobble another step.

"I can't quite believe it, either," he said ruefully. As far as he was concerned, this was a dream come true. A bona fide miracle.

More importantly, it was a miracle he wasn't going to let slip through his fingers.

"What happened?" she asked.

"It's a long story." Rather than dwell on that fateful day and the events leading up to it, he drank in everything about her, from her acorn-colored hair and eyes that reminded him of the Grand Canyon's various shades of brown to her retroussé nose and sensual mouth. She'd lost weight, too, if his hands hadn't deceived him.

The paramedic stepped close to interrupt. "I don't mean to cut short your reunion, Dr. Montgomery, but let's get you inside before you fall."

Whether she suddenly realized how heavily he was leaning against her or the paramedic's statement had reminded her of his injuries, his prim and proper wife—and she still *was* his wife, even if they'd lived apart for the last twelve months—unwrapped herself from him and took his good arm. Although he missed her embrace, he was glad she hadn't completely turned him loose. Granted, she'd fallen back into nurse mode, but he wanted to believe she needed the contact as much as he did to reassure herself that he was, indeed, alive and well.

Maybe not "well", he corrected as he lowered himself into a hastily provided wheelchair, but his aches and pains now seemed inconsequential. For the past month he'd fought his fears of failure—fears that the feelings she'd once had for him were gone—but he took heart that she hadn't rejected him. In the nightmares that had often startled him awake, he'd dreamt she'd take one look at him and walk away. Thankfully, none of those painfully vivid dreams had come true.

They still had issues to resolve but he was cautiously optimistic about success. If he played his cards right—and he intended to because he'd had a month to plan a strategy—there wouldn't be any more talk of a divorce. Fate had given him a second chance to correct his mistakes and undo the past. He would not fail.

Leah wanted to ask a hundred questions, but Gabe's slumped shoulders as she walked beside his wheelchair told her how exhausted he was. In all the years she'd known him, she'd never seen him so drained, even during his residency when forty-eight-hour shifts had been the norm. There would be plenty of time to hear his story after his medical needs were addressed—starting with how he'd survived a supposedly fatal accident.

It wasn't until he'd gingerly moved from his wheelchair to the bed with her help and that of a paramedic that she realized the awkwardness of the situation. As a nurse she belonged in the room, but as his estranged wife she certainly didn't. Unfortunately, by the time she'd come to that conclusion, the other nurses had already disappeared into their respective patients' rooms, leaving her no choice but to continue. Asking for a reassignment now would only draw unwanted and unnecessary attention. As soon as word leaked of Gabe's return, speculation would run rampant anyway.

In spite of resigning herself to her temporary fate, her awkwardness grew exponentially as Jeff Warren took that moment to walk into the room. The normally implacable blond physician stopped abruptly in his tracks, as if he hadn't realized the identity of his patient until now. Immediately, he glanced back at Leah and she shrugged helplessly, realizing that this moment was as uncomfortable for him as it was for her. The only difference was Jeff seemed to recover more quickly from his surprise than she had.

"Gabe," he said, reaching out to shake his hand. "Welcome back."

"Thanks. It's great to be home."

"I'll do my best to get you there," Jeff promised. "Let's have a look at what you've done to yourself, shall we?"

Leah had planned to act as usual, giving Gabe the same objective care she'd give any other patient. However, that was easier said than done. The minute he shrugged off his tattered shirt, she saw the physical evidence of what he'd endured. His bones stood out in stark relief to the scabbed-over scrapes and large, brilliantly colored patches of purple, yellow and green that dotted his skin, while other areas were rubbed raw.

"Oh, Gabe," she breathed.

"It looks worse than it is," he assured her.

Objectively speaking, he was probably right, but through the eyes of someone who'd once carefully and lovingly mapped every inch of his six-foot body, she wasn't as certain. It became far too easy to imagine how he'd earned each scrape and each bruise and then marvel at how he'd endured the trauma and still returned home. His obvious weight loss made her wonder what he'd eaten, if anything, which was another facet of his ordeal she hadn't considered until now.

Part of her wanted to hug him again, to erase those physical hurts with a soft and gentle touch. The other part of her wanted to rail at him, ask if his injuries had been worth those extra duties he'd assumed and the additional trips he'd taken on behalf of his family's charitable organization.

More importantly, though, she wanted to lock herself in the restroom so she could cry because, however illogical it seemed, she somehow felt responsible—not for the crash itself, or even for this particularly fateful international jaunt, but for sending him into the ever-eager arms of the Montgomery Medical Foundation. Had she not rejected his comfort after their adoption had fallen through, he wouldn't have found his purpose in his work. With the schedule he'd set for himself, both before their separation and after, it was almost amazing that disaster hadn't struck before now.

Regardless of where she laid blame or how she took responsibility, what mattered most for now was the state of Gabe's health, not rehashing the mistakes or hurts of the past.

"Leah?"

Hearing her name, she pulled her thoughts together and met Jeff's questioning gaze. He was obviously reading more into her inattentiveness than she wanted.

"Maybe you should take a break," he suggested softly.

She was tempted to take his advice, but she'd never deserted a patient before and she wouldn't start now. She shook her head and squared her shoulders. "I'm fine. Really."

Jeff simply shrugged, then listened to Gabe's chest sounds as he spoke. "You still have some nasty injuries. What did you do? Hit every tree in the jungle?"

"It seemed like it," Gabe mentioned ruefully. "I picked up about half of my bruises and bumps during the crash. Splitting my leg open came later."

"What happened?"

"In regard to my leg or the crash itself?"

"Both."

Curious about the details surrounding his experience, Leah listened closely.

"Minutes before we crashed, there was a thump, then an engine sputtered, and Ramon yelled something about birds. The next thing I knew, we were going down." He paused. "When it was all over, I had a dislocated shoulder and a bad wrist. Jack relocated the bone and immobilized my arm with the supplies out of our first-aid kit. Then we went to find help."

Leah tried not to imagine the pain he must have endured while Jack had worked on his shoulder without any anesthetic. As an internist, Jack's basic orthopedic skills were no doubt rusty, but he would have had to proceed because the potential complications like a lack of blood supply and damaged nerves were too serious to ignore. As she surreptitiously studied Gabe's fingers, the pink skin color and lack of swelling were reassuring signs of his success.

"Needless to say, it took us a while to find another human being," he added wryly, "although, technically, a few locals found us when they stumbled across our path. We stayed in their village overnight but before they took us to the next town, the search team had tracked us there. And here we are."

"You're lucky they found you at all," Leah interjected. "We were told you were dead." Thank goodness Sheldon had persisted with cutting through the red tape to send in their own team. If they'd accepted the official verdict and let matters lie... the idea of Gabe and his colleagues still wandering through the jungle sent a chill down her spine.

"I'm not surprised the authorities assumed the worst," Gabe said, his voice pained. "We'd stopped inches away from a ravine and thought we were on safe ground. Not long afterwards, the ground gave way and the plane slid over the edge. On its way down, the fuel tanks blew."

Mentally picturing the scene, Leah shuddered as her grip tightened on the blood-pressure cuff she was still holding.

"You three are celebrities now," Jeff remarked. "Not many people walk away from an experience like that."

Gabe's face became stoic, his expression shuttered. "Two of my group didn't."

"Who?" she asked, hating it that not everyone associated with Montgomery Medical would have a happy ending.

"Will. Will Henderson, and Ramon."

Will was an information technology guru Gabe had hired about eighteen months ago to facilitate the internet connections between remote medical clinics and hospitals to specialists at centers like Spring Valley. Leah had met him a few times but had never had any dealings with him.

Ramon Diaz, however, was a man she knew quite well. As the first pilot Gabe had ever hired and the organization's most senior pilot, Ramon had usually taken charge of Gabe's flights. He'd also begun dating Theresa, one of the foundation's nurses, right before Leah and Gabe had split up, and had recently proposed to her. No doubt they'd both been thrilled to go on this trip together. How sad it had ended so horribly.

"Oh, Gabe," she breathed, knowing how the loss of two people who had been more friends than employees must weigh heavily on him. She dropped the cuff and clutched his hand in sympathy. "Did they…suffer?"

"Will didn't. He died in the crash. Ramon…died later."

Gabe's tight-lipped expression suggested there was a lot more to his story, but she didn't press for details. "I'm sorry, both for you and the company. Theresa must be devastated."

"She's having a tough time," Gabe agreed.

Making a mental note to visit with Theresa as soon as she was able, Leah watched as Jeff unwrapped the bandage around Gabe's leg. The gash was red and swollen, but didn't look nearly as bad as Leah had anticipated.

"I've seen worse," the doctor remarked, apparently agreeing with her opinion. "How long ago did this happen?"

"About ten days. I slid down a hill and bumped into a few rocks along the way. One of them sliced my skin."

"Then it definitely isn't healing as fast as I'd like."

"We cleaned it as best we could but, as you can see, our topical ointment couldn't quite do the job." Gabe winced as his colleague probed the area and his grip on her hand tightened. "Sutures might have helped, but those weren't available, either."

Leah wasn't fooled by his innocent tone or his condensed version of events. He could probably talk for hours about their struggle for the things she took for granted—food, water, protection from the elements and safety from predators. And he'd definitely had a difficult time because his clothing appeared as if he'd walked through a shredder.

As for his injuries, he'd made them sound as if they were nothing more than minor inconveniences when they were visible proof of his harrowing ordeal. Cracked ribs and a dislocated shoulder were painful under ideal conditions and to "slide down a hill and bump into a few rocks" before they'd healed would have been agony. If the truth were known, it wouldn't surprise her to learn that his so-called "hill" could probably compete with Pikes Peak and his "few rocks" had probably been boulders.

She wanted to throttle him for acting as if his stint in the jungle had been as easy and effortless as a Sunday stroll through the city park. Making a big deal out of bumps and bruises, gashes and cracked bones went against his macho grain, even if he was speaking to a physician who recognized what it took to create this degree of damage. There were two females in the room, too, and it wouldn't do to appear weak in front of them. In essence, it was a guy thing—part of that caveman, show-the-woman-who's-strongest mentality.

It was also a Gabe thing. He'd always tried his best to insulate her from the harsh realities of life instead of treating her as a partner in the challenges they faced—and they'd had a number of personal difficulties and tragedies to contend with. Obviously, he still pictured her as being too weak to face the truth. While some women might appreciate being treated like a Fabergé egg, she wasn't one of them. After ten years of marriage, Gabe should have learned that, but he hadn't.

As soon as she recognized the familiar resentment building inside her, she wondered why her former frustrations were rearing their heads again. She should be elated Gabe was home safe and more or less sound and not dredging up old complaints. Her only excuse was that she could finally give herself permission to be angry about his decision to take this flight in the first place.

Yet, however one might psychoanalyze her reaction, Gabe's return didn't wipe their slate of problems clean. They still had to be addressed in some manner and the easiest and most expedient method was to get his signature on those divorce documents, wherever they currently were.

Realizing her fingers were still entwined with his, she pulled her hand free.

Jeff's gaze was speculative as he glanced at her. He'd clearly noticed how her touch had lingered longer than was actually necessary, but he didn't comment. Instead, he finished his exam and tucked his stethoscope back into his pocket with deliberate movements.

"All things considered," he said, "you're not in too bad a shape." He paused ever so slightly as his gaze slid sideways to Leah and then back to Gabe. "You're a lucky fellow in more ways than one."

"You don't have to remind me," Gabe answered fervently.

A meaningful note in his tone made Leah question if the two men were discussing Gabe's health or if this was some sort of private male discussion, but before she could wade into the conversation, Jeff fell back into his professional mode.

"You've probably diagnosed yourself, but I want X-rays to check your ribs and your arm as well as basic bloodwork and cultures. To be honest, I'm not happy with the way your leg is healing, so prepare yourself for a few rounds of IV antibiotics." He glanced at Leah. "I want those started immediately."

Considering the state of Gabe's leg, Jeff's treatment plan was not only sound, it was necessary to stop the infection from turning septic. Without a word, she began pulling the appropriate IV supplies from the cabinet.

Gabe sighed audibly, as if he also knew the IV was necessary but wasn't particularly happy about it. "I'd expected as much."

"I'm glad we agree. After I see the films and lab results, we'll talk again."

"Any chance I can shower in the doctors' lounge before you run me through the testing mill?" Gabe's expression was hopeful. He might be the full-time CEO of the Montgomery Medical Foundation but he was also a member of the surgical staff at Spring Valley Memorial and, as such, he filled in a few nights a month and the occasional weekend when the regular surgeons took time off.

"Of course," Jeff agreed, "but if we delay your tests, we also delay your treatment. So let's do the cultures, blood samples and X-rays first, then by the time you finish your shower, we'll have answers and can decide what comes next."

Knowing how Gabe hated to compromise, Leah expected him to argue, but to her surprise, he didn't. "Okay. If it means I'll get out of here sooner, we'll do it your way."

Jeff grinned. "I'm glad to hear it. While you're stuck in Radiology, I'll see about arranging for first-class bathroom accommodations." He turned to Leah. "He's all yours for now."

It was a throw-away statement, a figure of speech, but she wondered if his qualifier referred to tending Gabe's injuries or if it had more personal overtones. Because it was far easier to fall back on the comforting routine of following a doctor's orders, she did so, determined to leave the soul-searching for later when her mind had stopped reeling.

Thank goodness experience allowed her to perform her tasks without thinking as she still considered Gabe's return as nothing short of miraculous. Thankfully, and perhaps Jeff had alerted Marge to the situation, Jane came in to help.

"Stay," Gabe said when Leah tried to escape, and so she did, but by the time he'd finished the lab draws and X-rays, his face was white and pinched with pain. Clearly, he was in desperate need of rest.

"I think the shower should wait," she began.

His jaw squared. "No way."

"Not even until you've napped a few hours?"

"Not even then."

Seeing how unsteady he was on his feet, she offered, "How about a sponge bath instead?"

His eyes lit with an unholy gleam before it faded. "As intriguing as that sounds, I want a shower that lasts until I empty the hot water tanks. I *need* a shower because I'm tired of smelling myself."

"You smell fresher than some patients who've walked through our doors," she replied.

"Too bad. I know what I want and I want water. Gallons and gallons of it."

"But you can hardly—"

His gaze was determined. "Trust me. I can and *will* do whatever I have to."

She wanted him to be reasonable and take her advice, but if he'd found the fortitude to survive the jungle, he'd find the energy reserves to shower. However, as both his nurse and his wife, she'd watch to ensure he didn't over-extend himself.

"You always were stubborn," she remarked.

He nodded. "I'll take that as a compliment."

"Well, hang tight while I see what I can arrange."

After a short consultation in the hallway where she couldn't speak privately to Jeff because Jane was part of their group, Leah wheeled Gabe to the nearby med-surg wing and into a patient room. She expected him to protest at the obvious implication, but he was too intent on his prize and didn't.

While he brushed his teeth with the spare toiletry kit she'd commandeered from their supply cabinet, she located towels and soap so he could finally indulge in his much-wanted and much-needed shower in the wheelchair-accessible bathroom.

After removing his splint—the X-ray had shown the bones in his arm and shoulder weren't broken—she covered his IV site with plastic so it wouldn't get wet.

"I'll be out here if you need me," she told him. "Be careful with your leg and when you're finished, I'll dress it."

While he hobbled into the shower, she turned down his bed and double-checked the medications that Jane had delivered. When she had everything in place except for her patient, she returned to the bathroom and stood in the doorway.

"How are you doing in there?" She raised her voice over the rushing water, noting he'd had at least a seven-minute shower.

"Fine." A groan came from behind the curtain.

That didn't sound good. Instantly worried, she straightened, ready to invade his privacy. "Are you okay?"

"Yeah. God, this feels so good."

The awe in his voice reminded her of other times when

he'd said the same, under more intimate circumstances. She quickly stuffed those thoughts inside her mental box labeled "to be opened at a later date". "I'm sure it does, but Jeff wants those antibiotics started ASAP."

"Just a few more minutes."

"The shower will still be here, waiting for you, tomorrow," she coaxed.

"I know, but five more minutes. Please."

It seemed cruel to deny him this simple pleasure when those extra minutes probably wouldn't affect his treatment outcome. "Okay, but I'm timing you."

"You're the boss."

If that were only true.

"I'd get done faster if you scrubbed my back for me," he added.

He sounded so hopeful and so like the old Gabe—the Gabe before their lives had drifted apart—that she flashed back to those happier times when they *had* shared a shower. The memory of the subsequent lovemaking burst into her head, but it was more than simple recall. She replayed how it had *felt*—from the sensation of his rough skin against hers, the tickle of his breath and his lips on sensitive areas, his clean, sandalwood scent teasing her nose.

His suggestion was so very tempting...especially when she reflected on their stolen moments during the early days of their relationship. In his position as a surgical resident and hers as a newly minted ED nurse, as long as a deadbolt guarded their privacy, they'd been happy.

Unfortunately, they didn't have a locked door and Gabe had become a celebrity, which meant privacy was impossible. Although those details didn't present an insurmountable problem, making love at this point implied that their personal life was fine and dandy.

And it wasn't.

"Not a good idea," she pointed out.

"Why not?"

"You mean, other than that you're barely able to stand?"

"Yeah."

"This place will be like Grand Central Station before long," she reminded him. "Everyone wants to drop by and give you a personal welcome."

"They can wait. Besides, people will understand if we have a quiet, intimate reunion. They're probably expecting it, which means no one will interrupt us unless there's a fire."

The sad fact was he was probably right. Most people knew they were separated, but no one, other than Jane, knew the D-word had been floated between them. Everyone loved a happy ending, which meant everyone would speculate—if not hope—that Gabe's return would be the turning point in their relationship. Perhaps under other circumstances, it would have been, but their differences were more deep-seated than a conversation or a few promises could fix.

"They can expect all they want, but it isn't going to happen."

His sigh was audible. "I suppose not, but I really would like you to wash my back. I can't reach."

Instantly, she felt ashamed for not realizing how his bruised ribs and stiff shoulder made his request completely valid. Irritated at herself for jumping to the wrong conclusion, she shoved the curtain aside to see her dripping husband struggling to touch those hard-to-reach places.

"Turn around," she ordered, determined to handle her task with clinical detachment. Yet, as she ignored the spray of water on her scrub suit to run a soapy washcloth down his spine and over the lean muscles of his back before moving around to his front, her concern over what he'd endured grew. This wasn't the body of the man she'd last seen a month ago. Oh, the birthmark in the small of his back was the same, as was the general shape of his torso, but while he'd once re-minded her of a lean mountain lion with rock-hard muscles and sinew, now he resembled a starving wolf.

"If you keep that up," he said dryly, "our private reunion will be extremely one-sided."

Realizing she'd come dangerously close to an area of his body where she hadn't intended to go, she froze.

"Although," he added softly, "there's always later."

The promise in his voice sent an unexpected tingle through her body but, then, a mere glance, a simple touch, or a softly spoken word from Gabe had always carried enough power to melt her into a puddle. What truly surprised her was how she could respond so easily in spite of the issues that had driven them apart. Was she so starved for attention and affection that when he showered her with both, she would greedily accept it?

Disliking what her response suggested, she dropped the washcloth over the handrail. "Rinse off. I'll be waiting." Suddenly realizing what she'd said, she clarified. "Outside. I'll be waiting *outside*."

As he laughed, she flung the curtain closed and counted to twenty so Gabe could finish and she could recover her composure.

"Time's up," she called.

He didn't respond.

"Gabe?" she repeated. "Your time is up."

Still no answer.

"Gabe?" Although she hadn't heard a thump or other worrisome noise, his silence raised her concern. She flung back the curtain once again to find him leaning against the tiled wall, his eyes closed, his dark hair dripping.

"I knew it," she scolded as she cranked the taps until the water stopped. "You've stayed in here too long. You're about to fall on your face."

"Maybe, but being clean would be worth it."

CHAPTER THREE

GABE hated feeling weak. For a man whose body had never failed him before, it was a humbling experience to be at less than peak condition. However, if his injuries convinced Leah to give him another chance, he wouldn't complain too loudly.

Although, in spite of his aches and pains, he'd been relieved to discover one part of his body still worked quite well. If he hadn't stopped her from toweling him off like a child, he would have needed a second shower—an ice-cold one.

"I don't suppose I can wear a scrub suit instead of that," he said, eyeing the hospital gown she held out.

"We'd never be able to take care of your leg if you were wearing trousers."

"I could wear a pair of athletic shorts."

"You could," she agreed, "but a pair isn't available at the moment. You're stuck with this for now."

"You could cut off the legs and turn the pants into shorts," he coaxed.

"If you were going to stay a few days, I would, but I suspect you're not, so I won't. Now, stop arguing." She tied the string at the back of his neck then guided him to the nearby bed.

He sank gratefully onto the mattress before he rubbed his face. "Did you bring a razor?"

"Not this trip. Count your blessings for the toothbrush I found. Would you like to sit or lie down?"

"Sit."

She immediately adjusted the bed to accommodate his wishes then pulled the sheet over his good leg, leaving his injured extremity uncovered while she fluffed his pillows. "We'll tackle the beard later. You've done enough for the moment."

He hated to admit she was right, but although his spirit was willing, his flesh was weak. He'd been functioning on adrenalin for too long. Now that he'd enjoyed a hot shower, although a much shorter one than he would have liked, he'd crash soon. With any luck, after a rejuvenating nap, his IV would have run its course and he could convince Leah to drive him home, where he'd deal with the proverbial elephant in the room.

"Maybe," he conceded, fighting to keep his eyes open. "But the beard has to go. It itches."

"We'll get to it," she promised, "but first things first." She reattached his IV tubing to the port just above his wrist before he recognized his surroundings.

Suspicion flared. Patients weren't shown to a regular room if they were leaving the hospital in a few hours. "What am I doing here?"

"Jeff ordered IV fluids and antibiotics. Remember?"

"I know that," he snapped. "Why am I *here*, instead of back in Emergency?"

Jeff strolled in at that moment, carrying films and a fistful of paper. "You're here, Gabe, because I'm admitting you for observation."

"I don't need observing. I'm fi—"

Jeff held up his hands. "Yes, you're fine," he said in a placating tone, "but you could be better and that's what we're going to do—make you better. I showed your X-rays to Smithson in Orthopedics and he agrees with me. You suffered a severe sprain to your wrist when you dislocated your shoulder. According to him, your shoulder is okay but he recommends a wrist brace for a few weeks." He peered over his reading glass with a warning glare, "However, he still wants you to take things easy, so don't lift anything heavier than a pen for a while."

Gabe took the films to see for himself. "Fair enough."

"As for your ribs," Jeff continued, "they'll get better on their own, provided you slow down and rest. But you already know that."

Jeff's advice fell in line with Gabe's plans, as he'd hoped it would.

"My main concern," Jeff continued, "is infection and I want to hit those bugs hard." He glanced at the IV pole. "I see your antibiotics are running."

"Thanks to my ever-efficient nurses," Gabe quipped.

"I'm glad you agree because you're going to be at their tender mercy for a few days."

His jaw squared as he shook his head. "No can do. I'm going home."

Jeff shook his head. "Not a good idea, buddy."

"Good idea or not, I'm sleeping in my own bed tonight. I can either do it with your permission or I'll check myself out AMA." Gabe hated to play the against-medical-advice card against a colleague, but he was *home*, dammit, and he wasn't going to postpone his heart-to-heart with Leah another day. He had too much to say and he couldn't say any of it here where walls were paper-thin and interruptions were commonplace.

"I can't give you my blessing to leave in a few hours." Jeff emphasized his statement with a brisk shake of his head. "I honestly can't."

"Are you keeping Theresa and Jack?" Gabe demanded.

"No, but, unlike a certain person, they only need good food and rest to recover from their experience," Jeff said wryly, "not high-powered antibiotics."

"If the IV is stopping you, I can handle it. Or Leah can do the honors. Just give her the supplies and we'll take it from there." Gabe heard her muffled gasp, but ignored it to fix his gaze on his doctor.

Jeff pursed his mouth as his eyes darted between Leah

and Gabe. "She could," he finally agreed, "but you know the dangers of septicemia as well as I do. You belong here where we can monitor you." He held up his hands to forestall his objections. "At least until the lab gives me preliminary culture results."

"Sorry. I'll stay a few hours to finish this IV, but I'm going home tonight."

After muttering something about physicians being terrible patients, Jeff turned to Leah. "Talk some sense into him, will you?"

She shrugged. "Sorry, but you're on your own. If he won't listen to you, he certainly won't listen to me."

Her matter-of-fact tone surprised Gabe. Did she really believe that he didn't value her opinion? And yet, in hindsight, he could understand how she might feel that way. After they'd lost their son and their dreams of having a child of their own, he'd wanted to do *something* to make things right again. When the opportunity to adopt a baby had literally fallen into his lap, he'd gone full-steam ahead over her halfhearted objections when he should have allowed Leah—and himself—more time to deal with their first loss. In the end, they'd had *two* losses to cope with and clearly hadn't done well with either.

Regardless, he'd had weeks to reflect on their relationship and if he wanted to prove to her that he was giving his marriage and her opinions top priority, then this was his opportunity.

"I'm listening now," he pointed out, avoiding references to the past in order to avoid a potential argument. "What do *you* suggest I do?"

"Follow your doctor's instructions," she said bluntly. "Jeff isn't being unreasonable."

No, Jeff wasn't, but Gabe hated being tethered to a hospital bed when Leah was free to go about her business. If his mental radar was working correctly, her "business" probably involved his own physician.

"You also," she continued, "aren't in a position to fend for yourself. Taking a shower completely wore you out. How will you function on your own?"

"I'll manage," he said, unwilling to spring his plan on her just yet.

Now she looked exasperated. "Fine. Do whatever you want, regardless of what your doctor or anyone else suggests. Frankly, with your attitude, I'm surprised you bothered coming to the hospital at all for medical attention."

Her comment struck home as he realized she was right. He *had* gotten to the point where he assessed a situation and made a decision without asking for advice or input, and if any was given contrary to his opinion, he didn't follow it.

The question was, had he always been that way? He truly didn't think so. At one time he hadn't been able to wait to share everything in his day with her and he hadn't made any plans without consulting her first, but now that he thought about it, that aspect of their life had changed after they'd lost both babies. Granted, the second child hadn't died, but when the birth mother had taken her daughter home instead of putting her in their care, it had felt the same.

Conversation had dwindled when she'd been grieving and although he'd tried to get his feelings out in the open, he'd soon given up. Leah's sorrow had been so overwhelming he hadn't wanted to burden her with his own pain, so he'd bottled his emotions and carried on.

Instead of coping together, they'd coped separately. He'd focused on his job and expanding the foundation's services while she'd flung herself first into a remodeling project and then into her job at the hospital. Eventually, their diverging interests had allowed them to drift apart until their marriage had reached breaking point.

He should have done things differently but he hadn't. Fate, however, had given him another chance and he was determined to make the most of it. The first step, however, was to prove that he *was* listening and valuing her opinion, even if her opinion conflicted with his own wishes.

"If you want me to stay, then I'll stay, but only on an out-patient basis until tomorrow morning," he qualified.

"I can live with that," Jeff immediately agreed, as if he realized this compromise wouldn't remain on the table for long.

Gabe continued, "And only if Leah is my nurse. My private nurse."

Leah's jaw dropped, plainly surprised he'd included her as part of his conditional surrender. A moment later, her expression cleared. "I cover the ED, not this ward," she pointed out, somewhat smugly.

He steadily met his colleague's gaze. "Jeff?"

The other physician pressed his lips together, then nodded. "If she's what it will take to keep you in that bed, I'll work it out," he promised.

Leah's jaw immediately closed with a decided snap, her eyes flashing fire. It was a small victory and one that she clearly didn't support, so Gabe forced himself not to smile. As compromises went, he'd gained more than he'd expected, although it was less than he'd wanted. What really felt good, though, was finally seeing Leah with her normal spark instead of appearing as if all the life had been sucked out of her.

"Fine," she said a trifle waspishly, "but I'm adding a condition, too. You'll stay until he releases you."

"Okay, but he *will* release me tomorrow morning." He glanced at his colleague. "Won't you, Jeff?"

Jeff appeared more interested in the tug-of-war between Leah and Gabe than in Gabe's capitulation. "If nothing horrible shows up on your cultures and you don't spike any fevers, then you have my word you'll be out of here in twenty-four hours."

Gabe leaned his head against the pillows, too exhausted to complain about how their final agreement had as many exemptions as a bill before Congress. He'd face those scenarios when and if he had to. "I want to know everything the minute you do."

"I wouldn't expect otherwise." Jeff addressed Leah. "In the meantime, good luck with your patient."

Gabe tried not to be jealous of how easily she smiled at his colleague—his divorced, *single* colleague—the same divorced colleague who'd probably been more than happy to comfort Leah during the past year, especially during the month after he'd been presumed dead. However, jealousy was a good thing, he decided, because it gave him added incentive to win her back again.

"Not to worry," she said airily. "If he misbehaves, I have a sedative with his name on it."

"I'd rather eat a steak, medium-well, with baked potato," Gabe said as he eyed the tray of food Leah had organized from the unit's kitchenette.

A steaming bowl of chicken broth with assorted crackers, strawberry and lime gelatin squares, and chocolate pudding were the result of her raid.

"Maybe you'll get those for dinner tonight," Leah said lightly, knowing he wouldn't. As much as she'd like to reverse his weight loss as quickly as possible, his digestive system needed to acclimate first. "This is just a snack until then."

"There's nothing here for a man to sink his teeth into."

She ignored his grumbling as she studied his skin tone with clinical detachment. Now that he'd scraped off his beard with the disposable razor she'd provided, he was paler than she'd like. His face, although still handsome with his straight nose and strong chin, was thinner and his cheekbones more pronounced than the last time she'd seen him.

"For good reason," she answered. "You hardly have the strength to chew."

"I can find the energy if it's worth my while," he said. "A cheeseburger, fries and a milkshake would—"

"Come up as fast as they went down. Would you rather hug the toilet for a few hours? Now, just try this," she wheedled. "If your system can handle this without any problems, I'll personally deliver a greasy cheeseburger from your favorite fast-food restaurant later on."

His sigh was loud enough to be heard in the hallway, but he picked up a package of crackers. After struggling unsuccessfully to tear the Cellophane, he finally gave up and tossed the packet of crumbs onto the tray in disgust.

"Would you like me to open it?" she asked, reaching for the mangled package.

Hating to admit his weakness, he grimaced. "I changed my mind. A fellow can do that, can't he?"

"Of course you can," she soothed, aware of the hit the tiny packet had leveled against his dignity. It was also clear that her time in the kitchen would be wasted if she didn't take matters into her own hands, so she picked up the spoon and began feeding him soup.

"I can do this myself," he protested between swallows.

She doubted it. He was clearly exhausted from the poking and prodding, the round of X-rays and his stint in the shower, but for some reason he refused to sleep. Maybe a full stomach would work for him as well as it did for babies.

"I know," she agreed, "but I'm trying to earn my pay. I am your nurse, remember?"

It still rankled how Jeff had marched into the nursing vice president's office and when he'd come out again, it was official. Leah was assigned to one patient and one patient only— Gabriel Montgomery.

"This is all so pointless," she had railed at the emergency physician. "Gabe doesn't need nursing care. He only needs someone to fetch and carry and help him in and out of bed, and anyone can do that. He doesn't need me and I can't believe you agreed to this. We have a date coming up!"

"I did it *because* of our date," Jeff had told her kindly. "You've been riding an emotional roller coaster for the past few weeks. Now that he's back, you need to rethink exactly what you want—"

"I *know* what I want," she'd interrupted.

"You *think* you know what you want," he'd corrected, "but having Gabe return from the dead changes everything."

"It doesn't," she'd insisted, trying to convince herself as much as him.

Jeff had smiled benevolently at her. "It may not, but you owe it to yourself, and to me, to be absolutely certain of what you're looking for in a relationship. But I'll be honest," he'd said as he'd squeezed her shoulder. "As much as I respect Gabe, I won't be rooting for him."

And so she'd accepted the inevitable, even though she believed her skills were being wasted and that she knew her own mind when it came to her broken marriage.

Yet, after it had taken all of her concentration to reel her thoughts in far enough to figure out the microwave controls to heat his broth, she had to admit that perhaps she *shouldn't* be working in the ED right now. While she felt guilty over leaving her department short-handed, she shuddered to think of how ineffective she'd be in handling a trauma victim when a life hung in the balance. To her utter disgust, feeding Gabe seemed to be the only task her jumbled mind could handle.

"Are you ready to try the gelatin?" she asked, spooning a red cube into his mouth before he could refuse.

He swallowed. "Do you work with Jeff often?"

"Usually. Like I said, I normally work in Emergency."

His brow furrowed. "Don't PRN nurses work everywhere in the hospital?"

She spooned another bite into his mouth. "Some do, some don't. I haven't since I completed my advanced trauma nursing coursework six months ago."

His brow furrowed. "I didn't know that."

"You didn't notice the nursing textbooks on the coffee table before I moved out?"

"I did, but I thought you were boning up because you'd accepted this relief position."

"I was. Then I decided to take the next step." She hesitated, realizing that while he could have asked, she also should have volunteered the information. Now she wondered if the reason she hadn't said anything had been because she'd wanted *him* to notice and express an interest in what she was doing. And when he hadn't, she'd counted it as a strike against him.

"I should have told you," she said.

He shrugged. "We both had problems with communication, didn't we?"

At least he wasn't putting the burden all on her and if he could be magnanimous, so could she. "To be fair," she began slowly, "some of your staff had quit and you were trying to take up the slack. You had larger problems than wondering why textbooks had appeared on the table. More gelatin?"

He shook his head, his gaze intent. "Are you working full time?"

"Officially, no. Unofficially, yes, but I'm not reaping the benefits," she said ruefully. "However, the director of nursing told me yesterday that the next available position will be mine." She shoved another gelatin cube in his mouth.

He chewed, swallowed, then surprised her with his next question. "How was your cousin's wedding?"

She froze. "You knew about Angela's wedding?"

"She sent me an invitation. I would have gone, but I didn't want to make the day awkward for you. Things will be different, though, for your next family function."

Different? "Excuse me?"

"I want us to save our marriage, Leah. To fix what went wrong with our relationship."

At one time those were words she'd dreamt he would say, but too much time had passed. He was asking for the impossible.

"I know you went through a traumatic experience," she said slowly, "and as a result you want to right the perceived wrongs in your life as part of whatever foxhole conversion you experienced, but what happened to us—to me—can't be fixed."

"It can," he insisted.

"Not if our relationship is tied to my medical history."

"It isn't."

She raised an eyebrow because, to her, it was. "Oh?"

"It never was."

She eyed him carefully. "Maybe I should have Jeff order a CT scan because I think you suffered a concussion. In case you've forgotten, our relationship began its downhill slope when I lost Andrew and any chance for more children."

"It may have, but we can turn our life around. Children or not, we can make our marriage into whatever we want it to be."

His fierce determination was almost contagious, but his rhetoric didn't change one important fact. This man, who should have gone into pediatrics because he loved little people, was destined to remain childless because she refused to risk another adoptive mother changing her mind in the final hour. And he'd made it quite plain over the years that his biggest wish was to fill his house with children—children she couldn't give him, whether they were his or someone else's.

Neither did his sincerity change the fact that his work at the foundation was probably far more rewarding than simply coming home to her each night. And, yes, she could join him on his trips as she had when they were first married and she'd rearranged her hospital schedule, but deep down she was a homebody while he was a traveler. Eventually, the difference would become an issue again.

"For what it's worth, I *am* glad you're back," she said simply, "but now isn't the time to discuss what went wrong in our life." She rose to push his bedside table away. "Your only concern should be to give yourself time to heal."

He frowned, clearly not liking her response. "I can't believe you're giving up on us so easily."

"To you, I'm giving up, but to me, I'm finally putting the past behind me. Which is what you should be doing, too."

He paused. "How long have you been seeing Jeff?"

She froze, startled by his question. "Jeff? I'm not... We haven't... We're just friends," she finished lamely, wondering how Gabe had drawn that particular conclusion when she'd been so careful to hide her burgeoning interest in the other man.

"But you'd like it to be more."

"You're guessing," she countered, hating it that he could read her so well.

He shrugged. "I saw the way he looked at you. I only want to know what I'm up against."

She didn't know why she felt compelled to explain, but she did. "We went for a beer a few times with the rest of the ED crowd on a Friday night, but nothing more than that. You and I may have lived apart, but I still took my wedding vows seriously, which was why I was waiting to pursue a relationship with Jeff until after…"

"After I signed the divorce papers?" he finished.

"Yes."

"But once you heard my plane had crashed, you didn't need them. Why didn't you two take things to the next level right away?"

He sounded more curious than argumentative, so she answered as honestly as she could.

"If you must know, I wanted to wait until after the foundation's annual fund-raiser. I'd already decided it would be my last one—and it seemed appropriate for our chapter to end there. Now that you're back, there isn't any point in waiting, is there?"

He paused. "Is that what you want? For me to sign your papers?"

Was that what she wanted? Perhaps if their differences weren't irreconcilable, perhaps if they hadn't grown apart, perhaps if Gabe treated their marriage as a partnership rather than a boss-employee relationship, she could risk giving him another chance, but she couldn't.

"While I'm thrilled you aren't dead," she said softly, "you have to admit we're better off apart than we are together."

"I disagree."

"How can you say that?"

"Because we've *been* apart and it hasn't worked for me. I've missed you, Leah. More than you can imagine."

"How is that possible?" she asked, more curious than cynical. "You were busy with your work. We rarely talked or saw each other."

"That doesn't mean I didn't miss the days when we *did* talk and I spent more time at home than any place else. I want us to reverse course. To go back to the way we were. Before everything happened."

Before everything happened—such a polite way of saying *before her world went to hell in a handbasket*.

Her mind's eye flashed to the nursery they'd prepared on two separate occasions. The same room that remained closed to everyone except the housekeeper who periodically dusted and vacuumed. The sore spot in her heart had lessened from the day she'd given up and finally locked the door, but it hadn't completely disappeared. Her plans to avoid the OB and nursery wing were proof of that.

"As great as the idea sounds, I don't know if we can," she said honestly. "We aren't the same starry-eyed people we once were and no amount of magical fairy dust will change us back."

He tugged her arm until she didn't have a choice but to perch on the edge of his bed. "Maybe we aren't the young, naive kids we once were. Maybe the hopes and dreams we once had died, but that doesn't mean we can't create new ones. Together."

Darn it, but his grip was comforting and once again his voice was so sincere—so full of faith—that the wall she'd created in her heart to hold back her hurts and disappointments began to crumble. Quickly, she struggled to shore up those widening cracks before those emotions overwhelmed her.

"Life has seasoned us," he continued softly, "but deep down, we're the same two people who fell in love. Getting ourselves back on track won't be easy and won't happen overnight, but anything worth having is worth fighting for. I've had weeks to do nothing *but* think and I'm asking you to not give up on me or on us." He paused to caress her hand. "Please."

Once again, he'd surprised her. He could have so easily *demanded* this of her, but instead he'd spoken in a humble manner. Maybe Gabe *had* experienced a change of heart.... However, as he'd said, he'd had the luxury of time to think about their life while she had not.

"I love you, Leah," he added hoarsely. "I want another chance."

As his words soaked in, tears sprang into her eyes and the wall inside her completely gave way. Instead of being happy, she felt angry.

She jerked her hand out of his and rose as she clenched her fists and stuffed them into her pockets.

"What's wrong?" he asked, his gaze puzzled as he followed her retreat to the opposite end of the room. "I thought you'd be thrilled—"

"Do you know...?" She fought the tears clogging her throat. "Do you know how long...it's been...since you told me that?"

"Judging from your response, longer than I thought," he said wryly.

"I'll say. And I had to wait to hear it until after you were nearly killed in a plane crash! You can't spring that on me, out of the blue." She watched him struggle to swing his legs off the edge of the bed. "What are you doing?"

"I'm getting up," he said as he put action to his words.

"You can't. Your IV—"

"To hell with my IV," he said fiercely as his first step toward her pulled the tubing taut.

Fearing he'd rip out the needle and undo her hard work, she hurried close to survey his hand for signs of damage. She'd taped everything down to avoid accidental dislodging, but tape wasn't a deterrent to a man determined to escape his tether. "What are you trying to do?"

"I'm trying to get to my wife."

Before she could move, she found herself pulled into his

embrace. She resisted at first, but the moment his arms surrounded her, she realized this was where she wanted to be. Oh, how she'd missed times like this, when they'd simply been happy to hold each other for no reason, other than "just because".

He kissed her forehead before pressing his cheek against hers. "I'm sorry," he murmured, "but everything is going to be okay."

She didn't answer because she didn't believe it to be true. How could it? So much had happened, so much had been lost, and they couldn't regain any of it. Then, after she'd reflected on the bittersweet moment, she pulled away and cleared her throat.

"You'd better get back into bed," she fussed, falling into her nurse persona as she avoided his gaze.

He didn't quibble but simply allowed her to help him sink onto the mattress, which spoke of how much his gesture had cost him. "I liked where I was," he said instead as she covered his legs with the blanket.

How could she answer? She had enjoyed his embrace, too, but she shouldn't. She'd wanted a divorce, for heaven's sake! Ending their marriage was the only solution because she could no longer define their relationship. Were they friends or enemies, or just two hurting people who'd lived together until she'd realized the status quo wasn't enough? Did she still have feelings for him or was she just falling into old habits because she was relieved that he hadn't died? Did she respond because of those feelings, or because it had been so very long since someone had comforted her or held her in his arms?

"Didn't you?" he pressed.

She hadn't followed his conversation because she'd been so caught up in trying to answer her own questions. "Didn't I what?"

"Like where you were?"

Knowing his tendency toward persistence—he wouldn't stop asking until she answered—she intended to deny her feelings until she met his gaze. To her surprise, she didn't see a smirk or satisfaction in those dark depths. Instead, she saw hesitation and uncertainty.

Her strong, silent, take-charge husband suffered from the same doubts and insecurities she did, and she'd never noticed until now.

"Come on, Leah," he coaxed. "Talk to me."

"If I tell you the truth, will you hush and rest?"

He nodded.

"Yes, I enjoyed where I was, but—" she injected a firm note into her voice "—that doesn't mean anything. It can't."

"Because you still want a divorce."

She didn't necessarily *want* one; she simply didn't have any other option. "It's for the best," she prevaricated.

He fell silent. "Okay, then," he said. "I'll sign your papers."

CHAPTER FOUR

GABE looked on as Leah stared at him in mute surprise. Clearly, she hadn't expected him to give in so readily. "You will?" she finally asked.

"Yes, but I have some conditions."

One corner of her kissable mouth turned up in disgust. "Naturally. And they are?"

"We move back in together first and see if we can make our marriage work."

"No."

"It's the only way I'll sign."

She opened her mouth then snapped it closed before she glared at him. "This is blackmail."

"It's negotiation," he countered.

"Your idea is pointless."

"We'll never know if we don't try. Whatever we do, don't you want to be sure, absolutely *certain*, that we're doing the right thing?"

"I'm already certain," she told him. "I was certain weeks ago, when I came by and delivered that folder of documents."

"Well, I'm not." He softened his tone. "Come on, Leah. If you're so certain, think of this as your opportunity to convince me it's the right thing to do."

"We don't need to live together for me to convince you."

"Maybe not, but it's one of my conditions."

"*But—*"

"Next," he interrupted her to add, "we have to really *try* to heal our marriage. Not simply live together like we did before, as married singles with each of us going our own way. We'll spend time together and we'll talk. No more overworking, no more avoiding our emotions or minimizing our feelings. We say what we mean and we mean what we say. And if we can't open up to each other, we'll go to a professional counselor."

She fell silent and Gabe hardly breathed as he waited for her answer. "Is that a condition, too?"

He nodded. "We'll definitely fail if the effort is one-sided or if we focus on the negatives instead of the positives. Surely you can invest a few weeks to salvage a ten-year marriage?"

"And who's to say one of us isn't working 'hard enough'." She made quotation marks in the air.

"If you think I'm not holding up my part of the bargain, you have to say so. I'll do the same."

Once again, she hesitated. "How long do you want this ridic—this exercise to last?"

He had a feeling she'd intended to call his trial run "ridiculous" but the fact that she'd corrected her negative remark suggested she was warming ever so slightly to the idea. "Until the foundation ball."

"Six weeks?" she sputtered. "No. Impossible."

"Are you afraid?"

"Absolutely not. I'm objecting because six weeks is a long time to prolong the inevitable."

"Six weeks will pass by in a flash. As for the outcome being inevitable, maybe it is and maybe it isn't, but if you quit one day short of our agreement, I won't sign the papers," he warned. "We'll end up with the messiest divorce in state history."

Dividing their property wouldn't be the problem. Leah hadn't been interested in his family money and hadn't touched a dime in the account he'd created for her after she'd moved out. Her Achilles' heel was the notoriety and publicity associated with divorcing the heir to the Montgomery fortune. And from the resignation in her eyes, she realized he could turn their divorce into a headline or a simple record on the district court blotter.

"You aren't playing fair," she complained. "A month should be more than enough."

"Oh, I don't know. Six weeks doesn't seem like very long when you'll have the rest of your life to spend with Jeff, or anyone else for that matter."

Her shoulders slumped in obvious capitulation. "I suppose not."

"There's also one more thing."

She rolled her eyes. "Why am I not surprised?"

"I want you to go with me when I head to Ciuflores, Mexico, in three days."

"What?" she screeched. "You're going back to Mexico, and you want me to go with you?"

"Yes."

"That settles it," she said firmly. "You definitely need a CT scan. Heck, probably a neurologist."

"My head is fine."

"Fine or not," she snapped, "my answer is no. Absolutely *no*."

He shrugged, as if unfazed by her outburst or her objection. "Then no signature."

"Why in the world would you want to go on another trip?" she asked, clearly ignoring his comment. "You barely came back alive from the last one. You should be giving yourself time to recover, not rushing to jet around the world again."

"In three days, I'll have recovered."

"No one heals from cracked ribs that quickly. You'll be sore and bruised. And you'll still need antibiotics for your leg, too."

"I'll take the antibiotics with me. And with you there to make sure I take them I'll be fine."

"Fine or not, why you, Gabe? You can't be the only member of the Montgomery Foundation who can travel."

"No, I'm not, but Sheldon told me just before you came in with my lunch that Father David had called and asked for supplies. They're in the middle of a flu epidemic and the situation is dire. I can't refuse his request—he's my friend."

Father David Odell was Gabe's old schoolfriend and although they'd taken different paths in life, they'd kept in contact. For the past few years David had served as the spiritual advisor to a poor community and had been instrumental in introducing Gabe to the two physicians who were the sole medical providers in the remote area. It hadn't taken long for the local doctors to recognize the advantages being handed to them through the generosity of the Montgomery Medical Foundation. Eventually, Gabe had arranged for the tele-medicine link for which his organization was famous, and two months ago he'd delivered the equipment and trained the staff on its use.

"Fine. If you want to go, then go. But I'm—"

"I need you, Leah," he said simply. "The people of Ciuflores need you. An extra pair of medically trained hands is in as much demand as anything I can supply."

She rubbed the back of her neck in obvious indecision and he pressed on. "There was a time when you couldn't wait to go on one of my trips," he reminded her. "And if I recall, you loved the experience."

"Yes, but I have responsibilities of my own here," she argued.

"I've checked out your work commitments and I know that as of today you're officially off the work schedule for the next ten days," he said. "Plenty of time to go on a three-day mission of mercy."

"And what comes after that? There's always another deserving community waiting in the wings."

"Not for me," he said firmly. "Oh, I may go places once or twice a year, but for the most part my traveling days will be over."

"Oh, please," she scoffed.

"I don't mind if you're skeptical. I would be too if I were in your shoes, but it's true. Saving our marriage requires time and proximity." He paused. "Is it a deal?"

"When does this unholy pact start?"

"Tomorrow. As soon as we get home."

"And in six weeks, when you finally accept that we're incompatible, you'll sign the papers, no arguments?"

There was no way they were incompatible—they'd had too many good years together—but if she wanted to think their time together would prove it, then she could. He, on the other hand, intended to show her just how *compatible* they really were.

"No arguments," he said, "but this is an all-out effort on both our parts. No halfhearted attempts at reconciliation. We give it our best shot." He knew he was repeating himself, but he wanted the terms perfectly clear. She wouldn't be able to cry foul down the road.

She let out an exasperated sigh. "Fine. Then you'd better get some rest tonight. Tomorrow will be an extremely busy day for both of us."

Physically he was exhausted, but emotionally he felt as if he could move mountains. He'd gotten Leah to agree to one last-ditch effort to save their marriage and with far less effort and cajolery than he'd expected. He wanted to believe that she'd given in because she wasn't quite as convinced about her plan as she'd originally let on but, whatever the reason, he was getting his second chance and he intended to make the most of it.

He'd handled things poorly before and now, after replaying those scenes and imagining ways he should have acted differently, he could straighten out those kinks. He'd start with sharing his own fears and feelings instead of hiding them behind his work. Hopefully, time had faded enough of Leah's hurts so he wouldn't feel guilty for dumping his own pain on top of hers. His father had taught him to be tough at all costs, but in this case the lessons he'd learned had come at the expense of his marriage.

"Okay, but—"

She held a hand in the air. "We've talked enough for now. Get some sleep."

He'd pushed all he dared, but he'd gotten more than he'd expected on his first try. Even so, he was curious...

"Why are you so eager for me to doze off?" he asked as she adjusted his bedding once more. Her actions were completely unnecessary because there wasn't a wrinkle in sight.

"Gabe," she chided. "People sleep while they're in the hospital. Rest is part of every patient's treatment plan."

"What will you do?"

"I'll think of something."

"You won't leave?" He hated the plaintive note in his voice, but he'd awakened far too often to the disappointing discovery that Leah's presence had only been a dream.

"I'll be here when you wake up."

"Promise?" he asked, hiding his worry behind a light-hearted tone.

She nodded, offering him a slight smile. "I promise."

"Ramon! Hold on!"

Gabe's rising voice and restless movements brought Leah out of her catnap. As she had done so many times during the last twelve hours, she padded across the dark room to pull him out of his nightmare.

"It's okay," she repeated as she sat in the chair next to his bed and held his free hand. "It's only a dream."

"I'm sorry," he murmured, still in the grip of his memories. "'Sall my fault." Then, "Not Will, too!"

His anguish was almost palpable and all Leah could do was watch him relive those moments of horror with tears in her own eyes.

"So sorry, guys," he murmured as tears slipped out from behind his closed eyes and his shoulders shook. "So sorry. My fault. All my fault."

Slowly, he settled back into his uneasy slumber, although she didn't know if her voice or her touch had caused that particular scene to fade.

Oh, Gabe. You went through hell, didn't you?

As she lightly blotted the moisture from his face with a

damp washcloth, stroked the hard lines of his cheekbones and brushed aside the lock of hair on his sweaty forehead, she murmured what had become her litany. Idly, she wondered if Jack and Theresa were reliving their horrible memories, too. No doubt they were. Poor Theresa.

With his face freshened, she continued to hold his hand and stroke his fingers, thinking about how he'd glossed over his experience to her, to Jeff, and probably to everyone else he'd spoken to since he'd returned. Now, though, in the dark of night and without his full awareness, he'd given her a glimpse of the tragedy and trauma he'd endured.

She'd been so caught up in having him home again and worrying over what his return meant to her personally that she hadn't considered the emotional aftermath of his experience. For the past two years she'd thought him cold, unfeeling and insensitive, but he'd obviously been more adept at hiding his emotions, compartmentalizing his feelings and carrying on in the face of adversity and disappointment than she was.

Worse, though, was how, as a nurse, she should have *known* he would feel survivor's guilt, not only because he'd lived through his ordeal and his friends had not but also because *his* organization had been responsible for sending them on this trip in the first place.

No wonder he felt as if he were to blame.

He should have told her all this, she thought self-righteously, but almost immediately she understood why he hadn't. He couldn't blurt out the whole traumatic tale the moment he saw her, could he, especially when they'd lived separate lives for a year? Ever since they'd been reunited, they'd been surrounded by people and hadn't had the time or the privacy to delve into the details.

Had that been the problem with their own losses? Had they been surrounded by so many well-meaning friends and family that they'd never had the opportunity to deal with their pain as a couple? And when they'd tried, had they both buried it so far underground that they hadn't been able to reach it?

As she gazed at his face and smoothed away the agony

etched there, his vulnerability tugged on her heartstrings. No, she decided, she felt more than compassion for a traumatized patient. She felt the pain of seeing a loved one suffer.

A *former* loved one, she amended. She didn't love Gabe in the same eye-sparkling, heart-racing way she once had because there were too many hurts and philosophical differences between them, but underneath all the bad stuff, the stuff that had gone wrong, the affection they'd once shared was there.

Unfortunately, affection didn't make a marriage. Love did, and hers had faded. Gabe might think they could rekindle those feelings but even if that were possible, he'd still want the family she couldn't give him. And as she'd told her mother when she'd phoned her earlier in the evening to share the news of Gabe's miraculous return, eventually they'd wind up in the same untenable situation.

Her mother hadn't been as certain about the outcome as she was but with Gabe's parents having died years earlier—one in a car accident and the other of a heart attack—her mom had always carried a soft spot in her heart for her son-in-law. While she was willing to support Leah's decision, whatever it might be, she'd also thought Gabe's suggestion made sense.

Clearly, everyone was hoping she and Gabe would have a happy ending, although Leah had given up believing in them.

But happy ending or not, she'd made a deal in order to win the prize she wanted—his name scrawled across the bottom of legal papers. In the meantime, she'd follow the letter of their verbal contract. "Say what you mean and mean what you say," he'd said, and she intended to live by that rule.

Perhaps the best place to begin was with the deaths of his friends. Their loss obviously weighed heavily on him and if he would express his feelings openly on that subject, perhaps they could work their way into dealing with their personal issues.

Relieved he was finally resting easier, she stifled a yawn. She should go back to her recliner, but decided she didn't have the strength or the desire to let go of his hand. Perhaps it was wishful thinking on her part, but it seemed as if this small contact was enough to hold his nightmares at bay.

She'd never felt as if Gabe had needed her, but in this, at least, he apparently did. For now, it was enough.

Gabe drifted awake to find the sun shining through the half-opened mini-blinds covering his window. Leah stood in the sunlight, gazing into the courtyard, arms crossed, her brow furrowed as if contemplating a serious subject.

For a moment, he simply lay there, looking his fill. They'd lost so much these past few years and, if not for his accident, they might have continued down their separate paths to an irreparable end. In fact, during the first few days of his trip, he'd seriously considered agreeing to her suggestion of a divorce, not because he wanted one but because he'd felt like such a failure. After being unable to give Leah her heart's desire—a baby—in this, at least, he could give her something she wanted.

The plane crash, however, had changed everything.

As he stared at his wife, who was more beautiful now than she had been when they'd married, he knew he would do everything in his power to make her happy again.

Suddenly, she faced him and smiled, looking more relaxed than she had a minute ago. "You're awake," she said.

"Hello to you, too," he said, his voice rusty from disuse.

She approached his bed, clearly intent on his IV pump, but he reached out and snagged her hand. Her hand was soft, her bone structure fine and her eyes uncertain.

Gabe, however, had no doubts, no reservations about what he wanted. He tugged her just hard enough to shift her center of gravity in his direction.

"Gabe," she protested.

Before she could utter another word, he tipped his chin to meet her mouth. Gradually, her lips softened under his and a small noise escaped her mouth—the same small sound that came out as a satisfied sigh.

He wished he could give her the sort of kiss he wanted to, but he didn't want fuzzy-teeth breath when he did. "Good morning," he whispered.

"Same to you," she answered, her voice as husky as he remembered from their more lighthearted days. Then, as if she recalled where she was, she straightened and began fiddling with his tubing. "How do you feel?"

The nurse was back and the bride he remembered had vanished. No matter. There would be time to find her again—just as soon as he sprang himself from this joint.

He took stock of his aches and pains. They were still there, and a few new ones had cropped up, but his bone-weary exhaustion was gone. "Pretty good. How about you?"

"Me?" She seemed startled by his question. "I'm fine."

"I wondered. From your expression as you were staring out the window, I'd guess you were solving the world's problems," he said offhandedly.

She disconnected the tubing from the cannula in his wrist and draped it over the IV stand. "Not the world's, just the foundation banquet's."

"What's wrong?" he asked.

"Sheldon and I had planned a memorial ceremony, but with your return we should turn it into a celebration."

"Keep the memorial idea," he advised. "It doesn't seem right to celebrate when two of my group didn't come home."

"Okay, but your friends, associates and donors will want to hear about your experiences. You intend to speak as usual, don't you?"

"Only briefly," he said. "I'd rather review the year in pictures."

"Then we will." She flicked his blankets off his feet. "Are you ready for a stroll to the bathroom?"

"I thought you'd never ask," he said fervently as he levered himself up with his good arm and swung his legs off the edge of the bed.

"Take it slow," she advised. "You're probably stiff and sore."

Every muscle ached and his ribs protested his movements but he ignored the pain as he hobbled across the room to his destination, aware of his wife hovering beside him in case he should fall en route. "No kidding, I can manage from here."

He closed the door for privacy to take care of his most pressing needs. Then he studied his face in the mirror and rubbed at the stubble before proceeding to remove it.

Fifteen minutes later, he left the bathroom and found a meal tray waiting on his bedside table. "I'd rather eat at home," he said.

"Good luck with that," she said. "I emptied your refrigerator and pantry a few weeks ago when we thought you weren't coming…back. By the time we shop for necessities, it will be well past lunchtime. Besides, if you don't eat this, this delicious hospital cafeteria cuisine will only go to waste."

"Is that what you're calling it these days to make it taste good? *Cuisine*?"

"How did you guess?"

"You can have it," he offered.

"Sorry. You need the nutrition more than I do."

"Then I'll share. Remember when we shared a piece of pie?"

She smiled. "That was only so I could appease my sweet tooth at a fraction of the calories. This, however, is a *healthy* meal and you need to eat every bite. You should be starved."

"I am a little hungry."

"I would think so. You haven't eaten since the soup and crackers I'd fixed for you yesterday afternoon, so dig in before your eggs get cold."

"Okay, okay," he groused as he headed for the chair, "but I'll sit in the recliner. Lolling in bed makes me feel like I'm sick and I'm not."

"No, you're not," she said. "How did you sleep?"

He vaguely remembered her unhooking his IV before stumbling to the bathroom at some point, but other than the occasional murmur of Leah's voice, there was nothing he could focus on.

"Fine, I guess," he said slowly, watching as she whipped the stainless-steel dome off his plate to reveal several strips of bacon, two generous scoops of scrambled eggs and four pieces of buttered toast. "I can't believe I missed dinner, though. Eating is something we all looked forward to. Jack kept talking about his famous grilled chicken and Theresa wanted anything covered in chocolate."

"And what did you want?"

"Your Irish stew. Any chance we can have that one night?" he asked as he dug into the eggs and decided they didn't taste like hospital cooking. However, if she expected him to polish off the double portion, she'd be sorely disappointed.

"I'll see what I can do. Maybe I'll work on it while you're napping this afternoon."

He shook his head as he chewed. "If I nap, I won't be able to sleep tonight."

"You might surprise yourself. Being at home, in your own bed can make a big difference with how well you sleep."

Something in her tone put him on alert. Worry over what he might have said knotted his stomach. "I had a nightmare, didn't I?"

"It was pretty intense. Do you have bad dreams every night?"

He carefully placed his fork on his plate, his appetite gone. "At first, yes. The last week or so, not as often. I'd hoped they'd disappear once I got home."

"Would you like to talk about it?"

He let out a deep breath. "No," he said honestly. Then, because he noticed her stiffen, he finished his sentence. "But I should."

"You said we have to be more open and express our thoughts and feelings," she reminded him. "It's part of our contract."

"I know, and I will. The problem is, I don't know where

to begin." He pushed his plate back. "Here. I'm not hungry anymore."

She bit her lower lip, clearly not happy with his answer or his sudden loss of appetite, but she simply nodded. "Too much too soon?"

He wondered if she was asking about the food or the conversation, but he didn't press for clarification. "Yes," he admitted.

"Small meals more often is probably best."

She'd been talking about food, which was a relief. "Probably," he said.

"The same holds true for our conversation. Even if you can't share everything all at once, a little bit here and there is better than holding it all inside."

She'd caught him off guard, but her analogy was sound. He let out a deep breath. "I know."

"Good, because I'll let you slide this time, but once we're home, the kid gloves come off," she told him.

Relieved by his reprieve, he nodded. "I wouldn't have it any other way. By the way, when can I leave?"

"As soon as you have another blood test," she said. "In fact, someone from the lab should be here shortly."

As if on cue, there came a knock at the door and it was, as Leah had predicted, a phlebotomist. A few minutes later, the woman left with her vials and Gabe opted to enjoy the shower once again.

This time, when he came out of the bathroom, he felt like a new man and said so.

"You certainly look better than you did when you first arrived," she responded.

"I had nowhere to go but up," he quipped.

"On the contrary, you could have gotten worse," she said sternly, as if he needed the reminder. "Thanks to your overnight stay and the miracle of antibiotics, the redness on your leg has faded a lot already. I'm sure your ribs benefitted from the rest, too."

"Maybe so, but—"

"Jeff was right and you know it," she insisted. "In fact, if your roles had been reversed, you would have done the same."

"Okay, okay. I'll cry uncle. But I know Jeff has designs on you so don't expect me to praise him as if he's the next Albert Schweitzer."

The sound of her laughter caught him by surprise. It had seemed like forever since he'd heard it. "What's so funny?" he asked.

"You." She smiled. "You're jealous."

"Of course," he said smoothly. "I'm not embarrassed to admit it, either, especially when the prettiest woman in the hospital is my wife."

At first, she appeared taken aback, then a pink hue colored her skin, which suggested that he was long overdue when it came to paying compliments and giving attention to his spouse. He'd fallen down in that area, too, but that was another mistake he planned to correct.

Although, as he studied her, he noticed a few other details, too. Details like wrinkled scrubs, dark smudges under her eyes and an occasional stifled yawn.

"Did you stay here all night?" he asked, guessing her answer.

"I said I would."

"I can't believe you didn't go home."

"I didn't know when you'd wake up," she said simply, "and I promised I'd be here when you did."

The fact that she'd put her own comfort aside and gone to such lengths for him when he didn't deserve it was humbling.

"While I appreciate your gesture, you should have left at some point to get some rest," he chided.

"I should have," she agreed. "If I'd known your nap would stretch into eighteen hours, I would have."

"Why didn't you?"

"Glutton for punishment," she said lightly. "By the way, you had a steady stream of visitors, so I made a list because I didn't want to forget anyone." She grabbed the yellow steno pad lying on the table and held it out. "Would you like to…?"

He waved her offer aside. "I'll read it later."

"Sheldon came by several times. He insisted you call him the minute you're awake."

"He can wait."

"He won't be happy," she warned.

"I'll see him soon enough." He glanced at the wall clock. "Any chance you can call the lab and get my report?"

"Impatient as usual."

"If I have to sit and do nothing, I'd rather—"

"Sit and do nothing at home," she finished for him.

He grinned sheepishly. "I've said that before, haven't I?"

"Yeah, but you'll have to hold tight for a few minutes while I pester the lab for the results."

"Okay, but don't forget I want to see the report, too."

"As if you'd let me forget," she answered wryly, before she slipped out of the room.

CHAPTER FIVE

GABE found a pair of loose-fitting chinos and a button-down shirt in the tiny closet and decided to beat the proverbial rush and change now rather than later. He unhooked his IV, leaving the cannula in his arm for Leah to deal with, then slowly dressed. The process wasn't pain free by any means, but his struggles only gave him another good reason for needing Leah at home with him.

He was sitting on the edge of his bed, waiting for the sharp pain in his ribs to fade, when Dr. Taylor Ewing strolled in.

"How are you, Gabe?" the chief of surgery asked in his booming voice.

"Doing better now that I'm home," Gabe answered.

"Good, good. Getting dismissed soon, I take it?"

"As soon as my latest blood test is done."

"In that case, before you go, would you mind reviewing a case? It came via email through your medical organization and as it's my first official foray into your world of telemedicine, I'd like you watching over my shoulder. I'd hate to delete a crucial file by accident."

Gabe had signed Taylor as a consultant in exchange for filling in as a surgeon when the department was short-staffed. The arrangement had been in both of their best interests. It gave Gabe a break from his organization's administrative duties and kept his surgical skills from growing rusty. Not that becoming rusty was a problem…when he and his staff were invited into an area with their supplies and equipment, they often assisted the local medical community.

"Who's asking for a consult?" he asked.

"A Dr. Hector Aznar."

Hector was one of the two Ciuflores physicians Gabe had come to know quite well. He and his partner, Miguel Diego, were dedicated young doctors who'd returned to their village after completing medical school. Both were intelligent men who could have established their practices anywhere in the country, but they'd chosen to take care of hometown folks.

"I'd be happy to, but I'm waiting for Leah to get back."

"No problem. We'll stop at the nurses' station and tell her where you are. Do you want a wheelchair or can you walk?"

Just that easily, it was settled. Within minutes, Taylor had left a message for Leah with the ward clerk and Gabe was heading to the man's office.

"Let's see what you have," Gabe said as he pulled a chair close enough to Taylor's desk to view the monitor.

"A formerly healthy fifty-two-year-old woman with nausea, diarrhea, vomiting, jaundice and sudden weight loss."

Gabe's instincts went on full alert. The last time he'd been in Ciuflores and helped with a clinic, he'd run into a case very similar, if not identical. At the time, he'd had limited diagnostic capabilities and had urged Hector to send the woman to a more advanced facility. "Any palpable masses?" he asked, because at the time he'd seen this particular patient he hadn't found any.

"Yes," Taylor mentioned. "In her belly."

Gabe hoped this patient wasn't the one he knew... "Labs?"

"I have the basics. There are more abnormals than not." Taylor handed Gabe a sheet of paper. "Her conjugated bilirubin is elevated, along with the liver enzymes, including alkaline phosphatase. From what I can tell, there's a lot of organ involvement."

According to the numbers, it was clear the woman had

cholestasis—a blockage in her bile duct—as well as issues with her liver. Her amylase was also off the charts and her glucose was abnormal, indicating pancreatic problems, too. As Taylor had stated, very few of her results fell within the reference range.

"They also sent a few ultrasound pictures." The older surgeon clicked a few times with his mouse and the images appeared on screen.

In spite of the grainy quality, the mass in the region of the pancreas was unmistakable and the diagnosis grim. Eighty-five percent of pancreatic masses were aggressive cancers and of those sixty to eighty percent had tumors that had spread into surrounding tissue.

"I hate to make a definitive diagnosis with so little to go on," Taylor said. "According to Dr. Aznar's email, a CT scan and MRI are out of the question."

"Hector and his colleague operate a small clinic and their resources are extremely limited. They didn't even have an ultrasound until I gave them one two months ago."

"How well do you know this Aznar fellow?"

"He's a smart fellow. Cares deeply about his patients because he grew up in the area."

"Can he handle a biopsy?"

"If he doesn't have a choice then yes, but he doesn't have any pathology capabilities. He'll have to ship the specimen to another hospital, which will take time, depending on how far it has to go." Gabe tried to remember where the nearest pathologist might be other than Mexico City, but came up blank.

"I assume they can't send their patients to a larger facility?"

"They can, but the nearest one is a half day's drive away and is only a step above their own clinic. The problem is, most of the natives either won't travel the distance or can't afford the trip, which is why internet access to specialists is so important."

Gabe leaned back in his chair. "The question is, do you think the tumor is operable?"

"It's difficult to say for sure," the nearly sixty-year-old physician said soberly. "Considering the size, one would have to guess that the cancer has already spread. The lab results seem to support that theory. If so, surgery won't help." He paused. "I assume chemotherapy isn't readily available."

"It isn't."

"Then Dr. Aznar doesn't have a choice. His patient has to go where she can receive proper testing and an accurate diagnosis. We can't discount the possibility of a benign tumor, which can be a curable condition."

"No," Gabe answered, "but even if it *is* benign, we can't guarantee a positive outcome."

He glanced at the patient ID and the name immediately jumped off the screen. Carlotta J. Salazar. His gut churned as he pictured the woman who'd come to his clinic. The same woman who lived at the local orphanage with her three precious grandchildren as the facility's main cook. From what David had told him, the poor woman hadn't had an easy life, and now a serious illness had added to her troubles. It was a good thing he would be going to Ciuflores in a couple of days. While he was there, maybe there would be something he could do for the woman who'd always fussed over his team like a grandmother.

Immediately, her three grandchildren came to mind. If he couldn't do anything for Carlotta, maybe he could do something for her family.

Taylor looked thoughtful as he stared at the images. "I like to play the odds and until we have a biopsy report, we have to. I'll email Aznar and talk him through a biopsy procedure if necessary. Meanwhile, I'll send the case on to a pancreatic specialist I know, unless you already have one in your network." He raised an eyebrow.

Gabe thought a moment. "We do. Let me call Sheldon for his contact information."

A phone call and a few clicks of a mouse later—along with

several muttered curses as Taylor clicked the wrong buttons—Taylor had an address and phone number in his inbox.

Gabe watched as Taylor painstakingly typed a short message to Hector, then another to Dr. Stephen Wilkerson, before asking Gabe's help in attaching the digital files for the specialist's review.

Finally, Taylor leaned back and grinned. "Done. Medicine has certainly changed since I first became a doctor," he said ruefully. "Who would have thought we would send images and reports around the world and back in less time than it takes to dial a phone number?"

"Who would have thought?" Gabe echoed.

"Knock, knock," Leah's voice came from the doorway. "I hear you've stolen my patient, Dr. Ewing."

Taylor rose with a hearty smile. "You heard correctly, my dear. Come in, come in. How have you been?"

"I'm great. Thanks for asking. Did you two finish your business?"

"Just now," the surgeon informed her. "I imagine you're in a hurry to get our boy home."

In Gabe's opinion, her smile seemed a bit forced, but it was a smile, nevertheless. "He is rather impatient, as you can imagine," she said.

"Then I won't keep you." He shook Gabe's hand. "Stay in touch, okay?"

"I will," Gabe promised.

In the hallway, he tried to read Leah's reaction, but couldn't. "I'll bet you were surprised to get Taylor's message," he said, to test the waters.

"Surprised to learn that you were wandering around the hospital with Taylor? A little, but, knowing how eager you were to leave, I assumed you had a good reason."

"I did. He got his first tele-medicine consult and wanted me to walk him through it."

"How did it go?"

"From a technology standpoint, great. Not so good for the

patient, though. What's really unfortunate is that I know the woman."

"Someone you've worked with?" she asked.

"Not really. Whenever my team and I visited Ciuflores, she took care of us. Cooked, did our laundry, that sort of thing."

"I'm sorry to hear she's not well. Will she recover?"

"The odds aren't in her favor." He shifted gears. "Did you get my lab results?"

"I did. Your white count is down and Jeff says you can go."

"Hot damn!" he exclaimed, pumping his fist in the air.

She grinned. "I thought you'd be pleased. As soon as we get back to the room, I'll take out your cannula and we'll be on our way."

"Fa-a-a-ntastic!"

But as they meandered through the hospital corridors to return to his starting point, he realized Leah had taken the long route. He knew she wasn't trying to give him more exercise or to delay his departure. She'd done it purely to avoid passing by the OB unit and the nursery. He'd hoped she'd gotten past her aversion, but apparently she had not.

One day, soon, they would have to clear the air about that, but not today. Today, he was finally going home.

Leah drew a bracing breath before she stepped through the garage door into the house she and Gabe had built. As she clutched the two grocery bags in her arms, a hundred memories bombarded her—memories of feeding each other strawberries during a late-night refrigerator raid to the day when she'd plunked the packet of divorce documents on the counter. She'd half expected the pages to still be there, but they were gone. Either Gabe, or Carrie Erickson, their housekeeper for the past four years, had moved them.

Asking about the folder would subtly remind him of why she'd agreed to his unholy pact, but she couldn't do it. Not only had she vowed to herself that sniping and innuendo wouldn't make the next few weeks any more bearable, but the look of sheer delight on his face as he slowly turned a three-sixty wouldn't allow her to say anything that would mar his homecoming. Cruel, she was not.

"I was afraid I'd never see this place again," he said simply. "It's good to be home."

"I'm sure it is," she answered, still trying to decide if she felt the same way. She wasn't particularly happy about being here because of all the memories, both good and bad, but Gabe had insisted she move in with him instead of vice versa. It was infuriating to realize he'd stacked the deck in his favor but, as she'd told herself many times during the last eighteen hours, this wasn't any different than enduring a mammogram. According to her mother and others who'd had one, the aggravation—and the pain—didn't last long. In the grand scheme of things, six weeks wasn't long, either.

Although perhaps once Gabe recognized and accepted that they both had fundamental differences about what they wanted in their futures, he'd sign those papers much sooner. She could only hope.

"Yeah," he said with satisfaction as he glanced through the doorway into the living room before smiling at her like a kid on Christmas morning. "Just like I remembered."

She took stock of the gleaming black granite countertops, the shiny stainless-steel appliances and the glistening cream-colored ceramic tile floor that she and Gabe had selected during what seemed a lifetime ago. A simple jar candle of her favorite Fresh Rain fragrance rested on the round table in the breakfast nook.

Nothing had changed and yet everything had.

He sniffed the air. "It even smells fresh."

"Carrie came by yesterday to air out the house and get it ready for you. For us," she corrected.

"Did you call her?" he asked.

"After our little talk. From the way the kitchen looks, she must have worked through the night dusting and polishing. She always did take good care of things."

"I'll have to call and thank her." He leaned against the counter to gaze around the room again. "If you only knew how many times I pictured this. Your fresh flowers on the table, the dishes stacked in the sink, the shoes by the door, the smell of your banana bread."

The flowers on the table had disappeared two years ago. Several months later her desire to bake had vanished and the dishes in the sink had eventually dwindled down to a coffee cup, saucer and a spoon because they'd eaten out more often than not. The only shoes by the door were the ones she'd deposited there a minute ago.

And yet could she blame him for thinking back on happier times in order to survive the most stressful period of his life?

A wrinkle appeared on his forehead, as if he realized real life wasn't comparing to his memories. "It's been a while since those days, hasn't it?"

"Yeah." Then, because she felt awkward and didn't want to say anything that might sound petty, she changed the subject. "Would you like a cup of coffee?"

"That would be great."

"Why don't you relax in the living room and I'll bring it when it's ready?"

"I'd rather sit here." He pulled a chair away from the breakfast table and sat down, wincing as he did so.

She'd noticed. "Ribs still sore?"

"Afraid so. They're better than they were, though."

"After another week or two of rest, you'll be back at the gym as usual."

"Probably," he said. "Do you still go?"

She shook her head as she poured water into the reservoir and spooned several tablespoons of Gabe's special dark roast they'd bought on their way home from the hospital. "I prefer walking or jogging outdoors." Truthfully, she'd started that so she wouldn't risk running into Gabe because he didn't work out on a set schedule.

"When I'm able to, I'd like to join you."

Surprised by his suggestion, she blurted, "But you hate to run. You always lifted weights, or swam laps."

"Nothing says I can't try something new. And I'd like to jog with you. We used to go to the park together."

"To walk," she corrected, "and it was when we were first married. That was a long time ago."

"So? Going back will be like old times. Remember when I flagged down the ice-cream truck in the middle of traffic because you wanted a vanilla cone?"

"Yes, and you almost got run over by a vehicle for it."

"True, but my quick reflexes saved the day."

"Quick reflexes?" she scoffed. "I saw that car hit your leg."

"It was a tap, not a hit," he insisted. "I didn't even get a bruise, which, if you recall, we spent hours looking for."

She remembered the evening in question quite vividly. It had been the same evening that had ended in a midnight kitchen raid for strawberries, peanut butter and chocolate ice-cream topping. The next day she'd sent their comforter to the dry cleaners to deal with the sticky stains.

"I know what you're doing," she said suddenly.

"What?"

"You're hoping to get what you want by going through the back door when you normally tear down the front."

"Is it working?" he asked hopefully.

"Not so far."

"Too bad. But for the record, I know how difficult it is for you to move into our house when you weren't mentally prepared."

His insight caught her by surprise and she simply gaped at him.

"But we have to learn to talk to each other again and dusting off the good memories seems a good place to start."

Her eyes narrowed. "Did you read a do-it-yourself marriage counseling book somewhere?"

"No. I just spent a lot of time thinking," he said simply. "So, how does my theory sound? Shall we begin there?"

She didn't want to because she sensed what would follow. She'd drop her defenses and be vulnerable, but they couldn't spend the next six weeks limiting their conversation to the weather or medicine. To be honest, she'd like to know what had been going on in Gabe's mind during those days when life had become so dark and bleak because he'd appeared so…unmoved by it all.

Or, as she'd already considered briefly, had he simply been better at hiding his reactions? Or worse yet, had she pushed him away so completely that he'd felt as if he *couldn't* talk? The latter question was one that she hadn't considered before, and the potential answer didn't sit well on her chest now. But, as he'd said, they had to start somewhere…

"Sure, why not?" she said. "We can stroll down memory lane, but I never have denied that we had some great years together. However, all good things come to an end."

"That's debatable, but for now we need to deal with a few housekeeping issues first. Moving your things comes to mind."

"I thought after you were settled, I'd run home and—"

"I'm coming with you."

She raised an eyebrow. "Afraid I won't come back?"

"No," he said solemnly. "You gave your word and I trust you. I want to come along so I can help."

"You want to *help?* You're limping worse than a Saturday night drunk, your ribs hurt if you breathe too deeply or move suddenly, and you aren't supposed to lift anything heavier than a pen."

"It's not that bad," he defended.

She cast him a you've-got-to-be-kidding look. "No offense, but let's be realistic. How much help do you think you'll be?"

"Maybe not much, but I want to go with you."

"What for? To supervise?"

"No. To keep you company."

He wanted to keep her *company?* Once again, he'd surprised her. "Oh."

"Do you mind?"

Of course she did. The little house she was renting was her childhood home—her sanctuary. She didn't want Gabe's overwhelming presence to ruin that for her.

Yet, once again, it seemed cruel to make a fuss over something so trivial, especially when they wouldn't be on the property any longer than it took to empty out her refrigerator and throw a few clothes into a travel bag.

Letting out a soft sigh, she surrendered. "Suit yourself, but if I catch you overdoing things, I'll convince Jeff to re-admit you."

"Understood. Is the coffee ready?"

She found the cups in the same cupboard where she'd always stored them and filled two. As she carried them to the table where Gabe was sitting, a brisk knock at the back door caught her off guard.

"Are you expecting someone?" she asked.

"No."

There were few people who qualified as back-door guests and she already guessed their visitor's identity. She wasn't wrong.

"Sheldon." She greeted him halfheartedly, not entirely shocked by his appearance given his eagerness to talk to Gabe while he'd been in the hospital.

Gabe's second-in-command stood on the threshold, his face somewhat apologetic. "Sorry to bother you because I know this isn't the best time, but I'd like to talk to Gabe. I promise I'll be gone before you realize I've been here."

Heaving a sigh, she stepped aside wordlessly and tried not to read anything into the way Gabe's eyes brightened at the sight of the familiar face.

"What's up, Shel?" he asked.

"The memorial service for Will and Ramon is set for day after tomorrow," he said.

"You worked fast."

"The families wanted it this way," he said simply.

Gabe simply nodded. "Of course."

"And," Sheldon continued, "we've been trying to make head or tail out of your notes for our Ecuador project and haven't had any luck. We're scheduled to go there in two weeks, and to make matters worse the health ministry is dragging its feet over the permits again. Would you mind setting me on the right track?"

"Not a problem," Gabe answered.

"Wait a minute," she protested. "You just got home from the hospital. You're supposed to *rest*, not work."

"This isn't physical labor," Gabe pointed out. "I'm only answering a few questions."

"That's right," Sheldon chimed in. "As soon as Gabe brings me up to speed and we sort through the problems, I'll be out of here. Ten minutes, tops."

"Do *any* of your projects run smoothly?" she countered.

"Lots do, but not this one. While you're waiting, why don't you relax? Shoot, lie down for a few minutes. I know you didn't sleep much last night."

He wanted her to *lie down*? When she had so much to do, the least of which was changing her address? Wasn't it enough that he'd blackmailed her into spending the coming weeks together, simply because it was what *he* wanted? Disbelief instantly filled her.

"It's only for a few minutes," Gabe coaxed. "Sheldon wouldn't be here unless it was important."

And therein lay the rub. His work *was* important. She knew so many people who wouldn't have gotten the medical help they'd needed now did, and it was all because of Gabe. The problem was with her. She simply wasn't as philanthropic of his time as he was. Perhaps she needed to live in a third world country to get her husband's attention.

Deciding she was being petty, she sighed. "You're right. Everything else can wait."

His gaze searched hers and, apparently satisfied by the acceptance he saw, he cupped the side of her face. "I know this isn't working out the way we'd planned."

"It isn't the first time."

"I promise we'll hurry."

"Yeah," Sheldon interjected. "I only need a few minutes."

Leah had learned long ago that "a few minutes" was code for "a few hours", if not longer. So much for things being different…

On the other hand, Sheldon probably did have a lot of questions. Gabe was involved in every aspect of the foundation and unless he'd left copious notes—which he wasn't known to do because he carried so much of his information in his head— Sheldon had been left to unravel the mess left behind.

Resigned to the inevitable, she simply nodded before she addressed Sheldon. "Would you like a cup of coffee while you're working?"

"I'd love one," he said fervently.

As soon as she handed a fresh mug to Sheldon, Gabe stepped forward to brush a kiss on her cheek. Instant awareness shot through her as she felt his lips touch her skin and she inhaled the scent that was only Gabe. *Stop that*, she mentally chided her traitorous body.

"Thanks," he murmured. "Would you like to join us?"

Another first. Well, not really a first. At one time he'd included her when he'd discussed foundation business at home, but that had ended after their adoption had fallen through. Then he'd stopped asking, as if he couldn't bear to be around her any more than necessary.

"Maybe next time," she answered. "While I'm waiting, I'll make my lists."

"Good idea." He turned away, then stopped short. "Is my computer still here?"

"It should be. I haven't taken anything," Leah replied. In fact, she'd been postponing the task of cleaning out the house to list it with a real estate agent. Now, she was grateful she'd dragged her feet. It would have been awful for Gabe to suddenly find himself homeless. "Sheldon?"

He shrugged. "I haven't taken anything, either."

Gabe seemed relieved by the news, which was understandable. "I presume you didn't cut off my network access or delete my files?"

Sheldon grinned. "Do I look stupid, boss? Of course not."

As the two men headed toward Gabe's home office, Leah was certain they'd both lose track of time once they began discussing work.

She found a pencil and notepad in the drawer near the telephone and sat down to begin her list. Unfortunately, her mind couldn't get past the fact that they hadn't been in the house for five minutes and she was already competing with his job. Her temper simmered.

She wanted to march in and yell at him, to remind him of his "things will be different" speech, but doing so with Sheldon in the room would only make the situation uncomfortable for everyone. But if Gabe wanted complete and total honesty, she intended to give it to him. No more holding things inside, no more being the sweet, forgiving, *pushover* wife.

Yet as she stared blindly through the window into the garden she'd once loved, her irritation faded. She hated the way she'd overreacted, even though no one knew it except her. Sheldon wasn't purposely sabotaging their life. Deadlines had to be met and questions had to be answered so the job could go forward, but what would he have done if Gabe hadn't been here? He would have muddled through on his own and probably done a wonderful job.

On the other hand, did Gabe have to run every time Sheldon, or anyone else at his office, called? She had so many questions and so few answers, which, according to Gabe, was what the next few weeks was all about.

Six weeks suddenly seemed to stretch into forever.

Gabe had tried to watch the time—he really had. However, one thing had led to another and by the time he'd checked the clock, two hours had passed.

So much for his "few minutes" promise, he thought glumly. "Sorry, Shel, but that's it for today."

Sheldon glanced at his watch and cursed under his breath. "Hey, man, I'm so sorry. It's just been such a relief having you back that the questions just kept coming."

"I understand."

"Tell Leah I'm sorry, too, and that I'll make it up to her."

"I'll tell her," he said, before Sheldon let himself out. Unfortunately, he had more to tell her than Sheldon's promise of restitution. A sincere apology was in order. He'd vowed things would be different but so far he'd failed his first challenge. Now he had to hope she'd give him another chance, although he would wager his old Beamer that she'd simply been waiting for him to screw up so she could say "I told you so" before she walked out the door. She'd given him one pass already in the hospital when she'd questioned him about his nightmares. He didn't think she'd do it again.

Yet he wasn't willing to surrender so soon. If that was her plan, then he'd argue they were both bound to make mistakes on their way to getting things right.

Practicing his apology, he slowly made his way past the living room to the kitchen, but she wasn't there. Thinking she'd gone upstairs and taken a nap, as he'd suggested, he ignored the pain in his leg and grimly climbed the stairs, hoping to find her in their bedroom, tucked under the covers, fast asleep.

At least, he hoped she was there because *he* wanted to wake her and he knew exactly how he wanted to do it. He'd first run a light finger along the side of her face before moving down her neck to take a detour along her collarbone. From there, he'd meander through a most luscious valley until she finally reached for him.

Anticipation, coupled with his months of celibacy, created a physical response so strong he could hardly turn the doorknob. When he did, he saw the master bedroom's king-size bed covered in the familiar green-and-gold comforter she'd bought when she'd decorated the room. A variety of matching pillows were artfully arranged near the headboard, but the bed itself was empty.

Leah wasn't there.

He checked every room upstairs—the guest room and even the nursery—but she wasn't in any of them.

He went downstairs, through the house and into the back-yard where she'd once loved to sit and enjoy the butterfly garden.

No Leah.

Where had she gone? More importantly, was she coming back? His gut churned at the possibility.

No, he decided logically, she would be back. She wanted his signature too much to give up so quickly. She was prob-ably running an errand or, having grown tired of waiting for him, she'd left for her place without him. No doubt she was on her way back this very moment.

Reassured by that thought, he returned to his office—his favorite room of the house. They'd spent many comfortable hours within these four walls, he realized as he sat behind the oak desk Leah had given him one Christmas. Leah would often curl up in the overstuffed chair with one of her fiction books while he'd read through his stack of medical publi-cations or taken care of business paperwork. Music or the television would play in the background and when they had both tired of whatever it was they'd been doing, they'd put the smooth desk surface to good use.

Now, though, instead of being cluttered with medical and cooking magazines or her latest knitting pattern, the highly polished wood only held his pen and pencil set, a framed photo of the two of them, which had been taken shortly after she'd learned she was pregnant, and a desk calendar with its top page showing the day he'd left on his last trip.

He didn't need to open the top left-hand drawer to know what it contained. A phone book, the *Yellow Pages*, and the divorce papers she'd delivered. With any luck at all, those doc-uments would soon be shredded and residing in the trash.

He glanced at the wall clock and saw another hour had passed. Telling himself not to worry about things like car accidents, ambulances or the county morgue, he broke down and dialed her cell phone number from memory, but his call went straight to her voice mail.

He told himself to wait. Traffic could have snarled, check-out lines could have been horrific, or she'd simply got caught up browsing and had forgotten to watch the time. He hoped the latter was the case because then he wouldn't feel so badly about doing the same.

After another fifteen minutes he simply couldn't wait any longer. He had to do *something*, even if he had to drive from one end of the city to the other, but he'd find her.

One way or another, he *would*.

CHAPTER SIX

LEAH watched the play of Gabe's muscles underneath his cotton shirt as he soaped her little blue Mustang. It was still almost hard to believe he'd married her when he could have had his pick of all the beautiful women in the world, but the shiny new ring on her finger said it was true. So did their marriage license and the wedding picture proofs she'd picked up from the photographer that morning.

Suddenly, a blast of cold water struck her chest.

"Gabe," she protested. "Look what you've done. I'm all wet."

His appreciative glance suddenly wiped away her irritation.

"So am I," he reminded her.

"But I wanted to wear this to my parents' house," she protested without heat. "Now I'll have to change."

"Can I help?" he asked hopefully.

"You can't." She pretended to pout as she struck up a sultry pose. "You're busy."

"Not anymore," he said, immediately shutting off the tap.

In a flash, she was in their bedroom, entwined in the sheets as his mouth and hands roamed over her body. "Oh, Gabe," she murmured as he caressed her breast and nipped at her neck. "That feels..."

"Wonderful?"

"Yes."

"How about this?" His fingers skittered a path down her body to a secret spot only he had found.

She arched in his arms. "Oh, my..."

Suddenly, the pleasant, swirling sensation disappeared as she felt something solid underneath her.

That wasn't right. How had the mattress become that hard...and bony?

She wiggled, wanting Gabe to fly her back to the clouds before she'd been so strangely and rudely interrupted, but she couldn't get comfortable. She and Gabe had fit so well together, but now there was this thing between them.

She elbowed the object, but it wouldn't budge. Irritated now, she pushed harder, but it only moved a fraction. Determined to remove this strange obstacle, she raised herself on one elbow and opened her eyes to see just what had dared to ruin her romantic interlude—

Leah gasped as she realized Gabe was lying beside her. Lying in *her* bed, in *her* house, on top of *her* quilt. And right now he was watching her with his intensely dark eyes.

This is certainly awkward. "What...?" She swallowed. "What are you doing here?" she asked faintly.

"Looking for you."

Oh, dear. "Is everything all right?"

His gaze didn't waver. "You tell me."

Instinctively, she understood his unspoken question. "I'm not upset because Sheldon came by," she assured him. "Well, I was at first, but I got over it once I put myself in his shoes."

The intensity in his eyes faded and he visibly relaxed. "I'm glad."

"By the way, what time is it?"

"Quarter before five."

She sank onto her back and flung her arm over her eyes. If he was right, then she'd been here for over four hours, and had been sleeping for most of them.

"How...how did you get in?" she asked.

"I recognized your fake rock in the flower bed near the

front door. You really should find out a better place to hide your house key," he said.

"Apparently so, if all sorts of riff-raff can find it," she said meaningfully.

He laughed at her veiled barb. "Let this be a lesson to you."

"How long have you been here?" she asked.

"About an hour."

An hour? "You should have woken me."

"I could have, but you were tired."

She had been. She'd slept very little the previous night, watching over Gabe and helping him through his nightmares. Tired or not, though, she hadn't planned her afternoon to turn out this way, and she told him so.

"Oh?" he asked, more curious than skeptical.

"After you didn't show any signs of wrapping up your conversation with Sheldon, I decided to run here, pack my things and get back before you noticed I was gone." She offered a weak grin. "Obviously, my plans didn't turn out the way I'd hoped."

"I'll admit we took longer than I'd intended," he admitted, "but when Sheldon went home and you weren't in the house, I started to wonder…"

"I should have left a note," she said, "but, honestly, this was supposed to be a simple, thirty-minute errand. When I walked into the house, though, a shower sounded good, and then the bed looked so comfortable. I decided to lie down for a few minutes and, well, the next thing I know, you're here in bed with me."

She narrowed her eyes, but before she could question him he put on a complete air of innocence. "You told me I should rest, so I did."

"I didn't mean you should do it in *my* bed."

"It isn't as if we made love while you were dead to the world," he calmly pointed out. "Furthermore, we aren't breaking any moral or legal laws if we share the same mattress. If it makes you feel better, notice how I'm on top of the blanket and you're not."

She clutched the sheet to her chest, aware that only a flimsy piece of fabric was between them. Granted, he wouldn't see anything he hadn't seen before, but it was the principle of the matter. They were a hairbreadth away from a divorce, for heaven's sake!

"Just so you know—we may be sharing a house, but that's *all* we're sharing. I'm taking the guest bedroom."

"We're trying to make our marriage work, Leah," he reminded her. "As I recall, our bedroom was the one place we didn't have any problems."

"I don't deny how wonderful our sex life was, but making love now only clouds our issues."

He looked somewhat disgruntled, although not surprised. "I was afraid you'd say that," he said ruefully.

"Because you know I'm right."

"Okay," he agreed. "I'll accept your decision. "For now."

Which meant he would address this subject again, but at this moment he was backing off. She would be satisfied with that, although if Gabe ever got a glimmer of her dream, he'd do his best to change her mind. Quickly.

"Did I…?" She paused. "Say or do…anything?"

He grinned. "You mean, like crawl all over me and whisper sweet nothings in my ear?"

Oh, dear. "Did I?" she asked, bracing herself for the worst.

"All I can say is that your elbow should be registered as a lethal weapon." He rubbed his side.

She was too horrified by the possibility of having caused him serious damage to be embarrassed, and she began pulling at his shirt to look for evidence. "Did I hurt you? Oh, my, your *ribs*!" she wailed.

He caught her hand. "They're fine," he said. "You didn't hurt me. Well, maybe a little, but hearing you say my name was worth the pain."

She was mortified. She'd never convince him she wanted

him out of her life if he'd heard her moan his name or if he knew he'd starred in her erotic dream.

"So," he said matter-of-factly, "do we want to stay in bed or get up and gather your things?"

"Get up," she said promptly.

"Okay. Ladies first."

She raised her eyebrow. "Not a chance, buster. As you well know, I'm only wearing this sheet and I'm not dropping it. I'll see you downstairs."

"Spoilsport."

He gingerly swung one leg over the edge and rolled upright with a small grunt, reminding Leah of his injuries. "I assume you haven't packed anything yet?"

She was embarrassed to answer. "No."

"Then I'll put on a pot of coffee." With that, he limped from the room.

For a minute Leah simply lay there, realizing how her best-laid plan had gone awry. Gabe's presence had already tainted her safe haven, much as the spirits of the two children she'd considered hers had tainted the house she and Gabe had built. There, she'd done her best to confine the atmosphere by locking the door to the nursery, but the gloom had invaded the rest of the house like a noxious fume and nothing she did could dispel it. The only way she could break free had been to move where she didn't see memories everywhere she turned.

Now, thanks to not setting an alarm, to not returning before he'd realized she'd left, she wouldn't ever banish the image of him in this specific bedroom and in this specific bed.

Damage control was in order, which meant she had to get him out of there as quickly as she could. She dashed to the bathroom and shimmied into a fresh pair of jeans and a clean T-shirt.

Next, she pulled her suitcases out of the closet and began tossing in clothes haphazardly. A quick sweep of the bathroom's counter and medicine cabinet took care of her personal items and within minutes she was packed. Neatness, in this instance, didn't count.

Downstairs, she set her cases by the door. Through the window, she caught a glimpse of Gabe's SUV parked at the curb.

"Your vehicle's outside," she said inanely as she accepted the mug Gabe handed her.

"How else was I supposed to get here?" he asked.

"Sheldon didn't give you a ride?" she asked.

"No."

"You *drove*? Are you *crazy*?"

He snagged a butterscotch out of the candy bowl on the nearby end table and nonchalantly unwrapped it. "I may have been out of the country for a few weeks, but I still have my driver's license."

"This isn't about the legality. It's about your health," she scolded. "You shouldn't be behind the wheel with your bum leg and sore ribs. Your reflexes are compromised and what if you're in an accident? You could be seriously injured, even killed! Not to mention the damage an air bag could do."

"Those scenarios are possible," he said, clearly unconcerned at the prospect, "but after surviving a plane crash, a car wreck seems mild in comparison."

"For heaven's sake, Gabe. You were lucky once, but you aren't invincible."

He folded the wrapper in half then in half again, as if he had nothing else to concern him, but she knew his casual air belied his sharp-eyed gaze and keen powers of observation. "You seem worried over something that didn't and probably wouldn't happen."

She couldn't believe he was asking her that question. "Why wouldn't I worry when you do something foolish?"

He shrugged. "It's nice to know you care."

"Of course I care," she snapped. "You're my—" She stopped short, unable to supply the word he was obviously waiting to hear and feeling as if he'd led her down this path.

"Husband?" he supplied helpfully.

She raised her chin. "Yes. For now."

"Then, as your husband, don't you think I'd worry about you, too?"

"I already explained and apologized for not leaving a note," she pointed out. "If I'd known I was so tired, I would have taken a nap when you suggested it."

"But you thought you could get by without one."

She nodded as she sipped her coffee, pleasantly surprised he'd remembered her preference for peppermint creamer and two packets of non-calorie sweetener. "That and…." She debated explaining the rest, but he wanted honesty, so she'd give it to him. "It just seemed as if once again you were telling me what to do."

"I'm sorry you thought so because I was only offering a suggestion," he said slowly. "It seemed kinder to suggest a nap than to mention the bags under your eyes or your haggard appearance."

No doubt she *had* looked like death warmed over—a twenty-four-hour stint in the hospital tended to do that to a person. "You're right, it was," she admitted. "I was cranky and finding fault. I'll try not to be so sensitive next time."

"And I'll keep Sheldon's interruptions to a minimum."

"Do you really think it's possible?"

He grinned. "You bet, especially if I don't answer the phone or the door."

"So you'll let the phone screen your calls and I get to weed out your visitors."

"Precisely."

"The next question is, will *you* be able to stay away from the office?" she asked, thinking of the hours he'd devoted to his foundation. Twelve- to sixteen-hour days hadn't been uncommon during their last year together. "I know how difficult it is for you to relinquish the driver's seat of your organization."

"I can, and I will," he said. "During our time in the jungle, Jack and I speculated on what might be happening here at home without me, and neither of us saw a pretty picture. My father wouldn't have agreed with me, but it isn't good for the entire workings of the foundation to hinge on one person. Until I implement more permanent changes, Sheldon is in charge. After I take hold of the reins again, I plan to delegate more."

"I'm sure you'd like to implement your ideas, but I'm not convinced life will be any different than it was before."

"I haven't convinced you *yet*," he corrected. "But I will. In fact, I'm willing to dissolve the trust fund and turn the foundation over to someone else if time becomes an issue."

His news clearly caught her off guard because she stared at him with the same incredulity he'd seen on her face when the ambulance doors had opened. "You're kidding."

"I'm not."

"I can't believe you're offering to relinquish your family's legacy. You've helped so many people—"

"I learned what's important in life," he said simply. "Yes, the foundation fills a need for a lot of people, but in the end my wife has to come first."

"Why?" she blurted out. "I know you cut back on your hours when we thought we were starting our family, but our situation is different now."

"Not really," he mentioned. "We're still a couple and I want to spend time with you."

He made it sound as if their future was settled, but in her eyes it still wasn't. And yet, if they were to have any *hope* of a future, they certainly had to do more than see each other in passing.

However, being around each other twenty-four seven meant that certain subjects were bound to come up. Certain subjects on which she'd already made her stand. Certain subjects that had brought them to the brink of a divorce…

She studied him through narrowed eyes. "And what happens if, by some miracle, we restore our relationship? What then? What's next on your agenda?"

He frowned. "I don't have an agenda, other than avoiding the divorce court."

"It isn't in the back of your mind to convince me to try the adoption route again? If that's your end game, then we may as well visit my attorney now rather than later."

"That isn't my plan," he insisted. "Whether we have children or not, we can still have a wonderful marriage. Just the two of us."

He sounded sincere and nothing in his eyes hinted at subterfuge, but she knew how badly he'd wanted children and she said so.

"Yes, I wanted to raise a couple of kids and still do if the opportunity arises," he admitted, "but our relationship comes first. If that isn't healthy, there's nothing left."

His quick response and his calm gaze caught her off guard. She hadn't expected him to give up his heart's desire so easily and it startled her to the point where she couldn't find the words to reply.

"Is that why you've been digging in your heels about this divorce business?" he asked, clearly amazed. "You're trying to save me from myself, aren't you?"

"It isn't fair to ask you to give up something you've desperately wanted and dreamed of," she defended. "You'll wake up one morning and realize you've wasted all those years and then we'll be back in the same boat, sailing down the same river to nowhere. I can't go through that again—"

"Will you let me be the judge of what I want?"

"Children are all you've ever talked about. As an only child, you wanted a houseful, you said."

"I did, because I believe siblings teach life lessons that an only child doesn't learn. Things like sharing everything from toys to parental attention and getting along with others, even when they irritate the heck out of us. But, Leah, we have to play the cards we're dealt and if we don't have children, then so be it."

"Then why...?" She bit her lip in indecision.

"Why what?"

"Why did you push so hard for us to adopt right after we

lost Andrew? You'd lost your chance to be a father and you grabbed at the first opportunity that came along."

"Is that what you think?" he asked, incredulous. "That I rushed into the adoption only because I wanted to be a *father*?"

"Didn't you?"

"No," he exploded. "Absolutely, not! I did it for *you*."

"How was your decision for me, Gabe? I was still grieving for my baby and any future children, and the next thing I knew we're trying to complete home studies and prepare for another baby."

He raked his hair with his fingers. "Hindsight says we should have waited, but at the time the opportunity seemed heaven sent. It would have been, too, but no one anticipated Whitney changing her mind in the final hour."

Leah let out a sigh. No, no one had known or even guessed the outcome would turn out completely different than everyone had planned. Whitney Ellis, the birth mother, had been so sure of her decision—until the time came for her to live with it.

"I had to do *something*, Leah, because I was losing you. You wouldn't talk. You wouldn't tell me how you felt. Later, after we began discussing adoption and you met Whitney, you came around. You were happy again."

After she'd recovered from her initial surprise and the situation had felt real and not just a dream, she had been. Deliriously happy.

"Then," he continued, "as soon as she decided to keep her baby, everything fell apart again. And then, before I knew it, you were moving out."

Gabe had struggled with so many conflicting emotions during those long months, but the day she'd packed her bags had been the bleakest day of his life. The day she'd asked for a divorce hadn't been a high point of his thirty-eight years, either. However, this was the first time he realized she had attributed selfish motives to him.

Then again, how could he have guessed? They'd never expressed themselves this openly before.

He should have pushed her harder to unburden herself in the weeks and months after their adoption had fallen through. He'd waited for her to broach the subject, thinking she'd talk when she was ready, but she never had. On the other hand, he'd *wanted* to talk, to pour out his disappointment and his pain, but he hadn't known how or where to begin. Consequently, they'd never discussed what had obviously lain so heavily on their hearts until eventually they'd found solace in other ways. He'd taken refuge in his work and she'd accepted a relief position at the hospital.

In the end, they'd drifted apart. Now he was trying to steer them back together, unable to believe he might be too late.

"Regardless of what you were trying to do, I don't want to live through the same experience," she said in a flat tone. "Putting our lives on display to birth parents in the hope they'll choose us, being interviewed and trying not to sound over-eager, not to mention the waiting, the *interminable* waiting. Then, after all that, our hopes and plans can fall through at a moment's notice."

"I understand how you feel."

"Do you, Gabe?"

"I went through the same disappointments you did," he pointed out. "It wasn't easy for me, either."

She frowned and cocked her head to study him. "You didn't act upset."

"I was. I wouldn't let myself show it because I felt like I had to be strong for you."

"I see." She paused. "Now that you know how I feel, if we reconcile—and that's a big *if*—would you be satisfied with my decision?"

"Absolutely," he said firmly, "As long as you don't let fear influence your choice. But whatever we do, whichever route we take, we have to move forward. Doing what we've done before—avoiding the issue, locking off a room of our house— didn't work then and it won't work now.

"That said," he continued, "at this particular point in time we have to concentrate on *us*. When we're on track again, the rest of our concerns about families and homes and jobs will fall into place."

Her expression suggested that she was skeptical, but if she truly thought he'd only been trying to fill *his* emotional needs, then he simply had to prove to her how wrong she'd been. Their future wouldn't be secure until she trusted him to mean what he'd just said.

"You can say those other things don't matter, but they've influenced our marriage."

"Then we'll deal with those things as they come up. What do you say, Leah? I know you aren't a quitter."

She sighed. "I don't have a choice. I have to play your game."

Obviously, she still felt as if she was being blackmailed—that she simply had to endure all this unpleasantness so she could get what she wanted. And yet, after lying beside her on the bed, hearing her whisper his name in her sleep, he suspected she still harbored feelings for him. He simply needed to tap into those.

"Yes," he said bluntly. "For the next six weeks, anyway."

She nodded, plainly resigned to their agreement.

Then, because he didn't know what else to say, he gestured around the room. "How much of this shall we take with us?"

"Just the afghan and my knitting bag." She pointed to a corner where yarn spilled out of a canvas tote. "If I need anything else, I can always get it later. Meanwhile, the refrigerator comes next."

He followed her into the kitchen, noticing Leah's touch wherever he looked. Silk sunflowers and wheat stalks sprouted out of several slender vases and lined the top of the kitchen cabinets. The ceramic bowl they'd bought at a flea market held fruit in the middle of the table. Her purse lay on the counter, her billfold and keys spilling out of the open flap. And several pairs of shoes stood in a neat row by the back door.

This was how a house should be, he thought. It should look lived in, not sterile and lifeless, like his. In a few short hours their house would look like he remembered, filled with color and flowers and the organized clutter that had always seemed to follow Leah. He could hardly wait.

"What made you decide to move into your parents' house?" he asked. "I thought they were going to sell it when they moved to Oklahoma to be near your sister."

To spoil their grandchildren, Tricia Jordan, Leah's mother, had told him. Although Leah hadn't seemed to begrudge them their decision, it had to be difficult for her to know that her sister was as fertile as a bunny while Leah's branch of the family tree had withered.

"They'd intended to," she admitted, "but the Realtor suggested they'd get a much better price if they updated it. So, when I wanted a place of my own, I moved in with the understanding I'd redecorate and modernize."

He glanced around the room. "You did a wonderful job. You always did have a good eye for detail."

"Thanks."

"Can you show me the rest?"

He saw her hesitation—as if she didn't want to share this with him—before she finally shrugged. "Sure, why not?"

Gabe followed her through the dining room, back to the living room, then upstairs to the three bedrooms and a bathroom. The walls had all been freshly painted in neutral colors and airy curtains covered the windows.

"Quite an ambitious undertaking to work on by yourself," he remarked as they returned to the kitchen.

"I didn't mind. I needed to keep busy."

"I suppose." He noticed a collage of photos on the refrigerator and strolled over for a closer look. The pictures were all scenes he remembered, but one in particular stood out.

"I'd forgotten all about this," he said offhandedly as he pointed to the snapshot of the two of them at a summer carnival, posing in front of the duck-shoot booth. "I spent a small fortune trying to win this giraffe."

She came close to peer around his shoulder and smiled. "You were determined to win that prize. I think it cost you more than the animal was worth, though."

"Yeah, but we wouldn't have had nearly as much fun."

"Probably not," she agreed. "You were bound and determined to hit the grand prize duck."

The concept had been simple—to shoot the toy ducks floating past with a suction-cup dart gun. Knocking over specially marked ducks earned special prizes and he'd decided early on which one he'd wanted.

He grinned. "It took me, what—an hour? As I recall, you named it Gemma. Because of the purple jewel around her neck."

The jewel was actually a piece of colored plastic, but it was pretty and sure to catch a baby's eye, which was why Leah had insisted the giraffe would be the perfect addition to their nursery. Now the toy stood behind a closed door, gathering dust instead of occupying a child's attention.

An image of the nursery they'd designed flashed his mind's eye, accompanied by the scent of baby powder and the tinkling music of a crib mobile.

"Would it be easier if we started over in a new house?" he asked. "A clean slate, so to speak?"

"You're getting ahead of yourself again," she pointed out. "We don't even know if we can make a go of our relationship and you're already talking about new homes?"

She clearly still hadn't bought into the notion they could make their marriage work, but he refused to consider otherwise.

"I know everything between us is unsettled, but we have to approach our relationship as if it can and will succeed. If you recall, we both agreed we'd give this our full commitment, and that means we can't entertain thoughts of failure.

"Besides," he continued, "I'm not suggesting we sell our house and buy a new one next week. My idea is simply something to think about, especially when we both know there's one room you can't bear to enter."

"Going into the nursery isn't easy," she admitted, "but even if our life together was settled, I'm not certain a new house is the answer, especially if you spend the majority of your time either at the office or jetting around the world. Any marriage where one party is thousands of miles and three time zones away three weeks out of every four is going to suffer under the strain. Call me selfish, but I don't want to be philanthropic with your time."

"Like I said, Jack and Sheldon will be taking a more active role in the foundation," he assured her.

Wearing a puzzled wrinkle on her forehead, she met his gaze. "This sounds crazy, but I feel as if an imposter has replaced my real husband."

He smiled. "No imposter. I'm the real guy."

She paced a few steps before she faced him. "I appreciate your offer of a different house," she finally said, "but let's follow your advice to focus on us and deal with permanent living arrangements later."

"Fair enough," he said, satisfied with his first real sign of progress.

CHAPTER SEVEN

AFTER dinner that evening, Gabe pushed his empty plate aside and leaned back in his chair. "That was delicious, Leah. You always were a wonderful cook."

His praise brought a heated blush to Leah's face. "It was only scrambled eggs and toast," she chided. "Hardly an impressive meal."

"Maybe not to you, but it was to me. 'Impressive' is a matter of perspective."

"I suppose," she said, unconvinced by his assurance but grateful for his appreciation, "but I should have fixed something more substantial, like the chicken breast or the sirloin steak we bought this afternoon."

"Or we could have gone out for dinner, as I suggested," he said.

After hurriedly packing her necessities and driving them across town in their vehicles, she'd wanted to organize the kitchen and her closet before calling an end to the day. Visiting a restaurant would have taken far more of her evening than she'd wanted to spare.

Plus, she'd have been Gabe's captive audience while their meal was being prepared. She wasn't ready for that, yet. It was one thing to have a civil conversation in the privacy of their home. It was another to hold a conversation where they would be under public scrutiny.

"It would have taken longer to get ready than it did to scramble a few eggs," she remarked, "and chances were we would have run into someone we knew who would have wanted to visit. I still have a lot I'd like to accomplish tonight."

The real problem, in her eyes, had been the possibility of well-meaning friends congratulating them on being a couple again. She certainly didn't want to navigate that particular minefield.

"Whatever the reason, I appreciate the trouble you went to. Simple meal or not, what I had was perfect," he declared. "After all, just this morning you said I needed to go easy on my stomach."

"It seems like we had that conversation ages ago."

"Considering how hard you worked this afternoon, I'm not surprised," he said. "Where you found the energy to accomplish what we did, I'll never know."

"I didn't do that much," she said.

Gabe had wanted to empty her house, lock, stock and barrel, but she hadn't been ready to go that far. Fortunately, she'd been able to use the excuse of minimal storage and Gabe's sore ribs to dissuade him. However, she sensed he would have ignored his sore ribs to haul whatever she wanted, regardless of how big, bulky or heavy it was.

"We could have accomplished more if you'd let me," he complained good-naturedly.

"You heard the doctor's orders. No lifting."

"And I obeyed," he answered.

"Then why did I end up scolding you for carrying boxes you shouldn't?"

Remembering how she'd huffed whenever she'd caught him, then pull the load out of his arms, brought a smile to Gabe's face. At first, he'd been affronted by how little she'd allowed him to carry. Then it had become a game to see how much he could get away with. Best of all, being caught and hearing her scold only meant that she cared, even if she wasn't ready to admit it…

To his great relief, though, most of her things were back at home where they belonged, the refrigerator and pantry had been restocked, and the house that had previously looked like a model home now had a lived-in appearance.

He couldn't be happier.

Well, he could be, he amended, if Leah had moved into the master suite instead of the guest room, but being under the same roof was better than the alternative and with luck the hall would only separate them for a short time. Meanwhile, his vision of Leah tucking her finger under his collar and leading him upstairs would give him something to dream about and work toward…

"More coffee?" she asked as she rose to grab his mug.

"I've had enough caffeine for one day. I won't sleep tonight as it is." At her questioning glance, he added, "Too excited about being home, I guess."

"It doesn't quite seem real yet, does it?" she asked softly.

"No. I'm half-afraid I'll wake up and find myself still in the jungle," he confessed.

"I've been thinking along the same lines—that I'll discover your return was nothing more than wishful thinking."

He nodded, grateful she understood his fears so clearly. He only hoped she didn't press for details about the crash or the events afterwards. Yes, he'd answer because being open and honest was part of their agreement, but he'd really rather not revisit such a traumatic episode when he wanted to revel in her company on their first night together.

"I'm sure the truth will soak in soon enough," he said casually. "I certainly wouldn't be able to ignore the facts if you warmed your cold toes against my leg. How your feet can be such icicles, I'll never know."

Her answering chuckle was a melody he hadn't heard for a long while. He wasn't particularly surprised by how rusty it sounded—she'd had little to laugh about during the past few years. As for the smile she gave him…it was the sort that brightened a man's day no matter how difficult or ugly it had been, and reminded him of the girl in the carnival photo. The joyful woman with whom he'd fallen in love hadn't disappeared—she'd only been hiding behind a dark cloud.

Restoring their formerly close relationship suddenly seemed elementary. The key to rekindling their marriage was to rekindle Leah's spark, he decided, and he was just the man to do it.

"It's a gift," she said virtuously. "Although I recall offering to wear socks."

"My way of warming up your feet was more fun." He wriggled his eyebrows.

Once again, her face turned a familiar rosy hue. "It was," she agreed. "Good thing it's summer and cold feet aren't a problem. Shall we clear the dishes? I'm ready to relax for a while."

As she jumped up, he also rose. "Relaxing on the deck sounds good," he said, carrying his own place setting to the sink. "But do you know the best part about dinner tonight?"

"So few dishes?"

"Hardly. It reminded me of old times."

Her hands froze over the faucet and she stared at him as if he'd sprouted an extra nose. "Old times?"

"Yeah. Remember when we were first married? I'd come home from the hospital, starving to death but too exhausted to stay awake, and you'd fix this very meal for me so I could eat before I fell asleep on my feet."

She smiled, her tentative expression disappearing again. "And sometimes you did. I always said I should publish a cookbook—*101 Scrambled Egg Recipes*."

"Or created your own show on the Food Network."

This time she laughed, a full-bodied laugh that sounded like the carefree Leah she'd once been. The same Leah who'd found happiness in small things like sunsets, the neighbor girl's kitten, and the wildflower he'd pilfered from Mrs. O'Shea's garden near their garage before he'd walked in the door. The same Leah who hadn't been able to wait for their love to grow into a family.

"It wouldn't have been on the air long," she said lightly as she shut off the faucet and slid their plates into the soapy water. "Frankly, I was getting to the point where I thought I'd sprout feathers if I swallowed another egg, scrambled or otherwise. I shudder to think what our cholesterol levels were."

"Ah, but back then I didn't care. I was more interested in sleep, food, and…" he snaked an arm around her waist, pulled her close and planted a swift kiss against her mouth "…my wife, although not necessarily in that order."

Her small intake of breath proved that she definitely wasn't immune to his touch. "What are you doing?" she asked.

"What I should have done a long time ago," he told her. "I'm focusing on us."

Leah knew that for the next six weeks to be bearable, they had to find their footing when dealing with each other. Over the next two days they talked and they laughed, but controversial subjects were avoided, although she didn't know if that was by chance or design. Oddly enough, she found herself feeling…content.

She told herself it was only because she was within weeks of settling her life once and for all. She'd obtain Gabe's signature and that would be that. Her feelings had nothing to do with discovering how she could enjoy his company.

However well their temporary truce was holding, the door at the top of the stairs remained locked. She would have to venture inside to face her ghosts before long because her grace period would eventually run out, but in the meantime she'd lump that ugly bit of their past in with what he'd called "the rest of the stuff".

The only tense moments came when Leah followed Gabe into their house after the memorial service for his colleagues. Although he seemed to be bearing up well, she recognized the strain he'd been hiding underneath the smiles he'd shown to everyone.

"Would you like some coffee?"

He jerked at his Windsor knot as he headed into his office. "I've had enough caffeine, thanks."

She trailed after him. "A glass of wine?"

"No."

"Something to eat? I noticed you didn't sample any of the snacks after the ceremony."

"I don't want anything."

His clipped tone spoke volumes about his mood, but Leah knew how destructive brooding was. How ironic to find herself in circumstances where their former roles were reversed. This time *he* was the one hurting and *she* was the one who wanted to banish the pain but couldn't find the key to doing so.

"Okay," she said with equanimity as he sank into his executive chair. "When you are, let me know." She perched on the desk's edge. "You delivered a beautiful eulogy today. I know how difficult it was to share your personal stories and anecdotes."

"Their families deserved to hear them."

"You did an excellent job. I didn't know Will and Ramon as well as you did, but from the few times I'd been around them, I could tell you'd described their personalities and characters perfectly."

"They were good men."

"Theresa was especially grateful for your kind words. She said she has more wonderful things to tell her baby when he grows up." She paused. "I didn't know she was pregnant."

"She just found out. Ramon never knew."

"I'm sure he does now," she said softly.

He made a noise that could have meant anything from agreement to skepticism. "What did you feel when she told you?" he asked.

She thought for a moment. "Surprise. Sadness that she'd have to raise the baby alone and that Ramon would never enjoy being a father. Happiness that she'd have someone to remember him by, not that she'll need a child to help her remember the man she loved.

"And…" she drew a bracing breath, hoping Gabe would share his confidences if she shared hers "…I was a little angry. Angry at life for being so unfair."

He nodded slowly. "Me, too. I felt all of that, and then some."

"You did? I couldn't tell."

"I did," he assured her. "Just like before."

She finally faced a hard truth. "I was so wrapped up in my own pain that I didn't see yours, did I?"

He sighed. "Neither of us handled our losses well. Let's hope we've learned from our mistakes."

"I also felt something else," she added tentatively. "Disappointment."

"Because you can't get pregnant?"

"No," she said slowly. "I've accepted that. I was disappointed because my husband knew about Theresa's condition and didn't tell me. You don't have to protect me, Gabe. I can handle it."

He met her gaze. "Handle it, how? Like the way you still won't walk past the OB unit after nearly two years?"

Ouch. "Okay, maybe I don't deal with the excitement and joy as well as I should, but it would have been easier for me if I'd been prepared to hear her talk about the baby."

"You're right. I should have mentioned her news."

"You're forgiven," she said lightly. "Frankly, I'm overwhelmed just thinking of what she'll face as she raises this child on her own—dealing with hormones, teenage angst and hi-jinks. It won't be easy."

"She won't be alone," he said. "She'll have plenty of support from her family, Ramon's family, Jack, and all of us who worked with him."

Leah suspected he considered himself a large part of that support, especially when she thought about what he'd done for the single mother-to-be so far. He could say what he wanted, but guilt probably fueled a huge part of his motivation.

"You shouldn't blame yourself, you know."

"I don't. Not about the plane crash, anyway," he corrected. "Who could have known we'd fly into a flock of blasted birds?"

"But you still feel responsible."

He fell silent. "Yes."

At least he'd finally admitted it. "Because you survived and he didn't?"

He fell silent for several long seconds. "He was alive when Jack and I found him, you know. We did everything we could, but he didn't hang on like I begged him to. He just...slipped away."

"I gathered as much from your nightmares, but you're doing a nice thing, Gabe. You established a college fund for his child and paid off his mortgage so his son or daughter would always have a place to live."

"It would have been nicer if I could have saved him."

That, her intuition told her, was really why he was struggling with the tragedy. "You were in the jungle," she reminded him. "Not in a fully equipped emergency department or surgical suite."

"He had so much to live for. Why him? Why Will? Why them and not the rest of us?"

"That's one of the mysteries of life. The thing is, there were three medical professionals at the scene, and one of them was the woman he loved. If he couldn't hang on for her then he physically wasn't able to, and you shouldn't feel as if you failed."

He smiled at her. "For an amateur psychologist, you're a pretty smart gal."

"It's nice of you to notice."

"By the way, we're leaving tomorrow at seven a.m."

She sighed. She'd been hoping he'd had second thoughts about his latest trip. "Then we're still going?"

"Why wouldn't we?"

"Oh, I don't know. I guess because you haven't mentioned a word about it. I thought maybe you'd changed your mind."

"I haven't. Sheldon arranged for the cargo to be loaded today so we'll be ready for takeoff as soon as we arrive at the airport." He studied her a moment. "You really aren't happy about this, are you?"

"No," she said bluntly.

"Why not?"

"One, you seem awfully eager to go. Like you did before."
A cold, foreboding chill ran down her arms. This was the way
the distance between them had first started, and how it had
grown with each subsequent trip. She'd stayed at home with
nothing to occupy herself but her thoughts while he'd jetted
around the world, seemingly without a care.

"Eager isn't the right word. This isn't a holiday."

Her fears churning like Grand Canyon rapids, she began to
pace. "Exactly. You're working and you said you wouldn't."

"Leah—" he began.

She held up her hands to forestall his arguments. "I know.
This is only for three days."

"And it's strictly a mission of mercy," he told her. "Or are
you implying I can't ever respond to a critical need anywhere
ever again?"

"No, but I don't like the way you took away my choice,
Gabe. You reduced this Mexico trip to an obligation, a condition, when it should have been, at the very least, a mutual
decision."

He looked thoughtful, as if he realized his mistake. "Okay,
so I handled that poorly, but I was desperate. I wanted you
with me because I was afraid if I left, even for a few days, I'd
lose my advantage and, ultimately, I'd lose you, too."

"Gabe," she said softly, "we'd already negotiated to spend
the next six weeks together. Did you think so little of me that
I'd renege on our agreement?"

"I couldn't take that chance. Regardless of the way I forced
your cooperation, I really do need you there."

"You need a nurse," she corrected. "Not necessarily
me."

"The nurse I need is you." He leaned forward. "I'm not
looking forward to flying for obvious reasons and I'd travel
another way, if I could. Unfortunately, my other choices aren't
practical or timely. With you beside me, though, I can get on
that plane." He paused. "If I hadn't been coming home—to

you—I doubt if anyone could have forced me to board the last one."

She'd never considered how difficult his return must have been. No doubt every noise had had him thinking the worst. "Oh, Gabe."

"The point is, we have both seen how working with a common purpose builds a team, which is what I want for us. I'm hoping we can accomplish it, but…" He hesitated. "If you truly refuse to join me, I won't stop you."

His offer startled her. "You'd let me stay behind?"

"Yes. According to what I heard this morning, they have a tremendous amount of critically ill children, especially infants. It won't be easy on you."

She didn't know if she should be grateful for his understanding or affronted by the implication that she would be too affected to do her job. More importantly, though, knowing they had so many sick young patients and a shortage of nurses, how could she refuse and still be able to sleep at night? Besides, he had apologized and explained his motivations, misguided though they'd been.

If he'd been so desperate to fix their marriage that he'd resorted to blackmail, then he wasn't simply giving lip service to the idea.

"All right, I'll go." Seeing his suddenly broad smile, she added, "Someone has to make sure you don't overdo it."

"Thanks. You won't regret it."

She already did, not because she didn't want to help those people but because Gabe was obviously expecting more from her than she could give. "I'd better start packing."

He caught up to her before she reached the bottom step. "This could be the thing our relationship needs."

She stared at him with a sad smile. "It might also be the thing that breaks us."

CHAPTER EIGHT

LEAH accompanied Gabe onto the tarmac with mixed emotions. From a medical standpoint she wanted to be a member of his team, but from a personal standpoint she was afraid. He believed working together would foster teamwork and cooperation, and it could. However, it could promote dissension just as easily. This would be a stressful three days for both of them and stress didn't usually bring out the best in people.

Maybe this trip would be a game-changer for their relationship, but if it changed for the worse, it was better they learned it now, rather than later.

However, her thoughts of what might or might not happen faded as soon as she saw how Gabe struggled to climb on board the plane. He drew a deep breath, braced his shoulders and squared his jaw before he finally ducked through the doorway. His hands shook as he buckled his seat belt and on the strength of his reaction she wondered how he'd been able to fly home immediately after his accident.

Helping him cope became her top priority. Throughout the entire flight she held his hand and chatted about everything and anything, asking question after question about Ciuflores. If he noticed she repeated herself, he didn't comment.

Sheldon and Ben, their other team member, obviously anticipated Gabe's reaction, too, because when she was at a loss for words, they took up the slack. The two men kept up a steady stream of chatter through their headsets in a not-so-subtle effort to divert his attention from their position high above ground.

"Try to get some sleep," she advised.

He shot her an are-you-crazy look, but dutifully closed his eyes.

Luckily, the trip went without incident. As soon as the wheels touched down on the level patch of ground that constituted the small airstrip outside Ciuflores, the look of relief sweeping over Gabe's face told how agonizing this trip had been to him. She had to admit to a grudging respect for a man who faced his fears in order to help a friend...

"Thanks for being here," he said simply.

"I'm glad I could help." And she was, she realized. He'd needed her, which thrilled her to the point where she was almost glad she hadn't stayed at home.

Hating the slight tremor in his hands, she kissed his cheek. "Enough lollygagging," she said cheerfully. "It's time to go to work."

As she'd suspected, facing his mission and fulfilling his purpose for being there did wonders for his composure. He squared his shoulders and began issuing orders to Sheldon, Ben and Corey Walsh, their pilot, as he opened the door and exited the plane.

Leah stepped outside the new twin-engined Cessna and was immediately struck by the humidity and the earthy aroma. Flowering trees lined the eastern edge of the clearing, which probably accounted for the floral scent she detected. A hint of something more unpleasant—like the community dump— drifted in from the north, but the thick foliage hid it from view.

A man wearing jeans, a casual shirt and a clerical collar rushed to greet them.

"David!" Gabe exclaimed as he hugged the tall fellow, confirming the priest's identity as Father Odell, Gabe's old classmate who'd established this mission church some seven years earlier. "It's good to see you."

In his late thirties, David had light brown hair and crow's-feet around his eyes, and his skin was tanned from the Mexican sun. He also looked tired but, as Gabe had explained on the plane, David not only ministered to the spiritual needs of the area but also was the director of the only orphanage in the vicinity.

The idea of running across so many parentless children had troubled her, especially as this was the first mention of a local orphans' home, but if Gabe could face his fear of flying, she could deal with the children if it became necessary. She had to because by then she couldn't walk out with the plane at ten thousand feet.

"The feeling is mutual," he answered. "When we heard about your plane crash, I said a lot of masses on your behalf. Then, when you phoned, I could hardly believe our prayers had been answered."

"That makes two of us, David, but with a man of your spiritual pull on my side, how could it have turned out any other way?" he joked.

"All things considered, I didn't expect you to fly here yourself," David chided gently.

"I wouldn't have for anyone except you," Gabe said.

"I'm glad you decided to get back on the horse that threw you, although I wish you'd come under better circumstances."

"Me, too. By the way, this is my wife, Leah."

It was obvious the two were close friends. "Father," she said as she shook his hand. "Gabe has told me so much about you."

"Now, that's a scary thought," the priest teased. "But, please, call me David. What are titles among friends?" He turned back to Gabe. "I assume you brought the supplies Hector requested?"

"And then some," Gabe told him. "If you have a few strong backs, we can start unloading."

David waved forward a group of men standing near the edge of the field. In no time at all the cargo had been moved from the plane to the waiting trucks and they were bouncing their way into town.

Leah clung to Gabe and hoped she'd still have teeth and eardrums when they finally reached their destination.

"Still no shocks on this beast?" Gabe yelled over the noisy muffler.

David grinned. "Why bother with shock absorbers? They'd just wear out. Honestly, though, think of this as nothing more than a free carnival ride."

Because it was futile to talk, the rest of their short trip passed without conversation. Ten minutes later, they reached Ciuflores.

The village's poverty was painfully evident by the dirt-packed streets and ramshackle houses. Grass had long since given up its struggle to survive, although a small patch appeared every now and then. Chickens and dogs roamed freely through the town and goats remained tethered to their owners' yards. What surprised her most was seeing only one person and he had tied a handkerchief over his nose and mouth, bank-robber style.

"Where is everybody?" Gabe asked the same question Leah had on her mind.

"They're staying at home," David explained. "Normally, this is a bustling time of day but with the flu hitting so hard, most aren't venturing out for anything except basic necessities. We're following all precautions but the situation has gotten worse since I called you."

"And your kids?"

Concern spread across David's face. "They fall into three groups. Those who are recovering, those who are currently sick, and those who will probably show symptoms before long. We've also lost four to pneumonia. Because an illness like this spreads through group homes like wildfire, we've sent the sick ones to the hospital to try and contain the illness. Unfortunately, we don't have enough resources to care for everyone, which was why I called you."

He pointed ahead. "This is our clinic, Leah, which we only have because of your husband's generosity."

"And your arm-twisting," Gabe added.

David chuckled. "That, too."

The whitewashed building was unassuming and boxlike, in contrast to the graceful Spanish architecture of the neighboring church. Yet even if she hadn't noticed the simple sign in front that read "*Clínica*", it was obvious this was an important building in the community because of the satellite dish perched on the flat roof like an oversize bird.

Inside, four patient wards, which had been designed to hold five patients each, held double that number. Of those, nearly every bed contained a child. One of the rooms was filled with cribs and padded boxes to accommodate the littlest. A few had IV poles standing beside their beds. Some were coughing, some crying, and some were too ill to do either.

In the last room, Dr. Hector Aznar was sitting on a young boy's bed, listening to his lungs. As soon as the nurse beside him murmured in his ear, he looked in their direction and a relieved smile suddenly grew on his face.

"Gabriel, welcome," he said as he approached and shook his hand effusively. "You are a sight to see." He launched into Spanish, which Leah couldn't follow.

Hector seemed to be at least ten years younger than Gabe, but his eyes reflected wisdom and experience that went beyond his years.

As the two men talked, presumably touching on Gabe's accident because Leah understood a few words, she studied her surroundings. One woman in uniform who was obviously a nurse from the way she checked IV bags and listened to lung sounds cared for the twelve toddlers and infants. A few other adults—probably parents—sponged little bodies, held cups and cuddled those who needed cuddling.

"Gabriel says you are a nurse, no?" Hector asked her in his thick accent.

"I am," Leah answered, anticipating his request.

"Good. Any assistance you can give us will be appreciated. Our girls are, shall we say, exhausted."

"I'll do what I can," she said simply. "What strain of influenza are you dealing with?"

He shrugged. "We have not tested anyone, but the ministry of health tells us it is most likely H1N1 Influenza A. Regardless of what name we use, we are fighting an uphill battle. Now that you are here, we can hope to turn the tide, yes?"

"Yes," she said. "Are you the only physician on duty?"

"My partner, Miguel Diego, is here, too, but now that you have arrived, he hopes to travel to the towns we normally visit once a month. Those people are probably in the same dire straits we are but sadly there are more of them than of us."

"Then you have a large caseload," she remarked.

Hector nodded briskly. "Larger than we can adequately care for, but we do our best. Your husband has been what you would call our guardian angel."

Leah stole a glance at her husband. The local physician's praise had brought a tinge of pink to Gabe's face as he grinned sheepishly at her.

Suddenly, all those hours when she'd begrudged his work made her feel extremely small and petty. It was one thing to know her husband's charity made a difference in the lives of so many people and quite another to actually *see* the difference with her own eyes.

Hector spoke rapid-fire Spanish and eventually Gabe nodded before he translated.

"Here's the deal," he began. "Ben, because you're a pediatrician, he would like you to evaluate every child here, starting with the most ill. According to Hector, pneumonia is a real problem so we have to start the IV antibiotics ASAP. The nurses speak English fairly well so you should be okay on your own, but if you run into problems, let me know."

"Okay, but don't wander away too far," Ben said as he shrugged on a gown that Hector provided. "My Spanish is so rusty I could ask for a blood-pressure cuff and get an enema."

Gabe grinned. "Yeah, well, do your best."

As Ben strode off to begin, Leah asked, "Did we bring the IV supplies for—?"

"Pediatric infusion sets are being unpacked as we speak. As soon as we get a handle on the hospitalized, you and I are going on house calls while Hector covers the walk-in cases."

She raised an eyebrow. "Do you really think we're going to accomplish all that today?"

He grinned boyishly, looking far more energized than she'd expected, considering his emotionally and physically stressful journey. She was feeling overwhelmed and she'd slept on the plane for a few hours, whereas Gabe had hardly closed his eyes. "Welcome to my world."

After one of the nurses shyly identified herself as Elena, she steered Leah to her first patient—a three-year-old girl who cried fitfully but sucked greedily on the bottle Elena handed her.

"It is electrolyte drink. She is not as sick as others but now you are here, she will have IV, too. If you would sponge her down, please?"

Leah saw how the little girl lacked the strength to hold her own bottle. Immediately, she sat in the nearby chair, cradled the child in her arms and held the bottle. As the child relaxed against her, she brushed away the sweat-dampened dark curls from her forehead.

"Where are her parents?" she asked Elena, who was wringing out a wet rag in a nearby basin of iced water.

"At home with their other children," she answered, handing the cloth to Leah. "They are sick, too, but not as sick as Sofita." She stared down at Leah and smiled. "She rests. Good. When bottle *está vacío*, go to next."

At the rate Sofita was guzzling the fluid, it wouldn't take long for her to finish. In the meantime, Leah propped the drink against her chest and held it in place with the same arm she'd crooked around the child's head. With her right hand, she ran the cool cloth over her face and arms.

The small sigh of obvious pleasure and the twitch of a smile were all the thanks Leah needed.

A short time later, she gently laid the toddler in her crib. After washing her hands, she moved to the next patient, as Elena had instructed. The Spanish nurse had placed IV sets in or near every bed, and with her help they began inserting the lines into tiny veins. Most of the children were too ill to give more than a token protest, which threatened Leah's composure more than once. As soon as they had the fluids and antibiotics running, she gave each one a bottle, a cuddle and a cooling sponge bath.

Time didn't matter. Caring for these kids did.

Finally, she reached a five-year-old boy who was so severely dehydrated she couldn't raise a vein. When he hardly flinched at her failed attempts, she knew she was in trouble.

"How's it going?" Gabe asked. His timing couldn't have been more perfect.

"Thank goodness you're here," she said, frustrated. "He's so dehydrated I can't start his IV. I've tried twice and I can't poke him again. I was hoping you'd try."

"Okay." Gabe took her place on the bed and began his search for a suitable site. When he'd succeeded and the IV fluid dripped at a steady pace, Leah wanted to cheer.

"Are you ready for a break?" he asked.

She stared at him, horrified by his suggestion. "I'm not finished. I still have IVs to start and—"

"This is the last one," he told her gently. "See?"

She finally glanced around the room and, sure enough, an IV bag hung near every bed.

"But I haven't cuddled this one yet," she said. "Or bathed him, or—"

"I will do that, Señora Montgomery," Elena came up to say. "We have done well. Go with your husband."

"But you've worked longer than I have."

"Go." Elena tugged her away from the bed. "I will sit as I watch Felipe."

"Come on, Leah," Gabe coaxed. "You won't be much of use if you wear yourself out on the first day."

Reluctantly, she followed him. "Where are we going?"

"To eat," he said, leading her past the patient areas to an average-sized room that served as Hector's office and staff lounge. There, two covered plates of food were waiting, along with a pot of rich black coffee.

"Hmm," Gabe said, sniffing the air and whipping the napkins off the plates. "This smells like Carlotta's cooking. She makes the best tamales, beans and rice." His hand froze and a thoughtful expression crossed his face.

"Carlotta? Is this the woman you suspect has pancreatic cancer? The one who cares for her three grandchildren?"

"Yes."

"If she's in the kitchen, maybe she isn't as ill as you thought."

"Maybe. When I have a minute, I'll find out."

At first, Leah thought she was too keyed up to eat, but the delightful aroma convinced her otherwise. She tasted the beans while Gabe poured two mugs of coffee.

"Has everyone else eaten?" she asked as he rejoined her at the table for four.

"I assume so. We took the last two places."

"Is it always like this when you visit a place?" she asked.

"The experience is never quite the same," he said. "We've conducted clinics before and treated a lot more people, but never this many seriously ill cases at once."

"I almost feel as if I'm in the middle of a disaster drill, except this isn't a practice. These children are really sick. I haven't stopped until now and I haven't stepped out of the one ward."

"What's sad is how the patients in the other three are just as ill, if not more so."

"You realize that three days isn't nearly enough time to make a dent in treating these people?"

"Believe me, no one is more aware of that than I. What's more disconcerting is when you realize Ciuflores isn't the only village experiencing this scenario. What we're seeing is taking place across the country. A lot of those communities aren't as lucky as this one."

The picture he'd painted wasn't pretty.

"Because they don't have a Father David who has a personal connection to the CEO of a charitable organization?" she asked.

His mouth curved into a gentle smile. "Exactly."

Gabe polished off the food on his plate then leaned back. "Are you hinting you'd like to stay longer?"

Was she? "I'm only making an observation," she said. "But isn't it difficult to leave when you know your work isn't finished?"

"Definitely," he agreed, "but staying until the crisis ends isn't feasible. Hector and his staff know that, and they're grateful for every bit of help we provide because it's more than they had before. When you stop to think about it, Ben and I have literally doubled the number of medical professionals in a sixty-mile radius, so we can treat twice as many patients. We may be a mere stitch in a wound that needs ten, but sometimes one, if properly placed, is better than nothing."

He stared at her now empty plate. "Are you ready to tackle our next assignment, Nurse Montgomery?"

She was starting to get her second wind. "Sure."

"Good, because, house calls, here we come."

Armed with David and his knowledge of his parishioners, Gabe began his round of house calls. He found everything from a household with only one or two sick individuals to homes where the entire family was symptomatic. Fortunately, none required hospitalization, which was good because he didn't know where Hector and his staff would squeeze in another patient.

Leah, however, was a star in his eyes. She performed basic

nursing care from taking temperatures to giving sponge baths. She taught children and parents to sneeze into the crooks of their arms and, with David's helpful translation skills, encouraged them to wash their hands with soap and water for the same length of time it took to sing the happy birthday song.

As soon as it was too dark to see more than a few feet in front of them, Leah was lagging behind and even David appeared a little frayed around the edges. Gabe wasn't functioning on much more than adrenalin, either.

"We're calling it a night," he told his crew as they returned to David's truck.

"We can see a few more people," Leah protested.

"We could," he agreed, "but we won't. We're all exhausted and tomorrow is another day."

Leah dutifully climbed into the cab of the truck, allowing the two men relative privacy.

"Your wife doesn't know when to quit, does she?" David asked.

"Afraid not."

"Have you told her where you two are bunking down?"

Gabe should have, but the opportunity hadn't presented itself until now. "Not yet. I'm hoping she'll be too tired to care."

"Good luck with that. If we weren't having an epidemic, I could make other arrangements, but—"

"We'll be fine at the orphanage," Gabe said firmly, hoping he was right. "Leah will understand our choices are limited. Did you find places for Sheldon, Ben and Corey, our pilot?"

"They're bunking together down the hall. I'm sorry I only had two rooms to spare, one for you and your wife and one for the others."

"We won't spend that much time in them anyway," Gabe answered practically.

"True. By the way, in the morning, before you're torn in a hundred different directions, save a few minutes for me, okay?"

"A problem?"

David sighed. "Yes and no. It's too late to go into detail."

"I'll find you first thing," Gabe promised.

As it happened, Leah was too exhausted to notice her surroundings, or, if she did, the fact simply didn't register. Gabe gratefully ushered her into the room they'd been given, although he knew his moment of reckoning would come in the morning.

As soon as she saw the bed, she sighed gratefully and began stripping off her clothes. By the time Gabe had opened his duffle bag, Leah was curled beneath the covers.

"Sweet dreams," he said softly, but she was already fast asleep.

He undressed down to boxers and a T-shirt and slipped under the sheet beside her. Immediately, she snuggled against him and he tucked her under his arm, pleased she'd turned to him without being aware of it. Which only proved that subconsciously she knew she belonged at his side.

Holding her against him, Gabe reflected on their day. She'd been such a godsend. Not only had she kept him sane on their long flight, she'd been a great partner when they'd finally started to work. She'd anticipated his requests, offered suggestions, and both her smile and calm manner had soothed the most anxious parents and fretful kids. He'd accomplished a lot today and he owed it all to her.

As he began drifting off, he realized her presence had given him another benefit. Normally, on trips such as these, he had a hard time going to sleep. Between pushing himself to the point where he was simply too tired to doze off and thinking of everything he had to accomplish the next day, he had trouble shutting off his brain so his body could follow suit.

Now, though, having her in his arms, listening to her gentle breathing and feeling her steady heartbeat brought him peace.

Tomorrow would start early and end late, but one good thing had happened already as a result of their trip.

After so many months apart, Leah was finally sharing his bed.

CHAPTER NINE

A THUMP and a giggle teased Leah as she dreamed of a summertime picnic with three children. Another giggle, a loud whisper, a foot digging into her side and a happy-sounding "Shhh" jarred the pleasant scene in her head, and she slowly opened her eyes. The two little girls straddling Gabe's chest in their nightgowns startled her completely awake.

"What in the world—?"

"She is awake?" the oldest asked, and immediately a boy, who looked to be about four years old and was wearing cowboy-print pajamas, climbed aboard, too.

The youngsters all chattered a mile a minute at Gabe, who simply laughed and answered in Spanish. Although she couldn't follow the conversation, she recognized a few words—*desayuno*, breakfast, and *señora*, lady.

"Gabe?" she asked as the smallest girl suddenly leaned over Leah and smiled at her around the thumb in her mouth. "What's going on?"

"This is Anna, Rosa and José. They are Carlotta's grandchildren," he explained as he sat up, holding on to Rosa so she didn't tumble off the mattress. "Anna is the oldest. She's five. Rosa is almost two and José is four."

"Carlotta the cook?"

"Yeah. They all live here with the rest of the kids."

"The *rest* of the kids?" she echoed. "Where *are* we?"

"David gave us a room in the staff quarters at the orphanage."

"We're staying in the *orphanage*?" she asked, horrified.

"I know what you're thinking, but this is where we usually bunk down. Besides, David couldn't ask a family who's sick to take us in."

She exhaled, knowing she couldn't refute his logic. She could do this. She *would*.

"Fine, but do we have to stay in the same room?"

"David only had two available. We have one and the rest of our group is sharing the other."

"I don't suppose we can ask for another bed or a cot?"

"All extra beds and cots are being used by patients. Unless you'd like to kick one of them off their mattress so you can have one to yourself?"

She cast him a disgusted look. "Of course not," she grumbled. "Maybe one of us should sleep on the floor."

"Feel free," he said. "I'm the one with the sore ribs, remember? Besides, nothing will happen in here that you don't want to happen."

His comment wasn't completely consoling. Given the opportunity—and her own weakness where he was concerned—they'd do far more than sleep. The good news was that they'd probably both be too exhausted when they finally fell into bed to have the energy to make love.

Just then the children bounced on Gabe again as each one chattered louder than the other in an obvious attempt to get his attention.

So much for his sore ribs, she thought uncharitably, eying the youngsters. Yet their excitement was contagious. After seeing the seriously ill children yesterday, it was refreshing to see such happy, healthy ones.

"I'm sorry about the early wake-up call." He tugged on the oldest girl's pigtail. "The kids aren't supposed to barge in, but they'd heard I'd arrived and, well…" he shrugged helplessly "…they couldn't wait to see us."

He tickled José and the dark-haired imp laughed with delight.

"You have an exuberant fan club," she remarked.

Gabe's grin made him look like the man in their wedding photos. The shadow she'd seen in his eyes yesterday had lifted and joy shone in its place as he tugged on José's hair. "I'm a novelty," he said.

Leah watched as Anna leaned over and planted a sloppy kiss on Gabe's cheek. "For being a novelty, they're very comfortable around you." In fact, she thought they were more than comfortable—they all looked at Gabe as if he was their personal fairy godfather.

"They remember me from my previous trips and haven't forgotten that I usually bring candy."

Rosa's eyes sparkled with interest. *"¿Tienes chocolate?"*

"Later," Gabe promised, as he threw back the sheet and swung his feet onto the floor. "After breakfast."

Immediately the children screeched with delight. His next words sent the children scampering off the bed with several more enthusiastic bounces before they disappeared through the open door.

"What did you tell them?" she asked.

"Candy is for children who eat their oatmeal first. I also reminded them that Father David won't be happy if their grandmother reported them missing."

"Well, I guess this means we should get up and start the day, though I still feel like I need another few hours in bed!"

"Did you sleep well?"

"I must have. I don't remember a thing after I stumbled in here last night."

"I'm not surprised. You worked hard yesterday. Unfortunately, today won't be easier."

"I didn't expect a vacation when I left home," she told him. "So don't apologize."

"Okay." He rose and stretched. "Come on, lazybones. Breakfast and our adoring public are waiting."

The morning meal was a noisy affair. The trestle tables were full of youngsters of varying ages, all waiting for their food. Yet when David rose to say the blessing, the littlest to the oldest became so quiet Leah could have heard a mouse scamper across the floor.

While Sheldon and Gabe discussed their plans for the day—Ben apparently had spent the night at the clinic to monitor several patients who'd needed ventilator support—Leah sensed she was being watched. At first, she disregarded her suspicion because so many of the children kept glancing in their direction, but the feeling persisted. When she saw the trio of children who'd provided their early-morning wake-up call, she knew she hadn't been imagining things.

Rosa was studying her with a thoughtful expression and José watched Gabe with adoration. Anna's gaze drifted from Gabe to her, then back to Gabe again, and it held such longing that it nearly undid her.

There was no doubt about it. For whatever reason, these children loved Gabe. And seeing the sparkle in their eyes when they captured his attention made her realize how she, too, had once looked at him through those same eyes of love.

Curious about the children's story, she waited to ask until the meal was over and Gabe had left the table to deliver the promised treat. While he was swarmed over by the youngsters, she pressed David for answers.

"Their grandmother has been our cook ever since her husband died several years ago," David began. "After her son and daughter-in-law were killed when his fishing boat capsized about a year ago, the children came to live with Carlotta. She needed to keep her job to support herself, so we worked out an arrangement where she continued to cook at a slightly reduced salary in exchange for day care and a place for the three of them to live."

He sighed. "The really unfortunate thing is that Carlotta has recently been diagnosed with pancreatic cancer."

"Gabe suspected as much but I didn't realize her diagnosis was official."

"Unfortunately—her condition being what it is—we don't know how much longer she'll be with us."

Leah's heart went out to the three children. To lose their parents and, soon, their grandmother... Life would be tough for them. "I'm so sorry to hear that. Do they have any other family?"

"Carlotta has another son. The children's uncle. We're trying to locate him, but no one seems to know where he is, what he's doing, or if he's even alive. I've been told he was quite a hellion in his younger days and went to Mexico City, where he fell in with the wrong crowd. Carlotta hasn't heard from him in years."

"What happens to them, then, after...?"

"If we can't find their next of kin, they'll stay here. If we do find their uncle, the children will go with him, unless he doesn't want them." He sighed. "The odds aren't in favor of him accepting the responsibility, but it's hard to say what might happen."

Leah glanced at the children interspersed around the room. "I presume all the children have a similarly sad story."

He shrugged. "More or less. Some are orphans, others have parents who simply can't provide for them."

"They're all from Ciuflores?"

"No. We're the only orphanage in the area, so kids come here from miles around. If I had the space, we could easily double our number. Life in this part of the country is difficult and the children often pay the price."

"I see." She paused, watching the three as they clung to Gabe, but it was more for his attention than the candy he provided. "Those three seem to love Gabe," she remarked.

"They all do," David said simply, "although I have to admit he has a special rapport with these kids in particular. Their faces always light up when I mention his name. I'm not sure why because he doesn't single them out but I suppose it's the same for them as it is with us. There are some people we feel more comfortable with than others.

"The thing is, he's good with children, in general," David continued. "A modern-day Pied Piper. He definitely has a gift."

"He does," she agreed, trying to ignore the sudden ache his words caused in her chest. If not for her, Gabe would have a houseful of his own children.

A sudden scuffle at the opposite end of the dining room drew the priest's attention. Either he had eyes at the back of his head or being the director of an orphanage of fifty had given him a sixth sense for trouble. "Sorry for deserting you," David apologized, "but I have to play referee."

David hurried toward the two teenagers, who were shoving each other and occasionally throwing punches. Rather than observe the drama unfolding at that end of the room, she watched Gabe as he dug in his pockets and passed pieces of wrapped hard candy to the children who swarmed him.

He looked so happy as he laughed, joked and hefted the littlest ones into the air.

She thought of the instances when they'd visited friends with children or her own family gatherings with her sister's kids. Their children had always climbed over Gabe on their arrival and she'd attributed their attraction to his freely lavished and complete attention.

His affinity for little people didn't stop there, either. Sick children responded to his smile and quiet confidence in a way that many adults did not. She'd seen that scenario more often than not in the hospital. More recently, she'd seen it during yesterday's house calls.

David's description of Pied Piper seemed apt.

Her insecurities suddenly flooded over her. It was far too easy to wonder if Gabe regretted marrying her or if he wished he'd cooperated when she'd offered a divorce. A legal piece of paper would have given him the freedom to find someone who could fill the need for a child in his life.

Although she rapidly dismissed those ideas as foolishness because he'd said he would love her regardless, one hard truth stared at her.

She was the one holding up the adoption process. *She* was the roadblock to their dreams of a family. Gabe had given control over those dreams to her, and *she* now carried the deciding vote.

Don't let fear influence your choice.

Deep in her thoughts, she didn't notice Rosa had toddled over to her until she felt a small hand on her knee.

Leah stiffened, an instinctive reaction born from her reluctance to let herself grow too close to a child...*any* child...but the trust shining in those dark brown eyes and the featherlight touch that was both comforting and tentative made her smile come easily.

"Shouldn't you be with your grandmother?" Leah asked. Then, because the little girl didn't seem to understand, she fished for the right phrases in her limited vocabulary. *"¿Dónde está tu abuelita?"* Where is your grandmother? *"Debes estar con ella."* You should be with her.

Rosa simply popped a thumb into her mouth and grinned.

Unable to stop herself, Leah stroked the tousled jet-black curls. "Don't you want to play with your friends?"

Rosa didn't answer. Instead, she simply waited, as if she had faith in Leah's ability to eventually figure out what she wanted.

Oh, please, let something else grab her attention, Leah thought. It was one thing to share her love with nieces and nephews and quite another to give it to a child she'd never see again. And yet she couldn't send Rosa away, not when she was waiting so patiently for acknowledgment. This toddler had already known more rejection than any child at her age should. She wouldn't add to it.

"Do you want me to hold you?" Leah asked. She searched her limited vocabulary for the proper phrase and came up missing. She simply patted her lap and held out her hands.

As if Rosa had been waiting for the invitation, she immediately popped her thumb out of her mouth, climbed up and made herself comfortable.

With an awkwardness that came more out of emotional

uncertainty rather than a lack of the mechanics involved, Leah shifted positions to tuck Rosa under her arm.

With her thumb back in her mouth, Rosa melted against her, as if there wasn't another place she'd rather be.

Certain one of the staff would soon retrieve the toddler, Leah allowed herself to enjoy the weight of the little body in her lap and the special scent so common to babies. Slowly, tentatively, she began to rub her shoulder.

"I wonder what you're thinking," Leah said, aware that even if Rosa understood her, she couldn't answer. "You are definitely a snuggler, aren't you?"

Rosa smiled around her thumb as if she understood or was simply happy to have Leah all to herself.

"I'll bet you've wrapped Father David and everyone else around your little finger," she murmured.

It wouldn't have been difficult to do, she decided. She'd been holding the tyke for less than five minutes and already felt the gossamer ties ensnaring her.

Somewhat amazed by Rosa's decision to seek her out, Leah simply continued to hold her and savor the moments when suddenly Anna and José appeared beside her. He held out a small battered toy truck while Anna showed off her own precious possession, a doll that showed it had obviously been well loved by the threadbare dress, broken nose and missing index finger. Immediately, Rosa squirmed off Leah's lap and disappeared as fast as her short legs would take her.

Wondering what had sent Rosa away, Leah admired the other children's toys. "Does your truck make a noise?" she asked José, then made a few questioning engine sounds. The boy beamed and he knelt down to run the truck beside her feet to demonstrate.

While he was occupied, Leah touched the doll's face. "Does your doll have a name?" she asked. *"¿Nombre?"*

Anna's smile stretched from ear to ear. "Sarita," she answered, before launching into a conversation that Leah couldn't begin to follow. It obviously revolved around Sarita because Anna stroked what was left of her doll's pigtails.

Suddenly, a new lovey was thrust into her lap—a light brown teddy bear with matted fur, a frayed red neck ribbon and one eye. Apparently Rosa wasn't to be outdone because she waited for Leah to acknowledge her toy, too.

Conflicting emotions filled Leah's chest—pain that these children were so happy with so little, and awe that they wanted to share what obviously meant so much to them. Plus, they wanted to share it with *her.*

For an instant she couldn't breathe and her vision blurred. She was desperate to escape and began frantically looking around the dining hall for Gabe to rescue her, but Anna spoke and Leah knew she couldn't obey her instinct to run away. Leaving the three so abruptly would be a rejection they couldn't understand and didn't deserve.

So she forced herself to breathe slowly and deeply until the overwhelming feeling passed, leaving bittersweet longing in its wake.

If not for David's intervention, Gabe would never have been able to untangle himself from the children clamoring for his attention. Fortunately, after David had dealt with the two boys who'd clearly experienced a difference of opinion, he clapped his hands and ordered the children to their daily chores. Less than thirty seconds later, the noise level had dropped considerably and he saw Carlotta slowly approach, leaning heavily on the girl beside her.

"Shouldn't you be in bed?" He fussed over the woman, who didn't appear anything like she had when he'd last seen her. She'd lost weight and her skin color reflected the toll her cancer was taking on her. Perhaps if he'd been able to convince her to go to a major facility for tests when he'd first examined her, they might have been able to halt the disease and give her a bit more time, but now it was too late. According to David, Taylor had talked Hector through a biopsy procedure and a preliminary result had confirmed the aggressive nature of her disease. While surgery and subsequent chemotherapy were options, those treatments would only prolong the inevitable.

"I will go there soon enough," Carlotta told him with a smile as she accepted the chair he'd pulled out for her then tiredly waved away her helper. "I must do what I can now. Your breakfast was good?"

According to David, Carlotta had been teaching two girls to take her place in the kitchen. From the food Gabe had eaten so far, Carlotta's replacements were learning their lessons well.

"It was delicious, as was yesterday's meal," he answered.

"Good. I want to see my grandchildren. They seem happy, yes?"

Gabe turned to find his wife and saw her surrounded by the three familiar faces. For a moment he waited and watched the childless woman with three motherless children...and wished.

"Your wife has a mother's touch."

"She does."

"Yet, the padre says you do not have children."

He ignored the familiar twinge of disappointment. "We had a little boy, but he was too small when he was born. Then we tried to adopt, but things didn't work out. So, no, we don't have children of our own."

"I see. That explains why your wife isn't, what is the word, *comfortable* with my babies? She has too much pain inside."

"Probably."

"And yet she has a good heart."

"She does." Gabe watched as Leah planted a kiss against José's temple. As he squirmed, she laughed as if she found his reaction humorous.

"You carry your own sorrow, do you not, Dr. Gabriel?"

He hesitated. "A part of me always will," he said simply. Then, because he wasn't comfortable under the older woman's scrutiny, he motioned toward the scene before them. "Your grandchildren are great kids."

"Even when they wake you early?"

He chuckled. "You knew they'd paid us a visit?"

"Grandmothers have eyes everywhere."

"With those three, you need them," he said.

"Oh, yes." Her gaze drifted in Leah's direction and she smiled at José's demonstration of his truck. "He is my busy one," she said. "Always moving, even in his sleep. Anna is my noisy one because she talks, talks, talks. And Rosa…" Her face was a mixture of love and sorrow as Rosa rested in Leah's lap. "Rosa is my cuddly one. It is good they are familiar with everyone here."

"No one will ever take your place," he said kindly, "regardless of who cares for them."

"Thank you for that, Dr. Gabriel," she whispered. "You, too, have a good heart. Perhaps Father David will find someone like you and your wife to take my place."

Gabe froze. Was Carlotta hinting that she wanted Gabe to adopt her grandchildren? If so, would Leah be open to the idea, especially after she'd adamantly refused to adopt? As he glanced at the children, he admitted that in spite of telling Leah he'd abide by her decision he'd love nothing more than to take these children into their home. He truly wanted to make it happen—to barge in, full steam ahead, just as she'd accused him of doing—but he couldn't. He'd told her the choice was hers, and he'd stick by that, even if it killed him.

"Do not fret," Carlotta told him. "What will be, will be." She struggled to her feet. "Come. Those three will play all day with your wife if we let them. Shall we rescue her?"

CHAPTER TEN

LEAH knew they were pushing hard to see as many patients as possible because they were scheduled to fly home in the morning. She hated leaving when the residents of this community obviously needed her help and she consoled herself with the reminder that the assistance she'd provided had eased the regular staff's burden to a small degree.

She also had to admit that the Salazar children had captured her heart, and in such a short time, too. How could they not, especially when Rosa smiled hugely whenever she saw her, then toddled over and wanted to be held?

These aren't your children, Leah told herself as she played with Anna and José. *You're just—what did Gabe call it? A novelty. Yes. That's it.*

In one small corner of her mind she was glad they were leaving so soon. She didn't want them to become so entrenched in her affections that her departure would be traumatic. They'd have enough to deal with when their grandmother died because they were old enough to remember her—at least for a while—but too young to understand why the one constant in their lives had disappeared forever.

During her odd moments she wished she could take all three home with her, but it was impossible. Their uncle would assume responsibility, which was as it should be.

By mid-afternoon, she had lost track of the number of homes they had visited. Most had at least one parent healthy enough to care for the sick members of their household, but the very last family they visited—the Ortiz family—was in dire straits. Every member was ill and the mother, pregnant with her third child, had an advanced case of pneumonia. The father had left several weeks earlier to find work and no one knew when he would return.

Leah, David and Gabe stood off in one corner to discuss their options.

"We can't leave her here," Leah warned. "She has diminished lung capacity with the baby pressing on her diaphragm. She needs to be in the hospital with round-the-clock nursing care, not to mention ventilator support."

"The hospital is full," Gabe pointed out.

"But if she stays at home…" Leah left her sentence unsaid. The outcome, in her opinion, was obvious.

"I know," Gabe said tiredly. "She won't make it for sure."

"Then David will increase his occupancy by two, at least in the short term."

"He still might," he warned. "Being in the hospital doesn't mean we'll provide a magical cure."

She knew as well as anyone how hard this strain of influenza was on pregnant women. "Yes, but there she has a fighting chance. Left at home, she has none."

Her argument had its desired influence because Gabe turned to David. "What will we do with the children if we can find a bed for her? Can you find someone to stay with them?"

"Ordinarily, I'd say yes, but I'm running out of healthy adults," David said ruefully. "The best I can do is bring them to the orphanage."

"But won't we expose the others?" Leah asked, hating the thought of Rosa and the other children contracting the same disease.

"We'll quarantine them," Gabe said.

"But David doesn't have enough staff to separate these two from the rest," she protested.

He raised an eyebrow. "What do you want me to do,

Leah? The hospital doesn't have room—we're going to have to squeeze her in as it is—and we can't leave them here to fend for themselves."

"We have no choice," David added. "We'll do the best we can and pray it will be enough."

She exhaled, hating their lack of options. "You're right. Just be sure your staff understands how easily the flu can spread through the orphanage if they aren't careful."

"I'm counting on you to remind them," he said.

"Then it's settled," Gabe said. "We'll move her to the hospital and the children to the orphanage."

As they turned to leave, Leah held Gabe back while David went on ahead to make arrangements. "How are you doing?"

"Fine."

"You look tired."

His smile was lopsided. "Aw, honey, I'm way past tired, but thanks for asking."

"Maybe you should take a break."

"I can't. Not now. Not with Mrs. Ortiz in her condition." He rubbed his face.

"You're worried about her," she guessed.

"I'm worried about a lot of things," he admitted. "Can we help her pull through with limited resources? Can we give her the attention she needs when so many others need it, too? Frankly, how Hector and Miguel bear up under this on a daily basis boggles my mind."

"Maybe the epidemic will play itself out soon."

"We can always hope." He dropped a quick kiss on her mouth then straightened as he gave her a rueful smile. "Gotta run."

A short time later, Leah found herself not only selecting a room for the two far away from the others but also instructing all the adults and older children on proper hygiene. Through it all, Carlotta's grandchildren became her shadows, although she refused to allow them in the same room as the sick children. A few times she was certain she'd caught a glimpse of

Carlotta out of the corner of her eye, but when she looked, the woman was gone.

Leah felt guilty for enjoying Rosa and Anna's attention, especially when she knew their time with their grandmother was so short, but having three energetic children in the older woman's sickroom wouldn't be a pleasant experience for any of them. She was doing the woman a favor by looking after the three, she told herself. After tomorrow, someone else would take over, anyway. Until then she planned to store up memories of toothy smiles, sloppy kisses and gentle hugs.

Dinner was a semi-relaxed affair, eaten in the dining hall long after the children had finished and were playing outside. David had disappeared into his office and Sheldon and Ben were back at the clinic, leaving Gabe and Leah to enjoy another meal of tamales and beans.

"I can't believe we're going home tomorrow," she remarked.

"Time flies when you're having fun."

She reached across the table to cover his hand. "I wouldn't call this fun. I'd describe the trip as enlightening, challenging and overwhelming."

"But you're glad you came."

She nodded slowly. "I am."

"We make a pretty good team, don't we?"

"Is this where you say, 'I told you so'?" she asked lightly, aware that so far this trip seemed to be fulfilling Gabe's expectations. Working together had opened her eyes to many things, but most of all she'd finally been able to see Gabe's character without the vision being distorted by her own pain and resentment. In fact, she was seeing the man she'd fallen in love with and knew it wouldn't take much to push her over the edge.

"I hear the garden has a beautiful moonlit path," he said offhandedly. "Want to check it out with me tonight?"

"A moonlight stroll sounds perfect. Do you think we can disappear for a while, though?"

"I don't see why not. Everything seems to be under control."

Sheldon took that moment to approach and lean over the table. His face was solemn, his tone grave as he spoke. "You spoke too soon, boss. We have a problem."

Gabe's shoulders slumped slightly. From Leah's own experience with Gabe's second-in-command, Sheldon tended toward understatement rather than exaggeration. If he said there was a problem then the problem was usually major, not minor.

"Somehow, I'm not surprised," Gabe said wryly. "What's up?"

"Ben wants you in the hospital ASAP."

Gabe frowned. "We were just there. Did he say why?"

"Not really. Something about Hector."

Leah exchanged a glance with Gabe. "What could be wrong with him?"

Gabe rose. "Let's find out."

They found the clinic's physician lying on the small cot in his office. Ben was sitting beside him as he listened to Hector's ragged breathing while Elena sponged off his face in an obvious attempt to bring down his fever.

"What happened?" Gabe asked in a low voice.

Ben slung his stethoscope around his neck and motioned them into the hallway. "Influenza."

Gabe's heart sank. "Damn," he muttered, running his hands through his hair. "We don't need this on top of everything else."

"My sentiments exactly," Ben agreed. "I noticed he wasn't feeling well this morning, but he shrugged it off as exhaustion from too-long days and too-short nights. Then, about thirty minutes ago, he could hardly stay on his feet and wasn't making any sense when he talked. I thought maybe it was the language barrier, so I found Elena to talk to him. She was as clueless as I was."

Elena nodded, her dark eyes large with worry. "*Sí*. He was

out of his head, talking crazy talk." She made circular motions near her ear.

"Elena and I convinced him to go to bed, which didn't take too much effort, I might add. Then I sent Sheldon to find you." He hesitated. "We're going to need a Plan B."

Gabe pinched the bridge of his nose, already anticipating the repercussions Hector's illness would have. From the looks on everyone's faces, they were realizing them, too.

He turned to Elena. "Do you know when Dr. Diego will return? Is there any way we can reach him before then?"

"He will be back in a week, maybe more, maybe less." She shrugged helplessly. "I can send someone to find him, but he does not always follow the same path. Sometimes he goes here first. Sometimes there first. Is no way to tell."

"What about a cell phone?"

She shook her head. "It does not work where he is going."

Damn! Gabe felt everyone's gaze as they waited for his answer. He only wished he had one to give.

"Here are our options," he said. "We leave as scheduled—"

Leah gasped. "But we can't desert these people now, when they don't have a doctor and they're in the middle of a medical crisis. Even if the patients were all doing well, the nurses can't handle Mrs. Ortiz—the pregnant woman we brought in earlier."

"Or..." he cast a meaningful glance at her for interrupting "...we stay until Miguel returns, which could be a week or more. And that will affect our other commitments." He turned to Sheldon. "The clinic in Tennessee comes to mind."

"Don't forget the trip to Alaska," Sheldon reminded him.

Sensing Leah was about to explode with frustration, he glanced at Ben. "Your anniversary is a few days away, if I remember correctly."

Ben cleared his throat and looked apologetic. "Yeah. My wife planned a big party. It's our tenth, and I promised I'd be there," he said to Leah as she was the only one who hadn't heard.

Gabe glanced at Sheldon. "How are the supplies holding out?"

"We've used about two-thirds of what we brought," Sheldon admitted. "Under normal conditions for a community this size, what's left should last a while. But…" he shrugged "…these aren't normal conditions. Everything depends on how near we are to the end of this outbreak."

"What's your opinion, Ben?" Gabe asked. "Are we on the downhill slope?"

"You've seen as many if not more patients than I have," the other physician replied. "If I had to guess, from the number and severity of the cases who've landed in the clinic, I'd say we're still in the thick of things."

Gabe agreed, although he'd hoped Ben might have drawn a different conclusion. "Then we have a third option."

"Which is?" Leah asked.

"I'll stay behind while the rest of you head back as originally planned. Sheldon, you handle the business end of sending down another shipment. Corey can help."

Sheldon nodded. "I'll get back as soon as I can." He grinned. "If not before."

"I'm staying, too," Leah declared, her chin rising defiantly. "I may not be a physician, but I can help."

She'd be a welcome addition, but he wasn't worried about her ability to hold their pace. He had three objections to her remaining behind, and they were all under the age of six. "Yes, but—"

"If you're not going home, neither am I."

Knowing she wouldn't appreciate an argument in front of everyone, he simply shot her his best we'll-talk-about-it-later look. To her credit, she didn't say a word, but her eyes promised a heated discussion.

He turned to his team. "Then it's settled. You two will fly back in the morning. Sheldon, you'll return as soon as you can arrange for another supply shipment."

"Piece of cake," Sheldon boasted.

"In that case," Ben said, "I'll take tonight's shift. This may be the only night you'll get any sleep."

It probably would be. After Ben climbed aboard their plane, Gabe would be on duty twenty-four seven.

"Okay, but call if you get more than you can handle."

Throughout the rest of their conversation, Leah didn't say a word, which didn't bode well. Still, Gabe hoped their moonlight walk through the garden would help as it could easily be the only private time he'd enjoy with her until they flew back to the U.S.

As soon as he'd finished hammering out last-minute details with Sheldon, he grabbed Leah's arm and led her out of the clinic. Darkness had fallen and the usual nighttime noises surrounded them as he walked beside her to the orphanage.

She held herself stiffly under the guiding hand he'd placed at the small of her back.

"Nice evening, isn't it?" he asked, making conversation to soften her irritation.

"Hmm."

He glanced at the building looming ahead, noticing the bank of windows in the orphanage's dormitory wing was dark. "Looks like the kids are all in bed."

"I'd say so."

She'd said a complete sentence; he was making progress.

"The garden's around the back," he said. "Watch your step. The ground is uneven." He took her hand before he led her down a small footpath and held back shrubs and branches for her to pass by unscathed. Finally, they arrived in a clearing that boasted a stone bench and a multitude of flowers. The colors were muted in the moonlight, but the white blooms seemed to glow as if nature had saved their beauty for midnight lovers. Their fragrance filled the air with a heady, sensual perfume.

"Oh, Gabe," she breathed as she turned a complete circle. "This is beautiful."

Relieved at how their surroundings had broken through

her reserve, Gabe smiled. "Not as beautiful as the woman standing here."

She met his gaze. "Do you really think so?"

"I know so." He traced a line from her temple down to her jaw.

"Then why…?" She bit her lip in indecision. "Why don't you want me to stay here with you?"

The hurt in her voice was as painful to hear as it obviously was for her to say. "I want you to stay," he confessed, "because I like having you here. It simply isn't in your best interests."

"Don't yo-yo on me, Gabe," she warned. "Why isn't it in my best interests? After all the fuss you made to get me here, now you insist I go? And without you?" She shook her head. "I don't understand."

"You're growing too attached to Carlotta's grandchildren and you've only been around them for a couple of days. How hard will it be on you to leave after another week?"

"Yes, I'm fond of them. They're sweet kids." She spoke as if she weighed each word beforehand. "You're trying to protect me again but it isn't necessary. When we finally go home, I'll handle it."

"Are you sure?" Perhaps it was his job to be supportive instead of doubtful, but he wanted Leah to know exactly what she would face. "Leaving these kids won't be like leaving your nieces and nephews. Chances are you'll never see these youngsters again."

She nodded slowly, as if she'd already realized it. "They'll go with their uncle and that will be that."

Gabe didn't see any point in mentioning that no one had been able to locate Carlotta's son. Why give Leah something else to worry about, especially if knowing they had a family member who'd step in was a comfort to her?

She squared her shoulders. "Regardless, you need me and I'm not leaving until I absolutely have to."

"Leah…" he warned.

"Please, Gabe? Let me help you, and let me enjoy the extra time with them."

He hated to hear her beg, even though he knew she was only going to put herself through more anguish.

"Yes," she added as if she'd read his thoughts, "I'll probably get teary-eyed and cry most of the way home, but I'm preparing myself for that. I'll be okay. Truly."

Her assurances were convincing, but he knew the separation, when it came, would be far more difficult than she imagined. And yet, if she understood and accepted the risks, what could he do?

"If you're certain..." He was repeating himself again.

"I am."

He hesitated, still unsettled by her choice. "You know I can just toss you on that plane," he mentioned offhandedly. "As the team's leader, I'm responsible for everyone's safety and well-being, including their emotional health."

"You are," she admitted, "but this is my decision, Gabe. I *want* to stay." Her grin widened. "And if you make me leave at first light, I'll return when Sheldon does."

He chuckled as he hugged her tight. "This is against my better judgment, but okay. You can stay."

"Gee, thanks for permission."

He grinned at her wry tone then he added a teasing note to his own to hide his own trepidation. "Are those the only reasons why you don't want to leave—because of the kids and the patients?" He held his breath, hoping to hear she'd had a change of heart about their divorce.

"Oh, I don't know," she said airily. "It could be because you're starting to grow on me, too, but I haven't made up my mind yet."

"And when do you think you might know?" he returned.

"Maybe tomorrow. Maybe next week. Maybe—"

"Right now?" He bent down to brush his lips against hers, but his light kiss soon turned heated. Perhaps it was due to the moonlight or the heady fragrance in the air. Perhaps it was because he was glad Leah wasn't leaving or that this could be their last uninterrupted night for the foreseeable future. Perhaps it was simply because Leah was the one woman who could make his blood sing, but, whatever the reason, he wanted more and he sensed she might feel the same.

"Yes," she breathed. "Maybe now…"

He hauled her against him, eager to take what she was offering and relieved that the moment he'd been waiting for was finally upon him.

"Dr. Gabriel! Dr. Gabriel?"

Leah broke off their kiss. "You're being paged."

Gabe grimaced. "So I hear."

"Maybe it's something minor."

The hopeful note in her voice and the way she'd responded in his arms made him believe that she might be coming round. That she just might have started to look forward instead of backward. That she either had or was on the brink of wanting her future to include him. Those notions were enough for him to accept this most inopportune interruption with grace, even though he really wanted to grumble and complain.

"Are you willing to wager on that?" he asked.

She grinned. "No, but it's a nice thought."

A teenage boy burst into the clearing. "Dr. Gabriel. Dr. Ben says to come."

"Sorry to cancel on you," he told her. "Duty calls."

"I understand. I'm a doctor's wife, remember?"

Leah stretched on the too-thin mattress, noticing Gabe's side was still empty. She'd waited for him to return to their room, but had given up and gone to bed two hours ago. Now her watch dial showed it was nearly midnight and the sheets were cold, which meant the emergency requiring his attention was serious.

She curled around her pillow, feeling like a contented cat as she reflected on their evening. It had felt good to work with Gabe on a professional basis, with none of their old baggage between them. Seeing him in action was a vivid reminder of why she'd fallen in love with him ten years ago. His concern and tireless interest in the people he'd come to serve were glowing testimonies to his character. He was a man who'd move mountains if he could for the people he cared about.

He'd told her that he'd pressed for the adoption for *her*, but she'd never quite believed that, until now. After seeing him in action—seeing how quickly he responded to whatever need he found—she finally believed his motives. And, for the first time, she began to wonder if she might be wrong about other things. Maybe they *wouldn't* be better off being apart…

Although the joy on Gabe's face as he played with Carlotta's grandchildren lay heavily on her chest. Could she open herself up to the possible heartbreak if she agreed to reopen their adoption case file? And were they strong enough as a couple to weather another rejection? Was Gabe that sure that they would be okay so long as they were together? Was she?

These questions went unanswered as their bedroom door swung open and the light from the hallway spilled inside.

"You're awake," Gabe said.

"Barely." She stifled a yawn. "What's going on?"

He tugged on the blanket. "I need a scrub nurse and you're it."

"A scrub nurse? I haven't been in the operating room since I was in training."

"Which still makes you more qualified than the other nurses." He tossed a pair of jeans and a shirt at her. "Come on, sleepyhead."

Leah rolled out of bed and stepped into her jeans. "What sort of surgery?"

"Appendectomy."

"Someone we know?"

"No. Five-year-old boy with excruciating belly pain. His symptoms began two days ago and gradually got worse. I've monitored him for the last few hours because his symptoms weren't classic for appendicitis, but his temp has spiked. I don't want to wait."

"Do you think the appendix ruptured?"

"Let's hope not. Here are your shoes."

She slipped on the loafers then followed him through

the silent building as she finger-combed her hair. "Are they equipped to handle surgeries at the clinic?"

"Not really, but we'll make do. I've operated under worse conditions."

"What about instruments?" Her stomach flopped like a landed fish. "Don't tell me you're going to cut on someone with only a pocket knife and a sewing kit in hand."

"I won't. Luckily, I don't leave home without my own basic tools of the trade," he said with a grin. "I've learned that I never know when they'll come in handy. One of the nurses is sterilizing them now."

What a relief! "How's Mrs. Ortiz doing?"

"Not well," he said grimly. "In fact, Ben and Sheldon would have flown her to Mexico City an hour ago, but I need Ben to handle anesthesia. In any case, they're leaving just as soon as I'm finished."

"The baby?" she asked.

"The midwife thinks the baby's showing a few signs of distress. The obstetrician Ben called said Mrs. Ortiz needs a C-section to relieve the pressure on her diaphragm, but I'm hesitant to do it because we can't take care of a preemie. The sooner we can get her to a place equipped for her problems, the better."

Fortunately, the night-shift clinic nurse had followed Gabe's instructions to the letter. His instruments were sterile and the patient was ready. Leah scrubbed beside Gabe, intent on his last-minute instructions and refresher course. Finally, between the drugs Gabe carried as part of his emergency surgical kit and what they found locked in Hector's cabinet, they were ready and their patient was unconscious.

"If we were at home, we could do this laparoscopically," he said offhandedly. "We have to do this the old-fashioned way."

"He won't care," Leah advised. "Now he'll have a scar to brag about."

Gabe's gaze met Leah's. Although she knew he couldn't see it through the mask, she offered a tremulous smile and hoped she wouldn't make a mistake because of her inexperience. As if he'd read her mind, he said, "Take a deep breath. You'll do fine." His eyes twinkled. "I won't be grading you, either."

She chuckled. "Thanks."

"Okay, then." He flexed his shoulders then held out his hand. "Scalpel."

As soon as she slapped the requested instrument into his hand, she was amazed at how quickly she fell into a rhythm. It was mainly due to Gabe, she had no doubt. His skill was obvious as he cut through skin and tissue until, finally, the offending appendix was revealed.

It was swollen and red and ready to burst.

"Looks like we got here in the nick of time," Gabe said as he clamped, snipped, then eventually sutured. "How's he doing, Ben?"

"Great," Ben said from his place near the patient's head as he monitored vital signs. "Just the way I like surgery—in, out and no problems."

"You can say that again."

After closing his incision and bandaging the site, Gabe pronounced his work done and stripped off his gloves. Looking tired, but pleased, he said, "Let's settle him in his cot, then we'll load Mrs. Ortiz in David's truck. Are you guys ready to go?"

"Corey's at the plane, doing his pre-flight checks," Ben answered. "Sheldon's waiting outside to help us with our patient. Then it's wheels up."

Leah shouldn't have been amazed at their efficiency, but she was. If she didn't know better, she'd think Gabe's team had drilled on this exact scenario until they'd choreographed every step. This was Sheldon's first time in the field and Ben's third, but their united purpose, coupled with Gabe's experience, had pulled them into a well-functioning team.

This was what Gabe had wanted to achieve with this trip—to extrapolate the unity created by this unlikely group of individuals into their marriage—to basically give their relationship a sense of purpose.

Having a family had been part of that purpose and when that had failed, it had seemed pointless to continue the marriage. And yet before Andrew had even become a glimmer in his father's eye, her wish had been simple—to love Gabe and share their lives together. Had that most fundamental purpose changed?

It hadn't, she decided. She still loved him and wanted her life intertwined with his.

Blurting out her revelation was tempting, but it would have to wait. Not only did they have a patient to oversee, but after everything they'd gone through, they both needed to mark the occasion in a special way.

The trip to the airstrip proceeded at a tortoise's pace in deference to Mrs. Ortiz's condition, but eventually everyone and everything had been loaded. The sun was dawning as the plane took off.

Leah watched the aircraft disappear into the cloudless sky. "Strangely enough, I feel like we've been deserted."

Gabe flung an arm around her shoulders. "It does, but at least we have each other." He kissed her forehead. "So, my dear, shall we see if there's any breakfast left?"

Before she could answer, a boy about twelve years old burst into the clearing. "Dr. Gabriel," he called out, panting.

Leah paused, watching Gabe as he listened to the boy's rapid-fire Spanish. She caught a few words, *orphanage* and *hospital*, and guessed at the rest. Finally, he faced her and motioned to the truck. "The sun is barely up and we're already in high demand."

"I gathered as much."

"You're needed at the orphanage and Hector insists on seeing patients even though he can barely stand. I think breakfast is on hold."

"I'm going to predict we'll be busy today."

"So busy you may wish you'd left with the others," he said darkly.

Leah gazed at her husband's face, noticing the distinct shadow of whiskers on his jaw. They would be pushed to their limits, especially Gabe, but she would be there to watch over him and ease his burden as much as possible.

"Not a chance," she said. "I'm exactly where I belong. With you."

CHAPTER ELEVEN

WHEN Leah arrived at the orphanage a short time later, she discovered five more children were symptomatic, bringing her total of sick children to seven. After tending each one personally, it was nearly lunchtime. Anna grabbed her hand and led her to their table, so in between wolfing down her own meal she helped feed the crowd of little people by encouraging them to eat, filling cups, and wiping up the inevitable spills.

As she finished scrubbing the last face before sending them outside to play, one of David's assistants approached her, looking harried. That seemed to be a common trait among everyone she'd seen the past few days. No doubt she would look the same by the end of the week.

"Carlotta is asking for you," the young woman said. "She is in her room."

"I'll be right there."

"Oh, and she wants you to bring…" She mimicked holding something between her thumb and forefinger and made sweeping motions with her hand.

"Pencil and paper?" Leah guessed, wishing she had a better command of the language than she did.

"*Sí*. Pencil and paper."

"I'll bring them," she promised, before washing her hands thoroughly. If only she'd asked Sheldon to include a few gallons of waterless bacterial cleanser… Her skin was already chapped from the constant handwashing and harsh soap, but better to have rough hands than flu.

Inside Carlotta's room and armed with the requested paper and pencil, she was amazed at how quickly the older woman's condition had deteriorated. "Carlotta?" she whispered, lightly touching the woman's shoulder. "You wanted to see me?"

Immediately the woman opened her eyes and struggled to smile. "*Sí.*"

"How are you feeling?" Leah asked. "Do you need any pain pills or—?"

Carlotta waved aside her question. "No. Tell me, Leah, what do you think of my little ones? Do you have what you call a soft spot for them?"

"I do," she admitted, smiling. "They are special children, but you know that better than I."

The older woman's face held that soft, far-off expression, as if she were seeing into the past. "Their parents were special people, too."

"I'm sure they were."

"I want to tell you about them," she said.

Surprised by the request, and also curious, Leah nodded. "I'd love to hear your story."

"Write it down, please. So you do not forget."

Now she understood Carlotta's request, although why the woman would dictate her personal memories in English instead of in her native Spanish was a mystery. Rather than argue with the frail woman, she simply nodded and prepared to write.

"My son, Mario, was a beautiful baby and looked much as José does now," Carlotta began. "We knew his wife's family well, long before he and Jacinta took their vows. She was such a happy child and loved to sing and dance. Anna takes after her. Rosa…my Rosa is, what do you call it…?" She paused to think. "A mixture of both."

"And because of that, all three are a comfort to you."

"Ah, *sí.* That they are. Mario was such a busy boy and as a youth, he…"

For the next hour, Leah recorded everything Carlotta shared. By the time she'd finished her fifth page, Carlotta's voice had faded. "We will continue tomorrow," she said faintly.

"Of course." Leah rose. "Rest now." Before she could move away from the bed, Carlotta grabbed Leah's arm in a surprisingly fierce grip.

"You will watch over my little ones?"

Leah didn't have the heart to explain her stay in Ciuflores wouldn't last longer than a week, and with their uncle presumably on his way it wouldn't be necessary for long. However, she also understood the dying woman's concern, so she folded Carlotta's hand in hers. "Of course. We all will."

Carlotta closed her eyes and nodded. "Come tomorrow."

Suspecting she would continue her story, Leah nodded. "I'll be here."

"Padre."

She paused. "Do you want Father David?"

At Carlotta's weak nod, Leah said, "I'll send him to you."

Rosa was waiting for her outside Carlotta's room, so Leah hoisted her on one hip as she searched out the priest. Fortunately, she found him in the chapel, on his knees. She would have tiptoed away to leave him to his prayers but Rosa began babbling and caught his attention.

"I'm sorry to interrupt," she told him as he approached. "But I spent the last hour with Carlotta. She wants to see you."

"Okay, I'll drop by for a visit. How is she?"

"Weak."

David nodded, his concern obvious in his eyes.

Leah blew a raspberry against the little girl's neck, causing her to giggle. "Would you mind taking her?" she asked, passing Rosa to him. "I want to check on the boy who had surgery and Rosa doesn't belong in the hospital."

"Ah, yes. I heard about Tomas. How is he?"

"His surgery went well and now I want to monitor his post-op care. Not that your nurses aren't doing a good job," she hastened to explain, "but…"

He grinned. "But you want to see for yourself."

Leah felt her face warm. "Yeah."

"I'll tell you what I told Gabe. Don't bite off more than you can chew. We can't afford for you and Gabe to follow in Hector's footsteps."

"I'll be careful," she promised.

Three days later, she finally admitted she had failed to keep her promise. She had tried to follow David's advice—she really had—but there was so much to do and so little time. Between sick children at the orphanage, helping at the clinic, and playing with Carlotta's grandchildren, her days didn't end until she fell into bed each night and curled around Gabe for a few hours before the routine repeated itself.

Today, though, she had the added job of using her ER skills while Gabe tended a man with severe burns on his arms and face.

"Will you keep him here?" she asked Gabe after they left the fellow to rest.

"He'll need skin grafts and surgical debridement, which is beyond what we can provide. According to Hector, there's a town about a half a day's drive away which is the equivalent of our county seat. They have a small hospital that's better equipped than our clinic. One of his friends will deliver our patient and his wife there as soon as she packs a bag."

"One thing you have to admit," she mused aloud, "everyone in this community pulls together. They don't have much, but what they do have, they're willing to share."

"You'll find that attitude in a lot of places like this."

She thought of something else he'd said. "You'd mentioned Hector. Is he feeling better?"

"Yeah, but he's still weak. I told him to concentrate on regaining his strength because when we leave, he'll need to run at peak efficiency." He rubbed his whisker-darkened face, which obviously hadn't felt a razor yet today and it was already mid-afternoon. "I don't envy him at all."

At first glance, her husband looked as perky as he always

did, but she saw the tired set to his mouth and the faint smudges under his eyes. No doubt she probably looked worse.

"Why don't you take a power nap?" she suggested. "Thirty minutes and you'll feel like a new man."

"As tempting as it sounds, I'll have to take a rain check."

"Okay." She stood on tiptoe to deliver a kiss. "I'll see you at dinner in about an hour."

His face lit with curiosity, then satisfaction. "Count on it," he said.

She'd just walked through the door and into what passed as a street when a teenage girl ran up to her. "Señora Gabriel," she panted. "Come!"

Life in Ciuflores seemed to be one crisis after another. "What's wrong?"

"The midwife…she is sick and my sister needs her. We must hurry."

Surely she wasn't asking Leah to deliver a baby! She turned toward the hospital. "I'll get Dr. Ga—"

The girl tugged on her arm. "No time. We must go *now*."

After casting a longing look at the building where her husband was probably dealing with his own crisis, Leah decided to accompany the girl and assess the situation.

The bungalow at the south end of the village was like so many others in its need for repairs and paint, but inside she soon realized she was caught in the middle of a situation she'd always hoped to avoid…the young mother, a girl of about eighteen, was fully dilated and moaning in pain, while her young husband appeared as if he wanted to join in.

Sensing the man would handle a task better than he seemed to handle his laboring wife, Leah sent him to the clinic with a message for Gabe.

Obviously grateful and eager for something to do, he ran out of the house while Leah turned to the younger sister. "Do you have hot water and blankets, um, what's your name?"

"Isabella. My sister is Regina."

"Okay, Isabella. Do you have the things I asked for?"

The girl bobbed her head. "*Sí*. They are ready from the last time."

"The last time?" Leah echoed. It was comforting to know that Regina had gone through this before and wouldn't be a stranger to what was about to happen. "She has another baby?"

"No. It was born dead."

Oh, dear. No wonder both parents looked as if they were frightened out of their wits. The thought of being responsible for bringing their baby into the world with a history like that only added to Leah's pressure.

She couldn't cave in, though. She had to do this. While she wasn't a midwife, her skills were better than nothing until Gabe arrived.

Unfortunately, while Leah washed her hands and changed the sheets with Isabella's help, Regina's contractions began to run into each other without stopping. Another look showed the baby's head was crowning and there was nothing she could do to stop it. She only hoped there wouldn't be any complications before Gabe galloped to the rescue.

She glanced at the door, willing him to suddenly save the day, but he didn't. She was on her own.

"Okay, Regina," she soothed as she positioned herself between the woman's legs. "We're going to do this. You'll be fine and so will your baby. Are you hoping for a boy or a girl? I'm sure you don't care, as long as it's healthy," she chattered on, mainly to draw Regina's attention away from her pain. Although Leah had no idea if the young mother understood her or not, her soothing tone seemed to calm the stark fear in Regina's eyes.

A mighty push later, and the baby's head was free. While Leah suctioned out its nose and mouth, Gabe strode in.

"You seem to have everything under control," he commented as he gently nudged Isabella out of the way to stand beside Leah.

"Thank heavens you're here," she said, relieved she didn't have to do this alone. "You can take over."

"You're doing fine as you are," he said, making no move to usurp her place. "I'll look over your shoulder and talk you through the rest."

He spoke to Regina in Spanish and as she bore down again, one tiny shoulder slipped out, then the other, until finally the little body glided into Leah's hands, already wailing.

"Slippery little things, aren't they?" he commented.

"Yeah." It was an awesome moment, but she didn't have time to revel in it. "You can tell her she has a daughter."

The new mother leaned against the pillow, perspiring and obviously spent as she rattled on and on in Spanish.

Gabe answered calmly as he helped Leah cut the cord. "I told her the baby is fine," he said. "She was worried."

"Rightfully so. She lost her first baby. Stillbirth."

Gabe washed his hands while refreshing her memory on cutting the cord. As soon as she'd finished, and he'd wrapped the baby in the blanket Isabella had provided, he handed her the infant.

"Score her Apgar and let Mom and Dad meet their daughter. I'll finish up. You did great, by the way."

"Regina did all the work," she said. "I basically watched."

After assessing the baby at a ten on the Apgar scale which evaluated her breathing, heart rate, color, muscle tone and response to stimuli, Leah diapered and bundled her up to meet her impatient parents.

Just as she was ready to carry the baby back across the room to Regina, Gabe stopped for a look. "You have the touch," he commented. "She hasn't complained at all about leaving her little nest."

Leah grinned. "Not yet, anyway."

"And look at all that black hair," he commented. "I already see pigtails in her future."

Leah smoothed down the spiky tufts and slid an inexpertly knitted cap over her head. "Between her mom and her aunt…" she smiled at a beaming Isabella "…pigtails, braids and ponytails won't be a problem."

After staying long enough to help Regina freshen up, recite a list of do's and don'ts, and congratulate the new parents, she walked out of the two-room home with Gabe beside her.

"Are you ready to add 'midwife' to your résumé?" he teased.

"Not a chance," she said. "I'm happy with heart attacks, gunshot wounds and stabbings. Those aren't nearly as stressful. The entire time my hands were shaking and my knees wobbled."

"You didn't show it," he said.

"You weren't looking hard enough to see the signs," she responded. "All I could think about was what if this baby didn't survive, either? I didn't want them to blame me for doing something wrong."

Gabe couldn't have asked for a better opening. "Did you blame me when you lost Andrew?"

She froze in her tracks. "Blame you? Why?"

"Because I wasn't there when you started hemorrhaging."

"No." She began walking again. "You hadn't gone on a trip for months and my obstetrician said everything was fine. If she didn't anticipate a problem, why should you? Besides…" she grinned, as if remembering "…by then you were driving me crazy with all of your hovering and I didn't see why you shouldn't go."

He saw her smile fade. "The question is," she asked, "do you blame *me*?"

He frowned. "Why should I?"

"Because, ultimately, I'm responsible for what happened," she whispered, staring straight ahead as if unable to meet his gaze.

"You just said your doctor believed everything was fine. Why do you think you were at fault?"

She shrugged. "Logically, I know what everyone told me, but I can't help wondering if I'd done too much that morning. I'd wanted to prove to you that I might be pregnant but I wasn't helpless. Maybe crawling on the ladder to change a light bulb tore something loose when I reached for the fixture—"

He hated hearing her sound so defeated. He grabbed her arm and pulled her to a halt. "Stop that," he scolded. "It wasn't your fault. It could have happened if you'd been lying on the sofa all day."

Her eyes shimmered. "I know that in my head, but in here…" she tapped her chest "…it's still hard to accept. Especially when you acted as if you couldn't bear to be around me. Which was why I thought you blamed me…"

"I felt helpless because I didn't know how to break through your misery, but I never considered you at fault," he insisted. "What happened was a tragedy, but a divorce wasn't the solution."

"Maybe not, but it would have allowed you to have the things you always wanted."

"I have what I want, right here."

"That's sweet of you to say, Gabe." She began walking and he matched his pace to hers.

"It's true, not sweet," he corrected.

She fell silent, as if sorting things through in her mind, and he didn't interrupt.

"Do you think about them, Gabe?" she finally asked.

He hadn't expected that question. "Nearly every day. Especially when I see children about the same ages as they would be now."

"Really?" she sounded surprised. "You never mentioned a word or acted as if you gave them another thought."

"You weren't looking hard enough to see the signs." He repeated her earlier comment, hoping it would jar her memory.

"I suppose not," she answered ruefully.

"What about you? Do you think about them?"

"I do," she said as she tucked her hands back into her pockets. "I told myself I shouldn't, but different things would happen or be said and I'd be reminded, especially if I heard of another Andrew or an Elizabeth."

"You were going to call her Lizzie."

"Yeah," she said with a far-away expression on her face. "Of all the things we chose I had the most fun deciding on names. A name is so important to a child's self-image."

"It is," he agreed. "Andrew John and Elizabeth Anne, with an 'e'. 'A special spelling for a special baby', you said."

For a long moment they walked in silence, but it wasn't uncomfortable or oppressive. In fact, it seemed almost contemplative, as if it was finally okay to mention those names aloud.

"I didn't want the divorce because I hated you," she said without preamble. "Ending our marriage seemed like the best solution to a bad situation. You'd asked me before if I was trying to save you and, yes, I was. You'd done the same thing for me so many times and this was something I could do for you. I wanted you to be happy because subconsciously I loved you. How else could this trip have opened my eyes so quickly, unless the truth had been there all along, waiting for me to see it?"

"And now?" A combination of anticipation and dread made him unable to breathe.

"I still love you," she repeated. "I want what we had before, even though I have trouble believing it's within reach."

His pulse skipped a beat. "Our future is yours for the taking," he promised. "I'll show you."

"I want it all, Gabe. The love, the passion, the romance, the honesty, the sharing. *Everything*."

"You'll have it," he said. "And then some."

She stopped on the path leading to the orphanage's front door. "I want our future to begin now, Gabe. Not when we get home, but *now*. I'm tired of feeling empty inside."

He hesitated, not wanting to misinterpret. It would literally destroy him if they made love and she still demanded a divorce. "You said we wouldn't make love because it clouded our issues. Does this mean I can shred those papers in my desk drawer?"

"Yes, you can."

"And our marriage will begin right now," he pressed.

"Unless you're too tired." She raised an eyebrow in question.

His previous exhaustion vanished and he was positively certain he wore a goofy grin on his face. "I'm not too tired."

A tiny wrinkle marred her brow. "I'll bet you haven't eaten all day. Maybe we should—"

"The only thing I'm hungry for is you," he said.

With Gabe having earned her cooperation, he seemed as if he couldn't walk to their room fast enough. He grabbed her hand in an unbreakable grip and pulled her into the orphanage, through the common rooms and to the staff quarters without breaking his stride.

"Gabe," she warned with a smile, "if anyone sees us, they'll wonder if there's a fire."

"They'd be right," he answered with a wink and a smile.

Fortunately they didn't meet a single soul, although there had been two close calls. As soon as they shut the bedroom door, Gabe slid the deadbolt home.

"So we don't have three little interruptions," he said.

In the blink of an eye, buttons were undone, zippers unzipped, and Gabe was following her onto the hastily turned-down bed. Impatient for him, she wriggled underneath his lanky frame.

"We have to slow down." His voice was pained.

She froze. "I'm hurting you. Is it your ribs?"

As she made a move to roll out from under him, he held her firmly in place. "You're not hurting me. I just don't want this to be over too soon," he finished hoarsely.

She studied his lean face, noticing how time had added a few wrinkles around his eyes and a few strands of silver near his temples. In spite of those small changes, he was still the guy who made every other man pale in comparison.

"If it is, then we can look forward to next time."

"I want this to be good for you…" he mumbled in her hair.

"It will be."

As she trailed her hands along his body, the evidence of his previous ordeal seemed to be fading. The ridges, hollows and bumps she'd seen in the hospital weren't as pronounced, but none of that seemed important. Loving her husband was the only thing on her mind.

With the speed of a starving man eating his first meal, he drove her to the brink until she soared over the edge and took him with her.

Too spent to move, she was only vaguely conscious of Gabe drawing the sheet over them before he tucked her under his arm.

"Are you okay?" he asked.

"Oh, yes. You?"

"Never better."

"Your ribs? I didn't hurt you, did I?"

"You didn't and even if you had, the pain would have been worth it. Now, stop worrying about my aches. You're ruining the mood," he teased.

"Can't have that," she answered with a satisfied chuckle. As she rested against him, she saw the sun still shining through white cotton curtains covering the western window. It was far too early to turn in for the night, but she was content to lie in this very spot until morning and savor his touch during every moment. "I can't move," she said, certain he'd turned her into a boneless jellyfish.

"Good, because you're where I want you," he murmured as he nuzzled her temple. "That was…fantastic."

"It was pretty amazing," she agreed.

"What's really amazing is how badly I want you again."

She met his obsidian-eyed gaze. "Really?"

"Oh, really," he said firmly as he rolled slightly toward her so she could discover the truth for herself.

"Mmm," she said, pleased by his response. "Maybe we should pace ourselves."

"Pace ourselves? I don't think I can."

"Try," she ordered, pleased because she was responsible for

his lack-of-control issues. What woman wouldn't be thrilled to know she could drive her man wild?

"What if I don't want to?"

That was better yet. "We have all night," she reminded him.

"True." He kissed her collarbone before nibbling his way south. "But humor me. I'm making up for lost time."

The next morning Leah was certain everyone was wondering where she and Gabe had disappeared to the previous evening. They'd missed dinner and although Gabe had slipped out around nine to check on a patient, he'd returned shortly after and they'd spent the rest of the night enjoying each other, uninterrupted.

Although they hadn't slept very much, Leah felt energized and was pleased to see the spring in Gabe's step as they ambled to the dining hall for breakfast.

The Salazar children immediately descended on them and halfway through their meal, Gabe suddenly announced, "I forgot. David wants to talk to us."

"Oh, Gabe. You don't suppose someone heard us raiding the kitchen before midnight, do you?"

He grinned. "I doubt if he's calling us on the carpet for something so minor. He knows doctors don't always eat on schedule."

"Then I wonder what's on his mind?"

"I don't know, but he'd asked for us to meet him yesterday."

"Yesterday?"

"I got the message right before Regina's husband came barreling into the clinic, yelling for me. After that, for some strange, inexplicable reason..." he grinned "...David's request slipped my mind."

"Ah, so if he's unhappy with us, you'll say it was my fault?" she teased.

"Would you rather I said I was with a patient? For shame,"

he tutted melodramatically. "I can't believe you'd ask me to lie to a priest."

She leaned closer and kissed him, uncaring that Rosa, José and Anna were watching them with unabashed interest. "Whatever. But why do I feel as if we're being summoned to the principal's office?" she joked.

"I don't know. Have you done something wrong?" he returned in the same vein.

"Not that I know of."

Her feeling rose to full strength as David welcomed them into his private office thirty minutes later. He motioned them to take a seat before he perched on the edge of his battered desk.

"You two look chipper this morning," the priest said with a knowing gleam in his eyes.

"We finally got a good night's rest," Gabe answered, squeezing Leah's hand.

"I'm glad to hear it." His expression became serious. "Now, more than ever, you need to take care of yourselves."

David's tone raised Leah's suspicions. He'd called them in for a reason. A very important reason.

Gabe must have sensed the same thing because his smile died. "Why now, more than ever?"

"Because I visited with Carlotta yesterday afternoon," David said simply. "She wants to pass guardianship of her grandchildren to you."

CHAPTER TWELVE

GABE didn't have to see the surprise on Leah's face. From her sharp gasp he knew it was there. The problem was, he didn't know how Leah would respond to such a request and he wished he'd cornered David before this meeting. As much as he would be willing to say yes, he didn't want to pressure Leah one way or the other.

"What did you say?" she asked.

"Carlotta would like you two to be her grandchildren's guardians. Adoptive parents, if you will."

"Oh, my," she breathed. "How? Why?"

"As Gabe knows, Carlotta and I have talked about her grandchildren's future from the time she first became ill," David went on. "While growing up in the orphanage is okay because she knows all of the staff, she wants her grandchildren to be placed with a family. However, she doesn't want them split up, which poses somewhat of a problem. Not many people are willing to take on three youngsters under the age of five at once."

"Of course," Leah murmured.

"In any case," he continued, "after meeting you, Leah, and watching the way you interacted with them, she thought you and Gabe were the couple she'd been praying for."

Once again, Gabe exchanged a glance with Leah. "We're honored, but—"

"But is she sure about this?" Leah interrupted, looking as

if she wasn't willing to let herself believe her good fortune. "I mean, she hardly knows us. Or me anyway."

"She apparently saw enough to be satisfied," David replied. "When she asked my opinion, I agreed with her."

"Thanks for the vote of confidence," Gabe said.

"Anyone who is willing to put the needs of so many ahead of his own is a special individual," he said, "whether they're my friend or not. In any case, on the advice of the lawyer who handles orphanage business, Carlotta has signed a document indicating her wishes. She'll transfer guardianship of Rosa, Anna and José to you to become effective on her death, providing you agree to take all three."

Leah gasped then faced Gabe with something akin to fear in her eyes. "Gabe?" she asked tremulously. "As much as I'd like to say yes, I'm not sure."

He reached out and took her hand. "Like I told you before, the decision is yours."

She met his gaze, as if trying to read his thoughts, before her expression turned speculative. "David," she said quietly, "would you mind giving Gabe and me a few minutes of privacy?"

"Sure. I'll be outside when you're finished."

From Leah's expression, Gabe knew he was in for a rough ride. It began as soon as David closed the door behind him and she jumped up to pace.

For a few seconds Leah couldn't find the words to voice her displeasure, but when she did, she delivered them fiercely. "You don't seem very surprised by David's announcement," she accused.

"I am, and yet I'm not. I wondered if this might be coming."

Her eyes narrowed. "You did? How?"

"Remember the day you held Rosa and the other two showed off their toys? Carlotta and I watched you. In her next breath, Carlotta started talking, hinting actually, about how she wanted a couple like us to take her grandchildren."

"And you didn't say anything? Didn't you think this was something I'd be interested in knowing?"

"What could I tell you? Carlotta said she wanted a couple *like us*, she didn't say she wanted *us*, specifically," he defended.

"You're splitting hairs, Gabe. Admit it. You suspected this was coming." An unpleasant idea occurred to her. "Was *this* why you wanted me to come to Ciuflores with you? To manipulate me—?"

"There you go again, giving me motives I don't have and never did," he ground out. "Like I said before, the choice to adopt is yours. All you have to do is say no, and the discussion ends here. David will understand."

She wanted to run away and avoid facing the issue, but the picture of Carlotta as she'd reminisced about her children, then her grandchildren, stopped her. *David might understand, but will Carlotta?* she wondered.

Leah didn't realize she'd spoken her thoughts until Gabe answered. "She's bound to be disappointed. It isn't like she has plenty of time to put her affairs in order."

No, she didn't. When Leah had seen the woman yesterday, she'd been much weaker than the day before.

"I only know one thing," he continued. "As much as I'd love to accept those three, I won't do it at the expense of our marriage. It took us too long to get where we are today."

Immediately, she regretted her accusations. "I'm sorry for being so sensitive and jumping to the wrong conclusions," she said in a small voice. "I know you better than that. Will you forgive me?"

"You're my wife," he said simply. "We're going to make a mistake here and there." He paused. "Shall we call David back in?"

Don't let fear influence your decision.

"Please do."

Although Gabe seemed curious about her answer, he didn't press her. Instead, he simply squared his shoulders as if bracing himself for bad news.

As soon as David returned, Leah didn't delay in putting both men out of their proverbial misery. She met Gabe's gaze as she announced, "We accept Carlotta's offer."

"Don't do this for me, Leah," Gabe warned.

"I'm not. I'm doing it for *me*, and for *us*."

His smile immediately grew from ear to ear and the tension in his shoulders eased visibly.

"Taking on three is a big responsibility, even without the culture and language issues," David warned. "This will be a major adjustment for all of you."

"We'll handle it," Gabe assured him.

"Definitely," Leah added.

David rose. "I know you will," he said kindly, "but I had to ask. I'm happy for you both and I'm happy for the peace of mind you're giving Carlotta."

"I do have one question, though," Leah said. "What about Carlotta's son—the children's uncle?"

"No one has seen or heard from him in five years. Even if we found him, a judge should honor Carlotta's wishes. I'm not expecting any problems."

Relieved to hear that, she and Gabe headed for the door. "We'd like to thank her for her gift. No, *three* gifts."

David showed them to the door. "She'd like that. Even though I've assured her you'll accept, hearing it for herself will ease her worries. This situation, as sad as it is for her, is also a blessing in disguise for you. So, congratulations."

"Thanks." Gabe shook his hand. "Whatever you need, just say the word and it'll be yours."

David chuckled. "I'll keep your promise in mind. Run along, now, so I can take care of the paperwork to satisfy the legal eagles."

In the hallway, Leah suddenly stopped short. "Oh, Gabe," she wailed as she truly realized what they'd done. "Have we done the right thing? One child is a challenge and two is even more so. But *three*?"

"And here we thought we'd go home to a quiet existence," he joked. "Those days are definitely over."

Leah grinned, already picturing noisy days ahead. "Oh, but just think. Rosa, Anna and José will be *ours*." Her smile dimmed. "I only wish they wouldn't have to lose their grandmother for it to happen, though. I want to celebrate, but a celebration doesn't quite seem appropriate."

"I know, honey." He drew her close. "I think she'd like us to be happy about her decision, especially because her outcome will be the same whether we agree to her offer or not. At least this way she has peace about the future of her grandchildren and we're blessed with the family we've always wanted."

As Leah rested her head on his shoulder, one word reverberated through her mind. *Family*. She and Gabe would be more than a couple, they would be a family. They'd experience all the joys and trials that came with that. She only hoped she'd be worthy of the task.

Suddenly she pulled away. "Oh, my gosh. We have so much to do to get ready for them. Our house will be stuffed to the rafters."

"You always said the place was too big," he teased. "Now you're saying it's too small?"

Love shone out of her eyes. "No, our home is going to be just right."

"How is she?" Leah asked Gabe as he came out of Carlotta's room later that evening.

Gabe tugged her out of the children's earshot. "She's slipped into a coma."

She hated to hear that. She still had so many questions and knew the woman hadn't finished telling her stories. Leah hoped Carlotta had shared her most treasured memories and she took comfort in the notes she'd recorded. Those were definitely precious pages.

"How long?"

"It's hard to say. Could be hours, or days. Not more than that, I would think."

"I'm glad we were able to talk to her for a few minutes this afternoon." A lump formed in Leah's throat as she thought about the emotional scene when she and Gabe had whispered their thanks to the dying woman. Carlotta hadn't answered; she'd simply smiled and wiggled her fingers in their hands.

"I am, too."

"I don't want her to die, but I know she's suffering," Leah admitted. "And I feel selfish for wanting to take the children with us when we leave in a few days. I'd like to stay, and yet I know we can't."

"I wish we could," he said, "but we'll have to leave as soon as they unload the plane."

She didn't like the idea very much and told him so.

"Our mission goes on, Leah," he reminded her. "A long goodbye won't be possible."

"But—" She thought of disappearing from the children's lives without warning or explanation, but Anna was the only one old enough to understand, and even then, she wouldn't. As much as she hated what her attitude said about her, she hoped she could take the children when she left.

"What if Miguel isn't back?" she asked.

"We'll cross that bridge when we come to it." His grim tone suggested he'd already considered the possibility and wasn't looking forward to making the decision.

"On the bright side, the number of new cases seems to be dropping," she offered.

"Let's hope it stays on the downhill slope."

Leah agreed. While over half of the children in the orphanage had exhibited symptoms in the last two days, none of the cases were severe enough to require hospitalization. She and the staff had been able to push enough oral fluids to keep them from becoming dehydrated and with antibiotics readily available for those who'd developed bacterial complications, a lot of problems had been nipped in the bud. So far, Rosa, Anna and José—*her* three children, as she now thought of them—only had a minor case of sniffles.

He flexed his shoulders then threaded his arm around her waist.

"It's getting late, Mrs. Montgomery," he said with the

heated look in his eyes she recognized. "Shall we put our hooligans to bed?"

"Yeah, but after that, what will we do for the rest of the evening?" she asked innocently.

"Don't worry," he answered with a boyish charm. "I'll think of something."

Carlotta slipped away in the predawn hours two days later. Leah could only mourn the loss and marvel in the woman's foresight at requesting Leah write down her family history. At least the three Salazar children would know a little about their roots.

Twenty-four hours after that, Hector had improved to the point where he was working again, although Gabe refused to let him take up his duties for more than a few hours at a time. However, Hector's recovery came as a relief to everyone because their plane was due and Miguel still hadn't returned. Hector might not be functioning at one hundred percent, but if he limited himself to the seriously ill patients, he could manage.

Oddly enough, she'd hated to leave but with these new developments she was impatient for the MMF plane to arrive. First, though, she had to wait for David to return from court with the children's signed and sealed paperwork.

"Would you quit watching the road?" Gabe teased. "David will get back as soon as he can. He won't make you wait a minute longer than necessary."

She bounced José on one hip. "I know. I'm being silly, but we're so close to having everything official. You don't suppose the judge will go against Carlotta's wishes, do you? I mean, David's not an attorney and the document isn't typed up nice and neat."

"I don't know how the Mexican court system works in family cases," Gabe said honestly, "but if anyone can maneuver his way through the system, it's David. Let's not worry until he gets back, shall we?"

Unfortunately, that was the problem. Leah was ready to

make plans and until she could do so with the Mexican government's blessing, she would fret.

When the unmistakable roar of the twin-engined Cessna sounded overhead, Leah's heart sank. She'd privately hoped the plane would be a day or two, or even three, late, but it obviously wasn't meant to be.

By the time they'd greeted Sheldon, unloaded the plane and restocked Hector's supply room, Leah saw David's truck parked near the orphanage. "Oh, Gabe," she breathed. "He's back. I can't wait to hear what he has to say, can you?"

Unfortunately, David's expression was grim, and she didn't like his report.

"The judge went on his circuit this week," David announced.

"Which means?" she demanded.

"He wasn't there to rule on the transfer of guardianship."

"Then when—?"

"The clerk in his office said it will take him at least a month to review the case."

"A month?" She swallowed hard. She'd wanted so badly to take the children home with her now.

"Four weeks won't be so bad, will it?" Gabe asked. "The delay will give us plenty of time to get ready."

"Four weeks is forever to a child," she pointed out. "A veritable lifetime. They won't remember..." Her voice died.

"Yes, they will," Gabe assured her. "They remembered me and they hadn't seen me for several months. A few weeks will pass quickly. This is only a minor inconvenience."

She didn't agree, but arguing with Gabe and David wouldn't change the facts. They couldn't stay and the children couldn't leave. She had to deal with it.

"You're right. We'll need every day of that to get ready," she said, determined to be positive when she felt the opposite.

Gabe hugged her. "That's my girl," he said softly.

David's face remained grave. "Unfortunately, there's more."

Leah's heart sank as she watched Gabe's eyes narrow. "More what?" he asked.

"Carlotta's son Jorge is here." David paused. "He wants the children."

"But—but he can't have them," Leah protested. "Carlotta wanted us to—"

David held up his hands. "I know that. You know that, and Jorge knows that. He believes his mother wasn't in her right mind when she made her decision, especially since she went into a coma a few hours later."

"Is he suggesting she was coerced?"

"He isn't making that accusation directly, but he believes the children belong with the only family they have left. As he's the one in particular..." David shrugged.

Righteous indignation rose up inside her. "Where has he been all this time?" she demanded. "Can he care for three young children?" Her voice wobbled. "Provide for them. *Love* them?"

"That's for the judge to decide, Leah," David said gently. "I'm not happy with this development, either, but what can I do?"

A horrible thought came to her. "Will he...will he take them away? From Ciuflores?" If he did, she was certain she'd never see the children again.

"I've insisted they remain here at the orphanage until the matter is settled. As far as the children are concerned, he's a stranger and they don't need the upheaval right now." He patted her shoulder awkwardly. "I'll keep a close eye on them. I promise."

Leah bit her lip to keep it from trembling. Thankful for Gabe's steadying arm around her, she nodded. "Thanks."

"Should we talk to this clerk to plead our case?" Gabe asked.

"The only one who needs to hear your side is the judge and he's not available. All you can do—and I know this sounds trite—is to go about your usual business while you're waiting."

Inside, she was screaming, *Been there, done that*, but David's advice was sound, even if she didn't like it. As she glanced at Gabe, she saw the same resignation in his eyes.

She managed a tremulous smile. "Then that's what we'll do. If you two will excuse me, I have a bag to finish packing and a few goodbyes to say."

As soon as she'd disappeared, Gabe spoke to David. "There's more, isn't there?"

David exhaled slowly as he ran his finger around his clerical collar. "Yes, and no. I don't have any new information, but I've got to admit, my friend, that this particular judge isn't one I've dealt with before. Rumor has it that he's a tough cookie when it comes to placing children, especially placing them outside the country."

"Then we don't have a chance?" Gabe asked.

"Oh, there's a chance. You have a lot in your favor. Carlotta's blessing will carry a lot of weight."

"Then what's the problem? The judge should understand that if she wanted her son involved, she would have arranged for it."

"According to our attorney, a lot will hinge on Carlotta's health and state of mind at the time she dictated her wishes. Medical testimony will be crucial. Unfortunately—"

"I was the attending physician," Gabe supplied, recognizing the dilemma he was in.

"If Hector had been treating her at the time she faded," David went on, "his opinion would carry more weight than yours because he doesn't have a vested interest in the outcome. You, on the other hand, do."

"It might look that way, but if Jorge wants to reconnect with family, where has he been all this time?" Gabe demanded, incensed on Carlotta's behalf. Perhaps if good old Jorge had been around, Carlotta wouldn't have worked so hard the last several years. Perhaps she would have sought treatment sooner.

"According to him, he travels a lot." As Gabe opened his mouth to argue, David held up his hands. "I know, I know.

Mail goes both ways, but that's a question he'll have to explain to the judge's satisfaction. Personally, I'm hoping Carlotta's wishes will carry the most weight because she knew her son better than anyone. If Jorge argues that he's not the irresponsible man he once was, then the court's decision could rest on who has the most eloquent lawyer."

He cast a meaningful glance at Gabe. "Unless…"

Gabe understood immediately. "Unless we can prove that Jorge isn't the upstanding citizen he claims to be?"

David grinned. "I've met lots of people in my line of work and I can safely say that clothes don't make the man."

Grasping at the hope David had provided, Gabe asked, "What can I do?"

"Nothing. It's easier for me to snoop around because as the orphanage director, I oversee the home placement study." He smiled. "You'd be surprised what sort of connections I have."

"In high places, I hope?"

"To low ones, too." He rose. "I hope you don't mind if I don't see you off. I need to start making phone calls."

"Let me know if I can do anything to help."

"I will. In the meantime, expect the best but prepare for the worst."

Leah fought the tears as she hugged Anna, Rosa and José. "I'll come back," she promised hoarsely. "Be good while I'm gone. When I see you again, we'll have all sorts of fun. We'll read stories and play games…"

"*Adiós?*" Anna asked, her forehead wrinkled in thought.

"Yes, but not for long," Leah told her. "This is just temporary." She tried to think of the right word to use and came up blank. "It's only temporary," she repeated.

Those three words had become her mantra, but it was cold comfort. She had the feeling that once she left Ciuflores, the tenuous tie between her and the children would be cut.

"*Adiós mi abuelita?*" Anna asked.

"No. Not goodbye like your grandmother. I'll see you

SIX-WEEK MARRIAGE MIRACLE

again, soon." Knowing the three had seen plenty of weepy people since their grandmother's death, Leah was determined to put on a bright face. Yet as she wrapped her arms around each little wiggly body and received a sloppy kiss, her breath burned in her chest.

Overcome, she glanced at Eva, one of the orphanage's staff, who immediately spoke to the children in a lilting voice that didn't quite match her red-rimmed eyes. Herding the children in front of her, the girl left the room wearing an apologetic expression, leaving Leah alone.

She sat quietly and tried to regain her composure, but the memory of those precious hugs and their baby-clean scent, as well as the moisture remaining on her cheek from Rosa's open-mouthed smooch, made it impossible.

She couldn't leave them. She just couldn't.

Acting on instinct, she dumped her clothes out of her travel case before heading toward the children's room. She began stuffing their things inside with little regard for neatness.

"Leah?"

Ignoring her husband, she doggedly continued her self-appointed task.

He stepped inside. "What are you doing?"

"What does it look like?" She brushed past him to retrieve the two small picture frames on their dresser—pictures which she knew were of their parents. "I'm packing their things. I'd buy everything new, but having a few familiar pieces—"

"Leah," he said firmly, as she stuffed the frames in the suitcase underneath a pile of clothes for protection. "What are you doing?" he repeated firmly.

"I only need a few more minutes, Gabe, and then we can leave."

"If you're doing what I think you're doing—"

She paused, clutching Rosa's doll to her chest. "I'm taking my children home, Gabe. They're mine. Carlotta passed their guardianship to us. She asked me…" Her voice caught.

Gabe gently tugged the doll out of her arms and pulled her against him. "She asked you what?" he coaxed.

The knot of emotion seemed to grow in her throat and she swallowed hard. "Before I knew what she had planned, she asked if I'd watch over them and I promised I would. I can't do that if they're here and I'm not." She met his gaze defiantly. "I won't break my promise."

"Leah," he said kindly. "I understand about promises, but we can't take them with us. Without the proper *legal* papers, we'd be accused of kidnapping."

The sane part of her brain agreed with him, but her heart didn't want to listen. "We have Carlotta's blessing," she argued. "David has it in writing. Duly witnessed. What more do the authorities need?"

"Okay," he said, sounding quite calm, as if they were discussing a grocery delivery. "Say we do it your way. Do you really want to risk the law showing up on our doorstep to haul them away and send us to jail? Or did you plan to live on the lam?"

She wanted to deny the scenario he'd painted would ever happen, but she couldn't. And yet...

"Oh, Gabe, we're so close," she breathed. "I have this feeling that if they don't come with me now, they never will."

His dark-eyed gaze met hers. "It's because we *are* so close that we can't do this. We can't afford to make an impulsive mistake and screw this up."

Logic once again warred with her emotions. "But—"

"If we do everything by the book, we stand a far better chance with the court than if we do something stupid."

"But—"

"Leah," he urged. "Think about this."

"I have, and—"

"Leah." The pity in his eyes was her undoing.

Suddenly, facing the fact she would soon be leaving the children behind, she collapsed against him and wept until his shirt was wet and wrinkled. Once the pain finally subsided, she realized Gabe's strength and support had never wavered in spite of his own heartfelt anguish.

"I thought what we went through before was terrible," she

said when she could finally speak, "but that was nothing compared to this. It's worse because I've gotten to know these three—their likes, dislikes, the way Rosa sucks her thumb when she's tired, how Anna talks with her hands—"

"How José wrinkles his nose when he smiles," he finished as he continued to rub comforting circles on her back. "You're right. This time is much more difficult."

As she stole a glance at his face, his red-rimmed eyes proved he was as torn up about the change in circumstances as she was.

"The good news is," he continued, "our absence is only temporary."

"Only temporary," she echoed as she pulled away.

He rubbed away the tear tracks on her cheeks. "Better?"

"Not really." She managed a weak smile.

"Come on," he said tenderly. "Let's go home."

CHAPTER THIRTEEN

EXPECT the best but prepare for the worst.

Over the next week, Gabe tried his best to follow David's advice, but he hadn't been able to share the same counsel with Leah. If he suggested there was a chance the court wouldn't decide in their favor, he didn't know how she'd react. During the time they'd been home she'd jumped between chatting about what toy each child would like to fretting if they were eating properly, getting enough hug time and staying healthy.

Sitting on the sidelines, as David had also suggested, was impossible. Although he had plenty of faith in his friend, David wasn't the only man with connections and Gabe didn't hesitate to use them. Discreetly, of course.

But by the beginning of the second week his guilt demanded he pull Leah aside.

"I'm going to Mexico tomorrow," he told her.

Her hands flew to her mouth. "You have news?" she breathed, her eyes lighting up.

"No," he said. "I haven't wanted to tell you this because I didn't want to raise your hopes, but you deserve to know the truth. I promised complete honesty when we got back together and I haven't held up my part of the bargain."

"What are you saying, Gabe? What aren't you telling me?"

He drew a deep breath, glad she was more interested in his news than in his moral lapse. "David is trying to dig up information on Jorge Salazar and so far he's coming up blank. I'm heading down there to see what I can do."

"I'll go with you."

"No. Absolutely not."

"Gabe," she warned. "I have a vested interest, too."

"Yes, but David says the key is to be discreet. There are places I need to go where you'll stick out like a sore thumb. If Jorge tells the judge we're deliberately trying to sabotage him…we can't take that risk."

"Then I'll stay in Ciuflores."

He shook his head. "I'm headed to Mexico City. This is a fly-in and fly-out trip. I can't work in a detour for you. I'm sorry."

She let out a deep sigh. "Okay. I don't like it, but I understand."

"Good."

"Thanks for being honest," she said. "I know it would have been easier on you to keep me in the dark, but I'm glad I know what you're doing. Just keep me posted, okay?" She grinned. "I know how much you hate to fly."

"Count on it."

Although Leah was glad that Gabe had gotten past his overly protective attitude, she almost wished he *had* left her clueless. The very thing he'd worried about—putting her on an emotional roller coaster—came to pass. Over the next two weeks he flew four more times to Mexico and on the conclusion of each trip he simply shook his head.

Her optimism was fading, but she clung to the idea that on one of his fact-finding missions he'd finally have news that would be in their favor.

And yet she watched Gabe push himself harder and harder, as if he was determined to succeed at any cost. At times she felt as if she was losing him because he became so focused on his objective, which was to bring the Salazar children home. She didn't know what to do or say to warn him about the path they seemed to be on, but the words came to her after the foundation's fundraising gala…

"You're leaving again?" Leah stared at her husband as he stripped off his bow-tie and tossed his tuxedo jacket on their bed at two a.m. She still wore her black shimmery ballgown, minus the strappy heels she'd kicked off the minute they'd walked through the door.

"First thing in the morning."

"It *is* morning," she pointed out.

"At eight," he said. "That gives me…"

"Six hours," she supplied. "That's all the notice I get? Six hours?" She couldn't begin to describe the hurt she felt. "How long have you known you were leaving?"

"I planned this trip yesterday."

"You should have told me."

"You were busy with the last-minute plans for the ball," he pointed out. "Honestly, it slipped my mind."

"It may have, but it's no excuse," she insisted. "You have to slow down, Gabe. You can't keep up this pace."

"Don't worry. I'll sleep on the plane."

"This isn't about sleeping, although you *are* burning both ends of the candle," she said tartly.

"I'm doing this for you, Leah. For us."

"I understand." She sank onto the bed and began toying with a loose sequin. "Tonight, when I saw the picture of me and the children on the screen…" Her throat closed and unconsciously she knotted her dress in her fist. She hated getting emotional and had told herself she wouldn't, but here she was, doing the very thing she'd vowed she wouldn't.

"That photo is my favorite," he said as he sat beside her. "I don't know how or when Sheldon snapped it, but I'm grateful. He's going to give you a copy, by the way."

"Thanks," she said. Seeing the image was a bittersweet experience and would be until the Mexican court finally reached a decision. She was at the point where she was willing to propose they grease a few palms, although she could imagine Gabe's horrified reaction to the suggestion. If he'd nipped her kidnapping attempt in the bud, then he certainly wouldn't be open to her attempt at bribery.

She rubbed her forehead, wondering what her ideas said about her character if she was willing to resort to illegal activities. Then again, she was a desperate woman.

Pushing those thoughts away, she added, "The point is, after seeing those pictures, I…I need you, Gabe, here with me. Not jetting miles and miles away."

He caressed her cheek. "Aw honey, I'd like nothing more than to be here, but this trip is important. I feel as if I'm so *close*."

She held his hand to her face. "You said that last time."

"I know, but—"

"You'd tried to protect me from experiencing emotional ups and downs, but now it's my turn. Please, Gabe, don't go. I know you're trying to give me my heart's desire, but maybe it isn't your place to provide it."

"I want to, though."

She snuggled close. "And I love you for trying, but we need to step back and let David handle things." She paused. "He is still investigating, isn't he?"

As Gabe's nod, she smiled. "Then let him do his job."

He stared at her like a dog staring at a new dish. "What if David doesn't succeed? What if we lose our case?"

"I'll be crushed," she admitted, "but I won't be nearly as devastated as I will be if I lose you. So, please. Promise me this is your last trip."

He looked as if he was ready to protest, but instead he simply nodded. "Okay," he said wearily. "You win."

"Good," she said, relieved by his decision. "Would you like me to drive you to the airport?"

"Thanks, but Sheldon is tagging along so he's picking me up. Meet me when my plane lands on Monday evening?"

Greeting him at the airport when he returned had become part of her routine. She'd added it because she needed the reassurance that he'd arrived safely. The main reason, however, was because she missed him terribly and wanted to see him as soon as possible.

"I'll be there with bells on."

Leah puttered around the house after Gabe left, wanting to do something but unable to find anything interesting enough to hold her interest. She baked a cake, but when it didn't rise, she realized she hadn't added all the ingredients. It landed in the trash.

She sewed a couple of loose buttons on Gabe's shirts then discovered she'd stitched the placket closed. She ripped it out and started over.

She took their formal wear to the dry cleaner's and after arriving at the shop across town realized she had forgotten to bring Gabe's tuxedo pants.

Staying at home and reading a book was pointless because she couldn't remember what she'd read from one page to the next.

Unsettled for reasons she couldn't understand, although she attributed the feeling to Gabe's absence, she meandered again into what she'd tentatively decided would be the girls' room.

Idly, she wondered if Gabe had seen the changes she'd made in here. Granted, they'd only been small ones and had only occurred a few days ago, but for her they were a step forward.

As she looked at the space where the crib had once stood, she reflected on all the "what ifs". What if one or both of their previous adoption attempts had been successful? Gabe wouldn't have insisted she join him on his trip to Ciuflores. She wouldn't have met Carlotta or her three grandchildren.

But even before that, what if Gabe hadn't returned from his plane crash? Or what if he had, and they'd divorced?

Those ideas sent a cold shudder down her spine. Of all the people who'd come and gone in her life, Gabe was her anchor. Whether or not the Mexican government allowed her to keep her promise to Carlotta, she would still have Gabe. He was her rock and she couldn't imagine life without him.

Fortunately, Jeff had taken her announcement in his stride. He'd suspected she hadn't gotten over her husband and was glad he'd allowed her the space she'd needed to figure that out for herself.

As for the children, if fate exacted another pound of flesh and stole her dream again, she would grieve, just as Gabe would. The difference was, they'd do it together, not separately. She loved him too much to fall back into those marriage-destroying old habits. She might never raise children, but she had Gabe and she would fight to keep their marriage alive, even if she had to resign her job and donate her time to the Montgomery Foundation in order to see him.

Strangely enough, her decision chased away her gloom. Over the next twenty-four hours nothing spoiled her good mood or her inner peace—not even what Jane had affectionately termed "another shift from hell".

Fortunately, she was able to leave the hospital promptly at six p.m. on Monday. Forty minutes later, she'd been cleared to wait on the tarmac near their plane's hangar, where she polished off the bottle of soda she'd purchased from a vending machine. Finally, the familiar plane with its red and black markings appeared overhead, and a few minutes later taxied to a stop in front of her.

She stood, eager for Gabe to open the door and descend the stairs. He'd been gone less than forty-eight hours and it seemed like forever.

Finally, the door descended, but no one exited.

"What's taking so long?" she muttered impatiently as she stared at the empty opening.

No sooner had she spoken than Gabe appeared. She strode forward, determined to meet him at the bottom of the steps. "Gabe," she called, waving to capture his attention.

His answering smile was broad. Apparently his trip had turned out better than he'd expected because he seemed happier than he had on previous returns.

She watched him step out, but then, before he carefully descended the stairs, he hoisted a small figure onto one hip. Her steps slowed. What in the world…?

Behind him came a larger child wearing a floral print sundress. This one painstakingly took each step as she held onto the railing with one hand and clutched a familiar doll in the other. Sheldon brought up the rear, carrying another child—a boy.

Leah froze in her tracks as the group come forward. Gabe looked positively ecstatic and the children's eyes were filled with wonder as they took in their surroundings.

The crowning moment came when Anna saw her. A huge grin spread across her little brown face and she ran forward, crying *"Mamacita!"*

Mommy. Leah swore her heart skipped a beat, probably several. Could it be?

She crouched down to hug her. "My goodness, you've grown," she told the youngster in a tear-choked voice. "Gabe?" she asked, hardly able to believe the reality of the little girl in her arms.

Her husband's smile stretched from ear to ear. "Hi, honey. We're finally home."

The look of awe and pure joy on Leah's face made everything Gabe had gone through worth the effort. Gifting her with the Hope diamond wouldn't have made her this happy or been this satisfying.

"Gabe?" she said again as she rose, reaching out tentatively to stroke Rosa's hair, as if afraid the children were only an elaborate hallucination.

He bent his head to drop a swift kiss on her startled mouth. "How do you like the presents I brought?" He held out Rosa, who immediately dove into Leah's arms, confident in Leah's quick reflexes and ability to catch her.

"They're fantastic," she told him, "but how was this possible? Are they here for a visit? When do they go back? Where's

David? Did the judge finally hear our case?" Then, "*Why didn't you tell me?*"

He laughed at her rapid-fire questions. "First things first. Let's get these monkeys in the car."

"But we don't have three car seats," she wailed.

"Yes, you do," Sheldon piped up. "As soon as we knew we were bringing them, I called the office. Loretta found three and stuck them in my car."

It took a while to make the transfer, but she and Gabe soon had everyone buckled into the safety seats and they were on their way. Corey would deliver the rest of their things later.

The children were clearly tired and fussy from their experience, so Leah's questions had to wait. All except one.

"Are they ours, Gabe? To keep?" she asked as he drove out of the airport.

Determined to chase away the fear in her eyes, he nodded. "They're ours. No refunds allowed."

She let out a long, deep, heartfelt breath then turned the most brilliant smile on him as moisture glistened in her eyes. "Thank you," she said as she squeezed his elbow before she looked into the back seat for the tenth time in as many minutes.

Leah smiled at the children behind her. Rosa and José were dozing and Anna was fighting to stay awake, but soon the car's motion lulled her to sleep, too.

The nap during the short drive home completely restored their energy. They were more than ready to eat the crackers and sliced apples she hurriedly assembled before rushing off to play with the toys she and Gabe had purchased beforehand, in anticipation.

"We need an emergency grocery-store run," she informed her husband. "I don't have kid-friendly food in the house."

"I'll go," he advised her. "Or, better yet, call Loretta and give her a list."

She didn't think shopping for groceries fell under the duties of an office assistant, but the woman was a grandmother and under the circumstances, would most likely be thrilled to do it.

"Okay, tell me what happened," she demanded when the youngsters were entertaining themselves with both their old and new toys. "And talk fast because we have a thousand and one things to do."

"After we landed in Mexico City, David called to tell me the judge was holding a preliminary hearing. I wanted to be there to state our case and answer his questions, so we immediately flew to Ciuflores. As it turned out, the investigators David hired had turned up some rather damning information about Jorge. Once the evidence was presented to the court—at the eleventh hour, I might add—the judge ruled in our favor. I thought about waiting until we could bring them home together, but David thought the children would have a difficult time with another separation, even a short one. So, here we are."

"Why do I sense there's more to this story than you're telling me? And where did David find the money to hire an investigator? His services couldn't have been cheap."

Gabe shrugged innocently. "I heard he received an anonymous donation to help defray those costs, but it's purely a rumor. Of course, it would also be pure speculation to guess the identity of the man who personally called in a few favors from some of his own contacts."

"I should be upset with you for leaving me out of all the fun, but I'm not." She stood on tiptoe to swiftly kiss him. "I'm glad you're back, Gabe. If I forgot to tell you this, welcome home."

His midnight-black eyes reflected tenderness. "I know things will be crazy for a while, probably years," he tacked on wryly, "and we may feel harried and hassled, but I'll always make time for us."

She wrapped her arms around his chest. "I intend to hold you to your promise."

The sound of raised voices caught Leah's attention. Clearly, José and Anna were having a difference of opinion. "You may want to rethink your stance on work-related travel," she advised. "A trip may be the only time you experience peace and quiet."

"It might," he agreed, "but peace and quiet can't compare to having a family who needs me."

"And we always will."

RECKLESS NIGHT IN RIO

JENNIE LUCAS

To Pete

CHAPTER ONE

"Who is the father of your baby, Laura?"

Holding her six-month-old baby on her hip, Laura Parker had been smiling with pride and pleasure across her family's two-hundred-year-old farmhouse, lit with swaying lights and filled with neighbors and friends for her sister's evening wedding reception. Now, pushing up her black-rimmed glasses, Laura faced her younger sister with a sinking feeling in her heart.

Who is the father of your baby?

People rarely asked that question anymore, since Laura always refused to answer. She'd started to hope the scandal might be over.

"Will you ever tell?" Becky's face was unhappy beneath her veil. At nineteen, her sister was an idealistic new bride with romantic dreams of right and wrong. "Robby deserves a father."

Trying to control the anguish in her heart, Laura kissed her son's dark hair, so soft, and smelling of baby shampoo. She said in a low voice, "We've talked about this."

"Who is he?" her sister cried. "Are you ashamed of him? Why won't you tell?"

"Becky!" Laura glanced uneasily at the reception

guests around them. "I told you… I don't…" She took a deep breath. "I don't know who he is."

Her sister stared at her tearfully. "You're lying. There's no way you'd sleep around like that. You're the one who convinced me to wait for true love!"

The people closest to them had stopped pretending to talk, and were now openly eavesdropping. Family and friends were packed into the farmhouse's warren of rooms, walking across creaking floors, having conversations beneath the low ceilings. Neighbors sat on folding chairs along the walls, holding paper plates of food in their laps. And probably listening. Laura held her baby closer. "Becky, please," she whispered.

"He deserted you. And it's not fair!"

"Becky," their mother said suddenly from behind them, "I don't think you've met your great-aunt Gertrude. She's traveled all the way from England. Won't you come and greet her?" Smiling, Ruth Parker reached for her grandson in Laura's arms. "She'll want to meet Robby, too."

"Thank you," Laura whispered soundlessly to her mother. Ruth answered with a loving smile and a wink, then drew her younger daughter and baby grandson away. Laura watched them go, love choking her. Ruth was wearing her nicest Sunday dress and bright coral lipstick, but her hair had grown gray and her body slightly stooped. The past year had left even her strong mother more frail.

The lump in Laura's throat felt razor-sharp as she stood alone in the crowded room. She'd thought she'd put the scandal of her pregnancy behind her, after she'd returned to her northern New Hampshire village pregnant, with no job and no answers. But would her family ever get over it? Would she?

Three weeks after she'd left Rio de Janeiro, she'd been shocked to discover she was pregnant. Her burly, overprotective father had demanded to know the name of the man. Laura had been afraid he might go after Gabriel Santos with an ultimatum—or worse, a shotgun. So she'd lied and said she had no idea who her baby's father might be. She'd described her time in Rio as one gigantic shagfest, when the truth was that she'd had only one lover her whole life. And even that had been for a single night.

One precious night…

I need you, Laura. She still felt the violence of her boss's embrace as he'd pushed her back against his desk, sweeping aside paperwork and crashing the computer to the floor. After more than a year, she could still feel the heat of his body against hers, the feel of his lips against her neck, his hot brutal kisses against her skin. The memory of the way Gabriel Santos had ruthlessly taken her virginity still invaded her dreams every night.

And the memory of the aftermath still left a shotgun blast in her heart. The morning after he'd seduced her, she'd tearfully told him she felt she had no choice but to quit her job. He'd just shrugged. "Good luck," he said. "I hope you find what you're looking for."

That was all he gave her, after five years of her love and devoted service.

She'd loved her playboy boss, stupidly and without hope. It had been fifteen months since she'd last seen Gabriel's face, but she could not forget it, no matter how hard she tried. How could she, when every day she saw those same dark eyes in her child's face?

Her tears in the little white clapboard church an hour ago hadn't just been from happiness for Becky. Laura had once loved a man with all her heart, but he hadn't loved her back. And as the cold February wind whipped through their northern valley, there were still times she imagined she could hear his dark, deep voice speaking to her, only to her.

"Laura."

Like now. The memory of his low, accented voice seemed so real. The sound ripped through her body, through her heart, as if he were right beside her, whispering against her skin.

"Laura."

His voice felt really close that time.

Really close.

Laura's hands shook as she set down her glass of cheap champagne. Lack of sleep and a surfeit of dreams were causing her to hallucinate. Had to be. It couldn't be...

With a deep breath, she turned.

Gabriel Santos stood before her. In the middle of her family's crowded living room, he towered over other men in every way, even more darkly handsome than she remembered. But it wasn't just his chiseled jawline or his expensive Italian suit that made him stand out. It wasn't just his height or the strength of his broad shoulders.

It was the ruthless intensity of his black eyes. A tremble went through her.

"Gabriel...?" she whispered.

His sensual lips curved. "Hello, Laura."

She swallowed, pressing her nails into her palms, willing herself to wake up from this nightmare—

from this incredible dream. "You can't be here," she whispered. "As in *here*."

"And yet I am," he said. "Laura."

She shivered at the sound of her name on his lips. It didn't seem right that he could be here, in her family's living room, surrounded by friends and family eating potluck.

At thirty-eight, Gabriel Santos owned a vast international conglomerate that bought and shipped steel and timber across the world. His life was filled with one passionate, single-minded pursuit after another. Business. Adrenaline-tinged sports. Beautiful women. Laura's lips turned downward. Beautiful women most of all.

So what was he doing here? What could he possibly have come for unless…unless…

Out of the corner of her eye, she saw her mother disappearing down the hall with her baby.

Trying to stop her hands from shaking, Laura folded her arms around the waist of her hand-sewn bridesmaid's dress. So Gabriel had come to Greenhill Farm. It didn't exactly require a crack team unit to find her here. Parkers had lived here for two hundred years. It didn't mean he knew about Robby. It didn't. He couldn't.

Could he?

Gabriel lifted a dark eyebrow. "Are you glad to see me?"

"Of course I'm not glad." She bit out the words. "If you recall, I'm no longer your secretary. So if you've come five thousand miles because you need me to go back to Rio and sew a button or make your coffee—"

"No." His eyes glittered at her. "That's not why I've come." He slowly looked around the house, which was decorated with strings of pink lights and red paper hearts along the walls, and candles above the fire in the old stone fireplace. "What's going on here?"

"A wedding reception."

He blinked, then came closer to her, the wooden boards creaking beneath his feet. Laura's eyes widened as the shadows of firelight shifted across the hard angles of his face. He was so handsome, she thought in bewildered wonder. She'd forgotten how handsome. Her dreams hadn't done him justice. She could see why so many women chased after him all over the world…and why he was the despair of them all.

"And just who—" his black eyes narrowed into a glower "—is the bride?"

She was bewildered at the sudden harshness of his tone. "My little sister. Becky."

"Ah." His shoulders relaxed imperceptibly. Then he frowned. "Becky? She's not much more than a child."

"Tell me about it." Laura looked down at her bridesmaid's dress. In the gleam of the fire and pink lights swaying above, the pale pink gown appeared almost white. She looked up suddenly. "Did you think it was me?"

Their eyes locked in the crowded room.

"*É claro*," Gabriel said quietly. "Of course I thought it was you."

The idea of her having the time or the interest to date, let alone marry, some other man made her choke back a laugh. She smoothed her bridesmaid's gown with trembling hands. "No."

"So there is no one important in your life right now?" he asked, in a casual tone belied by way he held his body in absolute stillness.

There *was* someone important in her life. She just had

to get Gabriel out of here before he saw Robby. "You have no right to ask."

"*Sim.*" He paused. "But you're not wearing a ring."

"Fine." Laura's voice was painfully quiet as she looked down at her feet. "I'm not married."

She didn't have to ask if Gabriel was married. She already knew the answer. How many times had he told her he would never, ever take a wife?

I'm not made for love, querida. *I'll never have a little housewife cooking my dinner in a snug house every night as I read books to our children.*

Gabriel moved closer, almost touching her. She was dimly aware of people whispering around them, wondering who this handsome, well-dressed stranger might be. She knew she should tell him to leave, but she was caught in the power of his body so close to hers. Her gaze fell on his thick wrists beneath sharply tailored shirt cuffs, and she trembled. She remembered the feel of that strong body on hers, the stroke of his fingertips….

"Laura."

Against her will, her eyes lifted, tracing up his muscular body, past his broad shoulders and wide neck to his brutally handsome face. In the flickering shadows, she saw the dark scruff along his jaw, the scar across his temple from a childhood car accident. She saw the man she'd wanted forever and had never stopped wanting.

His eyes burned into her, and memories poured through her. She felt vulnerable, almost powerless beneath the dark fire of his glance.

"It's good to see you again," he said in a low voice. He smiled, and the masculine beauty of his face took her breath away. Their fifteen months apart had made him only more handsome. While she…

She hadn't seen the inside of a beauty salon for a year. Her hair hadn't been cut for ages, and her only makeup was lipstick in an unflattering pink shade that she'd worn at Becky's insistence. Her dowdy dishwater-blonde hair had been hurriedly pulled back in a French knot before the ceremony, but now fell about her shoulders in messy tendrils, pulled out by Robby's chubby fists.

Even as a girl Laura had always tended to put herself last, but since she became the single mother of a baby, she wasn't even on the list. Taking a shower and shoving her hair back into a ponytail was all she could manage most days. And she still hadn't managed to take off all the extra weight from her pregnancy. Nervously, she pushed up her black-framed glasses. "Why are you staring at me?"

"You're even more beautiful than I remembered."

Her cheeks went hot beneath his gaze. "Now I know you're lying."

"It's true." His dark eyes seared her. He wasn't looking at her as if he thought she were plain. In fact, he was looking down at her as if he…

As if he…

He turned away, and she exhaled.

"So this is Becky's wedding reception?" He glanced around the room with something like disapproval on his face.

Laura thought their home looked nice, even romantic for a country-style winter wedding. They'd scrubbed it scrupulously clean, tidied away all the usual clutter, and decorated their hearts out. But as she followed his gaze, she suddenly saw how shabby it all was.

Laura had been proud of how much she'd been able to accomplish for her sister on almost no budget. Flowers had been too expensive because of Valentine's Day, so Laura had gone to the nearest craft store and cut out large hearts of red tissue paper, festooning them on their walls with red and pink balloons and streamers. She'd decorated the house in the middle of the night, as she'd waited for the cake to cool. For the reception dinner, their mother had made her famous roast chickens and their friends and neighbors had brought casseroles and salads for a buffet-style potluck. Laura had made her sister's wedding cake herself, using instructions from an old 1930s family cookbook.

She'd been tired but so happy when she'd fallen into bed at dawn. But now, beneath Gabriel's eyes, the decorations no longer seemed beautiful. She saw how flimsy it all was, how shabby a send-off for her second-youngest sister. Becky had seemed delighted when she saw the decorations and slightly tilted wedding cake that morning. But what else could she have done, knowing how hard her family had tried to give her a nice wedding when there was never a dime to spare?

As if he could read her mind, Gabriel looked at her. "Do you need money, Laura?"

Laura's cheeks went hot. "No," she lied. "We're fine."

He looked around the room again, at the paper plates with the potluck dinner, at her homemade gown, clearly not believing her. He set his jaw. "I'm just surprised your father couldn't do better for Becky. Even if money is tight."

Laura folded her arms, feeling ice in her heart. "He

couldn't," she whispered. "My father died four months ago."

She heard Gabriel's intake of breath. "What?"

"He had a heart attack during harvest. We didn't find him on his tractor until later. When he didn't come home for dinner."

"Oh, Laura." Gabriel took her hand in his own. "I'm sorry."

She felt his sympathy, felt his concern. And she felt the rough warmth of his palm against her own—the touch she'd craved for the past year and all the five years before. Her fingers curled over his as longing blistered her soul.

With an intake of breath she ripped her hand away.

"Thank you," she said, blinking back tears. She'd thought she was done grieving for her father, but she'd spent most of the day with a lump in her throat, watching her uncle walk Becky down the aisle, seeing her mother alone in the pew with tears streaking her powdered face. Laura's father should have been here. "It's been a long winter. Everything fell apart without him. We're just a small farm and always run so lean, one year to the next. With my dad gone, the bank tried to refuse to extend the loan or give us anything more for spring planting."

Gabriel's eyes narrowed. "What?"

She lifted her chin. "We're fine now." Although they were just surviving on fumes, trying to hold on another week until they'd get the next loan. Then they'd pray next year would be better. She folded her arms. "Becky's husband, Tom, will live at the house and farm the land now. Mom will be able to stay in her home and be well looked after."

"And you?" Gabriel asked quietly.

Laura pressed her lips together. Starting tonight, she and Robby were moving into her mother's bedroom. The three-bedroom farmhouse was now full, since Laura and her baby could no longer share a bedroom with Becky, and her other sisters, Hattie and Margaret, shared the other. Ruth had loyally said she'd be delighted to share her large master bedroom with her grandson, but Ruth was a very light sleeper. It was not an ideal situation.

Laura needed a job, an apartment of her own. She was the oldest daughter—twenty-seven years old. She should be helping her family, not the other way around. She'd been looking for a job for months, but there were none to be had. Not even at a fraction of the salary she'd earned when she worked for Gabriel.

But there was no way she was going to tell him that. "You still haven't explained what you're doing here. You obviously didn't know about the wedding. Do you have some kind of business deal? Is it the old Talfax mine that's for sale?"

He shook his head. "I'm still trying to close the Açoazul deal in Brazil." His jaw tightened. "I came because I had no choice."

Over the noisy conversation nearby, Laura heard a guitar and flute play the opening notes of an old English folk song from somewhere in the house. She heard a baby's bright laugh over the music and a chilling fear whipped through her. "What do you mean?"

His dark eyes narrowed. "Can't you guess?"

Laura sucked in her breath. All her worst nightmares were about to come true.

Gabriel had come for her baby.

After all the times he'd said he never wanted a child, after everything he'd done to make sure he'd never be burdened with one, somehow he'd found out Laura's deepest secret and he'd come to take Robby. And he wouldn't even take their son out of love, oh no. He'd do it out of duty. Cold, resentful duty.

"I don't want you here, Gabriel," Laura whispered, trembling. "I want you to leave."

He set his jaw grimly. "I can't."

Ice water flooded her veins as she stood near the fireplace in the warm parlor. "What brought you? Was it some rumor—or…" She licked her lips and suddenly could no longer bear the strain. "For God's sake. Stop toying with me and tell me what you want!"

His dark eyes looked down at her, searing straight through her soul.

"You, Laura," he said in a low voice. "I came for you."

CHAPTER TWO

I CAME for you.

Stricken, Laura stared up at him with her lips parted.

Gabriel's dark eyes were hot and deep with need. Exactly as he'd looked at her the night he'd taken her virginity. The night she'd conceived their child.

I came for you.

How many times had she dreamed of Gabriel finding her and speaking those words?

She'd missed him constantly over the last fifteen months, as she'd given birth to their baby alone, woken up in the night alone and raised their child without a father. She'd yearned for his strong, protective arms constantly. Especially during the bad times, such as the moment she'd told her family she was pregnant. Or the day of her father's funeral, when her mother and three younger sisters had clung to her, sobbing, expecting her to be the strong one. Or the endless frustrating weeks when Laura had gone to the bank with her baby in tow, day after day, to convince them to extend the loan that would let their farm continue to operate.

But there had been happy times as well, and then she'd missed Gabriel even more. Such as the day halfway into her pregnancy, when she'd been washing dishes in the tiny kitchen and she'd suddenly clutched her curved belly and laughed aloud in wonder as she felt—this time for sure—their baby's first kick inside her. Or the sunny, bright August day when Robby had been born, when she'd held his tiny body against her chest and he'd blinked up at her, yawning sleepily, with dark eyes exactly like his father's.

For over a year, Laura had missed Gabriel like water or sun or air. She'd craved him day and night. She'd missed the sound of his laugh. Their friendship and camaraderie.

And now, he'd finally come for her?

"You came for me?" she whispered. Was it possible he'd thought of her even a fraction of the times her heart had yearned for him? "What do you mean?"

"Just what I said," Gabriel said quietly. "I need you."

She swallowed. "Why?"

His dark eyes glittered in the flickering firelight. "Every other woman has been a pale shadow of you in every way."

If her heart had been fluttering before, now it was frantically rattling against her ribs. Had she been wrong to leave him, fifteen months ago? Had she been wrong to keep Robby a secret? What if Gabriel's feelings had changed, and all this time he'd cared for her? What if—

He leaned forward as his lips curved into a smile. "I need you to come work for me."

Laura's heart stopped, then resumed a slow, sickly beat.

Of course. *Of course* that was all he would want. He'd

likely forgotten their one-night affair long ago, while she would remember it forever—in her passionate dreams, in the eyes of their son. Laura stared up at Gabriel's dark, brutally handsome face. She saw the tension of his jawline, the taut muscles of his folded arms beneath his suit jacket.

"You must want it badly," she said slowly.

He gave her a tight smile. "I do."

Out of the corner of her eye, she saw her mother coming back down the hall, holding Robby in one arm and a slice of wedding cake in her other hand. Laura sucked in her breath.

Robby. How could she have allowed herself to forget, even for an instant, that her son was counting on her to keep him safe?

Grabbing Gabriel's hand, she pulled him out of the room, dragging him out of the house, away from prying eyes and into the freezing February air.

Outside in the wintry night, cars and trucks were wedged everywhere along the gravel driveway between their old house and the barn, strewn along the country road in front of their farm. Across the old stone walls that lined the road, white rolling hills stretched out into the great north woods, disappearing now into the falling purple twilight.

Behind them, next to the old barn, she could see the frozen water of their pond, gleaming like a silver mirror under the lowering gray clouds. Her father had taught all his daughters to swim there during the summers of their childhood, and even though Laura was now grown, whenever she felt upset, she would go for a swim in the pond. Swimming made her think of her father's protective arms. It always made her feel better.

She wished she could swim in the pond now.

Laura looked down at her breath in the chilly air and saw the white smoke of Gabriel's mingle with hers. She realized she was still holding his hand and looked down at his large fingers enfolding her own. The warmth of them suddenly burned her skin, sizzling nerve endings the length of her body.

She dropped his hand. Folding her arms, she glared up at him. "I'm sorry you've come all this way for nothing. I'm not going to work for you."

"You don't even want to hear about the job first? For instance—" he paused "—how much it pays?"

Laura bit her lip, thinking of her bank account, which held exactly thirteen dollars—barely enough for a week's supply of diapers, let alone groceries. But they'd get by. And she couldn't risk Robby's custody—not for something so unimportant as money! She lifted her chin fiercely. "No amount of money could tempt me."

His lips quirked. "I know I wasn't always the easiest man to live with—"

"Easy?" she interjected. "You were a nightmare."

His eyes crinkled in a smile. "Now that's the diplomatic Miss Parker I remember."

She glared at him. "Find another secretary."

"I'm not asking you to be my secretary."

"You said…"

He looked down at her. His voice was dark and deep, his eyes burning though her with intensity. "I want you to spend a night with me in Rio. As my mistress."

His mistress? Laura's mouth fell open.

Gabriel continued to stare down at her with his inscrutable dark eyes, his hands in his pockets. She licked her lips.

"I'm…I'm not for sale," she whispered. "You think just because you are rich and handsome you can have whatever you want, that you can pay me to fall into your bed—and go away the next morning with a check?"

"A charming idea." A humorless smile traced his sensual mouth. "But I don't wish to pay you for sex."

"Oh." Her cheeks went hot. "Then what?"

"I want you—" he moved closer, his hard-edged face impossibly handsome "—to pretend to love me."

She swallowed. Then she tilted her head, blinking up at him in the fading light. "But thousands of girls could do that," she said. "Why come all the way up here, when you could have twenty girls at your penthouse in Rio in four minutes? Are you insane?"

He raked his dark hair back with his hand.

"Yes," he said heavily. "I am going slowly insane. Every moment my father's company is in the hands of another man, every moment I know I lost my family's legacy through my own stupidity, I feel I am losing my mind. I've endured it for almost twenty years. And I'm close now, so close to getting it back."

She should have known it had something to do with regaining Açoazul. "But how can I possibly help you?"

He looked down at her, his jaw clenched. "Play the part of my devoted mistress for twenty-four hours. Until I close the deal."

"How on earth would that help you close the deal?" she asked, bewildered.

He set his jaw. "I've hit a snag in the negotiations. A six-foot-tall, bikini-wearing snag."

"What?"

Gabriel ground his teeth. "Felipe Oliveira found out I used to date his fiancée."

"You did?" Laura said in surprise, then gave a bitter laugh. "Of course you did."

"Now he doesn't want me within a thousand miles of Rio. He thinks if he doesn't sell me the company after all, I'll go back to New York." Gabriel looked at her. "I need to make him understand I'm not interested in his woman."

"That doesn't explain why you'd need *me*. Thousands of women would be happy to pretend to be in love with you. For free." She took a deep breath, clenching her hands at her sides. "Some of them wouldn't even have to pretend!"

He set his jaw. "They won't work."

She exhaled with a flare of her nostrils. "Why?"

"Oliveira's fiancée…is Adriana da Costa."

"Adriana da…" Laura's voice trailed off, her eyes wide.

Adriana da Costa.

Laura could still see those cold, reptilian eyes, that skinny, lanky body. Gabriel had dated the Brazilian supermodel briefly in New York several years ago, while Laura was his live-in personal assistant. She could still hear Adriana's pouting voice. *Why do you keep calling here? Stop calling.*

Find the whiskey, you stupid cow. Gabriel always gets thirsty after sex.

Laura cleared her throat. "Adriana da Costa, the bikini model."

"Yes."

"The one *Celebrity Star* magazine just called the sexiest woman alive."

"She's a selfish narcissist," he said sharply. "And for the short time we were together, she was always insecure. Only one woman has ever made her feel so threatened. You."

"Me?" Laura gasped. "You're out of your mind! She would never feel threatened by me!"

Gabriel's dark eyes gleamed. "She complained to me constantly. Why did I always take your calls, but not hers? Why did I always have time for you, day or night? Why would I leave her bed at 2:00 A.M. in order to go home to you? And most of all, why did I allow you to live in my apartment, only you and no one else?"

Laura's mouth fell open.

"She never understood our relationship," Gabriel said. "How we could be so close without being lovers. Which we weren't." He paused. "Not until…Rio."

The huskiness of his deep voice whipped through Laura, causing a sizzle to spread down her body.

"Adriana has made it clear she wants me back," he said in a low voice. "She'd leave Felipe Oliveira in an instant for me, and he knows it. Only one thing will convince them both I am not interested in her."

Laura stared at him.

"Me?" she whispered.

He looked right at her. "You are the only woman that Adriana would believe I could love."

A roar of shared memories left unspoken between them washed over Laura like a wave, and her heart twisted in her chest. She'd been only twenty-one when, on her second day in New York City, the employment office had sent her to Santos Enterprises to interview in the accounting office. Instead, she'd been sent up to the top floor to meet with the CEO himself.

"Perfeito," the fearsome, sleek Brazilian tycoon had said, looking at her résumé. Then he'd looked at her. "Young enough so you will not be planning to immediately quit to have a baby. At least ten or twenty years before you'll think of that. *Perfeito."*

Now, Gabriel looked at her with dark eyes. She felt a cold winter wind sweep in from the north and shivered.

"Be my pretend mistress in Rio," he said. "And I will pay you a hundred thousand dollars for that one night."

Her lips parted as she breathed, "A hundred thousand!"

She almost said yes on the spot. Then she remembered her baby, and her heart rose to her throat. She shook her head. "Sorry," she choked out. "Get someone else."

His brow furrowed in disbelief. "Why? You clearly need the money."

She licked her lips. "That's none of your business."

"I deserve an answer."

She set her jaw. He didn't know what kind of trouble he'd made for her by coming here. *Didn't know and didn't care.* He couldn't see how Laura had changed through the anguish of the past year. Who would be the first neighbor to gossip that her ex-boss bore an uncanny resemblance to her son?

She exhaled, clenching her hands. He still thought all he had to do was tell her to jump, and she'd ask how high. But she wasn't his obedient little secretary anymore.

With a deep breath, she closed her eyes. It was time to let it all go.

Let go the sound of Gabriel's warm, deep voice for the last five years as his executive assistant. *Miss Parker, there's no one as capable as you.*

Let go the brightness of his delight when he came home at 6:00 A.M. to find her silently waiting with freshly made coffee and a pressed suit for his early meeting. *Miss Parker, what would I do without you?*

Let go the memory of their time in bed, when his dark eyes, so vulnerable and warm, had caressed her face with unspoken words of love. Let go the memory of his lips hot against her skin. Let go the feel of him inside her. *Laura, I need you.*

She opened her eyes.

"I'm sorry," she said, her voice shaking. "You don't deserve an explanation. My answer is just no."

Around them, the dusting of snow reflected light into the white-gray lowering clouds, in a breathless hush of muffled silence. He blinked, looking bewildered.

"Did it end so badly, Laura?" he said softly. "Between us?"

She pressed her fingernails into her palms to keep from crying. Robby. She had to think of Robby. "You shouldn't have come here." Her cheeks felt inflamed in the winter air, her body burning up and yet cold as ice. "I want you to leave. Now."

He took a step closer, looking down at her. A sliver of moonlight pierced through the clouds to illuminate his face. She noticed the dark shadow on his hard jawline, saw the hollows beneath his eyes. She wondered when he'd last slept.

Her heart twisted in her chest. No. She couldn't let

herself care. She couldn't! Choking back tears, she edged away. "If you won't leave, I will."

He grabbed her wrist. He looked down at her, and his eyes glittered. "I can't let you go."

For a moment, she heard only the panting of their breath. Then a door banged open, and she heard a baby's whine. A chill went down her spine and she whirled around with a gasp.

Too late!

"Where have you been, Laura?" her mother called irritably, holding a squirming Robby in her arms. "It took me ages to find you. What on earth are you doing out here in the cold?"

Ripping her arm from Gabriel's grasp, Laura gave her mother a hard, desperate stare. "I'm sorry, Mom. Just go back inside. Go back. I'll be right there!"

But her mother wasn't looking at her. "Is that—is that Mr. Santos?" she said tremulously.

"Hello, Mrs. Parker," Gabriel said, smiling as he stepped towards her and held out his hand. "Congratulations on Becky's wedding. You must be very proud of your daughter."

"I'm proud of all my daughters." She came closer to shake his hand. "It's nice to see you again."

Laura stared at them, her heart in her throat. Her mother had always liked Gabriel, ever since he'd paid for the family to take a vacation to Florida four years ago, one they wouldn't otherwise have been able to afford. The Parkers had traveled in his private jet and stayed at a villa on the beach. It had been a lavish second honeymoon for Laura's parents, a big change from their first at a cheap motel in Niagara Falls. Pictures of that Florida vacation still lined the walls, images of their family smiling beneath palm trees, building sand castles on the beach, splashing in the surf together. With that one gift, Gabriel had won her mother's loyalty forever.

"I'm glad someone had the sense to invite you to Becky's wedding," Ruth said, smiling.

He smiled back with gentle courtesy. "I've always asked you to call me Gabriel."

"Oh no, I couldn't," she said. "Not with you being Laura's employer and all. It just wouldn't be right."

"But I'm not her employer anymore." He flashed Laura a dark look before leaning toward her mother to confidentially whisper, "And I wasn't invited to the wedding. I crashed. I came to offer her a job."

"Oh!" Ruth practically cried tears of joy. "A job! You have no idea how happy that makes me. Things have been so tight lately and you should see some of the ridiculous jobs she's applied for, as far away as Exeter—"

"Mom," Laura cried. "Please take Robby inside!"

"So she's looking for a job, is she?" he purred.

"Oh, yes. She's totally broke," Ruth confided, then her cheeks turned red. "But then, we all are. Ever since… since…" She turned away.

Gabriel put his hands into his pockets. "I was sorry to hear about your husband. He was a good man."

"Thank you," Ruth whispered. Amid the lightly falling snow, silence fell. Gabriel suddenly looked at Robby.

"What a charming baby," he murmured, changing the subject. "Is he related to you, Mrs. Parker?"

Her mother looked at him as if he was stupid. "He's my grandson."

Gabriel looked surprised. "Is one of your other daughters married, as well?"

"Mom," Laura breathed with tears in her eyes, terrified, "just go! Right now!"

But it was too late. "This is Robby," her mother said, holding him up proudly. "Laura's baby."

CHAPTER THREE

As her mother turned to place Robby into her arms, Laura's heart fell to the snowy, frozen ground. The six-month-old's whine faded, turning to hiccups as he clung to Laura. Ruth leaned forward to hug her.

"Take the job," her mother whispered in her ear, then turned to Gabriel and said brightly, "I hope to see you again soon, Mr. Santos!"

Laura heard the dull thunk of the door as her mother went back inside. Then she was alone with Gabriel; their baby in her arms.

Gabriel's dark eyes went to the child, then back to her. The sound of his tightly coiled voice reverberated in the cold air. "This is your son?"

She held her baby close, loving the solid, chubby feel of him in her arms. Tears stung her eyes as she looked down at Robby. "Yes."

"How old is he?"

"Six months," she said in a small voice.

Gabriel's eyes narrowed. "So tell me." His voice was deadly and still as a winter's night. "Who is the father of your baby?"

She'd wished so many times to be able to tell Gabriel the truth, dreamed of giving her son his father. With their baby squirming in her arms between them, the truth rose unbidden to her lips. "The father of my baby is…"

You. You're Robby's father. Robby is your son. But the words stuck in her throat. Gabriel didn't want to be tied down with a child. If she told him her secret, nothing good would come of it. He might feel he had no choice but to sue for custody out of duty, resenting Robby, resenting her for forcing him into it. He might try to take their child to Brazil, away from her, to be given into the arms of some young, sexy nanny.

Laura would gain nothing by telling him. And risk everything.

"Well?" he demanded.

She flashed her eyes at him. "The identity of my baby's father is none of your business."

His own eyes narrowed. "You must have gotten pregnant immediately after you left Rio."

"Yes," she said unwillingly. She shivered, looking from father to son. Would he notice the resemblance?

But Gabriel turned on her, his dark eyes full of accusation. "You were a virgin when I seduced you. You said you wanted a home and family of your own. How could you be so careless, to forget protection, to let yourself get pregnant by a one-night stand?"

Gabriel had used protection, but somehow she'd gotten pregnant anyway. She said over the lump in her throat, "Accidents happen."

"Accidents *don't* happen," he corrected. "Only mistakes."

She set her jaw. "My baby is not a *mistake*."

"You mean it was planned?" He lifted a sardonic eyebrow. "Who is the father? Some good-looking farmer?

Some boy you knew back in high school?" He glanced around. "Where is this paragon? Why hasn't he proposed? Why aren't you his wife?"

Robby was starting to snuffle. Even in his long-sleeved shirt, he was getting cold, and so was she. Holding him close to her warmth, she shifted his weight on her hip. "I told you, it's none of your business."

"Is he here?"

"No!"

"So he deserted you."

"I didn't give him the chance," she said. "I left him first."

"Ah." Gabriel's shoulders seemed to relax slightly. "So you don't love him. Will he cause any trouble when you take the child to Rio?"

"No."

"Good."

"I mean—I'm not taking Robby there. I'm not going." Her baby started to whimper as she turned away. "Goodbye, Gabriel."

"Wait."

The raw emotion in his voice made her hesitate. Against her better judgment she turned back. He stepped toward her, and she saw something in his expression she'd never seen before.

Vulnerability.

"Don't leave," he said in a low voice. "I need you."

I need you.

She'd once loved him. She'd served him night and day, existed only to please him. She had to fight that habit, that yearning, with every bit of willpower she possessed.

"Is a hundred thousand dollars not enough?" He

came closer, his dark eyes bright in the moonlight, the white smoke of his breath drifting around them in the chilly night air. "Let's make it a cool million. A million dollars, Laura. For a single night."

She gasped. *A million…?*

Reaching out, he stroked her cheek. "Think what that money could mean for you. For your family." His fingers moved slowly against her cold skin, the lightest touch of a caress, warming her. "If you don't care what it would mean for me, think what it could do for you. And all you need to do," he said huskily, "is smile for a few hours. Drink champagne. Wear a fancy ball gown. And pretend to love me."

Pretend. Blinking up at him, she swallowed the lump in her throat. *Pretend* to love him.

"Although I know it might not be easy," he said dryly. Then he shook his head. "But you are not so selfish as to refuse."

With an intake of breath, Laura clenched her hands into fists. "Maybe I am. Now."

His sensual mouth curved. "The Laura I knew always put the needs of the people she loved above herself. I know that hasn't changed." His dark eyebrow lifted. "You probably stayed up all night making your sister's wedding cake."

Her lips twisted with a dark emotion. "I really hate you."

"Hate me if you will. But if you do not come with me to Rio tonight…" He clawed his black hair back with his hand, then exhaled. His dark eyes seemed fathomless and deep, echoing with pain. "I will lose my father's legacy. Forever."

Shivering in the cold night, cradling her whimpering baby in the warmth of her arms, Laura looked up into Gabriel's handsome, haggard face. She knew better than anyone what the Açoazul company meant to Gabriel. For years, she'd watched him scheme and plot to regain control of it. He hungered for it. *His legacy.*

Living in the house her great-great-great-great-grandfather had built with his own two hands, on the land her family had farmed for two centuries, Laura could understand the feeling. She looked at his face. It was a shock to see raw vulnerability in his dark eyes. It was an expression she'd never seen there before, not in all the years she'd worked for him. She could feel herself weakening.

One million dollars. For a single night of luxury in Rio, a night of beauty and pleasure. She looked down at her baby. What could that money do for her son? For her family?

But oh, the risk. Could she be strong enough to resist telling Gabriel the truth? For twenty-four hours, could she lie to his face? Could she pretend to love him, without falling in love with him again for real?

On the country road in front of their property, Laura saw a parked black sedan turn on its headlights, as if on cue. She heard the smooth purr of the engine as it slowly drove up the driveway. Over Gabriel's head, moonlight laced the ridges of the dark clouds with silver.

She closed her eyes. "You will never come back looking for me after this?" she said in a low voice. "You will leave us in peace?"

Gabriel's own voice was harsh. "Yes."

Looking at him, Laura took a deep breath and spoke

words that felt like a knife between her shoulder blades. The only words he'd left for her to say.

"One night," she whispered.

An hour later they arrived at the small private airport, where his jet waited outside the hangar. As they crossed the tarmac, Gabriel felt his blood rush in his ears as he stared down at her.

Laura was even more beautiful than he remembered. In the moonlight, her hair looked like dark honey. The frosty winter air gave her cheeks a soft pink glow, and as she bit her lower lip, her heart-shaped mouth looked red and inviting. For a single instant, when he'd first seen her at the farmhouse, he'd had the insane desire to kiss her.

He took a deep breath. He was tired, flying straight from Rio on his private jet. Even more than that, he was exhausted from the months of negotiations to buy back his father's old company in Rio, to gain back the business that had been his birthright before he'd stupidly thrown it away as a grief-stricken nineteen-year-old.

He wouldn't fail. Not this time. Gabriel glanced down grimly at his expensive platinum watch. They were still on schedule. *Just.*

As they climbed the steps to the jet, Laura paused, looking behind her. Shifting the baby carrier on her arm, she pulled her diaper bag up higher on her other shoulder and bit her lip. "I think we should go back to the house for a few more things—"

"You have enough for the flight?" he said shortly.

"Yes, but I didn't pack clothes. Pajamas—"

"Everything you need will be waiting for you in Rio. It will be arranged."

"All right." With one last, troubled glance, she followed him up the steps.

Inside the cabin, Gabriel sat down in the white leather seat. A flight attendant offered him a glass of champagne, which he accepted. It had been harder than he'd expected to convince Laura to come. She sat across from him, suddenly glaring at him beneath her dark lashes.

Was she angry at him for some reason? God knew why. He was the one who should be angry. She'd left him in the lurch a year ago. In an act of pure charity, he'd allowed her to quit her job. It had been the act of a saint. He'd barely managed to patch up the hole she'd left in his office.

"You'd better have a very trustworthy babysitter in Rio," she growled, refusing the offer of champagne.

He finished off the crystal flute. "Maria Silva."

She blinked. "Your housekeeper?"

"She was my nanny when I was young."

"You were young?" Laura said sardonically.

Gabriel's throat closed. Against his will, memories of his happy childhood washed over him, of playing with his older brother, of the wrestling and fighting, of his nanny's voice soothing them. Only a year apart in age, Gabriel had competed with Guilherme constantly, always seeking to best him in their parents' eyes. He'd started some stupid battles. Leading up to the night of the accident…

Turning away, he finished harshly, "I'd trust Maria with my life."

Laura no longer looked angry. Now she looked bemused, staring at him with her large, limpid turquoise eyes. She started to ask a question, then was distracted when the flight attendant suggested she buckle in the baby's carrier before takeoff.

Gabriel watched her smiling down at her son, murmuring soft words of love as she tucked a baby blanket into his pudgy hand. The little one yawned again.

A strange feeling went through Gabriel.

He'd won. He'd convinced her. They would make it back to Rio in time. His plan would work. He should be feeling triumphant.

Instead, he felt...on edge.

Why? It couldn't be the money he'd promised her. A million dollars was nothing. He would have paid ten times that to win back his father's company. He would have given every penny he possessed, every share of stock in Santos Enterprises, the contracts, the office building in Manhattan, the ships in Rotterdam. Everything down to the last stick of furniture.

So it wasn't the money. But as the jet took off, leaving New Hampshire behind, he looked out the window. Something bothered him, and he didn't know what it was. Was it that he'd let Laura see his desperation?

No, he thought, setting his jaw. She knew how much his father's company meant to him. And anyway, allowing his vulnerability to show had helped achieve his goal.

It was something else. His gaze settled on the drowsing baby's dark hair, his plump cheeks.

It was the baby. The baby unsettled him.

Gabriel's jaw set as he realized what the edgy feeling was. What it had to be.

Anger.

He couldn't believe that Laura had fallen into another man's bed so swiftly. When she'd quit her job and walked out of his life last year, he'd let her go for one reason only—for her own good. He'd come to care for her. And he knew he couldn't give her what she wanted. A husband. Children. A job that didn't consume her every waking hour. When, the morning after he'd seduced her, she'd suddenly said she was quitting and going back to her family, he'd given Laura her chance at happiness. He'd let her go.

But instead of following her dreams, she'd apparently jumped into a brief, meaningless affair with some man she didn't even care about. She'd settled for poverty and the life of a single mother. She'd allowed her child to be born without a father. Without a name.

Cold rage slowly built inside him.

He'd let her go for nothing.

Gabriel looked at her, now leaning back in her white leather seat with her eyes closed, one hand still on her baby in the seat beside her. She was even more beautiful than he remembered. Even in that unflattering, pale pink satin dress, with that horrible hot pink lipstick, her natural beauty shone through. With all its deceptive innocence.

Against his will, his eyes traced the generous curves beneath her gown. Her breasts were bigger since she'd become a mother, her hips wider. And suddenly he couldn't stop wondering what her body would look like beneath that dress. *What it would feel like against him in bed.*

Erotic memories flashed through him of the first time he'd kissed her, when he'd swept his laptop to the floor in his ruthless need to have her. Taking her against his desk, he'd lost data that had cost thousands of dollars.

He hadn't cared. It had been worth it.

He'd wanted Laura Parker from the moment she'd walked into his office, looking uncertain in her country clothes and wearing big, ugly glasses. He'd seen at once that she had a kind, innocent heart, coupled with the fearless bluntness he needed in an executive assistant. He'd wanted her, but for five years, he'd held himself in check. He needed her too badly in his office, needed her expertise to keep Santos Enterprises—and his life— running like a well-oiled machine. And he knew an old-fashioned woman like Laura Parker would never settle for what a man like Gabriel could offer—money, glamour, an emotionless affair. So he hadn't allowed himself to touch her. Not even to flirt with her.

Until...

Last year, during a helicopter flight from Açoazul's steel factory to the north of the city, Gabriel had looked up from a report to discover his pilot had flown them right over the sharp stretch of road where his family had died nearly twenty years before.

Gabriel had said nothing to the pilot. He'd told himself he felt nothing. Then he'd gone back to the office. It was late, and all his other employees were gone. He'd seen Laura Parker alone at his desk, filing papers in her prim collared shirt and tweed skirt, and something inside him had snapped. Five years of frustrated need had exploded and he'd seized her. Her blue eyes had widened behind her sleek, black-framed glasses as, without a word, he'd ruthlessly kissed her.

That night, he'd discovered two things that shocked him.

First: Miss Parker was a virgin.

Second: beneath her demure exterior, she'd burned him to ashes with her passionate fire.

He'd made love to her roughly against the desk. He'd been more gentle the second time, after they'd taken the elevator up to his penthouse and he'd kissed her for hours, lying across his big bed. The night had been… amazing. More than amazing. It had been the most incredible sexual experience of his life.

Now, looking at her, a cold knot tightened in Gabriel's chest. He'd given that up, and she'd just thrown herself away. She'd let some unworthy man touch her. Get her pregnant with his child.

Gabriel's hands tightened into fists. Perhaps it was hypocritical to feel so betrayed, since he'd enjoyed many women the past year since she'd deserted him. But *enjoy* was not the right word. All Gabriel had done was prove to himself, over and over, that no other woman could satisfy him as Laura had.

Turning away, he set his jaw. He'd get control of Açoazul SA and then send Laura and her baby back to New Hampshire. He'd thought he might ask her to stay in Rio after the deal was done, but now that was impossible. As much as he missed her in the office—as much as he missed her in his bed—he couldn't take her back now. Not now that she had a child.

He couldn't let himself feel, not even for a moment, as if he were part of a family.

"You look tired," he heard Laura say quietly.

He turned to her, and their eyes locked in the semi-darkness of the jet. "I'm fine."

"You don't seem fine."

"A lot has changed." He looked from her to the sleeping baby. He wanted to ask her again who the baby's father was. He wanted to ask how long she'd waited before she'd jumped into bed with a stranger. A week?

A day? What had the man done to seduce her? Bought her some cheap flowers and wine? Given her cheap promises?

What had it taken for the man to convince Laura to surrender the life she'd yearned for, and accept instead just the crumbs of her childhood dreams?

"Gabriel?"

He looked up to find her anxious eyes watching him. "What?"

"What will happen after we arrive in Rio?"

He leaned back in his seat, folding his arms. "Oliveira is hosting an afternoon pool party at his beachside mansion on the Costa do Sul. Adriana will be there."

Laura bit her lip, looking nervous. "Pool party? Like with a swimsuit?"

"And after that," he continued ruthlessly, "you will attend the Fantasy Ball with me."

"Fantasy, huh?" Her full lips twisted. "I hope Brazilian shopping malls sell magic fairy dust, 'cause that's the only thing that will convince anyone I can compete with Adriana da Costa."

"The first person you must convince is yourself," he said harshly. "Your lack of confidence is not attractive. No one will believe I'd be in love with a woman who disappears in the background like a wallflower."

He had the hollow satisfaction of seeing the light in her beautiful face fade. "I just meant…"

"We made a deal. I am paying you well. For the next twenty-four hours, Laura, you will be the woman I need you to be. You belong to me."

Her eyes narrowed with anger and resentment, and as she turned away, some part of him was glad he'd hurt her. He heard the soft snuffle of the baby's breath, and it was like a razor against his throat.

He'd once been comforted by the thought of Laura back at home with her family, following her dreams. Now she'd taken that from him. She'd betrayed him.

And he hated her for that.

CHAPTER FOUR

As they descended through the clouds toward Rio de Janeiro, Laura stared out the porthole window at the city shining like a jewel on the sea. She folded her arms with a huff of breath, still furious.

You belong to me.

Her hands gripped her seat belt. Looking past Robby's baby seat, where he was thankfully sleeping again after a fairly rough night, Laura glanced at Gabriel on the opposite side of the jet. She allowed herself a grim smile.

Poor Robby had been crying half the flight. Gabriel must have been gnashing his teeth to be trapped in his private jet with a baby. Karma, she thought with a degree of satisfaction. Folding her arms, she turned back to the window to see the beautiful, exotic city as they descended through the clouds.

It had been difficult for her to leave her mother and sisters in the middle of Becky's reception. But instead of being angry, her mother and sisters had seemed pleased. They'd hugged her goodbye for the quick weekend trip. "You were so happy working for him once," her mother had whispered. "This will be a new start for you and Robby. I can feel it. It's fate."

Fate.

Laura had barely gotten on this jet before he'd insulted her. Now, he glared at her as if she were a stranger. No, worse than a stranger. He stared at her as if she were scum beneath his feet.

As the jet finally landed at the private airport, her hands gripped the leather armrest. She would never again feel guilty about keeping their baby a secret from Gabriel. After this, she would never let herself feel *anything* for him. She would do her job, pretend to be his adoring mistress—ha!—then collect the check and forget his existence. She *would.*

As the door of the private jet opened, Robby woke up with one of his adorable baby smiles. His toothless grin and happy cooing were worth any amount of sleepless nights, she thought.

"We're just here for one night, Robby," she told her baby, kissing his forehead as she unbuckled his seat. "Just a quick night here and we'll go straight back home."

"Did he sleep well?" Gabriel said sardonically behind her.

She gave him a pleasant answering smile. "Did you?"

As they stepped out of the jet, Rio's sultry heat hit her at once. She went down the steps, blinking in the blinding sunlight and breathing in the scents of tropical flowers, exotic spice and tangy salt from the sea. Lush, white-hot Brazil was the other side of the world from the frigid February weather she'd left behind her.

Looking across the tarmac, Laura saw a waiting white limousine and snorted. The other side of the world? This was a different world entirely!

"*Bom dia*, Miss Parker," the driver said, tipping his hat as he opened the door. "I am glad to see you again. And what's this?" He tickled beneath Robby's chin. "We have a new passenger!"

"*Obrigada*, Carlos," Laura said, smiling. "This is my son, Robby."

"Is the penthouse ready?" Gabriel growled behind them.

The driver nodded. "*Sim, senhor*. Maria, she has organized everything."

"Good."

Laura climbed into the backseat and tucked Robby into the waiting baby seat, ignoring Gabriel climbing in beside him. Carlos started the engine and pulled the limo off the tarmac, going south.

As they traveled through the city, now crowded with tourists for the celebration of *Carnaval*, Laura stared out bleakly at the festive decorations. Gabriel didn't speak and neither did she. The silence seemed like agony as the car inched through the traffic. As they finally approached the back of Gabriel's building, Laura heard loud thumping music, drums, people singing and cheering.

"This is as close as I can get, *senhor*," Carlos said apologetically. "The *avenida* is closed to cars today."

"*Está bom*." Setting his jaw, Gabriel opened the door himself and got out of the limo.

Laura looked out her window in awe. Ahead of them, she saw the street blocked and people gathering on Ipanema Beach for one of the largest, wildest street festivals in Rio. She looked up at Gabriel's tall building above them. He had bought it two years ago, as a foothold in Rio while he wrestled his father's company back from Felipe Oliveira. The ground floors held restaurants and retail space. The middle floors held the South American offices of Santos Enterprises, still officially headquartered in New York. The top two floors of the building were apartments for his bodyguards, household staff and Maria. The penthouse was, of course, for Gabriel—and, the last time she'd been here, for Laura. She swallowed. She'd never thought she'd be back here.

Especially not with a secret. *A baby.*

The car door wrenched open. She looked up, expecting Carlos, but it was Gabriel. To her shock, the expression on his handsome face was suddenly tender and adoring. His eyes shone with passion and desire.

"At last you are home, *querida*," Gabriel murmured. He held out his hand. "Home where you belong. It nearly killed me when you left. I never stopped loving you, Laura."

She gasped.

Suddenly she could no longer feel the hot sun blazing overhead or the fresh breeze off the sea. Loud music, horns and drumming and singing from Ipanema Beach all faded into the background. Her heart thrummed wildly in her throat.

Gabriel's black eyes sizzled as he looked down at her, catching up her soul, collecting her like a butterfly in a net.

Then he dropped his hand with a sardonic laugh. "Just practicing."

Setting her jaw, she glared at him. "A million dollars is almost not enough to deal with this," she muttered.

His lip twisted. "Too late to renegotiate."

"Go to hell."

"Is that any way to speak in front of your baby?"

Turning back into the car, Laura unbuckled Robby. Her son cooed happily, reaching up his chubby arms for her embrace, and she was happy she had one person in Brazil who actually loved her. Leaving the baby carrier in the limo, she scooped him out of his seat. He giggled, clinging to her wrinkled satin bridesmaid's dress.

Laura felt tired, grungy, dirty. After her poor night's sleep on the jet, after traveling halfway around the world, and most of all, after the constant friction of having Gabriel near her, Laura's emotions were too close to the surface. The flash of his dark eyes, the slightest touch of his hand, the merest word of kindness from his sensual lips, still made her tremble and melt.

He was poison for her, she thought grimly. Poison wrapped in honeyed words and hot desire.

She held her baby close and walked around Gabriel with as much dignity as she possessed, her shoulders straight. Her pink high heels—picked out from a thrift shop by Becky for five dollars—clattered against the marble floor as Laura walked through the back entrance and past the security guards toward the private elevator.

Gabriel followed her without a word. The elevator doors closed behind them, and she breathed in his scent. She felt his warmth beside her. She didn't look at him. His tall, powerful body was so close and she felt every inch.

The last time they'd been together in this elevator, they'd been on the way to the penthouse, after they'd just made love downstairs on the desk in his office. It had been her first time. He'd been shocked she was a virgin, even apologetic. He'd kissed her so tenderly in this very elevator, taking her back up to the penthouse with whispered promises that this time would be different, that he'd make it good for her, that he'd make her weep with joy.

And he had.

The elevator dinged at the same instant Robby struggled in her arms with a plaintive whine. Looking down, Laura saw he was peeking behind her at Gabriel, reaching out his plump arms. Gabriel didn't move to take the baby, or even smile. Of course he wouldn't. Why would he take the slightest interest in his own child? She knew she was being unreasonable, but she still felt angry. Exhaling, Laura walked into the penthouse.

His modern, masculine, clutter-free apartment had two bedrooms, a study, a dining room and main room off the kitchen. The whole place had clean lines, white walls and high ceilings, and a stark decor. A wall of windows two stories high showcased the breathtaking view of the pool and terrace, with Ipanema Beach and the Atlantic visible beyond.

"I'm so glad to see you again, Senhora Laura." Maria Silva, Gabriel's housekeeper and former nanny, was waiting for them. Her gaze moved to Robby. "This must be your sweet baby."

"*Senhora*?" Laura repeated, confused at how she'd just gotten promoted to a married woman.

The plump-cheeked, white-haired woman blushed. "You're a mother. You deserve respect," she said, then held out her hands to the baby. Robby gave a gleeful cackle, and Maria took him happily in her arms.

Frowning, Laura slowly looked around her. The penthouse seemed the same, but it had changed somehow. She saw to her surprise that all the electric plugs and sharp edges had been covered. Peeking into the dining room, she saw it was entirely filled with toys.

Laura turned to Gabriel in wonder. "All this?" she said. "For one night?"

He shrugged. "Don't thank me. Maria did it."

Laura's heart, which had been rising, fell back to her shoes.

"We'll have a wonderful time this afternoon, won't we?" Maria said to Robby, whirling the baby around to make him giggle. "If you need us, Mrs. Laura, we'll be making lunch."

Laura turned to follow them into the kitchen, but Gabriel stopped her. "They'll be fine. Go freshen up."

She scowled at him. "Stop barking orders at me. You weren't this bad when I worked for you."

"Do you want a shower or not?"

From the kitchen, Laura dimly heard Maria getting out pots and pans as she sang a song to the baby in Portuguese. Robby started banging the pans with a wooden spoon, keeping the beat. They seemed fine. Laura set her jaw, then grudgingly admitted, "I do want a shower."

"You have ten minutes." When she didn't move, he lifted a sardonic eyebrow. "Need help?"

She saw his lips curve as he turned away, walking down the hallway. Pulling off his shirt, he dropped it to the floor as he stopped in the doorway of his bedroom. He looked back at her with heavy-lidded eyes. "Go. Right now. Or I will assist you."

"I'm going!" With a gulp, Laura ran for the safety of her old bedroom.

Her room had changed, as well. All the old furniture she'd had as his live-in secretary was gone, of course.

The space had been turned into a bland guest room. Except…

She saw the brand-new elliptical wooden crib beside the bed, the changing table with diapers and baby clothes and everything else Robby might need. She exclaimed with delight as she touched the smooth wood. In the closet, she saw new clothes for her, as well. Gabriel had truly thought of everything. Going to the closet, she touched a black dress with a soft, satisfied sigh.

Then she saw the size on the tag.

Well, she thought with dismay, he hadn't thought of *everything*.

CHAPTER FIVE

TEN MINUTES LATER, Gabriel paced beneath the hot sun across his rooftop terrace. He stopped, staring down at Ipanema Beach across the Avenida Vieira Souto. He could hear the loud music from the crowds celebrating below. Lifting his eyes, he looked past the throngs of people, past the yellow umbrellas and food vendors to the shining waves of the surf, trying to calm his pounding heart.

Now Laura was here, everything would soon be sorted out. Oliveira and Adriana would both believe that they were in love. They had to believe. Otherwise....

No, he wouldn't let himself think about failure, not even for an instant. He couldn't lose his father's company, not now that it was finally within his grasp. He gripped the railing, glaring at the bright horizon of blue ocean. All along the coastline, tall buildings vied with the sharp green mountains for domination of the sky.

He'd changed into khaki shorts and an open, button-down shirt over a tank top, with flip-flops on his feet, Carioca-style. He paced his private rooftop. Bright sunlight reflected prisms from the water of his swimming pool. Turning back, he stared down blindly at the scantily clad women on Ipanema Beach, to Leblon to the west, ending in the stark, sharp green mountain of Dois Irmãos.

Gabriel had been only nineteen when he'd lost everything. His parents. His brother. His home. His hands tightened on the rail. When he'd had the chance to sell his family's business the day after the funeral, Gabriel had taken it. He'd fled to New York, leaving his grief behind.

Except grief had followed him. Consumed him. Even as he created an international company far larger than his father's had ever been, the guilt of what he'd done—causing the accident, but being the only survivor; inheriting his father's company, only to carelessly sell it—never left him. Never.

"Well, I did it," Laura gasped suddenly behind him. "Ten minutes."

"Very efficient," he said, turning to face her. "You should know that—"

His words froze in his throat.

Gabriel's eyes traced over her in shock as he watched her towel off her long wet hair. He took in the erotic vision of her obscenely full breasts overflowing the neckline of her black dress. He couldn't look away from the fabric outlining her full buttocks and hips.

"Where," he choked out, "did you get that dress?"

She stopped toweling her hair to look at him, tilting her head with a frown. "It was in the closet. Wasn't it for me?"

"Yes." He couldn't stop his gaze from devouring her curvaceous body. He became instantly hard, filled with the memory of how it felt to have her in his arms, for the most explosive sexual night of his life. *He wanted her.* Here in Rio, beneath the Brazilian sunshine, suddenly he could think of nothing but taking her, right here and now. He licked his lips and said hoarsely, "But I didn't expect it to look like *that*."

An embarrassed blush rose to her cheeks as she pushed up her black-framed glasses in a self-conscious gesture. "I gained a little weight with my pregnancy," she mumbled. "I'm not so thin as I used to be."

"No." Gabriel stared at her, feeling his body tighten with lust. "No, you're not."

Willing himself to stay in control, he pulled out a chair at the table next to the pool. "Maria made breakfast. Come and eat."

Laura scowled. "Is that an order?"

"Sim."

Carefully folding her towel and setting it on a nearby table—instead of just dropping it to the floor, as he would have done—she sat down.

"I probably shouldn't eat anything. Not if I'm supposed to wear a bikini," she said in a low voice. "I've tried to diet, but…"

"Never diet again," he said tersely. "You are perfect."

He pushed her chair back under the table. He paused, allowing his hands to remain on the back of the chair, next to her shoulders. He could almost feel the warmth of her soft skin.

She looked up at him over her shoulder with a scowl. "You're just being nice."

He stared down at her. "When have you ever known me to be nice?"

Her full pink lips suddenly curved into a smile as her blue eyes twinkled. "Good point." She tilted her head, considering. "So you really think I look…all right?"

"Hmm." His eyes lingered on her spectacular figure. She'd been beautiful before, but now, it was almost like torture to see her perfect female shape. Those hips. Her curvaceous bottom. Those breasts—!

She was almost *too* attractive, he thought. He wanted to convince Oliveira and Adriana he was in love with Laura, not have every other man on the Avenida Vieira Souta enjoy the luscious spectacle of her body. "You're fine," he said, irritated. "But that dress is unacceptable. We'll buy you something else when we go shopping today."

"Shopping. Right." Pouring milk and sugar into her cup, she stirred her coffee with a silver spoon. "I can hardly wait."

He sat down across the table. "You have nothing to worry about." He pushed the bread basket toward her. "It'll be fine."

She took a roll and sipped her coffee, and as they ate, Gabriel couldn't stop staring at her. Once, their relationship had been easy. A friendship. A trust. Now, he couldn't quite read her.

Strange.

For five years, Laura Parker had been the perfect employee. She'd had no life or interests of her own. She'd always been ready and waiting to offer her competent assistance for his latest emergency, whether it was a billion-dollar drop on a foreign stock exchange or a broken thread on his tuxedo.

Now…there was something different about her. Something had changed in her over the last year. He felt as if he didn't know her.

"How is your meal?" he said gruffly.

"Delicious."

"Try this." He handed her a bowl of pastries. Their fingers brushed and she jerked away as if he'd burned her.

He scowled at her. "We're attending Oliveira's party in three hours. No one will believe we are a couple if you jump every time I touch you."

Putting down her fork with a clang, she looked at him. "You're right."

He held out his hand across the table, palm up.

With an intake of breath, she placed her hand in his. He felt her tremble. Felt the warmth of her skin. A rush of desire went through him as his fingers tightened over hers. Coming to her side of the table, he pulled her to her feet.

For a moment, they stood facing each other beneath the warm, bright sun. A soft sea breeze ruffled her damp hair. She wouldn't meet his eyes. Her gaze seemed fixated on his mouth.

She licked her lips, and he nearly groaned.

"I passed your test," she whispered. "I'm touching you without flinching."

"Holding my hand is not enough."

She visibly swallowed, looking up. "What—what else?"

He put his arms around her, pulling her close. He felt the softness of her body, felt her curves pressed against him as he rested his hands on her hips. Her tight black dress squeezed her breasts still higher in the force of his embrace, plump and firm and begging for his touch. He stroked her cheek, tilting back her head. "Now I need you to look at me," he said in a low voice, "as if you love me."

Beneath her glasses, her wide-set blue eyes glimmered in the sunlight, shining like the sea.

"And I," he continued roughly, "am utterly, completely and insanely in love with you."

She trembled. Then she fiercely shook her head.

"This isn't going to work. No one will believe you'd choose me over her."

"You're wrong," he said. "Adriana is beautiful, yes. But that's all she is. While you…"

Laura stiffened in his arms, lifting her chin.

He cupped her head with his hands. "You are more than just a pretty face." He stroked her bare neck. "More than just a luscious body." He rubbed his thumb against her full, sensitive lower lip. "You are smart. And too kindhearted for your own good. You sacrifice yourself to take care of others, even when you shouldn't." He pressed a finger against her lips to stop her protest. "And you have something else Adriana does not."

"What?"

He looked down at her. "You have me," he whispered.

Gabriel felt her hands tighten around him.

"Can you do it?" he asked in a low voice. "Can you pretend you're in love with me? Can you make everyone believe that all you've ever wanted is for me to hold you like this?"

Her face was pale as she looked at him, trembling like a flower in his arms. When she spoke, her voice was almost too quiet for him to hear above the noise of the music and street party below. "Yes."

"Then prove it." He felt her soft curves pressing against his body, felt how delicate and petite she was in his arms. Laura was so beautiful in every way. He felt the press of her full breasts against his chest. Felt the tendrils of her long damp hair brush against his hands as he gripped her back. He breathed in the scent of her, lavender and soap, wholesome and clean.

He was hard for her. Rock hard. And yet she seemed to think she was inferior to Adriana da Costa, who aside from her beauty was nothing but a shallow, spoiled brat.

Suddenly Gabriel knew he had to tell Laura the truth.

"I want you, Laura," he said in a low voice. "More than any woman. I've always wanted you."

She gasped, her eyes wide. "You…"

Then her expression grew dull as the light in her eyes abruptly faded. "You're practicing again."

"No." He cupped her face roughly. "This has nothing to do with our business deal. I want you. I've spent the last year wanting you. And now you're in my arms, I intend to have you."

He saw her eyes widen beneath her glasses, heard her harsh intake of breath.

"But for now," he murmured, "I will start with a kiss."

Then he lowered his head to hers.

He felt her soft, warm lips tremble against his own. For a single instant, her body stiffened in his arms. He felt her hands against his chest as she tried to push him away. He just wrapped his arms around her waist more firmly and held her tight, refusing to let go.

Kissing her was even better than Gabriel had imagined.

It was heaven.

It was hell.

With a shudder and a sigh she suddenly melted against him. He ruthlessly pushed her lips apart, teasing her with his tongue, plundering the warm heat of her mouth.

His kiss became harder, more demanding, their embrace tighter beneath the white heat of the sun. Slowly, she responded. Her hands stopped pushing against his chest, and moved up to his neck, pulling him down to her. When she finally kissed him back, with a hunger that matched his own, a low growl rose in the back of his throat.

He forgot their affair wasn't real. He forgot the deal entirely. He felt only his masculine, animal need to have her, the need he'd denied himself for too long. Lust swarmed in his blood, pounding through his brain, demanding he take total possession of Laura in his bed.

CHAPTER SIX

THIS *couldn't be happening.*

Gabriel couldn't be kissing her.

But the part of Laura's brain that was telling her to push away, push away now, was lost in the scorching fire of his embrace. As his lips moved against hers, mastering and guiding her, heat seared down her body like a hot jungle wind.

Pleasure whipped through her, pleasure she'd felt only once in her life before. But this was even better than her memory. As they stood on the penthouse terrace, she grasped his open shirt, clinging for dear life. She felt the warmth of his body, the hardness of his muscled chest beneath his cotton tank top. His strong thighs in khaki shorts brushed like tree trunks against her legs. He towered over her, making her feel womanly and petite as he folded himself around her.

The hot, hard feel of his lips seared hers, causing sparks to shoot down the length of her body. Her breasts felt suddenly heavy, her nipples taut. A fire of ache raced to her deepest core as tension coiled inside her. She felt the rough sandpaper of his chin against hers and breathed in his intoxicating scent of musk and spice. Her knees shook beneath her. Her world was spinning.

Everything she'd wanted, everything she'd dreamed about for the past lonely year, and five years before that, was suddenly in her grasp.

His hands stroked her back through her black dress.

"Come to bed with me," he whispered against her skin.

Bed.

She sucked in her breath as reason returned. He was seducing her. And so easily. She'd made the mistake of giving in to her desire for him once, and it had changed the course of her life. She couldn't let it happen again. Never again...

With a ragged gasp, she pulled away from his grasp. Breathing hard, she glared up at him. "You don't seriously expect me to fall into bed with you after one practice kiss?"

His half-lidded eyes were sultry with confidence—*arrogance*—and his sensual lips curved into a smile. "Yes. I had rather hoped you would."

"Forget it."

"It would make our pretend affair more believable."

"By turning it into a real one?" she whispered.

He shrugged, even as the intensity of his gaze belied that casual gesture. "Why not?"

The early afternoon was growing hot, the sun and humidity alleviated only by the cooling trade winds off the Atlantic and the Janeiro River, for which the city had been named. Laura took a deep breath of the fragrant, fresh air redolent of spices and tropical fruits. How many times had she prayed that by some miracle, Gabriel would come for her?

I want you, Laura, more than any woman. I've always wanted you.

She pushed aside her own longing. She couldn't let herself want him. She couldn't. She lifted her chin. "Thanks, but I'm not interested in a one-night stand."

His black eyes glowed like embers. "I don't want a one-night stand."

She licked her suddenly dry lips. "You—you don't?"

He shook his head. "I want you to stay."

"You do?"

"I've missed having you as my secretary. And," he added, as she folded her arms furiously, "as my lover."

"Oh." Her arms fell back to her sides. She whispered, "And Robby?"

His jaw hardened as he looked away.

"The two of you can live in the apartment below mine," he said. "Your child need not inconvenience me at all."

Your child. Hot pride and anger rushed back to her, stiffening her spine. "You mean you will kindly overlook my baby in order to have me in Rio as your 24/7 employee and late-night booty call."

He stared at her, wide-eyed. Then he gave a sudden laugh. "I've missed you, Laura," he said softly. "No one stands up to me like you do. You're not afraid of me at all. You see right through me. I like that."

She jerked away from him, near tears and furious with herself. She couldn't believe she'd let herself get seduced by his sweet kisses, not even for an instant. Absolutely nothing had changed. Gabriel didn't want a wife or child. And for her, only a real family would do.

"Sorry," she said coldly. "But my days of being your

work slave and casual late-night lover are *over*. Don't you dare kiss me again."

But his hands only tightened on her. "I can and I will."

She exhaled in fury. "You have some arrogance to think—"

Seizing her in his arms, he kissed her at once, roughly, hard enough to bruise. Showing mastery. Showing possession. And to her eternal shame, when his hot lips were against hers, she could not resist. She sagged in his arms—and kissed him back.

"I want you, Laura," he murmured against her skin when he finally pulled away. "And I will have you. If not this instant, then soon. Tonight."

She shoved her hands against his hard chest, his deliciously muscular, taut body beneath the tight cotton tank top… Maybe it hadn't been so much a shove as a caress. Angry at herself, she stepped back from him, her cheeks hot. With more confidence than she felt, she said, "Not going to happen."

"We'll see." His voice held a smug masculine tone.

"Our deal had nothing to do with sex."

"Correct."

"I don't have to sleep with you."

He had the temerity to give her a sensual, heavy-lidded glance. "And yet you will."

"Ooh!" Clenching her hands into fists, she gave a little stomp of her heel and went back into the penthouse. She found her son still playing on the spotless floor in the kitchen as Maria washed the dishes.

Gathering her baby in her arms, Laura took Robby into the living room and sat down in a new rocking chair by the wide windows overlooking the city. When Gabriel followed her, she glared at him, daring him to interrupt her time with her child. With a sardonic uplift of his brow, he just turned away, disappearing down the hall.

For long moments, Laura held her baby. She fed him, rocking him to sleep, and suddenly felt like crying.

She couldn't let Gabriel seduce her. She could *not*. No matter how much her body craved his touch. No matter how her heart yearned.

Because her heart yearned for a lie. Gabriel would never change. Getting close to him would only break her heart—again. Break her heart, and possibly risk custody of her son. If she fell into bed with Gabriel, if she gave him her body, she feared she would also give up the secret that had tormented her for over a year.

She looked down at the sweet six-month-old baby slumbering in her arms. Gently, she rose to her feet and carried him down the hall to her darkened bedroom and set him in his crib. She stared down at Robby for a moment, listening to his steady, even breathing. Then she stiffened when a shadow fell from the open doorway.

"Time to go," Gabriel said behind her.

Straightening her tight dress over her hips, she walked out of the bedroom and closed the door. She glared at him, then glanced behind her. "I hate to leave him."

"Your son will be fine. Maria will be looking after him. And anyway—" he lifted a dark eyebrow "—this one night's work will allow you to give him a comfortable life."

She took a deep breath. "You're right. A million dollars is worth it." She lifted her chin. "It's even worth spending a night with you."

His lips curved into a sensual smile. "The whole night."

"Not going to happen."

"We'll see." He turned without touching her, and after bidding farewell to Maria, they took the elevator downstairs. Carlos had the Ferrari waiting in the alley behind the building, engine running.

"Obrigado," Gabriel said to him in passing, then held open the door for Laura. "If you please."

She tottered into the low-slung Ferrari, feeling squeezed like a sausage by the tight black dress and half expecting to bust a seam. Gabriel climbed in beside her and the red sports car roared away from the curb.

As he drove through the crowded streets, Laura stared out in amazement through the window. Rio de Janeiro always lost its mind and found its wildest heart during *Carnaval,* and this year that was more true than ever. Music wafted through the air, horns and drums to accompany people singing. Impromptu parades marched through the streets, and even those not on carnival floats from the prestigious samba schools often wore costumes that sparkled with sequins—and barely covered enough to be decent. Everyone became sexier, more daring versions of their regular selves. Laura took a deep breath. Even her.

"I'm taking you to Zeytuna," Gabriel said as he drove. "From there we'll go directly to Oliveira's pool party."

"Zeytuna?" She'd heard of the large, exclusive boutique, but had never shopped there. She licked her lips and tried to joke, "They sell magic bikinis, right?"

As he changed gears in the Ferrari, he glanced at her from the corner of his eye. "Yes."

Yes. Just yes. No encouragement. No reassurance. Laura tried not to think of her looming bikini face-off with Adriana da Costa and the sheer humiliation that was sure to follow. She bit her lip and changed the subject. "So what is our story?"

"Story?"

"When did we fall in love? So I'll know when people ask."

He considered. "We had an affair last year," he said finally. "You quit your job and left me when I wouldn't commit."

"Believable."

He glanced at her. "But I missed you. I've been secretly pursuing you for months—video chats, flowers, sending you jewelry and love letters and so forth."

"Sounds nice," she said, looking away.

"You invited me to your sister's wedding, and we fell into each other's arms. You surrendered to my charm and agreed to be mine at last."

"A true Valentine's Day fantasy." Her lips twisted as she looked back at him. "And Robby?"

Gabriel blinked, then his hands tightened on the steering wheel as he stared at the road. "Ah, yes. Robby."

"Everyone knows you would never date a woman with a child."

"Yes." He set his jaw. Then, relaxing, he shrugged. "It will only add to the credibility of the story. It makes you unique. I wanted you so desperately, I was even willing to overlook your baby."

"*Overlook* Robby? Thank you," she said, folding

her arms as she glared out the window. "Thank you so much."

"I do not appreciate your sarcasm."

She looked at him. "I don't appreciate you saying you'll *overlook* my baby—like you're doing me some big favor!"

He set his jaw. "And I do not appreciate the fact that there is a baby living in my house."

"Because you must never be inconvenienced," she said mockingly. "The great Gabriel Santos must never have even a hint of family domesticity in his selfish bachelor's penthouse!"

Silence fell over the Ferrari.

"You love your son," Gabriel said. It sounded like a question.

Pushing up her glasses, she glared at him. "Of course I love him. What kind of question it that?"

Gabriel's black eyes burned through her. "So how could you allow yourself to get pregnant without also giving him a father? You always told me you wanted marriage, Laura. A home near your family. A career that would allow you time to raise your children. How could you toss all that aside for the sake of a one-night stand?"

She swallowed, blinking back tears. Yes, how could she?

His eyes turned back to the road. "You quit without notice last year," he said coldly. "*That* was inconvenient."

She stiffened. "Inconvenient to replace me in your office—or your bed?"

His lips tightened. "Both."

"So difficult, and yet you didn't bother to even try to talk me out of it."

They stopped at a red light. He turned on her, his eyes glinting with fury. "I let you go, Laura. For your own good, so you could have the life you wanted. But instead of following your dreams, you threw it all away. You made my sacrifice worthless. How could you? How could you be so careless?"

"It was an accident!"

"I told you." His eyes were hard. "There are no accidents. Only mistakes."

"And I told you, my baby is not a mistake!"

"Are you saying you got pregnant on purpose?"

Her mouth went dry.

He waited, then the light turned green. His lip twisted as he turned back to the road. "Every child deserves to be born into a stable home with two parents. I'm disappointed in you, Laura. You should have been careful."

Laura stiffened. "Careful like who? Like you?"

"Yes."

She longed to have the satisfaction of wiping that scornful, judgmental look off his face. She wondered what he would say if she told him that he was the father.

But she knew the satisfaction would be short-lived. If he knew Robby was his child, he might feel duty-bound to take responsibility for a child he couldn't love, and be pinned down to a domestic life he'd never wanted. And he would hate not just Laura for that, he'd hate Robby, as well.

She had to keep the secret. *Had to.* Leaning back against the black leather seat, she pressed her lips shut. *Just a few more hours*, she told herself desperately.

Tomorrow she and Robby would be on the plane back home, a million dollars richer.

"I thought family meant everything to you."

She opened her eyes, blinking back tears. "It does."

"I thought you were better than that."

"Don't you think I want a father for Robby? Don't you think I want to give him the same loving family I had?"

"So why didn't you?" Gabriel took a deep breath and said in a low voice, "Badly done, Laura."

She started to deliver a sharp retort; then stopped when she saw the stark expression on his face.

"Why are you like this?" she said. "Why do you care so much?"

"I don't," he said coldly.

"You do. You've always acted like you despise the idea of matrimony and commitment and children—all of it. But you don't," she said softly. "You care."

Gabriel pulled the Ferrari to an abrupt halt. He didn't look at her. "We're here."

Blinking in surprise, she saw they'd arrived at the enormous, exclusive Zeytuna boutique in the Leblon district. Her door opened, and she saw a young, smiling valet in a red jacket. Gabriel handed him keys, then held out his hand to her.

"Come," he said coldly. "We haven't much time."

Reluctantly, Laura placed her hand in his, and felt the same shock of sensation, the brush of his warm skin and strong grip of his fingers around hers.

"Are you cold?"

"No," she said.

"You're shivering."

She ripped her hand away. "I'm just afraid we will fail. That *I* will fail."

"You won't."

She looked down at her tight black dress, seeing her big hips and oversize breasts and a belly that was far from flat. She thought again of competing against Adriana da Costa in a bikini, and shuddered. "I don't see how."

Gabriel's sensual lips curved up into a smile. "Trust me."

He folded her hand over his bare forearm as if she were a medieval French princess and he was her honored chevalier. He looked down at her with eyes of love, and even as she told herself that he was only practicing, this time the shiver was not in her body, but her heart.

Pretending to love him was too easy. She was playing with fire.

Just a few hours more, she told herself desperately. Then she'd never see him again. Her family would never need to worry about replacing parts on the tractor or losing their home after a bad harvest. They'd never need to panic when a glut on the market suddenly lowered prices of wheat to nothing. Her family would be safe. Her baby would be safe.

Her baby.

Laura swallowed. This was the first time she'd left Robby with a babysitter since he was born. It felt strange to be away from him. Strange, and dangerous to feel this young and free, with Gabriel beside her. He smiled down at her, and for an instant she was lost in his eyes, so dark and deep against his tanned skin.

It would be so easy to love him when he treated her like this. Even after she went home, she knew she would always remember his low, husky voice saying, *"I want you, Laura, more than any woman. I've always wanted you."* She would feel the heat of his body against hers when he'd seized her on the terrace and kissed her. She had new memories to add to the time they'd first made love, when he'd pushed her back against his desk, sweeping everything aside in his reckless, savage need. When their sweaty, naked bodies had clung together, their limbs intertwined in explosive passion.

Now, Laura's legs trembled as Gabriel drew her toward the two tall brass doors held wide by doormen.

"Boa tarde, Senhor Santos," the first doorman said, beaming.

"Good to see you again, Mr. Santos," the second doorman said in accented English.

Once they were inside the foyer, Laura looked up in amazement at a center courtyard two stories high, with a dome of colored Tiffany glass on the ceiling. But if the glamorous architecture was straight out of the nineteenth century, the boutique's clothes were as cutting-edge as anything she'd find on Fifth Avenue.

A bevy of pretty shopgirls rushed to wait upon Gabriel. "Allow me to help you, *senhor*!"

"No, me!" a second one cried.

"Senhor, I have something wonderful to show you!"

Laura scowled. She could just imagine what the eager girls wanted to show Gabriel. Turning, she glared at him. "How often do you come here?"

He snorted, hiding a grin. "Once or twice a month."

"Lingerie for all your one-night stands?"

"Suits for work. I'm known to tip well."

Laura looked at the fawning shopgirls, who were all staring at him with undisguised glee. "I bet."

"Sorry, girls," he said. "We already have an appointment."

"Mr. Santos," an older woman said in English behind them. "Welcome." She stepped forward with assurance, her red suit a perfect match to her short, sleekly coiffed gray hair. "I am ready to be of assistance."

"This is Mrs. Tavares," Gabriel told Laura. His hand tightened around hers as he turned back to the other woman. "And this is the girl I told you about. Laura Parker."

"Certainly, sir." Mrs. Tavares came closer. Gabriel stepped back, and Laura found herself standing alone, bereft of his strength, beneath the older woman's scrutiny. She examined a long tendril of Laura's mousy brown hair, then nodded. "Very fine material to work with, sir."

"Dress her for the beach."

"Which beach?"

"A pool party at a luxurious mansion on the Costa do Sul. It will be attended by famous beauties and rich men. Make her shine above the rest."

Still staring at Laura, the older woman stroked her chin thoughtfully. "How obvious do you wish her beauty to be?"

"Completely," he said.

"It will require help from a salon."

"As you wish."

The woman pulled the black-rimmed glasses off Laura's face.

"Hey!" Laura protested.

"And an optometrist."

Gabriel smiled. "I leave her in your hands."

Laura's cheeks were hot. The perfectly coiffed, elegant woman continued to walk around her, looking her up and down in the tight black dress, as if she were a handyman and Laura were a sad, decrepit old house in need of a complete remodel.

"This isn't going to work," Laura said, fidgeting uncomfortably. "I think you should go to the pool party without me. I'll just go to the Fantasy Ball later."

"You go to the Fantasia tonight?" Mrs. Tavares gasped. "The *Baile de Gala*?"

"Yes, and she needs a ball gown," Gabriel said. "Casual clothes as well. But she must be ready for the party in two hours."

Mrs. Tavares froze. "So little time?"

"Desculpa."

The woman tilted her head, considering Laura. "It will not be cheap. Or easy."

"Cost does not matter. Just results. Satisfy my requirements and you'll be generously rewarded."

The older woman's expression didn't change, but Laura saw her sudden stillness. Looking at Gabriel, she gave a slow, respectful nod. "It will be done, *senhor*, as you wish."

"My driver will pick her up in two hours."

With a clap of her hands, Mrs. Tavares turned and started barking out orders to the young shopgirls in Portuguese. With a second clap of her hands she scattered them.

"Tchau," Gabriel said to Laura, kissing her on both cheeks before he turned away.

He was abandoning her to face the sharks alone? Laura gasped, "You can't leave!"

"Missing me already?"

"Hardly!" she retorted witheringly, even as she looked around her nervously.

"You're in good hands," Gabriel said. "Carlos will bring you to Oliveira's mansion. I have business to attend to, unfortunately. But I'll be waiting for you at the party."

"But what if…what if you're disappointed? What if my makeover is a failure? What if—"

Gabriel leaned forward to whisper in her ear, "Have fun."

Fun? Laura glared at him, her heart in her throat. What kind of fun would it be to look like a fool, to be nearly naked in front of Rio's notoriously body-conscious crowd, to be compared to Adriana da Costa in a bikini? She shook her head desperately and said for about the millionth time, "This isn't going to work!"

He gave her an annoyingly confident smile. "You're going to love this."

"You will not be disappointed, Mr. Santos," the older woman said, gently pulling Laura back into her clutches. Laura was suddenly aware that there were twenty sales-girls hovering around her, while all the other customers were being chased out of this expensive, exclusive store.

The two-story luxury boutique had just closed—for her.

"No," she whispered, feeling scared that she would let Gabriel down. "You're wrong about me. I'll never be a beauty."

"You are the one who is wrong." Gabriel's eyebrows

lowered fiercely as he looked down at her, his dark black eyes glittering. "Today, the whole world will see how beautiful you really are."

CHAPTER SEVEN

OLIVEIRA'S party was in full swing when Gabriel arrived.

Security was tight for this event, one of the most coveted private parties of the *Carnaval* season. Not for tourists or international celebrities, this was for well-connected Cariocas, the richest local tycoons and their glamorous mistresses and wives.

Gabriel was grimly sure he'd gotten this invitation only so that Felipe Oliveira could taunt him in public that he'd decided to sell Açoazul SA to someone else.

And where was Laura? Gabriel cursed softly under his breath. He'd arrived ten minutes late, after an urgent phone call from London. He needed Laura here at once, so he could introduce her to Felipe Oliveira and try to undo the damage that Adriana had spitefully caused.

Oliveira's mansion was on the most beautiful stretch of the Costa do Sul to the north of Rio. The sprawling house was a white classical confection like a wedding cake, surrounded by multilevel terraces, with a large pool that overlooked a private beach. Oliveira had been a workaholic all his life, but now that he was in his mid-sixties, he'd apparently lost interest in business in favor of possessing—and pleasing—a woman half his age.

It was the only reason he'd finally offered to sell the company back to Gabriel after almost twenty years.

Gabriel stood on the upper terrace, looking down toward the pool where he instantly saw Oliveira, wearing baggy shorts and a button-down shirt. The man was deep in conversation with French tycoon Théo St. Raphaël, who was definitely not a local, and whose presence here could be for one reason only.

Gabriel ground his teeth. The Frenchman wore a sleek gray suit. He alone among all the guests was not even pretending to dress for a pool party. Gabriel's hands tightened on the railing. The aristocratic French bastard excelled at breaking companies up for parts. The two had tangled before, and Gabriel knew St. Raphaël would like nothing more than to steal Açoazul from under his nose. All the assets of his father's company would be scattered around the world, coldly dissected for St. Raphaël's profit.

Gabriel narrowed his eyes. He couldn't let that happen.

But where was Laura?

Scowling, he glanced at his watch. Carlos had texted that they were on the way. But Gabriel would have to start on his own. Grimly going down the stairs to the lower terrace, he started walking toward Oliveira and his French rival.

"Gabriel," he heard a woman's voice coo behind him. Setting his jaw, he turned with a scowl.

Adriana da Costa smiled up at him from a poolside cabana, where she was holding court in her tiny bikini. Five half-naked young men surrounded her, offering her food she would never eat in a million years. Gabriel saw one particularly hapless youngster trying to tempt her with a platter of bread and cheese. Bread and cheese?

Adriana's idea of a fattening meal was menthol cigarettes and a handful of raisins.

Lounging in her chair, she lazily stretched her skinny arm up over her wide-brimmed straw hat as she looked up at him. In her other hand, she was holding a glass of something that looked like water but was likely vodka on the rocks.

"What a lovely surprise," Adriana drawled. Her eyes raked over Gabriel's shorts and short-sleeved shirt, now open over his bare chest without the tank top. "I didn't know Felipe invited you." She smiled slyly. "I heard the two of you ran into some sort of…trouble."

Gabriel set his jaw. She knew perfectly well why he hadn't been able to close the deal. Since Gabriel had ended their short tumultuous affair, Adriana had been determined to get his attention, and now she had it. She clearly wanted to either have him back in her bed, or wreak her revenge.

How he despised her.

Curving his lips into a smile, he walked past the young men clustered around her and stood at the bottom of her lounge chair, near her perfectly pedicured feet. "Does Oliveira know you are keeping such company?"

"Oh, these?" She shrugged, indicating her admirers with a wave of her hand. "They are just my friends."

"You are an engaged woman. You should not have such friends."

"Go away, all of you," she told them in English. Pouting slightly, she sat back in her chair. "It is easy for you to say. You pushed me into an engagement that I never wanted."

"I would never push anyone into marriage."

"Dropping me like you did, what did you expect me

to do?" She sat up straight in her lounge chair, leaning forward to expose her cleavage to better advantage. "No man has ever left me before. You wouldn't return my calls. I fell into the arms of the first rich man who proposed to me!"

Gabriel set his jaw again. "And that is why you are trying to destroy my business deal with Oliveira?"

She shrugged gleefully. "I just told Felipe the truth—that we were once lovers."

"You implied more than that," he said. "You made him believe if I moved permanently to Rio, I would make it my mission to lure you into my bed."

Adriana looked up at him like a smug Persian cat, fluttering her long dark eyelashes. "Wouldn't you?"

He stared down at her, unable to believe her vanity. She'd been a pain in the ass as a mistress, possessive and jealous. But clearly, she still believed that he, like any man, must be lusting after her as a matter of course.

He was tempted to correct that impression, but if he did, she might do some real damage and lie to her fiancé, tell him that Gabriel had made a pass at her. Clenching his hands with the effort it took to hide his dislike, Gabriel forced himself to say pleasantly, "I will always treasure our time together, but that time is over. I am with another woman now. In a committed relationship."

"Committed? You?" Adriana stared at him, her eyes wide and shocked. It was very satisfying. For several seconds all he could hear was samba music from the live band. Seagulls flew overhead, their cries mingling with those of the guests and laughter of the Cariocas lying out in the sun. She licked her lips. "That's impossible," she said faintly. "You will never settle down."

"And yet I have."

"Who is the woman?" she demanded. "Do I know her?"

"My former secretary," he said. "Laura Parker."

Adriana sucked in her breath. "I knew it," she declared. Her eyes glittered. "I always knew there was something between you. Every time you ran to her in the middle of the night, every time you explained why she was the only woman who could possibly live in your flat, every time you swore your relationship was innocent, I knew you were *lying*!"

"I wasn't lying," he said. "At the time, she was just my employee."

"She was always more than that!"

"All right. We were friends," he said tersely. "But never more. Not until last year, when—"

"Spare me the details!" Adriana hissed.

A wide shadow suddenly fell between them from the front of the cabana, blocking the sun's reflection off the pool. "Is there a problem?"

Gabriel turned to see Felipe Oliveira standing behind him. His shapeless shirt covered his large belly, and his eyes were hard as bullets in his jowly face. He must have seen Gabriel come down the terrace steps and apparently make a beeline for Adriana. *Perfeito*, Gabriel thought, irritated.

"No problem." He glanced at Adriana, who'd folded her arms to look away in sulky silence. "I was just telling your future bride that her love for you has inspired me to make a similar commitment. My secretary and I have had an on-off affair for the last year, and I've asked her to move in with me."

Silence fell, until Adriana cried, "Move in with you?"

Oliveira stroked his double chin with shrewd watchfulness in his heavy-lidded gaze. "So you've decided to make a commitment to another woman. How romantic. How very...convenient."

The older man was no fool. Deliberately, Gabriel shrugged. "Laura is everything I've ever wanted."

Adriana muttered a blasphemous curse. "I always knew the little mouse was in love with you."

In love? Gabriel frowned. Adriana was mistaken. Laura couldn't love him. She was too smart for that. She knew his deep flaws far too well. Laura wouldn't give her heart to an undeserving man who would break it.

Or would she? He paused, remembering how she'd let herself conceive a child by a man who wouldn't marry her, a man she didn't even love.

Adriana said scornfully, "With her adoring, sickening gaze on you all the time, I knew it was just a matter of time." She gave him a hard look. "But your relationship won't last. Because we both know you care about only one thing."

Aware of Oliveira watching them, Gabriel stared down at her coolly. "And what is that?"

"Power. Glamour. Blatant sex appeal. And your secretary does not have it." Adriana tossed her head. "She's nothing but a drab little nobody who..."

She paused, tilting her head. Gabriel frowned, then he heard it, too—a low hum of male voices behind them, rolling across the pool and terraces like gathering thunder. Adriana leaned forward to look around the doorway of her cabana. Oliveira and Gabriel slowly turned.

A woman had just stepped out of the mansion, and

was coming down the stairs from the upper terrace toward the pool. She was wearing a tiny bikini, typical attire for Rio. Carioca women were among the sexiest in the world, and the women at this party were among the most beautiful in the city. One new beauty should have been nothing, and yet something about this particular woman caused every man who saw her to stop in his tracks.

Even the young men who'd hovered around Adriana suddenly were craning their necks to stare. A waiter who'd come to refill Adriana's drink accidentally poured vodka on her bare thigh, causing her to curse aloud as she rose to her feet. "Oh, you stupid—get away from me!"

But no one was looking at Adriana. Not anymore.

The beautiful new guest was petite and curvy, her hips swaying as she moved. Long honey-blonde hair hung in waves down her bare back. She had creamy skin, and beneath the triangles of her top, the largest, most perfect breasts any man could imagine.

Gabriel's jaw dropped as he recognized her, this woman coming around the pool toward the cabanas with such effortless grace. The woman who had brought Felipe Oliveira's exclusive, glamorous party to a standstill.

Laura.

Laura trembled as she walked in her high heels. She felt naked in her bikini, passing through the crowds of beautiful, glamorous people who one by one turned to gape at her. Her legs shook as she walked down the stairs toward the lower terrace, where cabanas overlooked the pool and private beach.

She walked past the musicians, past the buffet table, where a handsome, hawkish man in a gray suit stood staring at her. She stiffened as she walked passed him, her head held high though her cheeks burned. People's heads were turning sharply enough to cause whiplash. Men's eyes widened. Women's eyes narrowed. Laura's hand shook as she pushed her mirrored aviator sunglasses a little higher up her nose.

Wearing this tiny bikini was almost worse than wearing nothing at all. It had been crocheted of natural, wheat-colored yarn. She'd never gone out in public dressed in so little before. She had barely ever seen *herself* this naked, always averting her eyes from the mirror when she came out of the shower. Now, she could feel the hot sun of Rio burning against her skin.

Or maybe it was just the flush of heat caused by all the eyes roaming every inch of her, tracing the lines of her breasts, butt and legs.

Laura swallowed, wishing the earth would swallow her whole. She threw a glance of longing toward the Atlantic on the other side of the terrace gate. She had the sudden yen to throw herself in the water and start swimming for Africa.

But she forced herself to keep walking, looking for Gabriel to the right and left. She couldn't run away. He was paying her a million dollars, and she couldn't quit just because she was scared. She was on a job and she would earn her money. Every penny.

But she wished she knew what people were thinking. Were they staring because they thought she looked nice? Or because she looked so hideously bad? As soon as she was out of earshot, would they all dissolve into scornful laughter?

Mrs. Tavares had taken her into the center of a whirlwind at Zeytuna, barking orders in quick-fire Portuguese, and there had soon been five stylists surrounding her, doing her hair, hands, toenails. An on-call optometrist had come to fit her eyes for contact lens. Laura had tried on hundreds of potential outfits for the pool party, for the Fantasy Ball, casual clothes for later, even lingerie. Though she had protested at the lingerie, her every complaint had been ignored. Laura's mousy brown hair had been highlighted. The stylists had started to prepare a spray-on tan to darken her skin, until Mrs. Tavares had stopped them.

"No. Leave her pale. Her creamy beauty will stand out from the fake tans of all the rest."

Laura's makeup had been done to perfection, so lightly as to be barely visible, and yet somehow making her look…good.

Mrs. Tavares had ordered her to try on many bikinis before she'd finally been satisfied with this one. Laura couldn't tell the difference—they'd all just seemed to be tiny triangles of fabric, barely covering anything at all. But the Brazilian woman had chosen this one, crocheted of soft beige yarn. *"Perfeito,"* she'd said. "It shows you off to perfection, Miss Parker. You are soft, womanly, with those curves. You are *real.*" Mrs. Tavares's thin lips had curved. "You will stand out."

It was true that Laura's breasts had always been somewhat on the generous side, and since she'd left New Hampshire to have a secretarial career in New York, she'd gone to a great deal of effort to hide them, to make sure it was her professional skills that attracted attention, not her body.

"You have the perfect figure," Mrs. Tavares had said

with satisfaction as they'd stared at the result of Laura's makeover in a full-length mirror. "A Marilyn Monroe for the modern age. The gold standard of femininity."

Laura didn't quite believe her. A lifetime of feeling plain and unfashionable, especially compared to the glamorous women of New York, had left it imprinted on her mind that she was the hardworking one. The smart one. Never in her whole life had she been the pretty one.

But of course Mrs. Tavares would give her compliments, Laura had told herself as Carlos drove her to the mansion. The woman had been hired to give Laura a makeover, so naturally she would try to make the best of things. Laura had taken her praise with a pound of salt.

But still, the older woman had almost managed to convince her. Laura had felt confident, even pretty, when she'd left the boutique. Now, beneath so many open stares, she felt shy.

And afraid. What if, after everything, she failed Gabriel? Would he refuse to pay her the million dollars he'd promised? Or worse, would he just shake his head and look at her with cool dark eyes and say in a low voice, "I'm disappointed in you, Laura. I thought you were better than this"?

It had taken more courage than she'd imagined even to get out of the Rolls-Royce. Carlos had held her door open for almost a full minute, conspicuously clearing his throat before Laura had gathered enough bravado to get out of the car and walk into the mansion with her shoulders thrown back. Now, beneath the eyes of so many glamorous people, she felt vulnerable. *Exposed*.

Where was Gabriel?

Laura's feet shook in her ridiculously high heels as she walked around the pool. She didn't dare meet anyone's eyes, for fear of the scorn or mockery she might see there. She kept walking, keeping her gaze over people's heads, looking for one man who would stand out above the rest. She ignored the low hum of voices around her. She held her hand above her forehead, shading her sunglasses, as she looked for him. Would he laugh when he saw her? Would he regret whatever madness had caused him to think, even for an instant, that she could convince the world she was the woman who'd finally vanquished his playboy heart?

The thought made her throat hurt. Her hand fell to her side. She swallowed, suddenly unable to take the strain of all those mocking eyes on her.

"Que beleza."

Hearing Gabriel's low, husky voice behind her, she whirled around. She saw him standing in the doorway of a large poolside cabana. He was wearing shorts and an open shirt that revealed his muscular chest, tanned and laced with dark hair. Beside him she recognized Felipe Oliveira, looking sweaty and suspicious. But she was so relieved to find Gabriel that she hurried forward, pushing her sunglasses up on her head with a relieved smile. "Oh, Gabriel. I'm so glad to find you. I—"

Then she saw the woman standing behind them in the cabana and drew back with an intake of breath. "Oh. Miss da Costa. Hello."

The supermodel folded her arms icily. "I think we're a little past the politeness of 'Miss da Costa,' don't you? You must call me Adriana now," she said, in the exact same tone one might say *Go to hell*.

Laura blinked beneath the woman's malevolent

gaze. Then she remembered Gabriel's words. *You have something Adriana does not. You have me.* Looking at Adriana's angry expression, Laura realized their plan was working. The supermodel clearly believed Laura was Gabriel's lover—and hated her for it!

Straightening her shoulders, she looked at Gabriel with a smile. "Sorry I'm late."

He kissed her cheek tenderly. "I waited thirty-eight years to find you, *querida*," he breathed. "What are a few minutes more?"

He put his arm around her. After smiling at each other, they both turned to see the effect.

Felipe Oliveira looked skeptical. Adriana was scowling, sticking out her lower lip.

"You can't really be moving in together!" she said.

Laura glanced at him. Moving in together?

"It's already done," Gabriel said. He looked down at Laura, and his dark eyes were hungry and tender as he stroked her cheek.

Adriana gave a forced laugh. "She's no one. Nothing."

Gabriel wrapped his arms around Laura's bare waist. She nearly gasped at the rough feel of his hands against her naked skin.

"I am the one who is nothing." His black eyes burned through Laura's soul. "Nothing without you."

It's an act, she told herself as her heart turned over in her chest.

"All this time, you were right in front of me," he murmured as his wide, rough hand traced softly down her cheek. "The woman of my dreams." He cupped her face, tilting up her chin as he suddenly smiled. "I would fight them all for you."

"Fight who?" she whispered.

Staring at her, Gabriel gave a sudden laugh. Turning, he silently pointed behind them.

Following his gaze, Laura saw all the gorgeous party guests whispering to each other around the pool, staring back at them.

Of course they would stare at Gabriel, Laura thought. He was the sexiest, most sought after bachelor on earth. But they weren't looking just at him. Even Laura, inexperienced as she was, could see that.

And she suddenly knew, down to her bones, that they weren't staring at her because she was *ugly*.

She suddenly blinked back tears. Her makeover had created the illusion that Laura was worthy to be Gabriel's mistress. For the first time in her life, she felt beautiful. It was dizzying. Electrifying.

But the feeling hadn't been caused by magic fairy dust. She looked up at him.

It was the magic of his dark, hungry gaze. The magic echo of his words.

All this time, you were right in front of me. The woman of my dreams.

She was dimly aware of Adriana's angry scowl. But Laura didn't care about her anymore. Everyone else around them faded into a blur.

She and Gabriel were the only two people on earth. His dark eyes met hers, and his gaze fell to her lips. With agonizing slowness, he started to move his head toward hers. She realized he was going to kiss her, and her heart pounded frantically in her throat.

"Am I to understand," Felipe Oliveira said in a gruff voice behind them, "that this girl, your supposed lover, used to be your employee?"

Straightening, Gabriel turned to him, and Laura was able to breathe again. She leaned her cheek against his chest, still dizzy from how close she'd come to being kissed.

"His employee?" Adriana sneered. "She was his *secretary*."

Gabriel gave her a cool smile before turning his focus back on his rival. "Laura was once my secretary, *sim*, for five years. But now she's so much more." Looking down as she nestled in his arms, he stroked her cheek and said softly, "Now…she's the woman who tamed me."

CHAPTER EIGHT

IT'S only an act. Only an act!

But in spite of the constant repetition of those words, Laura's heart still didn't believe it as she looked up into Gabriel's dark eyes.

"Really," the other man drawled in accented English. His eyes traced over Laura. "She's certainly beautiful. But this is all too convenient." He folded his arms over his belly. "You've fabricated this affair, so I'll still sell you Açoazul."

Laura's pulse hammered in her chest. Convinced that their plan had failed before it had half started, she pulled away from Gabriel. But he held her tight in his power-ful arms, even as he never looked away from the other man.

"Why would I do that?" Gabriel said coolly.

The man looked at Adriana's tall beauty, then back at Gabriel with a scowl. "You know why."

"You'd be a fool not to sell me Açoazul," Gabriel said sharply. "No other competitor has offered you a fraction of the price. Théo St. Raphaël certainly won't. Don't lose a fortune based on some unfounded fear!"

The older man stiffened. "I'm not *afraid*. And it's not unfounded."

Gabriel nuzzled her neck. "I'm not interested in any woman except Laura."

She leaned back against him, closing her eyes. The feel of his lips and the nibble of his sharp teeth against the sensitive flesh caused sparks to thrill down her body. She heard the other man hiss through his teeth, and opened her eyes. Felipe Oliveira and Adriana were staring at them with shock. Looking up at Gabriel, Laura shivered as a single bead of sweat trickled down her bare skin between her breasts. The air between them suddenly crackled with sexual energy.

"Come, *querida*," Gabriel said in a low voice. "It's getting hot. I need to cool off."

Wrapping her hand in his own, he pulled her away from the cabana and across the terrace through the open gate, past the security guards to the private beach. Turquoise waves pounded the white sand with a rhythmic roar. Laura glanced back at the party behind them. She and Gabriel were still in full view of the mansion and terraces as he led her across the sand.

"You did it," Gabriel said when they were out of earshot.

"Did I?" Looking up, she furrowed her brow. "He didn't seem to believe us."

"Of course he's suspicious. The man's not stupid. But we'll soon convince him we're in love."

"How?" she whispered.

He reached down and stroked a tendril of hair from her face.

"To think all this time I had such a beauty working for me," he breathed, then shook his head with a laugh. "I'm glad you didn't look like this when you were my secretary. I wouldn't have gotten any work done."

"You wouldn't?"

"It was hard enough as it was. You were always too pretty. I wanted you from the first day I met you, when you came up to my office wearing that old brown suit and big glasses."

He remembered the clothes she'd worn the day they met? "You don't have to talk like this." Her heart was hammering in her throat. "No one can hear us."

"That's why I'm saying it," he said. "Come on."

He yanked off his flip-flops and shirt, leaving them on the sand as he pulled her into the sea. Kicking off her high-heeled shoes, she followed him, almost willing to follow him into the very depths of the ocean as long as he kept hold of her hand.

He led her into the water, deeper and deeper still. She looked at him in front of her, and her eyes hungrily traced the hard curves of his muscular back, his strong legs. She felt the shock of cool water against her skin as they walked through the ocean waves, moving slower and slower until the water reached their thighs.

He glanced behind her. "They're still watching." He smiled. "You make this too easy. Any man would want you. Half the men here are in love with you already."

Laura swallowed, yearning to tell him she didn't care, that he was the only man she wanted, the only one she'd ever wanted. She'd once loved him with all her heart, this man with the warm dark eyes that made her melt, who whispered words of adoration, who made her body sizzle even when they weren't out in the hot sun.

Gabriel's sensual mouth curved. "And you've proved yourself every bit the skilled actress I hoped you'd be. The way you shivered and leaned back against me when

I kissed your neck, as if you were head over heels in love with me...they bought it all."

Except it hadn't been an act. Beneath the blazing sun, they stared at each other, thigh-deep in the cool turquoise water, swaying in the currents. She felt the splash of the cool waves against her hot, bare thighs.

He came closer to her. "The way you look at me sometimes..." His gaze searched hers. "It reminds me of something that Adriana said. As if you really..."

"Really what?" Laura whispered.

He pulled back, his self-mocking mask back in place on his darkly handsome face. "I think I really do need to cool off," he said with a laugh, and he fell back with a splash into the water.

When he resurfaced, Gabriel sprang from the waves like a god of the sea, scattering sparkling droplets as he tossed his black hair back. Rivulets streamed down his tanned, hard-muscled chest. She couldn't look away. She wanted him to kiss her. She wanted him to make love to her, hard and fast, slow and soft, and never stop. Most of all, she wanted him to love her.

He came toward her, his eyes dark. He took her in his arms, and she felt the hard muscles of his chest press against her bare skin. He looked down at her.

"I know what you're thinking," he said huskily. "I know what you need."

Her mouth went dry. "You—you do?"

Without warning, he lifted her up in his arms, against his wet, muscled chest. Her head fell back in surprise, and she had a brief image of the blue sea and distant green jungle before she realized what he meant to do. Holding her tightly in his arms, he fell back into the waves.

She had one instant to gasp in a breath before she felt the cool water splash against her skin and she was baptized by the waves.

When he lifted her back out of the sea, she sputtered in outrage, kicking her legs against his chest. "I can't believe you did that!"

"Why?" he said lazily. "Didn't it cool you off?"

"That's not the point!"

"It felt good. Admit it."

"It felt great," she muttered. "But you spent a fortune to get me to look pretty, and now you've ruined it. They spent ages getting my hair just right—"

"I haven't ruined anything." His arms tightened over her bikini-clad body. She saw they'd gone farther from the shore. The water now reached his waist, and she could feel the slide of the waves moving sinuously and languorously against her backside and thighs. Her cheeks grew hot as she realized the crocheted yarn bikini, with all its tiny holes, was transparent when wet. "I'm done with this party," Gabriel growled, looking down at her. His hands tightened. "I'm taking you home."

At the rough sound of his voice, a shiver went through her. Tension coiled low in her belly as his dark gaze devoured her with ruthless hunger.

As he started wading back through the waves, clutching her against his chest, she felt their overheated skin pressed together beneath the hot sun.

Against her will, Laura's gaze fell to his mouth, to the cruel, sensual lips that had kissed her with such passion. He looked down at her, then stopped. For several seconds, he just stood in the water, staring down at her.

Releasing her from his hold, he let her go, let her slide slowly down his body against him. She felt how much he desired her, felt his hard body beneath the water. His eyes were like fire.

Cupping her chin in his hands, he lowered his head to hers.

As he kissed her, she felt the hard press of his satin-smooth lips, the sweet, tantalizing taste of his tongue, the salty taste of his rough skin. She surrendered in his arms in the swaying ocean, floating on waves. Drowning in him.

As Gabriel kissed her, standing in the ocean, he felt the warmth of her naked skin in the swaying, cool water. He tasted the wet heat of her mouth. Suddenly, he knew he had to have her. Now.

He heard catcalls behind them in Portuguese and realized he'd forgotten about the party. He'd forgotten about Oliveira and Adriana. At this moment, he didn't give a damn about them.

He kept kissing Laura, even when she tried to pull away. She resisted. Relented. Surrendered. Then, with a gasp, she did pull away.

The waves rolled against their skin, pushing their bodies together as they stared at each other. Her eyes seemed to glimmer. With tears? Gabriel frowned. "Are you crying?"

"Of course not!" she said, rubbing her eyes.

He reached out to tilt her chin upward, forcing her to meet his gaze. "You're a terrible liar."

She looked away. "Don't women usually weep when you kiss them?"

Her tone was light, even sardonic. He felt as if he was in some strange dream as he looked down at her. This beautiful woman was Laura, and yet not Laura. "They usually weep when I leave."

She flashed him a glance. "If they're your employees, they're probably weeping with joy."

His lips tugged up into a grin against his will. *Meu Deus.* Even now, she could make him laugh, when all he could think of was dragging her back home, ripping off her tiny bikini and pulling her naked body into his bed. All he wanted was to be alone with her, to feel her soft limbs caress him, to pull her back into a red-hot kiss so explosive it burned him from within.

He would have her. Tonight.

I always knew the little mouse was in love with you.

He angrily shook away the memory of Adriana's words. Laura didn't love him. She couldn't. She was too smart for that. It wasn't love that existed between them. It was sex. Just sex. He shuddered. It would be, as soon as humanly possible.

"I'm taking you home," he said. "To bed."

The bravado fell from her beautiful face. She looked up, and her expression suddenly looked vulnerable. Young. The reflective waves of the water lit up her pale body, exposing her full curves, illuminating her beautiful face, which now seemed to hold new secrets.

"No," she whispered. "Please. I'm not like you. Making love…it means something to me."

Looking down at her beauty, Gabriel felt no mercy in his heart. She wanted him, as he wanted her. Why hold back? Why hesitate from taking their pleasure? Laura should belong to him, as she always had. She should be his. His unselfish act of letting her go last year had been a mistake.

And she'd had another man's baby. Sudden posses-
siveness raced through his body like a storm. Thinking
of another man touching Laura left him in a rage. He
wanted to get the memory of the other man off her skin.
To make her forget anyone else had ever touched her.

With iron self-control, he took her hand. He heard
her soft intake of breath as she stared up at him, her
lips deliciously parted. His gaze fell to her mouth, but
kissing her wouldn't be nearly enough. He led her out of
the water and back to the sand. Stepping into his shoes,
he grabbed his shirt, wadding it up in one hand.

"Where are we going?"

He glanced back at her. She looked as dazed as he
felt. Her cheeks were flushed with passion, her lips
bruised. "Home. Let Adriana believe we had to rush
back to my penthouse."

"For an emergency?"

"I told you." He gave her a sensual, heavy-lidded
look. "To bed."

He saw her shiver under the hot sun. Blinking, she
knelt to pick up her high-heeled shoes. "But it's just a
game," she whispered, sounding as if she were talking
to herself as much as him. "It's not real."

Yet Gabriel was no longer sure. She'd come to Rio
as his pretend mistress. Now he wanted to make it true.
Where did the fantasy end and reality begin?

As he led her past security and across the lower terrace, he heard the whispers of the crowd racing ahead
of them, a murmur rising like a wave of music. Gabriel
didn't bother to glance at Felipe Oliveira or Adriana as
he passed them. He was too infuriated by all the men
staring at Laura. She did look beautiful with her long
wet hair slicked back and beads of seawater sparkling

on her skin like diamonds. And—Gabriel flinched—the yarn of her bikini was translucent when wet. Something he'd appreciated when they were alone, but now...

He bared his teeth at the other men as he led her across the terrace, a male predator protecting his chosen female. He climbed the stairs two at a time and entered the mansion, dripping water across the marble floors. As he led her toward the front door, he held her hand tightly. It felt so right in his. *Too* right.

He grabbed two towels from a uniformed attendant. "Tell my driver we are ready to depart."

The man hurried away. Gabriel took Laura outside to wait in the warm sun, away from prying eyes. Kneeling before her, he skimmed one plush towel over her bare skin, over her legs, her arms, the plump fullness of her breasts. Rising to his feet, he licked his lips and realized he was breathing hard.

He saw her swallow. Felt her tremble.

"Gabriel," she whispered, her voice hoarse, "Please..."

The Rolls-Royce pulled in front of the mansion, and Carlos leaped out to open the door, looking dismayed at his boss's early departure. He'd probably been playing dice with the other servants, Gabriel thought, but at this moment, he didn't give a damn about any man's pleasure but his own.

"Get in the car," Gabriel ordered Laura, his voice sounding admirably civilized compared to the roaring animal he felt like inside. When she didn't move, he grabbed her arm and pulled her roughly into the backseat.

As the driver closed the door behind them, Laura ripped her arm from Gabriel's grasp. "You don't need to be so rude!"

"Rude?" he growled.

"Yes, rude!"

Gabriel could tell she was hurt and angry. She thought he was being cruel. She didn't know it was all he could do not to push her back against the leather seat, to lay her flat on her back and rip off the little triangles of bikini. That all he wanted to do was taste those luscious breasts, throw himself over her, fill her completely. He clenched his hands into fists, shuddering at the sensual images that overwhelmed him. He wanted her—now. And he almost didn't care who saw them.

As Carlos started the engine, Gabriel forced himself to release her. He could wait until they got home. He could wait…

He repeated the mantra again and again as the car drove through the city. His body ached from the effort it took not to seize her in his arms. The slow drive though crowded streets, with police diverting traffic around sections closed for early evening parades, seemed to take forever.

Gabriel glanced at Laura sideways. The towel had slipped from her hands and the air-conditioning in the limo was no match for the way his temperature climbed every time he looked at her. Especially when he saw what the cold air was doing to her nipples beneath the bikini.

Water was still trickling from her wet hair, running slowly down her bare skin, down the valley between her large breasts. He wanted to run the edge of his fingertip down that trickle of water. He wanted to lap it up with his tongue. He wanted her spread naked across his bed, his body over hers, as he lowered his head to taste her, thrusting inside her, so deep, so deep…

As if she felt his gaze, she turned. Judging by the expression on her face, she hadn't been having such sensual images of him—oh no. She wanted to skewer him with a knife.

But as their eyes locked, her expression slowly changed. The glare slid away and her face turned bewildered, almost scared. With a visible tremble, she pulled the thick white towel tightly over her naked skin and looked out the window.

With a dark smile, Gabriel turned away.

She knew.

She knew what waited for them at home.

Memories of their one night together had caused months of hot, unsatisfied dreams for him. Now that he finally had her in Rio, he wasn't going to let her go. Not until he was completely satiated. He was done being unselfish when it came to Laura.

The car pulled up behind their building, but she didn't wait for Carlos to open her door. She flung it open herself and dashed out, heading for the private entrance.

It gave her a head start.

A low growl rose from the back of Gabriel's throat as he flung open his own door and raced out in grim pursuit. As he came around the car in the street, heading toward the curb, a red sedan nearly hit him. The driver honked angrily, but Gabriel didn't even pause, just leaped recklessly over the hood. He ran into his building's private lobby, across the marble floor. Ignoring the greetings of the guards, he ran for the private elevator just in time to see the silver doors slide together in front of Laura's face. Their eyes met for a single instant, and he saw the small smile that curved her lips. Then she was gone.

Gabriel cursed under his breath. He pressed the elevator button impatiently, multiple times, then rushed inside as soon as the door opened. When he arrived at the penthouse, he followed her voice.

"So Robby had a good day?" he heard her say from the terrace.

"Yes, Senhora Laura," Maria replied. "He had a good lunch, good play and is now having his second nap."

Breathing hard, Gabriel saw them through the windows, out on the terrace. The older woman was sitting in a lounge chair, with a glass of lemonade and the baby monitor on the table beside her, placidly knitting in the warm Brazilian sunshine.

"Did he miss me?" Laura's voice trembled. "Did he cry for me?"

"No, Mrs. Laura," she said kindly. "He had a happy day. But of course he will be glad to see his mama. He should wake soon. Perhaps you would like to take him on a walk?"

"Yes, I would like that. Thank you, Maria."

Laura turned and headed back inside. Gabriel ducked into the corner as she opened the sliding glass doors. Still holding her towel over her body, she started down the hall toward her bedroom.

He moved fast, springing like a jaguar. He heard her gasp as he shoved her through the open doorway of his room, pushing her against the wall. The towel dropped from her hands as he closed the door behind him with a bang. Grasping her wrists, he held her against the wall.

Without a word, without asking permission, he kissed her.

He felt the heat of her skin, covered only by the tiny bikini as he crushed her against the wall with his bare chest. Releasing her wrists, he grabbed the back of her head with his hand. Holding her tight against him, he kissed her savagely, hard enough to bruise, ruthlessly taking his pleasure.

CHAPTER NINE

WITH a gasp, Laura pulled back her hand and slapped his face.

"How dare you!" she cried.

The sound of the slap echoed in the bedroom. He stared at her incredulously, his hand on his cheek. Then his eyes narrowed. "Why are you pretending it's not exactly what you want?"

Laura sucked in her breath, feeling overwhelmed by need for what she could not—*could not*—allow herself to have. "Even if I want you, Gabriel, I know you're no good for me. It nearly killed me last year after our night together when you kicked me out of your life—"

"Kicked you out of my life?" he demanded. "You're the one who left!"

"You didn't try to talk me out of it. You didn't even ask me to stay!"

"I was trying to do what was best for you," he said. "I knew you wanted a husband, children. You needed a boss who didn't demand your life and soul. You needed a man who could love you as I cannot. So I gave you up, when it was the last thing I wanted! And what did you do?" He glowered. "You let yourself get pregnant by some cold bastard who cannot even be bothered to pay child support or visit his son!"

Tears streamed down her face as she shook her head. "Why do you keep torturing me about my pregnancy?"

"Because it means I sacrificed you for nothing!"

"Sacrificed?" she cried.

He grabbed her shoulders. "Don't you know how much I've wanted you, all this time?" His eyes searched hers fiercely. "Do you know how I've dreamed of you? In my office. In my bed!" His fingers tightened painfully on her shoulders. "If I'd known you would settle for so little, I would never have let you go!"

Panting with anger, they stared at each other in the shadowy bedroom, the only sound the violent rasping of their breath. His eyes were dark and furious with denied desire. His gaze fell to her lips.

"Laura…" he whispered.

She jumped when she heard Robby suddenly crying on the other side of the wall. All the shouting and the banging must have woken him.

"I'm not that virgin secretary anymore," she murmured, "free to make whatever stupid choices I want. I'm a mother now. My baby comes first." Setting her jaw, she pulled away from Gabriel. Stopping at the door, she looked back at him. "I gave in to passion once before," she said quietly. "And it nearly killed me."

Leaving him, she went to her own bedroom and locked the door behind her before she gathered her crying baby in her arms. Robby's plaintive wail instantly stopped as she cuddled him close. She breathed in the sweet smell of his hair.

She heard a low knock on the door.

"Laura." Gabriel's voice was muffled.

"Go away."

"I want to talk to you."

"No."

Silence fell on the other side of the door and she thought he'd left. She sat down in the rocking chair and held Robby in the darkness of the shuttered bedroom. Then Robby started to squirm and complain. Clearly, his nap was over and he was ready to play.

Setting her baby down on the carpet, with a pillow beside him in case he suddenly forgot how to sit and toppled over, she looked through the shopping bags that Mrs. Tavares had sent and selected some dark jeans and a white tank top. Pulling them on over a new bra and panties, Laura lifted her son onto her hip and quietly unlocked her door. Holding her breath, she peeked out into the hallway.

Gabriel stood leaning against the wall, waiting for her in jeans and a black T-shirt. His eyes were dark, almost ominous.

"Planning to sneak out?"

She took a deep breath, then tossed her head defiantly. "I'm taking my son for a walk."

"You need to get ready for the gala."

"It will just have to wait."

He stared at her, then set his jaw. "Fine. Then I'll come with you."

"Come with me?" she repeated incredulously.

He moved toward her quick as a flash, scooping Robby from her arms.

"Hey!" she cried.

Gabriel looked down at the baby, who was staring up at him with a transfixed expression. A shadow of a smile passed over Gabriel's handsome face. Turning, he opened the front closet and pulled out a folded stroller, an expensive brand that she would never have purchased on her own. Still holding the baby with one powerful arm, Gabriel opened the stroller with his other, in one easy gesture.

Her jaw fell. "How did you know how to do that?"

He shrugged.

She tried again. "Have you ever been around a baby before?"

He looked away. "It's madness outside. You are my guests. I will keep you safe."

"To protect us from a festival on Ipanema Beach? We're just going for a walk!"

"Funny. So am I."

"You're being ridiculous."

Putting Robby into the stroller, he clicked the baby's seat belt, then without a word, pressed the elevator button. The doors opened and he pushed the stroller onto it. Looking at her, Gabriel waited.

Exhaling, she followed him onto the elevator. The doors closed, leaving the two of them with only a baby stroller between them.

"Why are you doing this?" she said through her teeth.

"For my own selfish reasons, no doubt," he said dryly. "That is why I do everything, is it not?"

"Yes, it is." She bit out the words, then looked at him. "Why? Is there a chance Felipe or Adriana might see us?"

"There is always a chance," he said. "It's not impossible."

The elevator doors opened, and she grabbed the

handle of the stroller and pushed it through the lobby. Gabriel held the door open for her and they were out on the street.

Since she'd last been outside, the *avenida* had become even more crowded, filled with people celebrating *Carnaval*. Music was blaring, tubas and drums, as people sang and danced in the street with their friends, some of them wearing extremely provocative costumes as they gulped down *caipirinhas*, the famous Brazilian cocktail of lime and distilled sugarcane.

Laura and Gabriel walked down the beach to a slightly quieter area and found an empty spot past a big yellow umbrella. She saw families splashing in the surf with their children, as nearby, groups of young people drank together beneath the sun as they waited for the nighttime party to really begin, the women wearing tiny thong bikinis, the men in skintight shorts.

Laura took Robby out of the stroller, and when she looked around, Gabriel was gone. She placed her baby in her lap and Robby reached to take a handful of sand in his fist. She saw Gabriel across the beach, talking to a *barraqueiro*. A moment later, he was walking back across the beach toward her. He held up a plastic shovel and pail.

"I thought Robby would like to play," he said gruffly.

"Thank you," she said, shocked at his thoughtfulness.

He smiled, and the warmth of his suddenly boyish face as he held out the pail and shovel to Robby nearly made her gasp. As the baby happily took the shovel, Gabriel stretched out beside them and showed him how to dig in the sand.

Laura stared at him in amazement.

First he'd known how to handle the stroller. Then he'd thought of buying toys for their baby. He claimed he disliked children, so why was he acting like this?

Robby responded to his father's tutelage by first trying to chew on the shovel, then to eat the sand. Gabriel laughed, and with infinite patience, again showed him how to dig. Soon he had the baby in his lap. Robby was very curious about sand and kept dumping it on them both, then laughing uproariously. Soon deep male laughter joined with the baby squeals, and for Laura it was the sound of joy. She looked at Gabriel's handsome face, watching him as he smiled down at the child he did not know was his, and her heart filled her throat.

How could he not realize that Robby was his son?

"He likes you," she whispered. "And you seem to know how to take care of a baby."

Gabriel's dark eyes met hers. Then his expression abruptly became cold. He handed Robby back to her, causing the baby to give a little whine of protest. "No, I really don't."

All around them, she was dimly aware of the noise of the street party, of half-naked Cariocas tanning themselves beneath the sun, of people laughing and singing and making music all around them.

It wasn't too late for her to tell Gabriel the truth. She could tell him now. *By the way, Gabriel, I never took any other man as my lover. You were so careful to use protection, but guess what? You're Robby's father.*

How would he take that news?

He wouldn't be glad. Even in her most fantastic dreams she knew that. He'd told her a million times, in every possible way, that he didn't want a wife or children. Even today, when he'd asked her to be his mistress for real, he'd said he'd be willing to "overlook" her child. That he'd allow her baby to live in the down-stairs apartment so he wouldn't be forced to endure his presence.

And worse. If there was one thing Gabriel resented almost as much as the thought of having a family, it was someone lying to his face. If he found out that Laura had lied to him for over a year, he would never forgive her. He would take responsibility for the child they'd created—yes—and he'd try to get some kind of custody. But he would not love their son. And he would *hate* her.

Tomorrow, she repeated to herself desperately. They would go home to their little farmhouse in the great north woods, safe and sound. She'd never have to see Gabriel again.

But that reassurance was wearing thin. Every moment she spent with Gabriel, seeing him with their son, she found herself wishing she could believe the dream. Wishing he could love them.

The truth about Robby hovered on her lips. But the rational part of her brain stayed in control, keeping her from blurting it out. If she told him the truth, only bad things could happen. And she'd no longer be in control of Robby's future.

Gabriel glanced at his watch. The sun had started to lower in the sky over the green Dois Irmãos mountain rising sharply to the west. "We should go. Your stylist is waiting at the penthouse."

"Stylist?"

He rose to his feet. "For the gala."

He held out his hand, and Laura hesitated. A wistful

sigh came from her lips. The brief happiness of feeling like a family was over. "All right."

She allowed him to pull her to her feet. Tucking a yawning, messy, sand-covered Robby back into the stroller, she followed Gabriel across the beach toward home. By now the avenue was so crowded that Gabriel had to physically clear a path for the stroller.

When they safely reached the opposite side of the street, he looked at her. "I'm looking forward to seeing your dress tonight." He gave her a sensual smile. "And seeing it off you."

He was so sure of himself it infuriated her. But as his dark eyes caught hers, her feet tripped on the sidewalk. He caught the stroller, grabbing her arm. Then, leaning forward, he kissed her.

"Nothing will stop me from having you," he whispered in her ear. "Tonight."

With an intake of breath, she felt butterflies of longing and sharp bee stings of need all over her body. Tightening her hands on the handle, she pushed the stroller as fast as she could toward the building. She told herself that the sexy, tender, strong man she'd just seen on the beach, playing with their baby son, was a mirage. She couldn't let herself be fooled by his act. Gabriel was always ruthlessly charming when he wanted something. And right now, he wanted her.

Gabriel Santos always won by any means necessary. Both in business and his romantic conquests. But once he'd had what he wanted, once he'd possessed her in his bed, he would be done with her. He would no longer be willing to tolerate the fact that she had a child. He would toss her out, or drive her out. He would replace her.

She licked her lips as he caught up with her. "What's going to happen tonight?"

His sensual mouth curved. "You already know."

She looked at his face. There was a five o'clock shadow on the hard edges of his jaw, giving his handsome face a barbaric appearance. "Felipe Oliveira is no fool. He's suspicious. What if after tonight, he still doesn't believe that you love me?"

"He will."

"And if he doesn't?"

Gabriel's dark eyes glinted with amusement. "Then I have a plan."

CHAPTER TEN

THE Fantasia gala ball was the single most sought-after invitation of Rio de Janeiro's *Carnaval*. Laura had read about it in celebrity gossip magazines in the United States. The glamorous event, held in a colonial palace on the Costa Verde south of Rio, attracted beautiful, rich and notorious guests from all around the world. And tonight, Laura would be one of them. Tonight, she would be Gabriel Santos's beloved mistress.

His *pretend* mistress, she corrected herself fiercely.

The door of the black Rolls-Royce sedan opened, and she and Gabriel stepped out onto the red carpet that led inside the palace, which had once been owned by the Brazilian royal family.

Gabriel looked brutally dashing in his black tuxedo. Laura felt his hungry gaze on her as he took her arm. She tried to ignore it, tried to smile for the benefit of the paparazzi flashing cameras around them, but her body shook beneath the palpable force of his desire.

I want you, Laura. And I will have you.

Liveried doormen in wigs opened tall, wide doors. Gabriel and Laura went down a gilded hallway, then entered a ballroom that sparkled like an enormous jewel box. Standing at the top of the stairs, Laura looked up in awe at the huge chandeliers glittering like diamonds overhead. From a nearby alcove, a full orchestra played, the musicians dressed in clothes of the eighteenth century, except with sequins and body glitter.

The guests milling around them drinking champagne, laughing, were in gowns and tuxedos that were even more beautiful. More outlandish.

As they paused at the top of the stairs, Gabriel turned to her. "Are you ready?"

Laura held her breath, feeling like a princess in a fairy tale, or maybe Julia Roberts in *Pretty Woman,* with her strapless red sheath gown and long white opera gloves that went up past her elbows. "Yes."

When Gabriel had first seen her in this dress, he'd choked out a gasp. "You are without question," he'd said hoarsely, presenting her with two black velvet boxes, "the most beautiful woman I've ever seen."

Now, Laura looked at him, tightening her hand over his arm as he escorted her down the sweeping stairs. A thick diamond bracelet now hung over her gloved wrist. Diamond bangles hung from her ears set off by her highlighted hair tumbling in soft waves down her shoulders.

She'd never felt so beautiful—or so adored. This ball was truly a fantasy, she thought in wonder.

Silence fell around them as Gabriel, the dashing, powerful Brazilian tycoon, led her onto the empty dance floor. Laura hesitated beneath the gaze of so many people. Then, seeing them, the orchestra changed the tempo of the music, and it was irresistible.

Within twenty seconds, other couples had joined them. By the second song, the floor was packed with people. But Laura hardly noticed. As Gabriel held her, she felt hot and cold, delirious in a tangle of joy and fear and breathless need.

He swirled her around on the dance floor, in perfect time with the music. She felt his heat through the sleek tuxedo that barely contained the brutal strength of his body, and all she could think about was the night he'd made love to her, when he'd pressed her against his desk and ripped off her clothes, taking her virgin body and making it his own. He'd filled her with pleasure that night. Filled her with his child.

Now, his dark eyes caressed her as he moved. Leaning her back, he dipped her, his handsome face inches from hers. Pulling her back to her feet, he kissed her.

His lips moved against hers, soft and warm, whispering of love that was pure and true. Promising her everything she needed, everything she'd ever wanted.

Promising a lie.

With an intake of breath, she jerked away from him, tears in her eyes. "Why are you doing this to me?"

"Don't you know?" he said in a low voice. "Haven't I made it clear?"

"We had a deal," she whispered. "One night in Rio. One million dollars."

"Yes." He looked down at her. "And now I'm not going to let you go."

She stared up at him, frozen, even as other couples continued to swirl around them in a dark, sexy tango.

"I'm not going to let you seduce me, Gabriel," she said, her voice shaking. "I'm not."

He looked down at her, his eyes dark with desire. He didn't argue with her. He didn't have to.

With a gasp, she turned and ran, leaving him on the dance floor. Looking wildly for escape, she saw open

French doors that led outside to some sort of shadowy garden. She ran for them, only to smack into a wall.

Except it wasn't a wall. A man grasped her shoulders, setting her aright as he stared down at her. "Good evening, Miss Parker."

"Mr. Oliveira." She licked her lips. Dressed in a tuxedo that only served to accentuate his bulk, he was drinking a martini beside the bar. Behind him, she saw the gorgeously pouting Adriana in a skimpy silver cutout dress that clung like spackle over her breasts and backside, leaving everything else bare down to her strappy silver high heels.

"Lovers' spat?" Felipe Oliveira said mildly.

Gabriel appeared behind her. He put his hands possessively on Laura's shoulders. "Of course not."

Swallowing, Laura leaned back against Gabriel, feeling the hardness of his body against hers, and tried her best to look as if her heart wasn't breaking. She forced her lips into a smile. "I, um, just wanted a little fresh air."

Gabriel wrapped his arms around her more tightly, nestling her backside firmly against his thighs as he nuzzled her temple. "And I wanted to dance."

Oliveira looked at them, his eyes narrowed. "You're both liars."

Gabriel shook his head. "No—"

"I'll tell you what is really going on," the older man interrupted. "You think I am stupid enough to fall for this. But if I sign those papers tomorrow selling you the company, you know what will happen?"

"You'll make a fortune?" Gabriel drawled.

His hooded eyes hardened. "You will end this charade and be once again free to pursue what does not belong to you."

Gabriel snorted. "Why would I possibly be interested in your fiancée, Oliveira, when I have a woman like this?"

The other man looked at Laura, then shook his head. "Santos, you change lovers with the rise of each dawn. Miss Parker is beautiful, but you will never commit to her for long. There is nothing you can say to convince me otherwise." He finished the last of his martini. "I will sell to the Frenchman."

"You will lose money!"

"Some things, they are more important than money."

Gabriel exhaled. Laura felt his body tense behind her, tight and ready to snap. "St. Raphaël is a vulture," he growled. "He will break my father's company up for parts, fire the employees, scatter the pieces around the world. He will crush Açoazul beneath his heel!"

"That is not my problem. I will not give you any reason to remain in Rio." Oliveira's jowly face was grim as he started to turn away, holding out his arm for Adriana, who could barely contain the smug look on her beautiful face.

They'd lost.

Laura's heart leaped up to her throat, choking her.

They'd failed. *She* had failed.

"You're wrong about me, Oliveira," Gabriel said desperately. "I can commit. I've always been ready to commit. I was just waiting for the woman I could love forever."

Frowning, the older man and Adriana glanced back at them. They stopped. Their eyes went wide.

As if in slow motion, Laura turned to face Gabriel, who was standing behind her.

Except he was no longer standing. He'd fallen to his knee.

He'd pulled a black velvet box out of his tuxedo pocket.

Opening it, he held up a ten-carat diamond ring.

"Laura," he said quietly, "will you marry me?"

Laura's jaw dropped.

She looked from the ring to Gabriel kneeling in front of her. She looked back at the ring.

I was just waiting for the woman I could love for-ever.

He'd changed his mind about love and commitment? Did he want her in his bed so badly he was willing to marry her?

He smiled, and everything else fell away. She was lost in his dark eyes.

"What is this?" Oliveira demanded. "Some trick? Now she's your pretend fiancée?"

Gabriel just looked at Laura. "Say yes. Make this an engagement party."

And Laura exhaled.

All her wedding dreams came crashing down around her. This proposal had nothing to do with love, or even sex. It was entirely about business.

This was his plan B.

Tears rose in her eyes, tears she hoped would appear to be tears of joy. Unable to speak over the lump in her throat, she simply nodded.

Rising to his feet, Gabriel kissed her. Tenderly, he placed the diamond ring on her finger. It fit perfectly.

Laura stared down at it, sparkling on her hand like an iceberg. It was beautiful. And so hollow.

"Hmm," Oliveira said, watching them thoughtfully. "Maybe I was wrong about you, Santos."

"You said you'd never marry anyone!" Adriana sounded outraged.

Never looking away from Laura's face, Gabriel smiled. "Plans change."

"But people don't," she spit out. "Not this much. You would never marry a woman with a baby!"

Stiffening, Gabriel turned to her.

"She has a baby," Adriana said spitefully to Oliveira. "They were seen together on Ipanema Beach. He just brought Laura here this morning, after they'd been apart for a year. Why would he suddenly decide he's in love with a woman after being apart for over a year? It's a trick, Felipe," she declared. "It's a lie. He's not committed to her. He won't commit to anyone."

"I can explain, Oliveira," Gabriel said through his clenched jaw.

Felipe Oliveira's jowly face hardened as he slowly turned to face his younger rival. "No," he said. "I'm afraid you can't. I don't appreciate this elaborate theater you've performed. The deal is officially off."

The man turned away. Laura saw Gabriel's frustration, saw his vulnerability and the desperate expression on his face as he lost his father's company forever.

"Wait," Laura gasped.

Snorting a laugh, Felipe Oliveira glanced back at her with amusement. "What could you possibly have to say, little one?"

"Everything that Adriana said is true," she whispered. "I have a baby. And I hadn't seen Gabriel since I left

Rio over a year ago. But there's a reason why he came for me. A very good reason he'd want to marry me."

Folding his arms over his belly, Oliveira looked at her with a shake of the head. "I am dying to hear it."

Laura didn't glance at Gabriel. She couldn't, and still say what she had to say. Closing her eyes, she took a deep breath. Then she spoke the secret she'd kept for over a year.

"Gabriel is the father of my baby."

CHAPTER ELEVEN

Trembling, Laura folded her arms.

"Ah," Felipe Oliveira said, stroking his chin with satisfaction as he looked from her to Gabriel with canny eyes. "Now I understand."

"No!" Adriana gasped. "It can't be true!"

Laura's gaze rested anxiously on Gabriel. His dark eyes were deep as the night sky. She saw him take a deep breath. Then slowly, very slowly, he came toward her. Never looking away from her face, he took her in his arms. Biting her lip in apprehension, Laura waited for his jaw to clench with fury and resentment. Waited for him to say something biting and cruel.

Instead, he gently kissed her cheek, then turned to face Oliveira and Adriana.

"We weren't going to tell anyone yet. But yes, Robby is my son. I wanted to wait until after our wedding to make it public. It seemed more proper."

"Proper?" Adriana sneered. "When have you ever cared about *proper*?"

Gabriel stiffened, glaring at her. "I have always cared about doing what is right," he said in a low voice. "I would never leave my child without a father, without a name."

"And yet," Oliveira said, shifting his savvy gaze between them, "you allowed your fiancée to raise your baby alone, for all these months."

Gabriel set his jaw. "I—"

"He didn't know about Robby," Laura interrupted in a whisper. "I didn't tell him. It wasn't until he came to my sister's wedding that he first saw his son. I knew Gabriel didn't want a family—"

"So he always insisted," Adriana said resentfully.

Gabriel's dark eyes glowed with warmth and love as he looked down at Laura, who was shivering in her red strapless gown and opera gloves. "But Robby changed my mind." He wrapped his warm, tuxedo-clad arms more firmly around her. "From the moment I saw Laura with our son, I knew I couldn't part with them. We were meant to be a family."

Laura blinked back her tears, hardly able to breathe as she heard the words she'd always dreamed of.

She'd told him the truth about Robby, and he knew it. She could see it in his eyes. Robby was his son. And this was Laura's reward for being brave enough to tell the truth. He wasn't rejecting her. He wasn't rejecting their baby.

All this time she'd thought it would be so hard to tell him the truth, but it wasn't. It was easy.

Staring at them, Felipe Oliveira stroked his chin. "You might be a bastard, Santos, but you wouldn't desert your son. Or your son's mother." He looked from Laura to Gabriel with a sly smile. "And I see the passion between you. I have been a doddering old fool to feel threatened. The two of you are in love." He gave a sudden decisive nod. "*Está bom*. We will sign the preliminary contracts tomorrow. Be at my lawyers' office at nine."

Gabriel put his arm around Laura's waist, smiling at the other man. "Sure."

Adriana glared at Laura. "You got pregnant on purpose! You tricked Gabriel into marriage!"

As Laura stiffened, Oliveira grabbed the supermodel's arm grimly.

"There's only one person you should worry about getting tricked into marriage," he said, "and that's me. I look at them—" he nodded toward Laura and Gabriel "—and I see love. I look at you, Adriana, and I see... nothing."

She stared at him, her eyes wide.

Oliveira lifted a white bushy eyebrow. "Our engagement," he said mildly, "is over."

He marched off across the ballroom. Adriana's cheeks went red as an amused titter flowed through the nearby crowd.

"Fine," she shrieked after him. "But I'm keeping the ring!"

Oliveira didn't even turn around. Frustrated greed filled Adriana's eyes, and with an intake of breath, she started to push forward. "Felipe," she whined, "wait!"

When they were alone in the crowd, Gabriel looked down at Laura. She took a deep breath, waiting for the onslaught of questions she knew were coming. "Oh, Gabriel. I know we have so much to talk about—"

"Wait." He glanced at the people around them, amused celebutantes and movie actors in designer clothes, rich and beautiful and dressed in sparkling, sexy gowns. "Come with me."

Grabbing two flutes of champagne from the tray of a passing waiter, Gabriel pulled her through the glorious, gilded ballroom, filled with music and magic, and out a side door.

The private garden was dark and quiet. Laura looked up and saw black silhouettes of palm trees swaying against the purple sky. The night was tropical and warm, and on the wild southern coast so far from the lights of the city, she could see stars twinkling down on them.

Biting her lip, she faced him. "So…so you don't mind?"

"Mind?" Smiling, he handed her a glass of champagne. His dark head was frosted with silvery moonlight as he leaned forward to clink his crystal flute against hers. "You are the most incredible woman I've ever met," he whispered. "Brilliant. Beautiful."

She stared up at him with trembling lips as joy flooded her heart. "You're not angry?"

"Angry?" His brow furrowed. "Why would I be angry? Because you lied?"

She licked her dry lips. "Yes."

He shook his head. "No, *querida.*" His expression was tender. "I've just gotten everything I ever dreamed of. Because of you."

He drank deeply from his champagne flute, and she followed suit, her eyes wet with tears of joy. She'd never imagined he would react this way, not in a million years. What had she ever done to deserve this miracle—that Gabriel would so easily accept their child as his own? That he would be glad to be a father after all?

"I'm so happy," she whispered. Smiling, she wiped tears from her eyes. "I never dreamed you would react like this."

He looked down at her with a frown. "*Querida*, are you crying?"

"I'm happy," she whispered.

"So am I, my beautiful girl." He stroked her cheek, his fingertips lightly caressing her flushed skin. "You sexy, incredible woman," he breathed in her ear, causing prickles to spread down her body. Cupping her face, he lowered his mouth to hers. "I will never forget this night."

When he kissed her, his lips were hot and smooth on hers. He seared her with the sizzle of his tongue against her lips, teasing her. She gripped his shoulders, instinctively pulling him closer.

They heard a sudden burst of laughter as other guests came into the garden. Grabbing her hand with a low growl, Gabriel pulled her deeper into the trees, into a shadowy corner. Above them, palm trees swayed in the violet-smudged night. The other voices continued to come closer, and he pushed her all the way back against the palace wall. She felt the hardness of his body, the roughness of the stone behind her.

Without a word, he slowly kissed her throat. She closed her eyes, tossing her head back with a silent gasp. She felt his teeth nibble her neck, felt his hands skimming from her bare shoulders down the length of her arms, over her long white gloves. He kissed her bare collarbone, his hands cupping her breasts below the sweetheart neckline of her strapless gown. Pressing her breasts together, he licked the cleavage just above the red velvet, and she sucked in her breath.

Samba music poured out of the palace as the doors to the garden continued to bang open and more guests discovered the garden. Voices grew louder, laughing and sultry, murmuring in Portuguese and French, as other lovers approached their corner. Gabriel pulled away from her. "Let's get out of here," he growled.

She blinked at him, dazed with desire. "Leave the ball already? It's barely midnight."

Jerking her back against his hard body, he leaned his forehead against hers and whispered, "If we don't leave, I will take you right here."

Drawing in a breath, she saw his absolute intent to make love to her right here in the dark garden, against the wall, with people on the other side of the foliage and samba music wafting through the warm air. She gave a single nod.

Gabriel instantly grabbed her hand and dragged her through the garden, back into the ballroom. He pulled her through the huge, crowded space, wading against the flow of new arrivals. Laura heard people shouting greetings to him in a variety of languages, but he didn't stop. He didn't even look at them. He just pulled her relentlessly up the wide, sweeping stairs to the front door, where he tersely summoned his driver.

As they waited, they stood at the end of the red carpet, not looking at each other. His hand gripped hers, crushing her fingers through her gloves. She heard the hoarseness of his breath. Or maybe it was her own. Her heartbeat was rapid. She felt dizzy.

"What's taking so long?" Gabriel muttered beneath his breath. She felt his barely restrained power, felt the grip of his hand as if only sheer will kept him from turning to her and ripping off her slinky red gown, pushing her against the wall and tasting her skin, in front of all the servants, the valets and flash of the paparazzi's cameras.

It took three minutes before the Rolls-Royce sedan

pulled up and Carlos leaped out. Laura stared at the man's crooked tie. She saw a smudge of lipstick.

"Finally," Gabriel growled, grabbing his door.

"Sorry about the delay, *senhor*," Carlos said, casting a regretful glance back at the palace. Laura followed his gaze and saw a housemaid looking down from the second-floor window. Laura was so filled with joy, she couldn't bear the thought of everyone not being happy tonight. Standing on her tiptoes, she whispered in Gabriel's ear, "Give him the night off."

"Why?" he snapped. "I don't want to drive. I want to be alone with you in the back—"

"He was enjoying his time here." She tilted her head toward the window. "Look."

Gabriel glanced behind them, then instantly faced his driver, who'd just come around the car. "Carlos, you're dismissed."

"*Senhor?*" the man gasped in horror.

"Enjoy your night," he said. "I trust you can get a ride home tonight?"

Delight flooded the older man's face. "Yes, sir."

"I have an early appointment tomorrow. Do not be late." After opening the door for Laura, Gabriel walked around the car and climbed into the driver's seat.

Smiling at Carlos's dumbfounded expression, Laura fastened her seat belt, and Gabriel pressed on the gas. They drove down the tree-lined lane with a spray of gravel, and the flash of cameras from additional paparazzi parked outside the gate.

"I know a shortcut," Gabriel said a moment later. Turning off the busy main road, he drove down the rocky coast, the luxury sedan bouncing hard over the rough road. Laura looked out her window. The landscape was hauntingly beautiful, filled with trees and thickets of jungle that wound along the sharp cliffs overlooking the moonlit Atlantic.

She looked back at the dark silhouette of Gabriel's brutally handsome face, his Roman nose and angular jaw. She saw the tight clench of his hand on the gearshift, saw the visible tension of his body beneath his tuxedo.

As a warm breeze blew tendrils of hair across her face, she was so filled with joy she thought she might die. Life was wonderful, incredible, magical. How had she never fully realized it before?

It was Gabriel. He was the dark angel who'd changed her life forever. Her heart was his. Forever.

She loved him.

"Don't look at me like that," he said in a low voice, glancing at her. "It's a two-hour drive back to the city."

She sucked in her breath. "Can't you drive any faster?" she begged.

With a curse, he suddenly steered the car off the road with a wide spray of gravel, taking a sharp turn past a thicket of trees that ended on a dark bluff overlooking the wide ocean. He slammed on the brake and turned off the engine. The headlights went black, and with a low growl he was upon her.

But the front of the sedan hadn't been made for this. The two luxurious leather seats were separated by a hard center console, and the steering wheel pressed against Gabriel's hip. He'd barely kissed her before he was jumping out with a low curse. Opening her door, he yanked her out. She had one glimpse of the moon-drenched ocean beneath the cliff, and then he pushed her into the backseat.

He kissed her, his lips hot and hard against her, and covered her body with his own. She felt his weight against hers in the tight confines of the backseat. His scent of musk and soap mingled with expensive leather, the forest, wild orchids and the salty sea. The notched satin collar of his black tuxedo jacket moved against the bare skin of her shoulders. He gripped her gloved hands, pulling them back over her head, against the car window.

He kissed down her throat, his hands cupping her breasts through the corset bodice of her red dress. But their feet still hung off the end of the seat. His legs were dangling out of the car. And though the seat was comfortable and wide, he had scant space to brace his arms around her. With a low growl, he moved away, so fast he hit his head against the ceiling. He gave a loud, spectacular curse. She saw the flash of his eyes in the moonlit night.

"It's still not enough," he growled. "Not nearly enough."

He kicked the door wide open behind them. Taking her hand, he roughly pulled her out of the car. Kissing her, he pushed her back against the hood.

Laura gasped as she felt the warmth of the hard metal beneath her. Gabriel moved over her, kissing her lips, kissing her bare neck. Overhead, she saw the twinkling stars of the night sky as he peeled off her long white opera gloves one at a time, tossing them to the soft earth. She felt the shock the warm air against her bare skin. Standing up straight, he looked down at her as he yanked off his tuxedo jacket and tie, and she realized that he did not intend to wait until they got back to Rio.

Right here. Right now.

Below the cliff, she heard the roar and crash of the ocean waves pounding the shore. She heard the sounds of night birds and the chatter of monkeys from the stretch of dark forest behind them. She saw the flash of Gabriel's dark eyes in the moonlight as he bent over her, reaching around her to unzip her dress. He slowly pulled it down the length of her body. She watched in shock as he dropped the expensive dress to the ground. She was now lying on the hood of his Rolls-Royce, naked except for a white strapless bra, silk panties, white garter belt and white thigh-high stockings.

He gasped as he softly stroked her naked belly. "So beautiful," he breathed.

Swallowing, she looked up at him. The bright moon illuminated his black hair as his hands stroked her skin. Reverently, he undid the front clasp of her bra, pulling it off her body and dropping it, too, to the ground. She felt his shudder of barely controlled desire as he cupped her naked breasts in his hands. "I've wanted you so long," he said hoarsely. "I thought I would die of it."

Moving down her body, he licked the valley between her breasts, then took her nipple in his wet, warm mouth. As his tongue ran over her taut peak like a caress of silk, she felt his hands slide down to her hips.

Her own hands moved of their own volition, beneath his white tuxedo shirt to feel the smooth warmth of his skin, to feel the hard muscles of his chest beneath the scattering of dark hair. She unbuttoned his shirt with trembling hands as he breathed against her ear, tasting the sensitive flesh of her earlobe. He kissed a trail down her neck, to her breasts, as his hands moved between her legs, along the top edge of her garter belt and thigh-high stockings.

His fingers stroked over her silken panties, and her breath stopped in her throat. He reached beneath the edge of the silk, and she felt him stroke her lightly, so lightly, across her wet core. Her hips strained toward him but he took his time, holding back, stroking her. He slowly pushed two thick fingers an inch inside her.

She arched her spine against the hood.

Pulling back with a growl, he ripped off his white shirt, popping the cuff links. With a low curse in Portuguese, he bent over her once more. His bare chest was rough and laced with dark hair, his skin so warm as his muscles slid against the softness of her breasts. She felt him between her knees, his thickly muscled hips rough against her spread thighs. He leaned above her, standing beside the car. She gripped his shoulders as he kissed her neck, nipping the sensitive corner of her throat. With agonizing slowness, he kissed down between her breasts to her flat belly, past her white garter belt to the sharp edge of her hip bone. He kissed the edge of her white silk panties. Then he stopped.

She felt his warm breath against her skin above her thigh-high stockings. His lips slowly moved over the silk, kissing down her legs. Pushing them farther apart, he took an exploratory lick of her inner right thigh. As she sucked in her breath, he switched to her left thigh. She trembled beneath him, her breath coming in increasingly ragged gasps as his lips moved slowly higher on each side. He held her hips firmly, relentlessly, not allowing her to move away.

Pushing the silk of her panties aside, he paused, and

she felt his warm breath against her slick, sensitive core. He lowered his head between her legs, and still did not touch her, except with the soft stroke of his breath.

"Please," she gasped, hardly knowing what she was asking for. She grabbed his head, twining her fingers in his hair. "I—"

With ruthless control, he slowly pushed her wide with both hands. Lowering his head even more, he tasted her with the hot, wet tip of his tongue.

Pleasure ripped through her. With a cry, Laura flung her arms wide, desperate to hold on to something, anything, to keep herself from flying headlong into the sky. Her right hand found the car's metal hood ornament.

Gabriel's tongue moved against her, licking her in little darting swirls. Spreading her wide, he lapped at her with the full width of his rough tongue. As she cried out, he drew back, using just the tip of his tongue again to swirl against her in progressively tighter circles, until she twisted and writhed with the sweet agony of her desire. It was building—exploding....

"Stop," she gasped. "No." She gripped his shoulders, frantically pulling him up toward her, and he lifted his head. Undoing the fly of his tuxedo trousers, he yanked them down with his boxers. They fell to his black Italian leather shoes as he sheathed himself in a condom he'd pulled from his pocket. Leaving on her garter belt and stockings, he grabbed Laura by the hips and pulled her down to the very edge of the car hood, where he stood. Ripping the fabric of her panties in a single brutal movement, he pushed inside her in a single thrust.

She felt impaled by the way he filled her completely, so wide and big and deep. He gave a hoarse gasp and gripped her backside, lifting her legs to wrap around his hips.

Holding her against the hood, he thrust again, this time even deeper. He pushed inside her, faster and harder, squeezing her breasts as her hips rose to meet him. She felt tension coil low in her belly and held her breath as the sweet tension built, soared and started to explode.

Throwing her arms back on the hood, she closed her eyes and surrendered completely to his control. His hands moved to grip her hips again, speeding the rhythm as he rode her, so deep and raw that the pleasure was almost pain. So deep. So deep. Her body was so tense and tight and breathless that she didn't know how much she could take.

Her eyes flew open and she saw his face above her in the night, his features shrouded by shadow as he thrust so deep inside her that her heart twisted in her chest. He gasped her name and she exploded, clutching his shoulders as she heard a scream she didn't even recognize as her own voice. A man's voice joined hers as he plunged deeper into her one last time, thrust with a hard, ragged shout that echoed across the dark forest and crashing sea, causing startled birds to fly from the trees and disappear into the night.

Afterward, he collapsed over her, clutching her to him. Their sticky, sweaty skin pressed together as they lay on the hood.

When Laura came to herself, she realized she was wearing nothing but ripped silken panties and thigh-high stockings, beneath the dark Brazilian sky, on a remote stretch of coastline where any passerby could see them. She'd totally lost her mind. And it had been so, so good.

But Gabriel had won. He'd seduced her, just as he'd said. He'd possessed her.

And not just her body, but her heart.

She pulled away, intending to find her red gown in the darkness, to try to cover herself.

But he pulled her back into his arms on the long warm hood. "Where are you going?"

"You got what you wanted," she said bitterly. "You won." She shivered in the warmth of his arms. She'd surrendered and now she knew exactly the power he had over her—the power he would always have. She felt suddenly afraid of how vulnerable she was. He had her heart in his hands. "Now it's done."

"Done?" He gave a low, sensual laugh, then his hands tightened on her as he murmured, "*Querida*, it's only beginning."

CHAPTER TWELVE

By the time they arrived back in Rio two hours later, one thought kept repeating in Gabriel's mind. One thought over and over.

"Here," he said to her, covering her shoulders with his tuxedo jacket as they entered the lobby of his building. She threw him a grateful glance. Her red designer gown now hung askew on her body, the zipper broken from when he'd ripped the dress off her earlier.

As they passed the security guards, Gabriel glanced at them out of the corner of his eye. His white shirt was rumpled, the cuffs hanging open, his tie crumpled in the pocket of his trousers. Laura was looking at him breathlessly, her eyes luminescent, her makeup hopelessly smudged and her lips full and bruised.

He saw the security guards nudge each other with a smirk, and he knew he and Laura had fooled no one. There could be no doubt what they had been doing.

Normally he wouldn't care if people knew he'd taken a woman as his lover. But this was different. This was Laura. And one thought kept going through his mind, no matter how he tried to avoid it.

He never wanted to let her go.

Gabriel exhaled. When he'd taken her on the hood

of the car, beneath the night sky and in full view of the dark moonlit sea, he'd thought he would die of pleasure. Touching her naked skin, thrusting inside her until she screamed, holding her tight, the two of them joined together as one...

He shuddered. After that, he should feel satisfied, at least for the night. He should be satiated.

But he wasn't. Now that he'd had one taste of her, he only wanted more. And more. *He never wanted to let her go.*

Silently, they took the private elevator upstairs to the penthouse. The doors slid open, and he followed Laura inside. They found Maria quietly reading a book by the light of the lamp in the main room, beside the wall of windows two stories high.

The housekeeper rose to her feet, smiling. "The baby is sleeping, Mr. Gabriel, Mrs. Laura..." And then the older woman got a good look at both of them. She coughed, closing her book with a thump. "I will wish you both good-night."

"Thank you, Maria," Gabriel said gravely, and his former nanny scurried out, the elevator doors closing behind her.

After she was gone, Laura turned to him, a frown furrowing her brow. "You don't think she guessed about us, do you? You don't think she could tell?"

"Absolutely," he said, then at her horrified expression, he added, "not. Absolutely not."

She sighed in relief. "I'm going to go check on Robby."

Laura turned and went down the hall. He watched her go, watched the curves of her back and graceful sway of her body in his oversize tuxedo jacket as she moved like music. She stepped into the bedroom and disappeared. *Gone.*

His feet moved without thought, and he was down the hall and suddenly behind her in the darkened bedroom. He watched as she crept up to the crib and stood silently, listening to her baby's snuffling breaths as he slept. Gabriel came closer.

In the dim light of the tiny blue night-light plugged into the far wall, he could just barely see the sleeping baby. Robby's chubby little fist was tossed back over his head. His plump cheeks moved as his mouth pursed, sucking in his sleep. Gabriel heard the soft, even breathing of the child in the darkness, and something turned over in his chest. He felt the sudden need to protect this little boy, to make sure he never came to any harm.

Just as he'd once felt about his family.

The thought caused a raw, choking ache in his throat. Without a word, he turned and left.

He stood in the hallway for long moments, shaking. But by the time Laura came out into the hall a few moments later, he'd gathered his thoughts. Come to some decisions.

She closed her bedroom door softly behind her, then looked at Gabriel in the darkened hallway. "I'm so sorry about Robby," she said in a low voice. "I never should have lied, Gabriel. I was just so...scared."

Clawing back his hair, he gave a sudden laugh. "To tell you the truth, I was almost scared myself for a moment." He looked at her. "But it was brilliant of you to say I was Robby's father. It saved the deal. That was a stroke of genius, Laura."

Her beautiful face suddenly looked pale. "What?"

"It was the perfect lie. But don't worry. If Adriana

spreads the rumor I'm his father—and she likely will—I will not deny it." He set his jaw. "Since your baby's real father can't be bothered to give him a name, somebody has to do it."

She bit her trembling lower lip. "Gabriel—you never thought…for one moment…that it might be true? That Robby might actually be your son?"

He snorted. "No, of course not. If Robby were really my child and you'd lied to me all this time…"

"Yes?"

He shrugged. "I've destroyed men for less." Reaching forward, he smiled and stroked her cheek, then lowered his head to playfully kiss her bare shoulder. "But I knew Robby couldn't really be mine. We used protection. And you wouldn't lie, not to me. Other than Maria, you are the only person I trust in all this world. You are…"

But then he leaned forward, frowning at her. "You are crying again." He tilted his head, trying to see her face. "Is it from happiness?"

She looked away sharply, wiping her eyes. "Yes. Happiness."

"Good," he said. "Now." He stroked her cheek. "We must celebrate winning the Açoazul deal tonight." He gave her a wicked smile. "I can think of one way—"

"No," she blurted out. "I just need to—I need to…be alone."

Turning abruptly, she ran down the hall. He heard the soft whir of the sliding doors as she fled out onto the terrace. When he followed her moments later, she'd dropped his tuxedo jacket from her body. Her strapless gown was barely hanging on her full breasts, askew with the broken zipper.

"What are you doing?" he asked. "What's wrong?"

"Just leave me alone," she said. Her voice was low, almost grief-stricken. "Go to bed. I'll see you in the morning."

Her red dress suddenly fell to the ground, but she didn't seem to notice or care. He licked his lips, unable to look away from her half-naked body in the white bra and torn panties and thigh-high stockings. "What are you doing?"

She looked away. "I'm going to take a swim."

He smiled. "Wonderful idea. I'll join you."

"No!" she cried vehemently.

He blinked at her, frowning. "Why?"

For long moments, she didn't answer. He could hear the noise and music of the street party below them. She finally said in a low, muffled voice, "I need some time alone." When he didn't move, she choked out, "Just go away, Gabriel. Please."

Looking away from the illuminated turquoise water of the pool, she stared out at the vast dark ocean beyond Ipanema Beach. He'd seen a glimmer of tears in her eyes. And there was *no way* they were tears of happiness.

But she wanted him to leave. She'd made that clear. Setting his jaw, he turned and left her on the terrace, opening the sliding glass doors with a whir and closing them behind him.

Once inside, he stopped, clawing his hair back with one hand. He couldn't let it end like this. Did she have so much regret that she'd allowed him to make love to her? He turned around, intending to go back and argue, to plead.

Instead, he froze.

He saw her on the moonlit terrace, sitting on a lounge chair, her face covered by her hands. Then she dropped her hands. Squaring her shoulders, she started to roll down her stockings.

He stared at her, transfixed. She pulled off her garter belt and tossed that, too, to the limestone floor.

Rising, she stood in the moonlight. Now wearing nothing but her bra and panties, she walked to the edge of the illuminated pool. Ripples of water reflected tiny shimmers of light that moved across her naked skin. Gabriel stared at her as he touched the window, unable to move or even breathe as she stood on the edge of the pool, looking down into the water.

Then in a graceful movement, she dived in. She stayed underwater for so long that he was suddenly afraid. Sliding open the doors, he ran out onto the terrace.

He saw her sitting on the bottom of the pool, her eyes closed. It seemed to take forever before she finally rose to the surface with a gasp, her hair sleek and sopping wet.

Laura was facing away from him, the moonlight frosting her bare shoulders in silver. Her thighs spread wide as her legs chopped the water, which moved around her in illuminated ripples of blue.

He choked back a groan. He was hard and aching for her. There was no way he was leaving her now. Walking to the edge, he said, "Laura."

She turned to face him with a gasp. Her eyes were luminous, a dark shade of blue, as she tried to cover her breasts, treading water with her feet. "What do you want?"

Sitting on a chair by the pool, he looked down at her. "I want you to tell me what you're thinking."

"I'm thinking I want to be alone!"

"Tell me," he threatened. "Or I'll kiss it out of you."

Her eyes widened. Then she turned away. "Just go away."

But in spite of her defiant words, he heard a sob in her voice that caused his belly to clench. Had he done that? Had he caused it? His jaw set. Pushing the chair away, he rose to his feet. He calmly kicked off his black leather shoes.

"What are you doing?" she said, alarmed.

He didn't answer. Fully dressed in his tuxedo shirt and trousers, he jumped into the pool.

He'd been on the swim team in school, and was a fast swimmer underwater. He rose to the surface directly beside her, pushing her back against the hard edge of the pool. She gasped as she felt his hands on her.

"Tell me," he said grimly.

"No."

"Now."

Her eyes became wide and tearful. "I can't."

Gabriel looked at her, and again he had that same strange feeling in his chest, like a twist in his heart. Holding himself suspended in the water, he gripped the edge of the pool with both hands around her, trapping her. She had nowhere to escape.

"You're going to tell me." He felt the warmth of her curvy body against the sopping wet shirt now clinging to his chest. "Whatever it is."

He heard her intake of breath. Then she lifted her chin.

"It wouldn't do any good," she whispered. "Not to you. Not to anyone."

He growled in frustration. Holding on to the edge of

the pool with one hand, he cupped her cheek with his other palm. "Remember," he said roughly, tilting her chin. "You left me no choice."

And he ruthlessly kissed her.

Her lips trembled beneath his, soft and warm and wet. He moved his mouth against hers in a seductive embrace, luring her without force, tempting her with their mutual hunger, with the insatiable need between them. Deepening the kiss, he softly stroked down her cheek, down her neck. His hand went below the surface of the water and he stroked the side of her body, her plump breast beneath her nearly invisible silk bra, her taut, slender waist, the full curve of her hip.

With a shudder of desire, he pulled back to look at her.

In the moving prisms of light from the pool, he could hear the music and noise of the street party on the *avenida*. But here on the terrace of his penthouse, in the moonlit night, he saw only her. They were connected in a way he didn't understand.

He never wanted to let her go.

Reaching beneath her, he lifted her out of the pool. She was warm in his arms and her weight was light, barely anything at all, as he set her down gently on the limestone. He climbed out beside her, his wet tuxedo trousers and white shirt clinging to his skin. Impatiently, he pulled off the shirt, then yanked off his trousers with awkward force as the fabric clung stubbornly to his legs, nearly tripping him.

Laura, still sitting on the terrace floor in her transparent bra and panties, choked out a giggle.

"Laugh at me, will you, *gringa*?" Gabriel growled. He threw his sodden trousers on the floor, and his socks swiftly followed. He lifted her into his arms, holding her tightly against his naked body.

The laughter faded from her eyes, replaced by something hot and dark. Looking at him in wonder, she reached up and stroked the rough bristles of his jawline.

Just the gentle touch of her small hand sent his senses reeling, spiraling out of control. He wanted to push her into a lounge chair—that one, there at his feet—and throw himself on top of her, grinding into her, filling her until they exploded.

But he'd already done that once, on the hood of his car. No. Now, he would take his time.

Now, he would do it right.

Water trailed behind them as he padded naked across the terrace and back inside. The expensive rugs were left sopping wet with every step.

He looked down at her, this beautiful, soft, loving woman who had her arms wrapped around his neck and looked up at him with a mixture of apprehension, desire and wonder. He went down the hall to the master bedroom and set her reverently on his large bed.

He saw her lying across his white comforter, nearly naked, and he shuddered with need. Lines of silvery moonlight from his half-closed blinds slatted across Laura's bare skin, emphasizing the shadows of her full breasts and hips, and his whole body shook with hunger.

He needed her. *Now.*

"I'm going to get everything wet," she whispered with a nervous laugh.

"Good," he said roughly.

Her eyes were looking everywhere but at his naked

body, everywhere but the hard, huge evidence of his desire. There was no hiding how much he wanted her. Let her see. Let her know. He put his hand on the valley of bare skin between her breasts, and exhaled.

He could see her nipples through her wet silk bra. Beneath her transparent, half-ripped panties, he could see the dark curls of hair between her legs. He reached to rip off her bra, then stopped himself.

Take it slow. Do it right.

With iron control, he gently undid her bra and peeled it off her wet skin before dropping it to the carpet. Her panties were next—easy to remove those, as they'd already been ripped and only a few threads still held them together.

Looking at her now, naked and spread across his bed, he took a breath, struggling to stay in check. He wanted to throw himself on top of her and push deep, deep, deep inside until he felt her shake with joy around him. Instead, he forced himself to climb up beside her on the bed. Turning her against his naked body, he reached for her cheek and gently kissed her, long and slow.

His hand skimmed her side, caressing her. He took his time, kissing her, relishing the sweet taste of her lips, the warm wet pleasures of her mouth. He heard a sigh come from the back of her throat as she wrapped her arm around him, pulling him closer.

He throbbed against her soft belly, thick and rock-hard. But he made no move to throw her back against the bed. Instead, he just kissed her as if he had all the time in the world, exploring her mouth, biting her lip, nibbling her neck and chin, sucking the tender flesh of her ear. It nearly killed him to wait, but he owed it to her to take his time…take it—

He suddenly gasped as he felt her hand wrap around his hard, thick shaft. He jerked in her hand as she slowly ran her fingertips down his length. Her thumb gently touched the tip, and it became wet beneath her touch as a tiny bead like a pearl escaped. He gasped out a groan.

"Querida," he said hoarsely. "Don't… I can't…"

In a sudden movement, she flipped him on his back, pushing him against the pillows. He felt her lips move down his throat to his chest. He was suddenly in her power, and he felt it as she kissed his body. When her head slipped down past his taut belly, he gripped the goosedown comforter with white-knuckled control. Then he felt her tongue brush his hot, throbbing skin, licking the bead of moisture at the tip.

He gave a rough gasp and nearly lost it right then. Grabbing her shoulders, he pulled her up with force and lifted her hips over his body. He was blind with need, ready to thrust inside her, to impale her. He only knew he had to take her or die.

"Wait," she panted. Wrenching away from his grasp, she opened a drawer beside the bed. He saw a condom in her hand and realized he'd forgotten all about it.

He'd forgotten about it. If Laura hadn't stopped him, he would have made love to a woman without a condom for the first time in his life. He exhaled as he broke out into a sweat.

"There," Laura whispered. Finally, she lowered her body over his, allowing him to impale her, inch by inch.

His eyes rolled back and he closed his eyes. Yes. *Yes.* He was losing his mind. The more time he spent with her, the more he lost. And it was worth it. So worth it.

Slowly, she moved against him, pulling him deeper

inside her. Her thighs were clamped around his hips as she increased her rhythm and speed, riding him. Opening his eyes, he looked up at her, watching the sway of her enormous breasts as she moved over him. Her face was luminous. Her eyes were closed in ecstasy as she bit her full, bruised lower lip. He heard the intake of her breath, and he never wanted to let her go.

Ever.

His heart clenched in his chest. He couldn't let himself feel that way. He couldn't let himself feel anything but lust. Pure, raw sex.

He had to teach Laura her place. Show them both the true nature of the passion between them.

With a violent movement, he rolled her over on her back, so he was on top of her. Her eyes widened as he roughly gripped her shoulders. Then with a grunt he thrust inside her, hard and deep.

He gasped as he felt her body around him, hot and tight and silken and deep. She cried out from the force of his possession, but he didn't stop. He only rode faster, filling her with each thrust, deeper and faster, ramming himself inside her. He heard her shocked intake of breath and then she, too, began to grip his shoulders, her fingernails sharp in her answering frenzy of desire.

But it wasn't enough. He wanted to take off his condom, to feel her from the inside with his naked skin—

No.

The answer was like a blow. It was the one thing he could not allow himself to do. Ever. He could not be that close. He could not risk her conceiving a child.

Furiously, he rode her harder—faster—desperate to feel her tight sheath completely around him, to lose himself utterly inside her. As he slammed into her, he felt her fingernails cutting into the skin of his back. The pain only increased his pleasure as he rode her harder and harder until beads of sweat covered his forehead. He wanted to leave her raw, until he was utterly spent, until they both collapsed into oblivion.

He heard her cry out, her voice rising in a slow crescendo of joy. Tension sizzled down his body, leaving every muscle taut, crying for release. With a violent thrust, he filled her deeply, then held her tight as she screamed his name. He felt her convulse around him and could hold back no longer. With a savage, violent thrust, he filled her. He felt her hot and wet all around him and poured himself inside her with a shout, as his vision went black.

CHAPTER THIRTEEN

LAURA woke up with a start to see the soft curl of a pink sunrise through the windows. She sat up in bed abruptly, the blanket falling from her naked chest. Had she heard her baby next door?

She listened, and heard nothing except Gabriel's even, steady breathing beside her in the shadowy bedroom. Then she heard Robby's voice again.

"Ma…ma…ma!"

Quietly Laura rose from the bed and pulled a robe off the bathroom door hook. Leaving Gabriel's room, she went down the hall to her own, where she found her baby son sitting up in his crib. Whispering soft words of love, Laura took him in her arms. Holding him tenderly, she fed him, rocking him in the rocking chair. The baby, now yawning with a full belly, swiftly fell back to sleep.

But Laura knew she would not.

Putting him back in his crib, she went to the ensuite bathroom, closing the door silently behind her. She turned on the shower and dropped the robe to the floor. As the steam enveloped her body, she climbed into the marble shower. She washed her hair and stared bleakly at the wall.

She'd been so happy last night.

She'd been so *stupid*.

Of course Gabriel had thought she was lying when she'd claimed he was Robby's father. It had seemed a useful fabrication. Just like his marriage proposal.

She glanced down at the enormous diamond ring still on her finger. Her other hand closed around it with a sob. It had all felt so real. She closed her eyes, leaning her head back in the hot water. When she'd realized he still didn't believe he was Robby's father, her heart had split in two. She'd fallen into the pool, sinking into the water, hoping to forget her pain the way she did at the pond back at her farm.

But it had been Gabriel's touch that had made her forget, the searing heat of his dark eyes as he'd carried her to bed. For a few hours, she'd managed to forget her heartbreak, forget that she was in love with a man who didn't want her or their child. She'd managed to forget she'd be leaving him in the morning, with a lie forever between them.

He'd taken her in his arms and kissed her, his lips so gentle and tender and true, and she'd forgotten everything but that she loved him.

His hands had stroked her naked skin as he'd kissed her, his body hard and hot against hers on the bed. She'd lost her mind. Then she'd taken things into her own hands. Literally. A half-hysterical laugh escaped her. She remembered the hard, silky smooth feel of him in her grasp. The taste of the single gleaming bead on the tip of his throbbing shaft. She remembered the rough way he'd reacted, pushing her down against the bed and savagely thrusting deep inside her until she exploded with pleasure, blinding sweetness tinged with bitter salt like tears.

She blinked back tears as she stared across the steamed-up shower. It was morning now. Her left hand closed over the ten-carat diamond sparkling beneath the running water. Their night in Rio was over. Time to give back the ring. Time to take back her heart.

As if she could.

She'd go back home to her family's farm. Back to her lonely bed. Only now it would be worse than before. Because now she knew she'd always love him. Now, she'd never be free.

Who is the father of your baby, Laura? Will you ever tell?

She turned off the water and dried her hair with a thick white towel. She put on the plush white robe and left her bedroom, closing the door softly behind her.

Going to the kitchen, she turned on a light and made coffee. As it brewed, she poured milk and sugar into a big mug, then filled it to the rim with the hot, bitter brew. Blowing on the steaming liquid, she stood for a moment, alone in the house of sleeping males.

This could have been her home. They could have been her family. If only she'd fallen in love with a man who actually loved them back, a man who wanted a wife and child.

Carrying her mug, she went outside to watch the sun rise over the Atlantic. It was the last morning she would ever spend with both Robby and his father under the same roof. The last day she'd ever see the man she would always love.

She felt the soft wind, the breeze off the sea, and looked down at the beach below. She looked down. The party had ended, leaving only litter rattling along the empty street.

"There you are."

She turned to find Gabriel behind her in drawstring pajama bottoms. Her eyes unwillingly lingered on his bare chest before she met his gaze. His dark eyes twinkled at her as he held up a steaming cup of coffee. "You made coffee. Thank you."

She took a sip from her mug, relishing the burn against her tongue. "Sure." She drew a deep breath and turned back to the view of the ocean. "It was the least I could do before I go."

"Go?" There was something odd in his voice.

She turned back to face him, startled. "In a few hours, you'll sign the papers to buy your father's company. And Robby and I will go home."

Gabriel's handsome face looked suddenly grim. Setting down his coffee, he put his hands on her shoulders and gazed down at her. "I don't want you to leave."

"We had our night. It's over." She swallowed back her own pain, tried to smile. "We both knew it wouldn't last."

"No."

Laura gave him a trembling smile. "It was always meant to be this way."

"No," he repeated roughly. "Stay."

"As what?"

"As...as my mistress."

She licked her lips, yearning to agree, yearning to say anything that would give her relief from this heartbreak. But she knew that staying here as Gabriel's mistress wouldn't end her pain. It would only prolong it.

"I can't," she whispered. "I would always be waiting for the day you'd tire of me, and move on to another."

He searched her gaze. "Can't you live in the moment? Just live for today?"

Blinking back tears, she shook her head.

"Why?" he demanded.

For an instant, she almost laughed. He looked like a spoiled child deprived of his favorite toy. Then she sobered. "I don't want to raise Robby that way. And because…"

"Because?"

She took a deep breath. Taking her heart in her hands, she looked up at him.

"Because I love you," she whispered.

His dark eyes widened. "You—love me," he repeated.

She nodded, a lump in her throat. "I left you last year because I knew you could never love me back. You've told me so many times you will never love anyone. Not a wife." She trembled, lifting her eyes to his. "Not a child."

He stared at her, and Laura waited, breathless with the hope that he might deny it, that he'd say his time with Robby had changed his mind.

"There's more to life than love, Laura," he said, pulling her into his arms. "There's friendship, and partnership, and passion. And I can't do without you, not anymore. I need you. Your truth. Your goodness. Your warmth." He gave her a humorless smile. "It warms even my cold heart."

She caught her breath, then rubbed her stinging eyes. "I'm sorry, but I can't do it, Gabriel. I can't," she choked out. "I can't just stay here, loving you, while you give me nothing in return but the knowledge that you'll someday leave—"

He gripped her shoulders. "Marry me."

Her eyes and mouth went wide. "What?"

"Marry me." He picked up her left hand, looking down at the diamond on her finger. His lips curved upward. "You already have the ring."

"But I thought your proposal was a lie!"

"It was."

She shook her head tearfully. "So why are you saying this? We're alone. You've already convinced Oliveira. You don't need to pretend, not anymore!"

"I'm not pretending." Bending his head, he kissed her hand, making her tremble with the sensation of his warm lips against her skin. He looked up. "I need you, Laura," he said huskily. "I don't want to lose you. Marry me. Now. Today."

She licked her lips, feeling like she were in a dream. "What about Robby?"

Setting his jaw, Gabriel straightened.

"Perhaps I can't love him. But I can give him my name. I can give you both the life you deserve. And I can be faithful to you, Laura. I swear it."

It was so close to everything she'd ever wanted. Gabriel would be her husband. He would be a father, at least in name, to their child. And if some part of her warned that this was a fool's bargain, to marry a man who could not love her, she still couldn't resist. Her heart overrode her reason and she succumbed to the temptation of her heart's deepest desire.

With a tearful sob, she flung her arms around him in her bulky white cotton robe, kissing him as the sun finally broke, vivid and golden, over the fresh blue Atlantic.

"Yes!" she cried with a sob. "Oh, yes!"

CHAPTER FOURTEEN

Two weeks later, Laura stared at herself blankly in the mirror.

An elegantly dressed bride in a long, white lace veil and satin sheath gown stared back at her. It still didn't feel right. She picked up her neatly bundled bouquet of white roses and looked back in the mirror.

It was the morning of her wedding. In less than an hour she would have everything she'd barely dared to dream of—she'd be Mrs. Gabriel Santos. Robby would have his father.

So where was the joy? She should have been ecstatic with bliss and hope. So why, looking at herself in this beautiful dress, standing in a suite of this beautiful rented mansion outside her village, did she feel so... empty?

Gabriel had wanted to marry her immediately, in Rio, but he'd quickly given in to Laura's begging when she'd asked to have their wedding in New Hampshire, so her family could attend.

"We can get married in New Hampshire, of course we can, if that's your wish," he'd told her. "But after the ceremony, we must live in Rio. Do you agree?"

She'd agreed. She'd been lost in romantic bliss, and

all she'd thought about was getting married to the man she loved, in a beautiful wedding surrounded by friends and family.

She hadn't bothered to think about what would happen afterward. Gabriel had already signed the preliminary contracts to acquire Açoazul SA, and he now planned to merge the company with Santos Enterprises and permanently move the headquarters from New York City to Rio de Janeiro.

Starting tomorrow, she and Robby would live far away from her family, far from the people who actually loved them. Laura would be the wife of a man who didn't love her, a man who would offer only financial support to the child he didn't know was his son. A child he could never love.

Now, Laura was dressed in an exquisite 1920s-style designer gown and her great-grandmother's old lace veil. In ten minutes, she would go downstairs to get married in this beautiful place. The Olmstead mansion was a lavish house of forty rooms built by a now-bankrupt hedge fund manager, currently rented out for weddings. It sat among acres of rolling hills with its own private lake, a winter wonderland. And after the elegant ceremony in the gray stone library filled with flowers, a reception would follow in the ballroom, a lavish sit-down dinner of steak, lobster and champagne.

Laura had fretted about having such a luxurious wedding, worrying she'd steal her little sister's thunder from two weeks ago. Gabriel had smiled and picked up the phone. Within minutes, he'd arranged to send Becky and her new husband to Tahiti on honeymoon, via his private jet. He'd created college funds for young Margaret and Hattie, to allow them to go to university.

For their mother, he'd completely paid off the mortgage on the farm, and even helped out Ruth's dearest friend, a neighboring woman with a sick child, by paying for medical care.

All of this, and he'd still deposited the agreed-upon million dollars into Laura's bank account.

"A deal's a deal," he'd told Laura when she'd thrown her arms around him with a sob of delight. "I will always take care of you. That means taking care of your family."

Laura bit her lip, furrowing her brow as she stared at herself in the mirror. She had everything she'd ever wanted. And yet…

"Your family," Gabriel had said. Not *our* family.

He didn't love her. He didn't love Robby. And he still didn't know the truth.

What difference does it make? she argued with herself. Her love for Gabriel could be enough for both of them. He would still provide for Robby financially, living in the same house, acting exactly like a father in so many ways. What difference did the truth make?

Except it made a huge difference. In fact, truth was everything. Because without truth, how could there be love?

Her troubled eyes looked back at her in the mirror.

But if she told Gabriel now that he really was Robby's father, if he knew she'd lied to him all this time, she might lose everything she had. He would never forgive her for the lie. He might—almost certainly *would*—call off the wedding. Why would he take her as his wife if he couldn't trust her? Then he might sue for custody of Robby, and take her baby away from her out of duty—or even a desire to punish her.

But her conscience stung her. Didn't Gabriel deserve to know the truth before he pledged himself to her for the rest of his life?

She heard a knock, and her mother's smiling face peeked around the door. "All ready, sweetling? Your sisters are waiting and eager to be bridesmaids."

Laura took a deep breath, clutching her bouquet in her cold, shaking hands. "Is it already time?"

"Just a few more minutes. The last guests are arriving now…" Then, as Laura turned to face her in her 1920s-style gown and her great-grandmother's long veil, Ruth gasped, and her eyes filled with tears. "Oh, Laura," she whispered. "You're beautiful."

Laura's lips trembled as she smiled. "You look amazing, too, Mom."

Her mother shook her head dismissively at the compliment, then came forward to embrace her, looking chic in pearls and a mother-of-the-bride suit of light cream silk. "I'm going to miss you and Robby so much when you're in Rio," she choked out. "You'll be living so far away."

Laura fought back tears. Though she adored the energy of Rio, the warmth of the people and the beauty of Brazil, the thought of moving permanently to the other side of the Equator, far from her family and home, caused wrenching pain in her heart. If her husband loved her, it might be endurable. But as it was… Choking back a sob, she squeezed her mother tight and tried to reassure her. "We'll be just a quick plane ride away."

"I know." Her mother pulled away with a smile, even as her eyes glistened with tears. "My consolation is that I know you're going to be happy. Really, truly happy." She paused. "Gabriel is Robby's father, isn't he?"

Laura sucked in her breath. "How did you know?"

Her mother's smile widened. "I've got eyes, haven't I? I see how you are together. How you've always been. He's crazy about you."

Apparently her mother didn't see as much as she thought. Blinking back tears, Laura swallowed and said over the lump in her throat, "We have some...problems."

Her mother laughed. "Of course you do. There were times I was ready to kill your father. But now—" her voice broke "—the problems we had seem small. I would give anything to have him here again, arguing with me." She paused. "I know love isn't simple or easy. But you'll do the right thing. You always do."

Laura swallowed yet again. "Not always."

Ruth smiled. "Your father used to call you Little Miss Trustworthy. Of all my children, you were the easiest to raise. And now, the hardest to let go." Her mother shook her head, wiping away her tears. "Look at me. Here I am, making a mess of myself after Gabriel bought me this expensive dress."

"You're calling him Gabriel," Laura said.

"Well, what else would I call my son-in-law?" She kissed her daughter on the cheek. "He's not your boss now. A husband is quite a different matter." With a little laugh, she turned to leave in a soft cloud of lavender perfume. "Husbands need to be reminded not to take themselves too seriously."

"Wait," Laura whispered.

Her mother stopped at the door. "Yes, sweetie?"

Laura clenched her hands. The bodice of her wedding gown suddenly felt inexplicably tight.

She was standing on a precipice and knew it. The

choice she made today would change the entire course of her life. And her son's life, as well.

You'll do the right thing. You always do.

"I need to see Gabriel," she choked out. "Will you send him up to me?"

Her mother frowned. "Right now? It's bad luck to see the bride. Can't it wait an hour?"

In an hour, they'd be married. Not trusting her voice, Laura shook her head. With a sigh, her mother closed the door. Five minutes later, Gabriel appeared.

"You wanted to see me, *querida*?" he said huskily.

A lump rose in Laura's throat as she looked at her handsome husband-to-be, at the brutal power of his body barely contained in the sophisticated tuxedo. She was suddenly reminded of the last time he'd been in a tuxedo, when he'd kissed her in the shadowy gardens at the Fantasia Ball, then made love to her on the hood of his car overlooking the dark, moonlit ocean...

She set her bouquet on the vanity. "I need to ask you something."

His lips curved as he came up to her, stroking her face. "What is it, *minha esposa*?"

His wife. She swallowed, looking up at him.

"Do you love me?" she whispered.

He stiffened. Staring down at her, his handsome eyes became expressionless and dark. She waited, her heart pounding.

"I thought we agreed," he finally said. "I care for you, Laura. I admire you and I always will. I lust for you and want you in my life."

Her heart fell to her white satin shoes.

"But you don't love me," she said softly.

He set his jaw. "I told you from the start. I can't love anyone. Not a wife. Not children."

"But we will have them…"

"No," he said. He came closer, putting his hands on her shoulders as he searched her gaze. "Is that why you sent for me before the ceremony, to ask if I might want children someday?"

She nodded tearfully.

He took a deep breath. "I'm sorry, Laura. I thought you understood. Though I can offer you marriage, nothing else has changed. I still cannot offer you love. Or more children."

She blinked, staring up at him in shock. "No more… no more children?"

He shook his head.

"But why?" she cried.

He dropped his hands from her shoulders.

"You should know, before you marry me, why I will not change my mind." His jaw clenched as he turned away from her. Outside the windows, rolling white fields were dotted with black, bare trees. "My parents and brother died when I was nineteen. Because of me."

"I know you've spent your whole life trying to regain what you lost," she said. "But it wasn't your fault they died!"

"I was driving the car that killed them." His black eyes were bleak. "My brother had just eloped with a waitress who'd had his baby while we were away at university. He'd been living with her for months, keeping it secret from our parents that he'd dropped out of school. I visited their flat in São Paulo, where they were living with their baby daughter, barely surviving on the wages he could make as a laborer. This from my brother—who should have been a doctor!"

Laura took a deep breath. "So that's how you know how to play with a baby," she whispered. "You'd spent time with your niece."

He gave her a smile that broke her heart. "Yes," he said in a low voice. "But when my brother decided to marry the woman, I was sure she was a gold digger. I dragged my parents to São Paulo to break up the wedding, and we convinced Guilherme to come back with us to Rio. I hated the thought of my brother giving up all his dreams, just because he'd accidentally gotten some woman pregnant."

"Right," Laura said over the lump in her throat. "A child doesn't matter to you. Not like a career."

His jaw clenched as he turned away. "It was raining that night," he said in a low voice. "I was driving the car so my parents could convince my brother to see reason." Gabriel gave a hard laugh. "But instead, Guilherme convinced *them* he needed to go back and marry Izadora. 'Turn the car around,' they told me. I looked into the rearview mirror to argue. I looked away from the road only for a second," he whispered. "Just a single second."

He stopped, his face grief-stricken.

Laura stared at him, feeling sick.

"I slammed on the brakes. I turned the wheel as hard as I could. But the tires kept sliding, right off the cliff. I heard my mother scream as the car rolled, then we hit the bottom. They all died instantly. But not me." He looked at her bleakly. "I was lucky."

"Oh, Gabriel," she whispered, coming close to him.

She tried to put her arms around him, to offer comfort. But his body was stiff. He pulled away.

"I was wrong about Izadora. At my brother's funeral she wouldn't even look at me. I offered to buy her a house, set up a trust fund for my niece, but she refused with angry words. I'd taken her husband from her, taken the father of her child, and she told me she hoped I would rot in hell."

Laura shuddered.

"She eventually married an American and moved to Miami. My niece is grown now." He took a deep breath, and she saw that his eyes were wet. "She's almost twenty, and I haven't seen her since she was a baby."

"You haven't?" Laura said in shock. "But she's your only family, your brother's child!"

His jaw clenched. "How could I see her?" he demanded, turning on her. "Why should I be allowed to spend time with my niece, when it was my thoughtless action that caused her to lose her father? Her grandparents? They never got to see her grow up. Why should I?"

"But, Gabriel…it was an accident. You were trying to help your brother. We all make mistakes with the people we love. Your brother would forgive you. Your family loved you. They would know your heart. They'd know you never meant to—"

"I'm done talking about this," he growled, raking his hair back with his hand. He set his jaw, and his dark eyes glittered. "You wanted to understand why I never want children. I've told you why."

She closed her eyes, drew a deep breath. Tears streamed down her face as she opened her eyes.

"It's too late," she whispered.

"What do you mean?" he demanded. "Too late? What are you saying?"

She lifted her chin. "I've never had another lover, Gabriel. How could I, when I never stopped loving you? It's always been you. Just you."

He stared at her. His dark eyebrows came together like a storm cloud. "That's impossible," he said angrily. "Robby—"

"Don't you understand?" She shook her head tearfully. "Robby is your son."

The echo of her words hung in the air between them like a noxious cloud.

Gabriel stared at her, then staggered back.

"What?" he choked out.

"Robby is your—"

"I heard you," he cried, putting his hands over his ears. But he couldn't stop his mind from repeating those words. *Robby is your son.* "You're wrong. It's impossible."

"No," Laura said quietly. "Didn't you notice how he looks so much like you? That he was born exactly nine months after our night together? How could you not know? How could you not see?"

He shook his head. "But—but it can't be," he gasped. "I was careful. I used protection."

She shook her head. "Condoms have been known to fail—"

"Only to people who use them incorrectly," he muttered. "I do not."

"But even then, three percent of the time they—"

"No." He held out his hand, blocking her words. He

felt as if he couldn't breathe, and loosened the tie on his tuxedo. "I can't be his father. I can't."

Laura took a deep breath. She looked so beautiful in her white gown and veil. He'd never seen her look so innocent, so beautiful. So deceitful.

"I know this must come as a shock to you," she said softly. She gave him a tremulous smile. "It was a shock for me, too. But Robby's not an accident. He's not a mistake."

"Then what is he?" Gabriel demanded.

She looked up at him, her blue eyes luminous.

"A miracle," she whispered.

Images of Robby's chubby, smiling face went through his mind. His dark hair, his inquisitive dark eyes. *Of course* Robby was his son. Pacing, Gabriel raked his hair back with his hand. How could he have not seen it before?

Because he hadn't wanted to see it, he thought grimly. Because having a child, when he'd killed his parents and prevented his brother from raising his, was the one thing he could not allow himself to do.

"I destroyed my own family," he said in a low voice, staring blindly through the windows toward the wintry hills. "I don't deserve another."

Laura came slowly toward him, her beautiful face filled with tenderness and love, her eyes glowing with light.

"What happened that night was an accident. It wasn't your fault. But you've buried yourself in the cemetery with them, not allowing yourself to be happy or loved, always punishing yourself—"

"Not punishment. *Justice*," he said in a low voice, feeling as if his heart were being ripped out of his chest. "If I hadn't tried to talk Guilherme out of having a family, if I hadn't tried to talk him out of committing to his wife and baby, they would all be alive. Why should I enjoy the life I denied my own brother?"

"Your brother is gone. He forgave you long ago. But we're still here, and we need you," she said. She took a deep breath and lifted her tearstained eyes to his. "Please, Gabriel. I love you. Love me back."

His jaw hardened as he stared down at her.

"Don't use the word *love*," he said harshly. "You lied to me. And you turned me into a liar, as well. I said I would never have a wife. Now look at me." Rage burned inside him as he gazed down at his tuxedo. He ripped the tiny rose boutonniere out of his lapel. "Just look at me!"

She went pale beneath her wedding veil, and the beautiful light in her eyes dimmed. "I'm sorry. It's why I didn't tell you I was pregnant. I knew it wasn't what you wanted, that you'd feel trapped by duty to a child. But—" she took a deep breath "—I couldn't marry you. Not without telling you the truth."

"Thank you," he said coldly, pacing the carpet. He stopped. His body felt chilled, as frozen as a New Hampshire winter. Maybe because of the icy dagger she'd just plunged through his back. "Thank you, Laura, for being so trustworthy and decent."

She flinched. Her eyes were red, her beautiful face swollen with tears. "I understand if you want to back out."

"Back out?"

"Of the wedding," she whispered.

He saw the way her petite, curvaceous body was shivering in her wedding dress. He forced himself not to care. What difference did her feelings make to him anymore? His lips curved as he looked at her scornfully. "I'm more determined to marry you now than ever."

She licked her lips and he saw a tremulous hope in her blue eyes. "Because you love Robby?"

He stared at her. "Because he's my duty."

Tears fell unchecked down her face as she clutched her arms together over her exquisite beaded gown. "Can't you even try to love him?"

"The deal stands," he said coldly. "I will still marry you. I will still take care of your son."

"*Our* son!"

For a long time, she stood, staring at him. Her lips parted to speak, and his cell phone rang in his pocket. Emotionlessly, he turned away from her. "Santos."

"I'm afraid I have to back out of our deal, Santos."

Gabriel recognized the voice at once. Felipe Oliveira. His eyes widened in shock as he stepped away from Laura. "Is that some kind of joke, Oliveira?" he growled into the phone. "Some attempt to drive up the price? Because you've already signed the papers."

"Just the preliminary papers. And Théo St. Raphaël has just offered me three million euros more for Açoazul than you. Best of all, he's throwing in his prize vineyard to sweeten the offer." The man gave a laugh. "I've always wanted to make my own champagne, and his vineyard is legendary."

"You can't do that!" Gabriel exploded. "We signed a contract!"

"A preliminary contract," the man pointed out gleefully. "All I need pay for reneging on the terms is a small penalty—a million American dollars. Which St. Raphaël has also offered to cover."

Gabriel cursed aloud. "But why? Why betray me like this, Oliveira, after we helped you see Adriana's true nature?"

The older man cackled. "Now that I'm rid of her, I suddenly find I'm interested in business again. Sorry, Santos." He paused, then said with greater seriousness, "Sorry, young man. But you'll live to fight another day."

"I'll leave within the hour," Gabriel said desperately. "I can be in Rio by tonight, and we can talk further—"

But Oliveira had hung up. Gabriel stared for a long moment at the phone in his hand. He felt dizzy with the vertigo of how much he'd lost in the last two minutes.

He'd lost...*everything*.

He whirled on Laura, who was staring up at him with big eyes. "Let's get the wedding over with," he growled, stomping toward the door. "As soon as it's over, we're leaving for Rio."

Her trembling voice stopped him. "No."

He frowned, looking back at her from the doorway. "No? What do you mean, no?"

She licked her lips, coming closer. Her eyes were luminous in the morning light.

"I could accept you not loving me," she said. "I told myself that my love could be enough for both of us." Her eyes narrowed, glittering like a frozen blue sea. "But I can't accept you not loving Robby. He can't just be your *duty*."

"I just found out he's my son," he retorted, "after a year of your lies. What do you expect from me? That I declare my love and fall at your feet?"

She looked at him, and her lips trembled in a smile. "That would be nice."

He shook his head angrily. "Accept what I can give you. And be grateful!"

"Grateful?" she cried. With an intake of breath, she held up the hem of her wedding dress and marched right up to him. Her beautiful face was outraged. "I waited five years for you to love me," she said. "I dreamed of you for the whole last year! All I wanted was for you to marry me…"

"And I will," he said impatiently. "Come on."

"But I was wrong." She lifted her chin. "Love is what matters. Without love, this marriage is nothing but a lie." She shook her head fiercely. "And I won't let Robby settle for that. I won't let him grow up wondering why his father doesn't love him, why his parents' marriage is so strained, what he's done wrong!"

Gabriel stared at her. It suddenly seemed as if an ocean divided them. He reached out his hand. "Laura…"

She slapped it away. "No!"

He glared at her. "I don't have time for this."

"So go."

He briefly considered the idea of dragging her forcibly down the aisle. But she was surrounded by farmers and ranchers and strong neighbors with guns, while to their eyes he was just some stranger who was taking her and Robby away.

But he wasn't just a stranger. He was Robby's father.

Gabriel sucked in a deep breath, overwhelmed by the flood of emotion in his heart. He couldn't give in to the feeling. *Couldn't…*

Grabbing her wrist, he started to pull her towards the door. "We will marry, then leave for Rio—"

She ripped her arm out of his grasp. "I'm not going."

"You're being ridiculous. Don't you understand? Oliveira is backing out of the contract! If I don't change his mind, I'll lose everything!"

"I understand," she said softly. "You should go."

"I'm not leaving the country without you and our son."

"I'm not marrying you. Not like this."

"You're being selfish!"

Laura swallowed, her cheeks pink. He could see he'd hurt her with the accusation. But she wasn't going to let him manipulate her so easily. "I'll never try to stop you from seeing Robby whenever you want. Our lawyers can work out some arrangement. But I won't marry you, and I won't leave the people who love us for someone who doesn't."

"So that's it?" he said incredulously. "You're giving me an ultimatum?"

"Yes." Her eyes filled with tears as she gave him a trembling smile. "I guess I am."

Gabriel swallowed against the sudden lump in his throat. He couldn't force her to marry him. He couldn't seduce or charm or bully her into it. When did she get so steady? When did she get so strong?

Raking his hair back, he looked at her. "Laura," he said slowly. He exhaled a deep breath. "I can't do it. What you're asking. I wish I could, but I can't. I can't... love you."

Pain flashed across her face, raw and sharp. Then she straightened her shoulders in her wedding gown.

Reaching up, she pulled the vintage lace veil off her elegant blonde chignon. Her blue eyes were stricken but steady.

"Then I'm sorry," she said quietly. "But if you can't love us...you can't have us."

CHAPTER FIFTEEN

GABRIEL had to hurry. Every second he wasted with Laura was like a grain of sand falling through a fatal hourglass. He had to leave at once.

And yet he couldn't.

Leaving her felt like a death. He took a deep, shuddering breath. "This isn't over," he said hoarsely. "I'll be back after I close the deal in Rio."

"Of course." Laura's shoulders straightened, even as her lower lip trembled. "I will never stop you from seeing Robby. I hope…I hope you'll see him often. He needs his father."

Gabriel heard the music start to play downstairs and thought of the guests surrounded by white roses and candlelight, waiting for the wedding ceremony to begin. He clenched his hands, feeling that same strange spinning, sinking feeling in the region of his chest.

"Remember," he said tersely, looking at her. "This was your choice. I wanted to marry you."

She swallowed as tears streamed unchecked down her pale cheeks. "I'll never forget that."

No, he thought suddenly. It couldn't end like this. Not like this!

With a sudden, ragged breath, he seized her in his

arms. Pressing his lips against hers, he kissed her with every ounce of passion and persuasion he possessed. He never wanted to let her go.

She was the one to pull away. He saw tears falling down her cheeks as she stepped back, out of his reach. "Goodbye."

He sucked in his breath. But there was nothing he could do. Nothing to be done. "I'll be back," he said heavily. "In a few days."

She gave him a wan smile. "Robby will be glad whenever you choose to visit."

He left the room. Went out the door. Walked past her mother, who was waiting at the bottom of the stairs. He went outside into the cold winter air to the limo waiting outside. Gabriel felt a sudden pain in his chest when he saw that someone—one of Laura's friends, perhaps—had written Just Married across the back window in white shaving cream, and attached aluminum cans to the back bumper to drag noisily down the road.

His hands clenched as he flung himself heavily into the backseat of the limo. Carlos, who'd apparently been texting someone as he waited in the driver's seat, jumped.

"Mr. Gabriel! What are you doing, so soon...? And where is Mrs. Laura?"

"She's not coming," he replied tightly. His throat hurt. "And she's not *Mrs.*"

"But *senhor...* What happened?"

Gabriel looked bleakly out the window, at the beautiful fields of endless white. "Just go."

Laura stood by the closed door until the sound of Gabriel's footsteps faded away.

Sagging into a chair, she covered her face with her hands. She'd been happy to be a bride, a single mother no longer—so pleased to finally leave the scandal behind her. She thought of her baby, downstairs now with one of her cousins, and a sob came from her lips.

But she'd had no other honorable choice. If she'd been willing to accept a life without love forever, what would that have done to her soul? What would that have taught her son?

She'd done the right thing. So why did she feel so awful?

She heard the door squeak open and looked up with an intake of breath.

Her three sisters, all dressed in elegant bridesmaid gowns, stood in the open door with their mother. "Why did Gabriel storm off like that?" Ruth asked tremulously. Then she saw Laura's tearful face. "Oh, sweetheart!"

A moment later, Laura was crying in their arms as they hugged her, and her scowling little sister Hattie was cursing and offering to go punch Gabriel in the face. That made Laura laugh, but the laughter turned to a sob. Wiping her eyes, she looked up at them.

"What do I do now?" she whispered.

Her mother searched her gaze. "The wedding is off? Is it for sure?"

Laura nodded with a lump in her throat. "He said he didn't love me, that he would never love me. Or Robby, either."

Her mother and sisters stared at her with a unified intake of breath. Then Ruth shook herself briskly.

"Well then. I'll go downstairs, tell everyone to head home."

Laura folded her arms, her belly sick with dread and

grief. "It'll cause such a scandal," she whispered. She stared at the patterns on the carpet as the full horror built inside her. "Just when all the rumors were coming to an end."

"Weddings get canceled all the time," Becky said staunchly. "There's nothing scandalous about it."

"Zero scandal," Hattie agreed quickly, pushing up her glasses. "It's totally uninteresting."

"Not even as interesting as when Mrs. Higgins's cow knocked over the Tast-E Burger truck," Margaret added.

"It'll be all right, sweetheart," her mother said, softly stroking Laura's hair as she sat beside her. "Just stay here. I'll handle everything."

It was very tempting. But with a deep breath, Laura shook her head.

"I'll ask your uncle, then," Ruth said quickly. "He's waiting to walk you down the aisle. He can simply make a little announcement and—"

"No," Laura choked out. "I did this," she whispered, rising to her feet. "I'll end it."

Climbing onto his private jet at the airport five miles away, Gabriel nearly bit the stewardess's head off when she offered him champagne. As she scurried off to the back cabin, he grabbed the entire bottle of Scotch from the galley and gulped straight from the bottle, desperate to feel the burn. But when he pulled the bottle from his lips, he realized the pain in his chest had only gotten worse.

It was his heart. His heart hurt.

"Ready, sir?" the pilot said over the intercom.

"Ready," Gabriel growled. Falling into the white

leather seat, he took another gulp of the bottle and stared out his window.

He felt as if he were leaving part of himself behind. His wife. His child.

Robby. His *son*. Gabriel still couldn't believe it.

He didn't want to go.

I have to, he told himself angrily. *I have no choice.* He remembered how his parents had taken Gabriel and Guilherme to visit the factories of Açoazul Steel. It had been truly a family company. His father had been president, his mother vice president of marketing. "Someday, boys," his father had said, "this company will be yours. Your legacy."

The jet's engine started. Closing his eyes, Gabriel leaned his head into his hands. He still remembered the sound of his father's laugh, the tender smile in his mother's eyes. They'd been so proud of their strong, handsome, smart sons. He could still hear his brother saying, at twenty years old, "I never intended to have a family so soon, but now I can't imagine it any other way. I'm happy, Gabriel. I am."

Grief gripped Gabriel's chest. Why hadn't he believed him? Why had he been so sure that *he* was right, and his brother wrong?

"Robby's not an accident. He's not a mistake."

He suddenly saw Laura's beautiful face as she'd stood in the morning light, wearing a wedding gown as luminescent as New England snow.

"Then what is he?"

She'd looked up at him. *"A miracle."*

He blinked, staring at the porthole window as the jet's roar increased. Last year, he'd let Laura go because he'd wanted her to find a man who could love her. He'd wanted her to be happy. He'd been so angry when he'd thought she'd thrown her dreams aside and fallen into bed with a man who didn't deserve her.

But she'd loved Gabriel himself all this time. She'd loved him without hope. She'd taken care of their baby all on her own, while carrying such a heavy weight on her shoulders at home. She'd assumed from the start that she and Robby were on their own.

Gabriel was the man who didn't deserve her.

He'd tried to offer her money. His name. But that wasn't what Laura wanted. She wanted his love. She wanted…a family.

Gabriel set down the bottle. His body felt hot and cold at once.

The jet lurched forward, taxiing toward the runway.

He gripped the armrests. He had to go back to Rio, or he'd lose his family's company forever. Açoazul SA would be dismantled. He would lose his last link to his family.

The jet started to go faster down the runway, and he sucked in his breath.

His family.

He'd told himself for twenty years that he didn't deserve another family. And yet, like a miracle, he had one.

He had a family. Right here and now. And he was choosing to leave them.

He sat up straight in his chair. His breathing came hard and fast. What about his family's legacy?

Legacy.

He had a sudden flashback of a million small memories of warmth and joy and home. Visiting the steel factory. Sitting on his father's shoulders at *Carnaval*, watching the parades go by. Vacations in Bahia. Dinner together each night. A life of love and tenderness. Until he'd made one dreadful mistake.

"Your brother would forgive you. Your family loved you," he heard Laura's warm, loving voice say. *"They would know your heart."*

The jet hit full throttle, racing down the runway faster and faster, preparing for takeoff.

And Gabriel suddenly realized he was about to make the worst mistake of his life. And this time it wouldn't be an accident, a car spun out of control on a rainy road by a nineteen-year-old boy. This time it would be a stupid, cowardly decision made by a full-grown man.

He hadn't wanted another family.

But he had one.

Gabriel saw the white fields fly past the window. The jet started to rise, lifting off from the ground, and he leapt to his feet with a scream.

"Stop!"

CHAPTER SIXTEEN

LAURA hesitated outside the closed doors of the huge, flower-strewn library, frightened out of her mind.

She could hear the rumble on the other side of door, the mutters and whispers. The wedding had been scheduled to start thirty minutes ago, and everyone was obviously starting to assume the worst.

But there was no way around it. She had to get through it. With a deep breath, she pushed the doors open.

The enormous two-story library had been modeled after an old English abbey with walls of gray stone. It was now festooned with white roses and candles, with hundreds of chairs set up to create an aisle down the middle.

At the sight of the bride standing at the end of the aisle, musicians hastily began to play "Jesu, Joy of Man's Desiring" on guitars and violins. Laura stopped the music with a chopping gesture across her neck.

Silence fell. She could have heard a pin drop as three hundred pairs of eyes turned to her.

She trembled, passing a hand over her eyes. Then she heard her baby cry out halfway down the aisle. Going swiftly to her cousin Sandy, who held him in her lap,

Laura took her son in her arms. Robby looked dapper in a little baby tuxedo just like his father's, complete with rose boutonniere. She smiled through her tears. For an instant, she just held her baby in her arms, feeling his soft skin and breathing his sweet smell.

Then, squaring her shoulders, she slowly turned to face her family and friends.

"Thank you all for coming," she said loudly, then faltered. "But I'm afraid… Afraid that…"

"What?" her great-aunt Gertrude demanded loudly from the back. "Talk louder!"

Laura's knees grew weak. Did she really have to announce to all her friends and relatives that the only man she'd ever loved had just left her at the altar? How had she ever thought this was a good idea?

"Did he leave?" one of her hotheaded cousins demanded, rising to his feet in the front row. "Did that man desert you?"

"No," she cried, holding up her hand. Even now, she couldn't bear for them to think badly of Gabriel. He'd always been honest with her from the beginning. She was the one who'd arrogantly tried to change him, who'd thought that if she loved him enough, he might love her back. She was the one who'd thought if he knew Robby was his son, he might change, and love the child he'd never wanted. "You don't understand," she whispered. "I told him to go. I made him leave—"

"You couldn't," a husky voice said behind her. "Though you tried."

With a gasp, she whirled around.

Gabriel stood in the double doorway, dark and dashing in his tuxedo. And most incredible of all, he was smiling at her, smiling with his whole face. Even his black eyes held endless colors of warmth and love.

"What are you doing here?" she murmured. "I thought you were gone."

He started walking toward her.

"I couldn't go," he said. "Not without telling you something."

"What?"

He stopped, halfway down the aisle.

"I love you," he said simply.

She swayed on her feet. She was dreaming. She had to be dreaming.

He caught her before she could fall. "I love you," he murmured with a smile, and he looked down at the baby between them. "And I love my son."

There was an audible gasp. Gabriel looked around him fiercely.

"Yes," he said sharply. "Robby is my child. Laura was afraid to tell me about Robby, afraid I wouldn't be able to measure up to be the man—the father—he needed." Gabriel looked back at her. "But I will. I will spend the rest of my life proving I can be the man you deserve."

A sob escaped Laura's lips. Reaching up, she put her hand to his cheek, looking up at him. "You love me?"

He pressed his hand over hers. She saw tears in his eyes. "Yes."

She blinked, sucking in her breath. "But what about the deal in Rio?"

He looked down at her. "I don't care about it. Let the Frenchman have it."

She gasped, shaking her head desperately. "But you've tried to get the company back all these years.

It's all you wanted. All you've dreamed about day and night!"

"Because I thought it was my family's legacy." He reached down to cup her cheek. A smile curved his sensual lips. "But it wasn't."

"It wasn't?" she whispered.

"My family loved me, and I loved them," he said. "No accident can ever change that. I will honor their memory for the rest of my life. I will honor them by living as best as I can until the day I die." He took her hand tightly in his own, looking down at her. "And today, I will start the rest of my life loving you."

"I love you…." she choked out. "So much." She swallowed, then shook her head. "But we can get married later. We should leave for Rio at once. I don't want you to lose your company, your family's legacy—"

"I haven't lost it. I've found it at last. My family's legacy is love," he said. "My family's legacy—" he lifted his shining eyes to her face "—is you."

The autumn leaves of New Hampshire were falling in a million shades of red, gold and green against the cold blue sky when Gabriel and Laura returned home from New York.

Laura sighed with pleasure as their SUV rounded the bend in the road and she caught her first glimpse of the old Olmstead mansion on the hill. It was the Santos house now. The day after their wedding, Gabriel had bought it for her as a present.

"It's too big," she'd protested. "We can't possibly fill all those rooms!"

He'd given her a sly, wicked smile. "We can try."

And they had certainly done their best. In fact, they'd

done excellent work on that front. Laura blushed. Since they'd moved into the house in March, they'd made love in all forty rooms, and also in the secret nooks of the large sprawling garden. They'd shared many warm evenings on the banks of their private lake, swimming and talking and watching the stars twinkle in the lazy summer night. One big pond, she thought, for what was sure to be one big family. She smiled. She would someday teach her own children to swim there, as her father had taught her.

She'd been in New York City with Gabriel for only a single night, but she was already glad to be back home. She hadn't known it was possible for a man to fuss so much over his wife.

As the SUV stopped, she started to open the door, but Gabriel instantly gave her a hard glare. "Wait."

Laura sat back against her seat with a sigh.

He raced around the SUV and opened her door. Gabriel held out his hand, and his dark eyes softened as he looked down at her. She placed her hand in his, and felt the same shiver of love and longing that she had the very first time she'd touched his hand, in the days when she was only his secretary.

After helping her from the SUV—it wasn't as easy as it used to be—he closed the door behind her. He followed her constantly, anxiously, always concerned about her safety and comfort. It might have been irritating, if it wasn't so adorable.

"I can close my own door, you know," she observed.

He stroked her cheek, looking down at her fiercely. "I have a lot to make up for. I want to take care of you."

Glancing at the sweeping steps that led to the front

door, she lifted her eyebrow wickedly. "Want to carry me up the stairs?"

Grabbing her lapel, he pulled her against his dark wool coat. "Absolutely," he whispered, nuzzling her hair. He gave her a sensual smile. "Especially since the next flight of stairs leads straight to our bedroom."

Lowering his head to hers, he kissed her.

His lips were hot and soft against her own, and a contented sigh came from the back of Laura's throat. As he held her, a cold wind blew in from the north around them, scattering the fallen leaves and whispering of the deep frost that would soon come to the great north woods. But Laura felt warm down to her toes.

"You're a furnace," Gabriel said with a laugh as he pulled away. Then he smiled. "I think the baby is glad to be home."

"So am I," she said, then laughed. "For one thing, you won't be trying to throw yourself in front of trucks, trying to protect me on the crosswalk."

"Fifth Avenue is insane," he muttered.

"Yeah, all those crazed tourists and limo drivers," she teased. Turning, she started to walk toward the front steps. She was excited to see Robby, after his first overnight apart from them. He'd had two loving babysitters fighting over him, Grandma Ruth and nanny Maria. "Thanks for a lovely night. It was nice."

"Yeah." Lifting a dark eyebrow, he grinned wickedly, clearly remembering their time alone together in front of the fire last night.

She elbowed him in the ribs. "I meant with the girls."

"Right." He cleared his throat. "Your sisters seem to

be settling well. It's the first time I've seen them since they started college."

"You're not in New York very much these days," she teased.

"I have better things to do than work," he growled. "Like make love to my beautiful wife." Grabbing her again by the lapels of her warm camel-colored coat, he kissed her again, long and hard, before she pulled away.

"You are insatiable!"

He gave a dark, wicked grin. "I know."

A flash of heat went through her. After they'd married that blustery day in early March, he'd made love to her without protection for the first time. The sensation was so new to him that they hadn't left the bed for a full week after their wedding. In some ways, Laura thought, she'd been his first, just as he'd been hers. And they'd gotten pregnant on their honeymoon.

Laura put a hand on her jutting belly. Their baby, a little girl, was due in just a few weeks.

"Thanks for moving up here," she whispered. "I am so happy to be close to my family."

His eyes met hers. "So am I. And I have you to thank for that."

Maybe it was pregnancy hormones, but Laura still felt choked up every time she thought of the three girls now living in the same city, all going to college. Two of them were her sisters. Brainy Hattie had transferred to Columbia University, and eighteen-year-old Margaret had opted for NYU.

But the greatest miracle of all—Gabriel's young niece, Lola, was now at Barnard.

Last spring, shortly after Laura had found out she was

pregnant, she had tracked down Izadora, Lola's mother, and invited their family to come up for a weekend visit to New Hampshire in the private jet. To Gabriel's shock, they'd accepted.

After twenty years, Gabriel had finally made peace with Izadora and met her American husband, a restaurant owner in Miami. Gabriel had hugged his young niece for the first time since she was a baby. And he'd convinced Izadora to allow him to create a trust fund for Lola. "It's what Guilherme would have wanted," he'd said gravely, and put like that, how could Izadora refuse? Lola was now at Barnard College studying art.

"All this family around us." Wiping away her tears with a laugh, Laura shook her head and teased, "And you paying for three students at college already. Robby will probably want med school. And now this little one. Are you sure you're ready for more?"

Gabriel put his hands on her swelling belly beneath her long T-shirt. At nearly nine months along, she could no longer button her wool coat. Half the time she was too hot to wear it, anyway. "Just a few weeks now," he whispered. Dropping to one knee, he impulsively kissed her belly.

"Gabriel!" she gasped with a laugh, glancing up at the big windows of the house.

Her husband looked up at her. His eyes glowed with tenderness and love. "I'll be here this time, *querida*," he said in a low voice. "Every step of the way."

"I know," she said, her throat choking with tears of joy. Tugging him to his feet, she wrapped her arms around his neck and kissed him. And as the cold wind blew, carrying dry leaves down their long driveway, she felt only warmth and love in the fire of their embrace.

And Laura knew two things.

The fire between them would always last.

And second, that they had an excellent chance of filling all forty rooms.

THE MAN SHE COULD NEVER FORGET

MEREDITH WEBBER

To Linda and Alison and the writing friends we share and love—long may Maytone survive!

CHAPTER ONE

As THE SMALL plane circled above the island, the hard lumps of pain and worry that had been lodged in Caroline Lockhart's chest for the past months dissolved in the delight of seeing her home.

From the air, the island looked like a precious jewel set in an emerald-green sea. The white coral sand of the beaches at the northern end gleamed like a ribbon tying a very special parcel, the lush tropical forest providing the green wrapping paper.

Coming in from the west, they passed over the red cliffs that lit up so brilliantly at sunset that early sailors had called the island Wildfire.

As they flew closer, she could pick out the buildings.

The easiest to find was the palatial Lockhart mansion, built by her great-grandfather on a plateau on the southern tip of the island after he'd bought it from the M'Langi people who had found it too rough to settle.

Lockhart House—her home for so many years—the only real home she'd known as a child.

The house sat at the very highest point on the plateau, with views out over the sea, ocean waves breaking against the encircling reef, and beyond them the dots of other islands, big and small, settled and uninhabited, that, with Wildfire, made up the M'Langi group.

Immediately below the house and almost hidden by the thick rainforest surrounding it was the lagoon—its colour dependent on the sky above, so today it was a deep, dark blue.

Grandma's lagoon.

In truth it was a crater lake from the days of volcanic action in the area, but Grandma had loved her lagoon and had refused to call it anything else.

Below the house and lagoon was the hospital her father, Max Lockhart, had given his life to building, a memorial to his dead wife—Caroline's mother.

Around the main hospital building its cluster of staff villas crowded like chickens around a mother hen. And below that again lay the airstrip.

Farther north, where the plateau flattened as it reached the sea, sat the research station with the big laboratory building, the kitchen and recreation hut, small cabins dotted along the beach to accommodate visiting scientists.

The research station catered to any scientists interested in studying health issues unique to this group of isolated islands, and the tropical diseases prevalent here.

The most intensive research had been on the effects of M'Langi tea—made from the bark of a particular tree—and why the islanders who drank this concoction regularly seemed to be less affected by the mosquitos, which carried a unique strain of encephalitis.

As she frowned at what appeared to be changes to the research station, she wondered if anyone was still working there. Keanu's father had been the first to show interest in the tea—

Keanu.

She shook her head as if to dislodge memories of Keanu from her head and tried to think who might be there now. According to her father, a man she knew only as Luke had been working there for a short time but that had been four or five years ago.

Circling back to the southern end of the island, past the little village that had grown up after Opuru Island had been evacuated after a tsunami, she could just pick out the entrance to the gold mine that tunnelled deep beneath the plateau.

The mine had brought wealth not only to her family but to the islanders as well, but the only sign of it was a huge yellow bulldozer, though it, too, was partly hidden beneath a cluster of Norfolk pines and what looked like a tangle of vines.

Weird.

Dropping lower now, the sea was multicoloured, the coral reefs beneath its surface visible like wavy patterns on a fine silk scarf. Images of herself and Keanu snorkelling in those crystal-clear waters, marvelling at the colours of the reef and the tiny fish that lived among the coral, flashed through her mind.

An ache of longing—for her carefree past, her childhood home—filled Caroline's heart, and she had to blink tears from her eyes.

How could she have stayed away so long?

Because Keanu was no longer here?

Or because she'd been afraid he might be…

'Are you okay?' Jill asked, and Caroline turned to her friend—her best friend—who, from seven hundred miles away, had heard the unhappiness in Caroline's voice just a short week ago and had told her she should go home.

Insisted on it, in fact, although Caroline suspected Jill had wanted to show off her new little plane, *and* her ability as a pilot.

'I'm fine, just sorry I've stayed away so long.'

'In recent times it's been because you were worried that

rat Steve would take up with someone else if you disappeared on him for even a week.'

The words startled Caroline out of her sentimental mood.

'Do you really think that? Do you believe I was that much of a doormat to him?'

Jill's silence spoke volumes.

Caroline sighed.

'I suppose he proved he didn't really care about me when he dropped me like a hot cake when the story about the Wildfire gold mine being in trouble appeared in the paper.'

But it was still upsetting—wounding…

Could the man who'd wooed Caroline with flowers, and gifts and words of love, who'd wrapped her in the security of belonging, really be the rat her friends thought him?

Had *she* really been so gullible?

'Maybe he *did* meet someone else,' Caroline answered plaintively. 'Maybe he was telling the truth.'

'That man wouldn't know the truth if it bit him on the butt,' Jill retorted, then fortunately stopped talking.

Caroline wasn't sure if it was because Jill was concentrating on her landing, or if she didn't want to hurt her friend even more.

Although she'd realised later—too late—that Steve *had* been inordinately interested in the mine her family owned…

The little plane bumped onto the tarmac, then rolled along it as Jill braked steadily.

'Strip's in good condition,' she said as she wheeled the craft around and stopped beside the shed that provided welcome to visitors to Wildfire Island.

But the shed needs repainting, Caroline thought, her elation at being home turning to depression because up close it was obvious the place was run-down.

Although the strip had been resurfaced.

Could things have come good?

No, her father had confirmed the mine was in trouble when she'd spoken to him about the article in the paper. Although all his time was spent in Sydney, working as a specialist physician at two hospitals, and helping care for Christopher, her twin, severely oxygen deprived at birth and suffering crippling cerebral palsy, the state of the mine was obviously worrying him.

He had been grey with fatigue from overwork and his fine face had been lined with the signs of continual stress from the hours he put in at work and worry over Christopher's health, yet with the stubborn streak common to all Lockharts he'd refused to even listen when she'd asked if she could help financially.

'Go to the island, it's where you belong,' he'd said gently. 'And remember the best way to get over pain is hard work. The hospital can always do with another nurse, especially now clinical services to the outer islands have expanded and we've had to cut back on hospital staff. Our existing staff go above and beyond for the island and the residents but there's always room for another pair of trained hands.'

Losing himself in work was what he'd done ever since her mother had died—died in his arms and left him with a premature but healthy baby girl and a premature and disabled baby boy to look after.

'Maybe whoever owns that very smart helicopter has an equally smart plane and needed the strip improved.'

Jill's comment brought Caroline out of her brooding thoughts.

'Smart helicopter? Our helicopters have always been run-of-the-mill emergency craft and Dad said we're down to one.'

But as she turned in the direction of Jill's pointing finger, she saw her friend was right. At the far end of the strip was a light-as-air little helicopter—a brilliant dragonfly of a helicopter—painted shiny dark blue with the sun picking out flashes of gold on the side.

'Definitely not ours,' she told Jill.

'Maybe there's a mystery millionaire your shady uncle Ian has conned into investing in the place.'

'From all I hear, it would take a billionaire,' Caroline muttered gloomily.

She'd undone her seat harness while they were talking and now opened the door of the little plane.

'At least come up to the house and have a cup of tea,' she said to Jill.

Jill shook her head firmly.

'I've got my thermos of coffee and sandwiches—like a good Girl Scout, always prepared. I'll just refuel and be off. It's only a four-hour flight. Best I get home to the family.'

Caroline retrieved her luggage—one small case packed with the only lightweight, casual summer clothes she owned. Her life in Sydney had been more designer wear—Steve had always wanted her to look good.

And I went along with it?

She felt her cheeks heat with shame as yet another of Steve's dominating characteristics came to mind.

Yes, she'd gone along with it and many other 'its', often pulling double shifts on weeknights to be free to go 'somewhere special' with him over the weekend.

The fact that the 'something special' usually turned out to be yet another cocktail party with people she either didn't know or, if she had known them, didn't particularly care for only made it worse.

But she'd loved him—or loved that he loved her…

Jill efficiently pumped fuel into the plane's tank, wiped her hands on a handy rag, and turned to her friend.

'You take care, okay? And keep in touch. I want phone calls and emails, none of that social media stuff where everyone can read what you're doing. I want the "not for public consumption" stuff.'

She reached out and gathered Caroline in a warm, tight hug.

'You'll be okay,' she said, and although the words were firmly spoken, Caroline heard a hint of doubt in them.

Dear Jilly, the first friend she'd made at boarding school so many years ago, now back in the cattle country of Western Queensland where she'd grown up, married to a fellow cattleman, raising her own family and top-quality beasts.

Caroline returned the hug, watched as Jill climbed back into the plane and began to taxi up the runway. She waved to the departing plane before turning to look around her.

Yes, the shed was a little run-down and the gardens weren't looking their best, but the peace that filled her heart told her she'd done the right thing.

She was home.

Bending to lift her suitcase, she was struck that something was missing. Okay, so the place wasn't quite up to speed, but where was Harold, who usually greeted every plane?

Harold, who'd told her and Keanu all the legends of the islands and given them boiled lollies so big they'd filled their mouths.

Her and Keanu…

Keanu…

She straightened her shoulders and breathed in the scented tropical air. That had been then and this was now.

Time to put the past—all the past—behind her, take control of her life and move on, as so many of her friends had advised.

And moving on obviously meant carrying her own suitcase up the track to the big house. Not that she minded, but it was strange that no one had met the plane, if only out of curiosity.

Had no one seen it come in?

Did no one care any more?

Or was Harold gone?

How old had he been?

She didn't like the tightening in her gut at the thought that someone who had been so much part of her life might have died while she'd been away...

Impossible.

Although all adults seemed old to children, she doubted Harold had been more than forty when she'd left—

The blast of a horn sent the past skittering from her mind, and she turned to see a little motorised cart—the island's main land transport—racing towards her from the direction of the research station.

'Are you the doctor?' the man driving it yelled.

'No, but I'm a nurse. Can I help?'

The driver pulled up beside her and gestured towards his passenger.

'We phoned the hospital. Someone said the doctor would come to meet us on the way. My mate was fine at first but now he's passed out, well, you can see...'

He gestured towards the man slumped in the back of the little dark blue vehicle. He had no visible injury—until she looked down and saw his foot.

Clad only in a rubber flip-flop, the foot had a nail punched right through beneath the small toe, and apparently into a piece of wood below his inadequate footwear.

Caroline slid in beside the man and put a hand on his chest. He was breathing, and his pulse— Yes, a bit fast but obviously it had been a very painful wound.

'I think we should get him up to the hospital as quickly as possible,' she said, as a figure appeared on the track they would take.

A figure she knew, although the intervening years had stretched him from an adolescent to a man—and for all her heart was bumping erratically in her chest, she certainly didn't know the man.

Caroline slid out of the cart and took the spare seat in front while Keanu, without more than a startled glance and a puzzled frown in her direction, took over in the back, fitting an oxygen mask to the man's face and adjusting the flow on the small tank he'd carried with him.

'Give me a minute to get some painkiller into him.'

Prosaic words but the deep, rich voice reverberated through Caroline's body—a man's voice, not a boy's...

This was Keanu?

Keanu was here?

She didn't know whether to hug him or hit him, but with witnesses around she could do neither. What she really wanted was to turn around and have another look at him, but the image of that first glimpse was burned into her brain.

Keanu the man.

Now grown into his burnished, almond-coloured skin, his grey eyes—his mother's eyes—strikingly pale beneath dark brows and hair.

Straight nose, tempting mouth, sculpted shoulders, abs visible beneath a tightly fitting polo shirt.

He was stunning.

More than that, he projected a kind of sexuality that would have every female within a hundred yards going weak at the knees just looking at him.

'Come back for a break from Sydney society?'

The cold wash of words obviously directed at her fixed the trembling knee thing, while the sarcasm behind them replaced it with anger.

She turned, chin tilted, refusing to reveal the hurt his words had caused.

'I'm a nurse, and I've come back to work, but I *am* surprised to see you here after the way you cut your connection to the islands so many years ago.'

Fortunately, as Caroline had just realised their driver was listening to this icy conversation with interest, they pulled up at the front of the hospital.

The patient was awake, obviously benefiting from the oxygen and the painkilling injection.

Keanu asked the driver to lend a hand, and the two of them eased the man out of the vehicle.

'Sling your arms around our shoulders and we'll help you in,' Keanu said, and Caroline guessed he was concentrating on the patient so he wouldn't have to look at her.

Or even acknowledge her presence?

What had happened?

What had she done?

Steely determination to not be hurt by him—or any man—ever again made her shut the door firmly on the past. Whatever had happened had been a long time ago, and she was a different person, had moved on, and was moving on again...

But walking behind Keanu, she couldn't *not* be aware of his presence. This man who'd been a boy she'd known so well was really something. Broad shoulders sloping down to narrow hips, but a firm butt and calf muscles that suggested not a workout in gym but a lot of outdoors exercise—he'd always loved running, said he felt free...

She was looking at his butt?

Best she get away, and fast.

But once they had the man on the deck in front of the hospital, Keanu turned back towards her.

'Well, if you're a nurse, don't just stand there. Come in and be useful. Hettie and Sam are on a clinic run to the outer islands and there's only an aide and myself on duty.'

He stood above her—loomed really—the disdain in his voice visible on his features.

And something broke inside her.

Was this really Keanu, her childhood friend and companion? Keanu, who had been gentle and kind, and had always taken care of her when she'd felt lost and alone?

Back then, his mother's mantra to him had always been 'Take care of Caroline', and Keanu, two years older, always had.

Which was probably why his disappearance from her life had hurt so deeply that for a while she'd doubted she'd get over it.

Head bent to hide whatever hurt might be showing on her face, she took the steps in one stride and followed the three men into the small but well-set-up room that she knew from the hospital plans doubled as Emergency and Outpatients.

Having helped lift the patient onto an examination table, the driver muttered something about getting back to work, and hurried through the door.

Which left her and Keanu...

Keanu, who was managing to ignore her completely while her body churned with conflicting emotions.

'Nail gun?' Keanu asked the patient as he examined the foot.

The patient nodded.

'Never heard of steel-capped workboots?' Keanu continued. 'I thought they were the only legal footwear on a building job.'

'Out here?' the man scoffed. 'Who's going to check?'

'Just hold his leg up for me, grasp the calf.'

An order to the nurse, no doubt, but even as he gave it Keanu didn't glance her way.

'No "please"?' Caroline said sweetly as she lifted the man's lower leg so Keanu could see just how far through the wood the nail protruded.

She must have struck a nerve with her words, for Keanu

looked up at her, his face unreadable, although she caught the confusion in his eyes.

So she wasn't the only one feeling this was beyond bizarre.

'Okay, let it down,' he said, the words another order.

Maybe she'd been wrong about the confusion.

Only then he added, 'Please,' and suddenly he was her old Keanu again, teasing her, almost smiling.

And the confusion *that* caused made her wish Jill hadn't taken off again so quickly. She had come here for peace and quiet, to heal after the humiliation of realising the man she'd thought had loved her had only been interested in her family money.

What was left of it.

'Here's a key.'

Keanu's fingers touched hers, and electricity jolted through her bones, shocking her in more ways than one. 'You'll find phials of local anaesthetic in the cupboard marked B, second shelf. Bring two—no, he's a big guy, maybe three—and you'll see syringes in there as well. Antiseptic, dressings and swabs are in the cupboard next to that one—it's not locked. Get whatever you think we'll need. I'm off to find a saw.'

The patient gave a shriek of protest but Keanu was already out of the room.

Slipping automatically into nurse mode, Caroline smiled as she unlocked the cupboard and found all she needed.

'He's not going to cut off your foot,' she reassured the man as she set up a tray on a trolley and rolled it over to the examination table. 'Hospitals have all manners of saws. We use diamond-tipped ones to cut through plaster when it has to come off, and we use adapted electric saws and drills in knee and hip replacement, though not here, of course. I'd say he's going to numb your leg from the calf down, then cut through the nail between your flip-flop and the wood. It's easier to pull a nail out of rubber and flesh than it is out of wood.'

Their patient didn't seem all that reassured, but Caroline, who'd found where the paperwork was kept, distracted him with questions about his name, age, address, any medication he was on, and, because she couldn't resist it, what he was doing on the island.

'Doing up the little places down on the flat,' was the reply, which came as Keanu returned with a small battery-powered saw and a portable X-ray machine.

'The research station,' he said, before Caroline could ask the patient what little places.

'They're doing up the research station when there's not enough money to keep the hospital running properly?'

The indignation in her voice must have been mirrored on her face, for Keanu said a curt, 'Later,' and turned his full attention to his patient.

After numbing the lower leg—Caroline being careful not to let her fingers touch Keanu's as she handed him syringes and phials—he explained to the patient what he intended doing.

'Nurse already told me that,' the man replied. 'Just get on with it.'

Asking Caroline to hold the wood steady, Keanu eased it as far as it would go from the flip-flop then bent closer to see what he was doing, so his head, the back of it, blocked Caroline's view. Not that she'd have seen much of the work, her eyes focussed on the little scar that ran along his hair-line, the result of a long-ago exercise on her part to shave off all his hair with her grandfather's cut-throat razor.

Fortunately he must have been able to cut straight through the little bar of the nail, for he straightened before she could be further lost in memories.

Caroline dropped the wood into a trash bin and returned to find Keanu setting up a portable X-ray machine.

'We need to know if the nail's gone through bone,' he explained, helping her get back into nurse mode. 'And the picture should tell us if it's in a position that would have caused tendon damage.'

'Why does that make a difference?' Now he was pain-free—if only temporarily—the patient was becoming impatient.

'It makes the difference between pulling it out and cutting it out.'

'No cutting, just yank the damn thing out,' the patient said, but Keanu ignored him, going quietly on with the job of setting up the head of the unit above the man's foot.

Intrigued by the procedure—and definitely in nurse mode—Caroline had to ask.

'I thought the hospital had a designated radiography room,' she said, remembering protocols at the hospital where she'd worked that suggested wherever possible X-rays be carried out in that area, although the portables had many uses.

Keanu glanced up at her, his face once again unreadable.

'There is but I doubt you and I could lift him onto the table and with his leg already numb he's likely to fall if he tries to help us.'

Which puts me neatly back in my place, Caroline thought.

'Move back!'

Ignoring the peremptory tone, she stepped the obligatory two metres back from the head of the machine, watched Keanu don a lead apron—so protocols *were* observed here—and take shots from several angles.

That done, he wheeled the machine to the corner of the room, hung his apron over a convenient chair and checked the results on a computer screen.

'Come and look at this. What do you think?'

Assuming he was talking to her, not the immobile patient, she moved over to stand beside him—beside Keanu, who had been the single most important person in the world for her for the first thirteen years of her life. Important because, unlike her father, or even Christopher, he'd always been there for her—her best friend and constant companion.

Until he'd disappeared.

But this Keanu…

It was beyond weird.

Spooky.

And, oh, so painful…

'Well?' he demanded, and she forgot about the way Keanu was affecting her and concentrated on the images.

'By some miracle it's slipped between two metatarsals and though it's probably hit some ligament or tendon, because the bones are intact it shouldn't impact on the movement of the foot too much.'

'And don't look at me like that,' she muttered at him, after he'd shot yet another questioning glance her way. 'I *am* a trained nurse, and have been a shift supervisor in the ER at Canterbury Hospital.'

'I don't know how you found the time,' he said as he headed back to the patient.

She was about to demand what the hell he'd meant by that when she realised this was hardly the time or place to be having an argument with this man she didn't know.

Her friend had been a boy—was that the difference?

It certainly was part of it given the way her body was reacting to the slightest accidental touch…

'Okay, so now I need you to swab all around the nail then hold his foot while I try to yank the nail out. I'd prefer not to have to cut it out.'

Caroline put on new gloves, cleaned the areas above and beneath the foot, changed gloves again and got a firm grasp of the man's foot, ready to put all her weight into the task of holding on if the nail proved resistant.

But, no, it slid out easily, and as the wound was bleeding quite freely now, it was possible the risk of infection had been limited.

'Antibiotics and tetanus injections in the locked cupboard,' Keanu told her as he examined the wound in the patient's foot. 'And bring some saline and a packet of oral antibiotics as well. Everything's labelled as we get a lot of agency nurses coming out here for short stints. I'll use the saline to flush the wound before we dress it.'

He worked with quick, neat movements, cleaning the wound, putting the dressings on—usually, in her experience, a job left to a nurse—before administering the antibiotic and a tetanus shot. He even pulled a sleeve over the foot to keep the dressings in place and keep them relatively clean.

'Now all we have to do is get you back to your accommodation,' Keanu said. 'Keep off the foot for a couple of days and find your workboots before you go back on the job. If you don't have any you can phone the mainland and have some sent out on tomorrow's plane. Nurse Lockhart and I will help you out to a cart and I'll run you back down the hill.'

'I've got workboots,' the man said gruffly. 'And I'll phone my mate to come and get me, thanks. The foreman on the job doesn't like strangers on the site.'

'Strangers on the site? What site? What's happening at the research station, Keanu?'

He touched her on the arm.

'Leave it,' he said quietly, and the touch, more than his words, stopped her questions.

Since when had her body reacted to a casual touch from Keanu's hand?

It was being back on the island…

It was seeing him again…

Remembering the hurt…

Caroline closed her eyes, willing the tumult of emotions in her body to settle. She was here to heal, to find herself again, but she was also here to work.

She cleaned up, dropping soiled swabs into a closed bin marked for that purpose and the needles into a sharps box. Their patient was now sitting on the examination table, chatting to Keanu about, she found as she edged closer, fishing.

Well, it wasn't something she wanted to discuss right now, and as she needed time to sort out her reactions to seeing Keanu again, she slipped away, heading back down the track to the airstrip to collect her suitcase.

She could walk up to the house on the path behind the hospital and so avoid seeing the source of her confusion again. And once she was up at the house—home again— she could sort things out in her head—and possibly in her body—and…

And what?

Make things right between them?

She doubted that could ever happen. He had disappeared without a word, returned her letters unopened.

But now she'd have to work with him. Was she supposed to behave as if the life they'd shared had never happened?

As if his disappearance from it hadn't hurt her so badly she'd thought she'd never recover?

Impossible.

She'd reached the airstrip and grabbed her case by the time she'd thought this far and as further consideration of the problem seemed just that—impossible—she put it from her mind and started up the track, feeling the moisture in the air, trapped by the heavy rainforest on each side, wrap around her like a security blanket.

She was home, that was the main thing.

The track from the strip to the big house led up the hill behind the hospital and staff villas.

Staff villas?

Keanu.

Forget Keanu!

For her sanity's sake, she needed to work—she'd already sat around feeling sorry for herself for far too long as a result of another desertion.

And another nurse would always come in handy on the island even if they couldn't afford to pay her. She had her own place to live and some money Steve hadn't known about tucked away in the bank.

And wasn't this what she and Keanu had always planned to do?

He would become a doctor, she a nurse, and they'd return to Wildfire to run a hospital on the island. As children, they'd shared a picture book with a doctor and a nurse that had led to this childhood dream. Had it seemed more important because they had both lost a parent who possibly could have been saved if medical aid had been closer?

Half-orphans, they'd called themselves…

But as she hadn't existed for Keanu once he and his mother had left the island permanently, seeing him here, *and* seeing him carrying out *his* part of their dream, had completely rattled her.

Trudging up the track, she shook her head in disbelief at his sudden reappearance in her life, especially now when all she wanted to do was throw herself into work as an antidote to the pain of Steve's rejection.

Could she throw herself into work with Keanu around? Even seeing him that one time had memories—images—of their shared childhood flashing through her head.

Helen, his mother, had died not long after leaving the island. Caroline's father had passed on that information many years ago, but he'd offered no explanation the year

Caroline had found out she wouldn't be going to the island for her holidays as Helen and Keanu had left and there'd been no one to care for her.

And despite her grief at Helen's loss, she'd felt such anger against Keanu for not letting her know they were leaving, for not keeping in touch, for not telling her of his mother's death himself, that she'd shut him out of her mind, the hurt too deep to contemplate.

'I'll take that.'

Keanu's voice came from behind her, deep and husky, and sent tremors down her spine, while her fingers, rendered nerveless by his touch, released her hold on the case.

Why *had* he come back?

And why now?

But it was he who asked the question.

'Why did you come back?'

Blunt words but something that sounded like anger throbbed through them—anger that fired her own in response.

'It is my home.'

'*One* of your homes,' he reminded her. 'You have another perfectly comfortable one in Sydney with your father and your brother—your twin. How *is* Christopher?'

She spun towards him, sorry she didn't still have the suitcase to swing at his legs as she turned.

'How dare you ask that question? As if you care about my brother. People who care for others keep in touch. They don't just stop all communication. They don't send back letters unopened. I was twelve, Keanu, and suddenly someone who had been there for me all my life, someone I thought was my friend, was gone.'

Keanu bowed his head in the face of her anger, unable to bear the hurt in her eyes. Oh, he'd been angry at her reappearance, but that had been shock-type anger. He'd returned to Wildfire thinking her safely tucked away in Sydney, enjoying a busy social life.

Then, seeing her appear out of nowhere, so much unresolved anger and bitterness and, yes, regret had churned inside him he'd reacted with anger. But that anger should have been directed at another Lockhart. It was regret at the way he'd treated her—his betrayal of their friendship—that had added fuel to the fire.

Guilt...

And now he knew he'd hurt her again.

He'd learned to read Caro's hurt early. He'd first read it in a three-year-old looking forward to a visit from her daddy, the visit suddenly cancelled because of one thing or another.

Usually Christopher's health, he remembered now.

Throughout their childhood, she'd suffered these disappointments, a trip back to her Sydney home put off indefinitely because Christopher had chicken pox and was infectious. Going back to Sydney at ten when her adored grandmother had died, and learning it would be to boarding school because her father worked long hours and Christopher's carers could not take care of her as well...

'I'm sorry,' he said, apologising for all the hurts she'd suffered but knowing two words would never be enough.

'I don't want your "sorry" now, Keanu. I'm here, you're here, and we'll be working together, so we'll just both have to make the best of it.'

'You're serious about working in the hospital?'

Had he sounded astounded that she glared at him then turned away and stalked off up the path?

He followed her, taking in the shape of Caroline all grown up—long legs lightly tanned, hips curving into a neat waist, and long golden hair swinging from a high ponytail—swinging defiantly, if hair could be defiant.

The realisation that he was attracted to her came slowly.

Oh, he'd felt a jolt along his nerves when they'd accidentally touched, and his heart had practically somersaulted when he'd first set eyes on her, but surely that was remnants of the 'old friends' stuff.

And the attraction would have to be hidden as, apart from the fact that he was obviously at the very top of her least favourite people list, he was, as far as he knew, still married.

Not that he could blame Caro—for the least favourite people thing, not his marriage.

They'd both been sent to boarding school while still young, she to a school in Sydney, he to one in North Queensland, but the correspondence between them had been regular and intimate in the sense that they'd shared their thoughts and feelings about everything going on in their lives.

Then he and his mother had been forced to leave the island and there had been no way he could cause his mother further hurt by keeping in touch with Caroline.

She was a Lockhart after all.

A *Lockhart*!

He caught up with her.

'Look, no matter how you feel about me, there are things you should know.'

She turned her head and raised an eyebrow, so, taking that as an invitation, he ventured to speak.

'There's your uncle, Ian, for a start.'

Another quick glance.

'You must have known he came here, that your father had left him in overall charge of the mine after the hospital was finished and he, your father, that is, was doing more study and couldn't get over as often.'

She stopped suddenly, so he had to turn back, and standing this close, seeing the blue-green of her eyes, the dark eyebrows and lashes that drew attention to them, the curve of pink lips, the straight, dainty nose, his breath caught in his chest and left him wondering why no one had ever come up with an antidote for attraction.

Cold blue-green eyes—waiting, watchful…

'So?'

Demanding…

Keanu shifted uneasily. As a clan the Lockharts had always been extraordinarily close to each other and even though Ian was the noted black sheep, Caroline's father had still given him a job.

'Ian apparently had gambling debts before he came— a gambling addiction—but unfortunately even on a South Sea island online gambling is available. From all I heard he never stopped gambling but he wasn't very good at it. Eventually he sacked Peter Blake, the mine manager your father had employed, and took whatever he could from the mine—that's why it's been struggling lately and your father's having to foot a lot of the hospital bills. Ian stopped paying the mine workers, closed down the crushers and extractors and brought it to all but a standstill.'

He paused, although he knew he had to finish.

'Then he ran away. No one knows for certain when he went but it was very recently. One day his yacht was in the harbour at the mine and the next day it was gone.'

Blue-green eyes met his—worried but also wary.

'Grandma always said he was no good,' she admitted sadly. '"In spite of the fact he's my son, he's a bad seed," she used to say, which, as a child, always puzzled me, the bad-seed bit.'

He heard sadness in Caroline's words but she seemed slightly more relaxed now, he could tell, so he took a deep breath and finished the woeful tale.

'The trouble is, Ian's damaged the Lockhart name. I don't know how people will view your return.'

'What do you mean, view my return?'

Her confusion was so obvious he wanted to give her a hug.

Bad idea.

He put out his hand and touched her arm, wanting her calm enough to understand what he was trying to tell her. Though touching her was a mistake. Not only did fire flood his being, but she pulled away so suddenly she'd have fallen if he hadn't grabbed her.

And let her go very swiftly.

'Lockharts have been part of M'Langi history since they first settled on Wildfire,' he said gently. 'Your grandfather and father helped bring prosperity and health facilities to the islands and were admired for all they did. But Ian's behaviour has really tainted the name.'

He could see her confusion turning to anger and guessed she wanted to lash out at him—well, not at him particularly…or perhaps it was at him particularly, but she definitely wanted to lash out.

She turned away instead and trudged on up the slope, spinning back when she'd covered less than three feet to reach out and say, 'I'll take my bag now, thank you.'

Cool, calm and collected again—to outward appearances.

But he knew her too well not to know how deeply she'd been affected by his words. She'd never been a snob, never seen herself as different from the other island children with whom they'd attended the little primary school on Atangi, but she'd felt pride in the achievements of her family, justifiably so. To hear what he was telling her would be shattering for her.

But all he said was, 'I'll carry the bag, Caroline, and maybe, one day soon, we can sit down and talk—maybe find our friendship again.'

In reply, she stepped closer, grabbed her bag and stormed away, marching now, striding, hurrying away from him as fast as she could.

And was it his imagination, or did he hear her mutter, 'As if!'?

CHAPTER TWO

KEANU RUSSELL WALKED swiftly back down the track. He probably wasn't needed but the hospital was so short-staffed someone had to be there. The situation at the hospital was worse than he'd imagined when, alerted by the elders on Atangi, the main island of the group, he'd come back.

He touched the tribal tattoo that encircled the muscle of his upper arm, the symbol of M'Langi—of his belonging.

'Come home, we need you.'

That had been the extent of the elders' message, and as the islanders—with help from Max Lockhart—had paid for his high school and university education, he'd known he owed it to them to come.

He'd tried to contact Max before he'd left Australia but had been unable to get on to him. Apparently, Max's son, Christopher, had had a serious lung infection and Max had been with him in the ICU.

Trying the hospital here instead, Vailea, the hospital's housekeeper, had answered the phone and told him the islands—and the hospital in particular—were in big trouble.

'That Ian Lockhart, he's no good to anyone,' Vailea had told him. 'Max has been paying for the hospital out of his own money, because the mine is run-down and any money it does make, that rotten Ian takes.'

There was a silence as Keanu digested this, then Vailea added, 'We need you here, Keanu.'

'Why didn't *you* call me? Tell me this? Why leave it to the elders?'

There was another long pause before Vailea said, 'You've been gone too long, Keanu. I did not know how to tell you. I thought with me asking, you might not come, but with the elders—'

She broke the connection but not before he'd heard the tears in her voice, and he sat, staring at the phone in his hand, guilt flooding his entire being.

M'Langi was his home, the islanders his people, and he had stayed away because of his anger, and his mother's inner torment—caused by a Lockhart...

But if he was truly honest, he'd stayed away because he didn't want to face the memories of his happy childhood, or his betrayal of his childhood friend.

But home he was, and so aghast at the situation that memories had had no time to plague him. Although sometimes when he walked through the small hospital late at night he remembered a little boy and even smaller girl holding hands on about the same spot, talking about the future when he would be a doctor and she would be a nurse and they would come back to the island and work in the hospital her father had, even then, been planning to build.

Okay, so the ghost of Caroline did bother him—had bothered him even as he'd married someone else—but there was enough work to do to block her out most of the time.

Or had been until she'd arrived in person. Not only arrived but apparently intended to work here.

Not that she wasn't needed...

The nurse they had been expecting to come in on the next day's flight had phoned to say her mother was ill and she didn't know when she might make it. Then Maddie Haddon, one of their Fly-In-Fly-Out, or FIFO doctors, had phoned to say she wouldn't be on the flight either—some mix-up with her antenatal appointments.

Sam Taylor, the only permanent doctor, was doing a clinic flight to the other islands, with Hettie, their head nurse—another permanent. They didn't know of the latest developments but as Keanu himself had come as a FIFO and intended staying permanently whether he was paid or not, he could cover for Maddie.

And, presumably, Caroline could cover for the nurse.

Caroline.

Caro.

He had known how hurt she would have been when he'd cut her out of his life, but his anger had been stronger than his concern—his anger and his determination to do nothing more to hurt his already shattered mother.

Caroline discovered why Harold hadn't met the plane. He was in the front garden of the house, arguing volubly with his wife, Bessie. It had been Caroline's great-grandfather, autocratic old sod that he must have been, who'd insisted that all the employees working in the house and grounds take on English names.

'You come inside and help me clean,' Bessie was saying.

'No, I have to do the yard. Ian will raise hell if the yard's not done, not that I believe he's coming back.'

Watching them, Caroline felt a stirring of alarm that they had grown old, although age didn't seem to be affecting their legendary squabbles.

'Nor do I but someone is coming. Some other visitor. We saw the plane on a day when planes don't usually come, and anyway it was too small to be one of our planes.'

'Might be for the research station. Plenty of people coming and going there,' Harold offered, but Bessie was going to have the last word.

'In that case you don't need to do the yard.'

Caroline decided she couldn't stand behind an alle-mande vine, wild with shiny green leaves and brilliant yellow trumpet flowers, eavesdropping any longer.

'Bessie, Harold, it's me, Caroline!'

She passed the bush and came into view, expecting to be welcomed like a prodigal son—or daughter in her case—but to her utter bewilderment both of them burst into tears.

Eventually they recovered enough from their shock to rush towards her, arms held out.

'Oh, Caroline, you have come back. Now we have you *and* Keanu back where you belong, everything will be good again.'

Wrapped in a double, teary hug, Caroline couldn't answer.

Not that she would have been able to. Although she knew he was here—knew only too well—hearing Keanu's name knocked the breath out of her. But it had been the last part—about everything being good again—that had been the bigger shock.

But it also gave her resolve. If the trouble was so bad the islanders thought she, whom they'd always considered a helpless princess, could help, things *must* be bad.

She eased out of their arms and straightened up. Of course she had to help. She didn't know how, but she certainly would do everything in her power to save the islanders' livelihood and keep much-needed medical care available to them.

Enough of the doormat.

M'Langi was her home.

'But why are you working in the house, Bessie? What happened to the young woman Dad appointed after Helen left?'

With Keanu, a voice whispered, but she had no time for whispering voices right now.

'That was Kari but from the time that Ian got here we

thought it would be better if she kept her distance,' Bessie explained. 'Ian is a bad, bad man for all he's your family. In the end I said I'd do the housework. I mind Anahera's little girl too, but she's no trouble, she plays with all your toys and loves your dolls, dressing and undressing them.'

Caroline smiled, remembering her own delight in the dolls until Keanu had told her it was girl stuff and she had to learn to learn to make bows and arrows and to catch fish in her hands.

'Anahera?' she asked, as the name was vaguely familiar.

'Vailea, her mother, worked as the cook at the research station while we were caretakers there. But there's all kinds of funny stuff going on there too, so now she's housekeeper at the hospital and Anahera—she's a bit older than you and went to school on the mainland; her grandmother lived there—well, she's a nurse here so I mind her little one.'

It was hard to absorb so much information at once, so Caroline allowed herself to be led up to the house, where a very small child with dark eyes, olive skin and a tangle of golden curls was lining up dolls in a row on the cane lounge that had sat on the veranda for as long as Caroline could remember.

The cane lounge, potted palms everywhere, a few cane chairs around a table, once again with a smaller pot in the middle of it, and the swing she and Keanu had rocked in so often—*this* was coming home…

'This is Hana,' Bessie said, leading the little girl forward. 'Hana, this is Miss Caroline. She lives here.'

Caroline knelt by the beautiful child, straightening one of the dolls.

'Just Caroline will do,' she said, 'or even Caro.'

Caro.

No one but Keanu had ever called her Caro, but now wasn't the time to get sentimental over Keanu, for all he looked like a Greek god, and had sent shivers down her spine just being close to him.

She was here to…

What?

She'd come because she was unhappy, seeking sanctuary in the place she'd loved most, but now she was here?

Well, she was damned if she was going to let things deteriorate any further.

But first she had to find out exactly how things stood, and whether whoever ran the hospital would give her a job, and most importantly of all right now, she had to find the steel in her inner self to work with Keanu…

'Are you being paid, Bessie?' she asked, thinking she had to set her own house in order first.

Bessie studied her toes then shook her dark, curly hair.

'Anahera pays me for looking after Hana, but it's been a while since Harold got a wage.'

Caroline was angry. She knew their fondness for the Lockhart family and gratitude for what her father had done for the islands would have kept them doing what they could whether they were paid or not.

Knew also that the couple wouldn't be starving. Like all the islanders, and many people she knew on acreage on the mainland, they had their own plot of land around their bure—the traditional island home—and Harold would grow vegetables and raise a few pigs and chickens, but that didn't make not paying them right.

'Well, now I'm here we'll shut off most of the rooms and I'll just use my bedroom, bathroom and the kitchen. I can pay you to keep them clean and I'll vacuum through the rest of the place once a fortnight.'

Bessie began to mutter about dust, but Caroline waved away her complaint.

'Lockharts have been eating dust since the mine began,' she said, 'so a little bit on the floor of the closed rooms doesn't matter. And now,' she announced, 'I'm going down to the hospital to ask whoever runs it for a job. Even if they can't pay me, they can surely find me something to do.'

She left her case and headed back down the way she'd come. Work would give her the opportunity to find out what was going on. Even small hospitals were hotbeds of gossip.

Although...

Of course she could work with Keanu. She didn't know the man he'd become so she'd just treat him like any other colleague.

Male colleague.

Friendly, but keeping her distance...

Definitely keeping her distance, given how the accidental touches had affected her...

Lost in her muddled thoughts, she was halfway to the hospital when she remembered the only people there had been Keanu and an aide. What had he said? Hettie and Sam were on a clinic run? Caroline knew the hospital ran weekly clinics on the other inhabited islands of the group and today must have been one of those days.

That was probably the only reason Keanu had accepted her help with the injured man earlier.

She walked back up the hill, wondering why she'd thought returning to the island was such a good idea.

Wondering how things had gone so wrong, not only with the island but between herself and Keanu.

Had she judged him too harshly?

Refused to accept he might have had a good reason for stopping communication between them?

But surely they'd been close enough for him to have given her a reason—an explanation?

Hadn't they?

Totally miserable by the time she reached the house, she

went through to her old bedroom and unpacked the case that either Bessie or Harold had left there.

Then, as being back in her old room brought nostalgia with it, she slowly and carefully toured the house.

Built like so many colonial houses in those days, it had a wide veranda with overhanging eaves around all four sides of it. She started there, at the front, looking down at the hospital and beyond it the airstrip, and onto the flat ground by the beach, and although she couldn't see the research station, she knew it was there, sheltered beneath huge tropical fig trees and tall coconut palms.

As she knew the village was down there, on the eastern shore, nestled up against the foothills of the plateau. The village had been built on land given by her father, after the villagers on another island had lost their homes and land in a tsunami.

Now some of the villagers worked in the mine and at the hospital, and worshipped in the little white church they'd built on a rocky promontory between the village and the mine. A chapel built to celebrate their survival.

She knew the beach was there as well, but that too was hidden, although as she turned the corner and looked across the village she saw the strip of sand and the wide lagoon enclosed by the encircling coral.

On a clear day, from here and the back veranda, she'd have been able to see most of the islands that made up the M'Langi group, but today there was a sea haze.

The western veranda formed the division between the main house and the smaller copy of it, an annexe where Helen and Keanu had lived.

No way was she going there now, although their home had been as open to her as hers had been to Keanu.

This time she entered the house through the back door, through the kitchen with its different pantries opening off it and the huge wooden table where she and Keanu had eaten breakfast and lunch.

The pantries had provided great places for hide and seek, although Grandma's cook had forever been shooing them out, afraid they'd break the precious china and crystal stored in them.

Caroline opened the door of one—empty shelves where the crystal had once reflected rainbows in the light.

The sight sent her hurrying to the dining room, on the eastern side of the main hall. Looking up, she saw with relief that the chandelier still hung above the polished dining table.

Grandma had loved that table *and* the grandeur of the chandelier. She had insisted Caroline, Keanu and Helen join her there for dinner every evening, the magic crystals of the chandelier making patterns on the table's highly polished surface.

Helen would report on anything that needed doing around the house, and talk to Grandma about meals and what needed to be ordered from the mainland to come over on the next flight.

Grandma would quiz Keanu and Caroline about their day at school—what they'd learned and had they done their homework before going out to play.

Ian might have sold her grandmother's precious crystal to cover his gambling debts but at least he'd left the chandelier.

He must have been desperate indeed to have packed the delicate objects before sending them out on the boat that made a weekly visit to the harbour at Atangi.

Before or after he'd started skimming money from the mine?

Taking away the livelihood of the workers?

Shame that she could be related to the man brought heat to her cheeks, but what was done was done.

Unless?

Could she do something to help set things to rights?

Refusing to be waylaid, she continued with her exploration. Next to the dining room was the big entertaining room Grandma had always called the Drawing Room—words Caroline still saw in her mind with capital letters. Here, at least, things remained the same. The furniture, the beautiful old Persian carpets—Ian couldn't have known they were valuable.

But the elegant, glass-fronted cabinets were empty. Grandma's precious collection of china—old pieces handed down to her by *her* mother and grandmother—was gone.

That was when tears started in Caroline's eyes. Ian had not only stolen physical things, he'd stolen her memories, memories of sitting on the floor in front of the cabinet while Grandma handed her one piece at a time, telling her its history, promising they would be hers one day.

That she'd lost them didn't matter, but the treachery of Ian selling things he knew had been precious to his mother turned her tears to anger.

Taking a deep breath, she moved on into Grandma's sitting room.

The little desk she'd used each day to write to friends was there, and Caroline could feel the spirit of her grandmother, the woman who, with Helen, had brought her up until Grandma's death when Caroline was ten.

Opening off the wide passage on the other side were large, airy bedrooms, all with wide French doors and folding shutters that led onto the veranda. The filmy lace curtains still graced the insides of the windows, although they were beginning to look drab.

Grandma's was the first room, the huge four-poster bed draped with a pale net, the faint scent of her presence lingering in the air. There'd always been flowers in Grandma's room, as there had been on the dining-room table and the cabinets in the drawing room...

Leaving her exploration, she hurried out into the garden, minding the thorns on the bougainvillea as she pulled off a couple of flower stems, then some frangipani, a few yellow allemande flowers, some glossy leaves, and white daisies.

Back inside she found vases Ian must have considered too old and cracked to fetch a decent price. She filled them with water and carried them, one by one, into the three rooms where flowers had always stood.

Soon she'd do more—head into the rainforest for leaves and berries and eventually have floral tributes to Grandma that would rival the ones she used to make.

But there was still half a house to explore.

Her father's room was next, unchanged although the small bed beside her father's big one reminded Caroline of the rare times Christopher had come to the island. The visits hadn't lasted long, but she and Keanu had always shared their adventures with him. They would put him in his wheelchair and show him all their favourite places, probably risking his life when they wheeled him down the steep track to Sunset Beach.

The next room must have been Ian's, then three smaller, though still by modern-day standards large, rooms—hers in the middle.

But as she poked her head into Ian's room it was obvious he hadn't been living there as the furniture was covered in dust sheets that seemed to have been there for ever.

'He lived in the guesthouse.'

Bessie had come in and now stood beside Caroline, looking into the empty, rather ghostly room.

The guesthouse was off the back veranda opposite Helen and Keanu's suite of rooms, but detached and given privacy by a screen of trees and shrubs.

'I don't think I'll bother looking there,' she said to Bessie. 'It was about the only place on the island Keanu and I weren't allowed to play so there'd be no memories.'

She was back on the front veranda when she heard the *whump-whump-whump* of a helicopter.

Now she could go down to the hospital and ask for a job.

Right now before she'd let her doubts about working with Keanu solidify in her head.

Or perhaps tomorrow when she'd worked on a strategy to handle working with him…

He had to go up to the house and make peace with Caro, Keanu decided, not skulk around down here at the hospital.

Sam and Hettie would employ her, that much was certain, so he would be working with her. But doctor-nurse relationships needed trust on both sides and although all his instincts told him to run for his life, he knew he wouldn't.

Couldn't.

M'Langi was more important than these new and distinctly uncomfortable reactions to Caro. Finding out what had been happening and trying to put things right—that was what the elders expected of him.

So he was here, and she was here, and…

He sighed, then began to wonder just why she was here. He'd never totally lost touch with what Caro was up to, being in contact with her father all through his student years, asking, oh, so casually, how she was doing.

And friends from the islands, staying at the Lockharts' Sydney house on a visit or while studying, would pass on information. So now he thought about it, he'd known she'd studied nursing, because he'd smiled at the time to think both of them were fulfilling at least the beginning of that childhood promise.

But he'd never expected her to return to Wildfire to actually finish the job, especially as he'd known a little of the life she'd been leading. Known from the Sydney papers he would buy up in Cairns, for the sole purpose, he realised, of torturing himself.

He might pretend he'd bought them for the business section, which was always more comprehensive than the one in the local paper, but, if so, why did he turn to the social pages first, hoping for a glimpse of Caro—a grown-up, beautiful Caro—usually on the arm of a too-smooth-looking bloke called Steve, to whom she was, apparently, 'almost' engaged.

What the hell did 'almost' mean?

It couldn't have been jealousy that had made him feel so bad—after all, he'd been the one who'd not almost but definitely married someone else. Someone he'd thought he'd loved because she'd brought him out of the lingering misery of his mother's death, his loneliness and his homesickness for the island.

So kind of, in a way, he'd betrayed Caro not once—in disappearing from her life—but twice, although that wasn't really true as trysts made between twelve-and fourteen-year-olds didn't really count.

Did they?

It was all this confusion—the unresolved issues inside him—that was making him angry, and somehow the anger had made her its target.

Which was probably unfair.

No, it was definitely unfair.

Especially as she was obviously unhappy. He'd put that down to her seeing him again, which would be natural after the way he'd behaved towards her.

So maybe he should stay well out of her way.

Except he'd always hated it when Caro was unhappy. And if he'd caused or even contributed to that unhappiness, which he must have, cutting her off the way he had so long ago, then shouldn't he do something about it?

At least see if they could regain a little of their old friendship.

Friendship?

When one glimpse of the grown-up Caro had sent his pulses racing, his entire body stirring in a most un-friend-like manner?

Not good for a man who was probably still married…

On top of which, he was torn between two edicts of his mother. The childhood one, always spoken when the two of them as children had left the house, plainly spoken and always understood: take care of Caroline.

Then, as his mother had been dying from pancreatic cancer that had appeared from nowhere and killed her within six weeks, while he, a doctor could do nothing to save her. *Then* she had *cursed* the Lockharts…

Well, Ian Lockhart anyway.

Anyway, wasn't he beyond superstitions like curses?

He shook his head to clear the memories and useless speculation, checked the few patients they had in the hospital, then let out a huge sigh of relief when he heard the helicopter returning.

He almost let himself hope it was bringing in a difficult case, something to distract him from the endlessly circling thoughts in his head.

Hettie and Sam had left the hospital's makeshift ambulance down near the helicopter pad so Keanu walked down to the airstrip, not really wishing for a patient but ready to help unpack anything they might have brought back. And it would be best to break the news about the FIFO nurse and Maddie not coming now, rather than leaving it until the morning.

Would he tell them about Caroline's arrival?

He'd have to at least mention it.

Sam would be only too delighted to have an available nurse.

And he would be doomed to work with the woman he didn't really know but had been instantly attracted to in a way he'd never felt before.

It was because of the old friendship. The attraction thing. It had to be, but with any luck, after the way he'd treated her, she'd want to have as little to do with him as possible.

He was almost at the helicopter now, and could see Sam and Jack Richards, the pilot, lifting out a stretcher.

Good! That means work to do, Keanu thought, then realised how unkind it was to be wishing someone ill. But it was only when he saw the patient that he felt a flush of shame at his thoughts. It was old Alkiri, from the island of Atangi, the elder who had been one of his and Caro's favourite people and true mentor when they had been young.

He moved closer and greeted the elder in his native language, touching the old man's shoulder in a gesture of respect.

Even through the oxygen mask, Keanu could see the blue tinge on their patient's lips and he wondered just how old Alkiri might be.

'He had a fall, perhaps a TIA as apparently he'd been falling quite a lot recently.'

TIA—transient ischemic attack—often a precursor to a full-blown stroke. Had Alkiri been putting these falls down to old age? He was a private man, unlikely to seek help unless he really needed it. Yet, as Caroline's grandfather's boatman, he had not only lived here at Wildfire but had taken two small children under his wing. It was he who had taken them and the village children to and from the school on Atangi, teaching them things about the islands, and life itself, that to Keanu were as important as the learning he'd had at school.

He should tell Caro Alkiri was—

He stopped the thought before it went any further. It had been automatic for he knew she'd loved the old man as much as he had—and probably still would...

But he was no longer the boy who'd run through the house, calling for his friend to pass on a bit of news.

And she was no longer the girl he'd always wanted to find so he could tell—

They strapped the stretcher into the converted jeep, especially modified for just that reason, then Jack and Hettie rode back to the hospital, Sam walking with Keanu to check on any news and pass on information from the clinics on the other islands.

The scent of a nearby frangipani hung in the air, but today such a reminder that he was home didn't soothe Keanu as it had on other days, on other such walks with Sam, or Hettie or whoever had done the clinic run.

He gave Sam the news that neither Maddie nor the FIFO nurse would be arriving the next day, assured Sam he was happy to work full time, then hesitated.

'More?' Sam asked quietly.

'There *is* a nurse,' Keanu answered, and something in his voice must have alerted Sam.

'She's a problem? Drinker? Chain smoker who'll insist on cigarette breaks? Axe murderer?'

'She's a Lockhart,' Keanu answered, and watched as Sam smiled and shook his head.

'That doesn't make her a bad nurse, Keanu. I assume she's Max's daughter, the girl you grew up with. And don't look at me like that—nothing stays secret on this island for long.'

Sam stopped walking and turned towards Keanu, his usually smiling face set in a frown.

'Are you saying you can't work with her?'

'Of course not,' Keanu responded, possibly too quickly. 'But the Lockhart name isn't held in much regard here at the moment. I was wondering about the patients.'

'Of course you were.'

Sam smiled again.

'Considering all the good Max Lockhart and his parents and grandparents before him have done for the islands, I doubt the one bad apple will have totally ruined the name. I do hope not, because we need her. But speaking of Ian, Hettie and I discovered he'd stopped in at Raiki after he left here and took not only the locked box of drugs we kept in the clinic there, but also the clinic nurse.'

'Why on earth?' Keanu had trouble taking in this information. 'Drugs, maybe—he's on a boat, could have injuries and presumably anything he doesn't use he'll sell—but the nurse? I assume she went willingly.'

'Apparently so, but it leaves Raiki without a nurse. The drugs we can replace, but she was one of the first nurses trained when Max set up the programme to help any islanders wanting to do nursing. Most of them lived in his house in Sydney while they were at university, but she was one of the few who came back here to work.'

'But the others will be helping people even if it's not here,' Keanu pointed out, mainly to cover the stab of guilt he'd felt at Sam's statement. It had reminded him that he, too, hadn't come back—well, not until he had been reminded of his duty...

'So, when do I get to meet her?' Sam asked.

'I imagine she'll come down in the morning. She did help out soon after she arrived earlier today when we had a bloke come up from the research station with a nail from a nail gun in his foot. It wasn't much of a test of nursing but she seemed to know what she was doing.'

Sam smiled again before walking on.

'Poor girl!' he said. 'Already damned with faint praise.'

Poor girl indeed, Keanu muttered to himself. If she was still a girl everything would be okay.

Or would it?

She'd been nothing more than a girl when he'd hurt her and for all he'd told himself she wouldn't miss his letters, and would probably be relieved not to have to write back, given all the friends she would have made at school, he'd never quite believed it.

'I could take you up to the house and introduce you this evening if you like,' he offered.

Sam studied him for a minute.

'Let's just wait for her to come to us,' he suggested, then he grinned. 'And let's hope she's early as apparently she'll have to start work straight away.'

CHAPTER THREE

A BEAUTIFUL YOUNG woman with long, lustrous, dark hair piled up beneath a dodgy-looking nurse's cap, and wearing what was apparently a uniform of green tunic and green three-quarter-length pants greeted Caroline with a smile and, 'Can I help you?'

'I'm looking for Sam,' Caroline explained.

'Rather you than me,' the woman replied. 'He's in the little room he calls his office, probably setting fire to the paperwork. Straight along the passage and on the left.'

Caroline turned to follow the directions.

'I'm Anahera, by the way, but everyone calls me Ana,' the dark-haired woman added.

Caroline turned back.

'Oh, I've met your daughter. She's adorable. I'm Caroline Lockhart.'

Caroline held out her hand but couldn't miss the hesitation or the look of wariness in Anahera's eyes before she took the proffered palm and shook it.

But 'Oh!' was all she said, turning back into the small ward behind her where Caroline could see four occupied beds.

Farther down the passage she found the room, knocked briefly then answered a peremptory 'Come in.'

'Caroline Lockhart, I presume?'

The good-looking man behind the desk looked up briefly from the paperwork he was shoving from one pile to another, then frowned down at it.

'Never become an administrator,' he muttered, pushing the lot back together into an untidy heap.

'Don't like paperwork?' Caroline asked, but she was smiling as she said it. There was something immensely likeable about this man.

'Who does? The problem is I'm already short on staff and I've still got to waste time doing blasted paperwork.'

'Can't you get the dog to eat it? Isn't that the classic homework excuse?' Caroline suggested, seeing the warm brown eyes of the Labrador lying on Sam's feet under the table.

Sam flashed her a grin.

'I did try that but the wretch keeps spitting it out. Hospital dogs are too well fed. But let me introduce you. This lazy, too-well-fed beast is Bugsy, Maddie Haddon's dog. Maddie is one of our FIFO doctors but rather than fly Bugsy back and forth she leaves him here. Unfortunately she can't make today's plane and as he usually knows when she's due in, he's decided I'm the best substitute for his owner.'

Sam paused and studied Caroline for a moment.

'I'm also a nurse short, and Keanu told me you were here. Want a job?'

'As long as it doesn't involve sorting that mess you've made of those papers you're shuffling. I can certainly help in other ways.'

Humour lit his eyes.

'Nice back massage? Rub my feet?'

'In your dreams!' Caroline retorted, deciding she quite liked this rather strange man.

'But I could fill in for your missing nurse,' Caroline

added, refusing to be beguiled by gleaming eyes. 'I'm a nurse and you're apparently one nurse short.'

'Keanu said you're a socialite.'

One more black mark against the man who'd hurt her so badly.

'Well, you may not have noticed but there's not that much social life around here, and a socialite without a social set is superfluous to requirements, while a nurse might just fill in for the one who isn't coming, if you're willing to give me a chance.'

Now she had his attention.

'Touchy, are you?' He looked her up and down. 'I suppose you have the right bits of paper—degree, references.'

'Right here,' she said, pulling the paperwork she'd grabbed and stuffed in her back pocket before leaving the house.

Caroline began to relax.

Well, not *relax* relax—that would never happen with Keanu somewhere near—but some of the tension she'd been feeling drained slowly out of her.

'It seems you've been away from the island for a long time,' Sam said, riffling through the papers but, she suspected, speed-reading every word. 'Why have you come back?'

'I don't think that's relevant but I did hear the island was in trouble.'

'And you thought coming here to nurse would cure things?'

Caroline shook her head.

'Boy, are you a grump! I didn't even know there'd be a nursing position available, although I had intended working here for nothing if necessary, but this place was my home—*is* my home—and I'll be damned if I'm going to sit back and let it fall apart without at least trying to find out what's been happening and what can be done to save it. My dad would be here as well, only he— Well, there's a family problem.'

Sam raised his head and looked at her.

'He's a great man, your father. He does the best he can. Lobbying for government support, fundraising. Ever since the mine stopped paying its promised share for the hospital, I think he's put his entire salary into it. I just do what I can.'

'So, do I get a job?'

Sam studied her a little longer.

'The nurse who was coming was a FIFO—Fly-In-Fly-Out—the term more commonly used in mining communities. It means you're on duty for two weeks then off for one, and you can take the flight to the mainland for that week off if you wish.'

'Which leaves you with only one nurse—Anahera— for a week?'

'Not really. The FIFOs overlap and we have another permanent. You haven't met Hettie yet—Henrietta de Lacey— only don't dare ever call her Henrietta, she'll lop off your head with the nearest implement. She's our head nurse and is permanent staff and she's the one you should be speaking to about this job, but she's doing another clinic run. It's not usual to do two in one week, but there's a lot to sort out. The clinic on Raiki is short of drugs, not to mention a nurse, so Hettie's gone out there to replace the drugs then scour the islands to see if she can get one of the nurses from another island to cover Raiki for a while. How are you in a helicopter?'

Caroline was wondering what had happened to both the drugs and the nurse from Raiki when she realised she'd been asked a question. She grinned at him.

'Do you mean can I fly one or do I throw up in one?'

'Definitely the latter. Pilots we have.'

'I'll be fine, but do nurses always do the clinics or do the doctors go out to the other islands as well?'

'Doctors too,' came the swift reply, although Caroline had already forgotten what she'd asked as she'd sensed a presence in the room behind her, and every nerve in her body told her it was Keanu.

'Sorry to butt in, boss.'

His deep voice reverberated around the room.

'But Alkiri, the old man you brought in from Atangi, is having difficulty breathing—I think his end is very near. Okay with you if I sit with him?'

Sam nodded, then turned to Caroline.

'If you want to start work now, go sit with Keanu. Just see Alkiri is propped up in a comfortable position and moisten his lips for him if he needs it. Turn his head a little—'

'So saliva can drain out,' Caroline finished for him. 'I *have* done this before, you know.'

Sam nodded again, then added softly, although they were already alone in the room, 'I'd like you there for Keanu. He's known the old man all his life. He's the elder who asked Keanu to come back to the islands. It will be hard for him.'

Caroline nodded.

'Alkiri would have known he was dying,' she murmured, remembering the uncanny sense the islanders seemed to have about death. 'Maybe he wanted Keanu by his side.'

She left the room to be with Alkiri and Keanu, though she doubted *he'd* take comfort from her presence.

Sitting on the opposite side of the bed from her child-hood friend, she took the old man's dry hand, feeling bones as fragile as a bird's beneath the papery skin.

'It's Caroline,' she said very quietly. 'Do you remember teaching me to weave fish traps?'

To talk or not to talk to the dying was a much-argued topic, but Caroline thought Alkiri deserved to know she remembered, and perhaps to let his mind drift back to happy times he'd had with the two children.

'Then you'd take us out in your old boat to show us where to put them up against the reef.' Keanu took up the story equally quietly, but looking at him, Caroline wondered if the sadness in his eyes was not all caused by the elder's approaching death.

Caroline swabbed the saliva from the old man's mouth, while Keanu started a story about Alkiri's frustration at not being able to teach Caro to split a coconut properly.

'I still can't,' Caroline admitted, 'although they're everywhere in the city shops now and people are going crazy for coconut water.'

'I've been looking into that and have talked to the elders,' Keanu said quietly. 'Wondering if the craze for it might provide a viable source of income for the islanders. After all, it's not just the water but every bit of a coconut is used in one way or another. I've got an accountant who's done a lot of set-up work on new businesses looking at the figures.'

Her thoughts hadn't quite got that far but the splitting of coconuts had started her thinking that way.

She risked a glance towards him. Surely they were not still going to be able to read each other's thoughts, especially now, when her thoughts, since meeting him again, had been almost wholly taken up with how magnificent he looked.

Keanu was as fine a specimen of manhood as she'd ever seen, and although just looking at him generated unwelcome reactions in her body, she couldn't resist a sneaked glance now and then as she tried to analyse her reactions.

She turned her attention back to Alkiri, speaking quietly again, more memories tumbling into her head. Keanu offered some of his own, adding to hers—shared lives.

At some stage she heard a plane come in—bringing

stores but not the staff that had been expected, Caroline guessed. Then some time later it took off again. They talked on...

There were long silences between Alkiri's rattly breaths, some so long she feared their old friend had already died. Until suddenly he roused, opened his eyes and looked from one to the other, smiling.

'With both of you here, I am at peace. Please keep me here when I am gone. Wildfire was always my true home,' he whispered in a thin papery voice, and then the breathing did stop.

For ever.

Caroline couldn't bring herself to pull the sheet up over the old man's face. Very gently, she closed his eyes, and straightened the sheet across his body.

'*Can* we bury him here or would his family want him back on Atangi?' she asked, finally meeting Keanu's eyes across the bed.

Keanu shrugged, and, sensing the grief he was trying hard to hide she went to him, unable not to offer comfort to her old friend, and put her arm around his wide shoulders.

'Come on, let's have a cup of tea while we think about the arrangements.'

He walked with her, but blindly, although the fact that he was not aware of her didn't bother Caroline one bit. She was far too busy battling all the reactions just touching Keanu's body had caused in hers—hoping the deep breaths she was taking to suppress the weird emotions were going unnoticed by her companion.

But her heart raced, her head spun, and every nerve in her body tingled with excitement.

Ridiculous, she told herself. This was 'old friend' reaction and not sexual at all, although it *did* feel...

Sexual?

Vailea was in the kitchen. She took one look at Keanu's stricken face and pulled out a chair for him.

'I heard you were back,' she said, her voice cold enough to douse the fires just touching Keanu had set alight. 'Come to bring more trouble to us?'

'No, of course not. I've come to work.' Caroline tried to sound reassuring, but Vailea's words and attitude had stung.

What on earth had been going on? Was it more than Ian's poor management? Selling off the family heirlooms wouldn't have affected anyone outside the family, so what else had happened or was happening? What had Bessie said about the new housekeeper? Something about Ian...

'I've come to make Keanu a cup of tea,' she said as Vailea's eyes continued to study her, a malevolence Caroline couldn't understand clear within them.

'I'll take care of him,' the older woman snapped, and Caroline, only too pleased to escape the extremely uncomfortable atmosphere, left the kitchen.

'Boy, this is going to be fun,' she muttered to herself as she made her way out of the hospital.

Keanu could deal with Alkiri on his own—do whatever needed to be done. She was damned if she was going to stay around and be insulted. Once Hettie, the head nurse, returned later today and gave Caroline her roster, she could work out how best to avoid Vailea altogether.

Vailea *and* Keanu.

Although there was something about Vailea's reaction to her that seemed more personal than a general hatred of all Lockharts...

Keanu walked up to the house at six. He'd spent two hours talking to the elders on Atangi, making arrangements for Alkiri's funeral. The elders had agreed he could be buried on Wildfire and they would send over people to help with the practicalities and some cooks to prepare the food.

'Is there somewhere we can all gather?' the man he'd been speaking to had asked. 'I think the little church and its hall would be too small.'

Keanu thought of the big longhouse that had once been the centre of the research station and assured the elder that somewhere could be found. There was always the Lockhart house if nothing else worked out.

They settled on a service at ten in two days' time.

Now, given that they might need the house, he had to make peace with Caro, although he doubted he could ever explain his angry reaction to her arrival—far too complicated and quite unwarranted, really.

Caroline was sitting on the veranda, watching the sun sink into the sea, dropping below the western cliffs lit up with the brilliant fiery red that gave the island its name.

He took the steps three at a time in long, deliberate strides, then slumped down on the top one, not looking at her but out at the dying colours of the sunset.

'Why *did* you come back?' he asked, almost gently, although being this close to her had started all the physical reactions again, and the confusion of that made him feel…

Angry?

Not really, more unsettled…

'Why did you?' she countered.

'I was asked,' he said, trying desperately to pretend that this was just a conversation between two old friends. Which, of course, it was—wasn't it?

'The island was in trouble, the community was in trouble. It's my home and I love it. Of course, I had to come back.'

'And yet you ask me why I came? To tell you the truth,

I didn't know things were this bad until I got here. I just wanted—needed—to come home.'

'And now you're here?

She turned towards him, her eyes alight with determination.

'I have to find out what's been happening. How everything's gone so terribly wrong. Do you honestly believe the island means less to me than it does to you? That this isn't my community as well?'

Her gaze drifted back to the sunset, so he guessed there was a bit more to the answer than that. But whatever it was it had caused a break in her voice and he wanted more than anything in the world—more even than saving the livelihood and well-being of the islanders—to comfort her, to take her in his arms, hold her close, smell the Caro scent of her, and never let her go.

Like she'd want *that*!

He also wanted to ask her about Christopher. She hadn't answered earlier. But he knew it was too painful a subject to bring up when they were so estranged, so he stuck to practicalities.

'So, what do you think you can do?' he asked instead, his voice rougher than it should be as it scraped past the emotion in his throat.

'Find out what's been going on, for a start,' she said. 'All the predictions from the geologists showed the mine had many years to run. I don't doubt Ian's been embezzling the money it's been earning but it can't *just* be that.'

Keanu hid a smile. That sounded so like the young Caroline—his Caro—on the trail of some possible crime—suspected cruelty to some chickens being only one of her campaigns.

Memories were dangerous things…

Better to stick with the present and practicalities, discuss what facts he *did* know, although they were few enough.

'Did you know Ian leased out the research station?' he asked.

'He's leased the research station? Why on earth would he do that?'

'Money, why else! It had been run-down for a while. Fewer and fewer people using it. Then he somehow found this wealthy Middle Eastern guy who wants to set up an exclusive resort. The local residents are a bit uneasy about it, but heaven knows we need all the income and employment we can get.'

'Well, it explains the guy with the nail in his foot. Does my dad know?'

'I assumed he did but the negotiations certainly went through Ian, and no one here seems to know anything about it.'

'Dad would never have trusted Ian to negotiate, and he'd never have made a decision without consulting the elders. He sent Ian here mainly to keep him out of trouble. It's the way Dad feels about family. He thinks even the black sheep deserves a chance to redeem himself, but from all I'm hearing about our particular black sheep, it's impossible.'

She sighed then added, 'The guy with the nail in his foot—he's working there? Work's going on now?'

Keanu nodded. 'And has been for some time.'

'I want to have a look.'

'You can't. The whole place is fenced and gated. That patient yesterday wouldn't even let us drive him back down there. He had his mate come back to the hospital, remember?'

'But this is our home! We can go wherever we like.'

Keanu hid a smile. This was Caro at her most imperious. And hearing her, hearing the old Caro sent a piercing pain through his chest.

'You want to argue with the guards? They'll never accept your authority. Besides, legally, I would think now this man has leased it, it's his land for as long as the lease states.'

'But Dad doesn't know anything—if he did he'd have told me. Come on, Keanu, you must know something.'

'All I know is that some rich man is turning it into a resort. A chap called Luke Wilson was doing some research here a few years ago and apparently this rich bloke knew Luke from somewhere. That was enough for Ian to make contact with him and that's what happened.'

Keanu paused, trying to think—to get it right.

'I wouldn't be surprised if he's already achieved his aim for the resort—there's been a hell of a lot of activity going on around the place. Container loads of stuff taken off huge ships and ferried ashore on barges, imported workers everywhere.'

'But the research station? That was my great-grandfather's legacy to the whole of M'Langi, designed to provide facilities and housing to anyone who wanted to investigate or study ways to improve the health of the islanders through science. Your father was one of the first to work there. I know my grandfather and Ian resented putting money into it, but I'm sure it was legally tied up so the mine had to keep supporting it.'

'And if the mine couldn't?' Keanu asked. 'Isn't it better to lease it to someone with money than let the idea die completely?'

Caroline stared at him, trying to work out what might be going on behind this conversation.

As far as she was concerned, there was a lot of very strange stuff lingering in the deep recesses of her mind and fluttering along the nerves in her body, yet Keanu was sitting there, about as sensitive as a boulder.

Whatever. She was finding out things she needed to know so she had to set aside all the physical manifestations of the boulder's presence and seek more information.

'You mean this mystery millionaire is going to keep the research station going? So why build luxury accommodation?'

Keanu shrugged.

'Who knows, but that's what's happening because Sam's been carrying on with some of Luke's research into why the islanders don't suffer from encephalitis to the extent their counterparts in other island groups do and he's been wanting to use the laboratories there. Apparently, they've said he can as soon as the renovations are completed.'

'Weirder and weirder,' Caroline muttered, but the worst of the weirdness was what was going on in her body. She'd been, what, thirteen when she'd last seen Keanu? And with her isolated life on the island then boarding school, had probably been a late developer. And although his disappearance from her life had devastated her—even broken her heart—it had been a child's heart that had been broken, a child's love betrayed.

What she was feeling now had nothing childish about it, and if she was going to be working with him, seeing him every day, she'd better get over whatever it was PDQ.

Practicalities—they would be the best antidote to this Keanu business.

'Let's go and see,' she suggested. 'I'll grab some bottled water and a torch, and we'll go take a look.'

'We can't,' Keanu answered flatly, killing the small spark of excitement taking some action had lit.

'And why not?' she demanded, the young Caroline again.

'I've already told you, it's fenced off. Visitors to the resort won't be bumped along a rocky track—they'll travel down there by helicopter.'

'They can't have fenced the whole place. Not the beach and the reef and that rockfall around the corner of Sunset Beach.'

'So?'

'We'll just have to find our way either around or over this fence and see what's happening for ourselves. We'll go down to the beach for a start, and walk to the rockfall then figure it out from there. We've swum around it in the past, but it might be low tide. We should at least go and have a look.'

She was twelve again and grinned at him.

'Come on, Keanu, it will be an adventure, just like old times!'

Keanu studied the beautiful, *smiling* woman in front of him and knew that while her features might have changed as she'd matured, her determination obviously had not.

He heard his mother's voice, back when they'd been young, saying look after Caroline—words to a child that were now coming back to haunt him. He'd *have* to go along on this ridiculous escapade because there was no way he could let her go alone. The very thought of her prowling around down there made his blood run cold, not to mention what might happen if she tried to climb the rockfall on her own.

Apart from which, he had to admit, he *would* like to know what was going on at the northern end of the island, and he could check out if they'd rebuilt the longhouse and if it would be suitable for Alkiri's funeral feast—should they get permission to use it.

'Are you going like that?' he asked, looking at the short shift dress she wore.

'Of course,' she replied. 'It's faded so much it almost

looks like camouflage, although I didn't choose it for that—just pulled it out of the cupboard. I'll slip on some soft dive boots in case we have to swim.'

He hoped like hell they wouldn't have to swim, because the thought of seeing that shift wet and clinging to her body was already causing a definite stirring in his lower abdomen.

The thought of helping her down the cliff path, taking her elbow on a tricky bit, touching her at all, had been bad enough, but the wet shift image was torturous.

Yet he'd seen Caroline naked often enough, when they'd shucked off their clothes to swim in the lagoon by the house—but that had been boy-girl stuff, kid stuff—and she hadn't had breasts then...

Dear heaven, was he losing his mind?

He knew his mother had had good reason for leaving the island—Ian Lockhart had made sure of that—but he wondered if she'd also been thinking of what might happen as he and Caroline went through puberty? Feeling as she did about Ian, his having a relationship with Ian's niece might have been too much...

Caroline was back, soft dive boots—more like ballet slippers—on her feet and a small backpack on her back. She passed a second one to him.

'A camera with a long-distance lens,' she announced. 'Apparently, Ian didn't know of Dad's interest in photography or he'd have found them and sold them off as he seems to have done with everything else of value in the house.'

Keanu thought of the beautiful pieces of porcelain Caro's grandmother had collected—and Caro had loved—and knew without asking that they'd be gone.

Well, he hadn't been able to save her treasures, but he sure as hell was going to do everything he could to keep her safe in her mad quest to save the island. At least in *that* quest they'd be partners once again.

He slung the backpack over his shoulder and reached out to take her arm.

'Let's go,' he said. She moved away from his outstretched hand, but undeterred he added, 'It *will* be like old times!'

Except all his senses were on full alert, his body buzzing just being near her, so who the hell knew what would happen if she actually swam!

CHAPTER FOUR

THEY WALKED SWIFTLY to the clifftop, muscle memory in their feet remembering the path possibly better than their brains did. Above them, in the thick rainforest, birds were settling down for the night, rustling among the leaves. Then down the rocky track with its views out over the reef to the ocean beyond. The path they took was now overgrown in places as if it had been rarely used since two adventurous children had left the island.

'How long have you been here?'

Caroline, following him with one hand on his backpack, asked the question.

'Three weeks.'

The answer came easily. Three weeks of shock as he'd tried to accept the island as it was now and work out what had happened.

'Have you seen the Blakes?'

Keanu shook his head.

'They were long gone when I got here. The old man, your grandfather, appointed Peter not long before he died and your father was happy to leave him in charge of the mine when you were born and he had to take Christopher to the mainland for constant medical supervision.'

'Dad liked the fact that Peter was an engineer as well

as having practical knowledge as a miner, and he was as honest as they come.'

'Probably too honest for Ian,' Keanu said. 'He decided he could do the job better and sacked Peter. Then, with Peter gone, Ian announced he'd take over the running of the mine as well as everything else on the island.'

'No wonder it's run-down,' Caro said tartly. 'Ian couldn't manage his way out of an open door.'

'Harsh!' Keanu said, turning to take Caro's hand and help her over a particularly tricky bit of the path.

'Well, you know he couldn't. The only things he was ever interested in were money and women and gambling, although I imagine the order changed according to the situation.'

And even in the dim light of early evening reflected off the sea she saw the pain on Keanu's face, the stricken look in his eyes. She remembered something strange that Bessie had said about it being better if Kari kept her distance from Ian, and started to connect the dots...

'Oh, Keanu, not your mother?' She reached for his shoulders and pulled him close, wrapping her arms awkwardly around his body. 'Is that why you left? Why didn't she tell my father? Or the elders? Or the police? Do something to get him stopped?'

Keanu eased out of her grasp and looked down at her, his face now wiped as blank as she'd ever seen it.

'He didn't assault her, if that's what you're thinking,' he said. 'What he did was worse.'

Bitterness as harsh and hurtful as Caroline had ever heard leached from every word so each one was a separate prick of pain—into her skin, through her flesh and into her heart.

But worse than rape?

What could she say?

Much as she longed to know more, she knew by the cold finality in Keanu's voice that the conversation was finished.

He had turned and was moving on and although she longed to ask him if that's why he'd never contacted her, she knew she wouldn't—couldn't. In fact, she knew the answer.

Somehow or other, a Lockhart had hurt his mother— an unforgiveable sin.

They stumbled their way down to the beach then, staying in the shadows of the fringing coconut palms, made their way to the rockfall.

The tide was in, the small ripples of water inside the reef splashing up against the rocks.

'So we swim,' she said brightly, wishing they could get back to the not easy, but easier atmosphere they'd shared as they'd started down the cliff. 'But I doubt Dad's camera's waterproof so what if I go around first then climb up on the lower rocks on the other side and you pass it to me, then you swim around?'

'Haven't changed much, have you? Bossy as ever!' Keanu muttered, and Caroline hid a smile—the old Keanu was back with her again, if only temporarily.

It was far worse than he'd expected, Keanu realised as Caro, the thin wet shift clinging to every curve of her body, appeared on the other side of the rockfall, reaching up and out for the rucksack.

He'd taken off his shirt but his shorts would be wet as he clambered ashore, so his reaction would be obvious, though it was darker now and maybe she wouldn't notice...

Well, he could hardly leave her alone on the other side of the rockfall—not with his mother's order, the 'take care of Caroline' one, still echoing in his ears.

He swam, emerging from the lagoon and flapping at his shorts to conceal the evidence of his reaction.

'We'd better move into the shadows of the palm trees,'

he said, deciding it was time to take charge. 'And walk quietly. You don't know who might be around.'

'What, like fierce Alsatian guard dogs that will rip us to pieces without a second thought?' Caroline muttered. 'I wonder if I can still shin up a coconut palm.'

Keanu smiled at the image, although he was thinking more of the darkness the shadows would provide. At least in the shadows beneath the palms he wouldn't be able to see the way her full breasts were outlined by the wet shift, or the way it was indented into her navel, and raised slightly over the mound of her sex.

He had to stop thinking about wet shifts and sex and concentrate or they'd be caught for sure.

As they approached the first of the bures that had once housed visiting scientists they heard voices, but not close.

'That sounds like people over beyond the kitchen where the little staff bar used to be,' he murmured to Caroline.

The helicopter pilots, back when there had been three or four and so they'd had more time off than other staff, had always frequented it, not by creeping down the cliff and swimming around the rockfall but by walking down the track from the airfield—the track now fenced off, guarded and gated.

A lone light shone in the first of the bures, but even from outside Keanu could see the place had had a lot of money spent on it. Stone walls where mud had been, a marble deck with a deep spa bath shaded by thick vegetation.

'This isn't accommodation for visiting scientists,' Caro whispered to him. 'It's luxury accommodation for the very wealthy who want absolute privacy and can afford it. See how each bure has been separated from the next by a thick planting of shrubs, most of them scented, like that huge ginger plant over there.'

'But what of the laboratories and the communal kitchens and dining rooms?' he argued. 'Surely people paying the kind of money they'd pay to stay here aren't all going to eat together?

'Let's see.'

Keanu took her hand, ignoring the shock of excitement such an impersonal touch had caused. He led the way towards the kitchen area, although always off the path that, even in the dark, looked freshly raked and would show their footprints.

What had been the kitchen and adjoining open eating area seemed shrouded in scaffolding, until they crept closer and realised the old longhouse had been included in the renovations. It was now a longer, wider building, still open at the sides to catch the breezes, exactly like the meeting halls on the other islands, where feasts were held and elders met to make rules or administer judgment. Only better—fancier...

The kitchens must be behind it, but so was the bar because the noise was louder now.

'We can't go farther,' Keanu said firmly. 'We'd be caught for sure. We'll have to rely on Sam to report on the laboratories when he's able to go back to work in them. And there's no way we can take photographs, the flash would alert someone for sure.'

He half expected Caro to argue—she'd always been the one more willing to take risks—but to his surprise she turned back into the bushes.

'Come on, we'll go back the way we came before someone finds us.'

Caroline smiled to herself, realising Keanu was now as intent on this expedition as she had been.

But holding Keanu's hand was distracting, and he was pulling her along, far too close to his body, which was beyond distracting. She began to tremble and suspected it wasn't nerves or cold, although he stopped in a particular dense patch of shadow and pulled her into his arms.

'You're cold,' he whispered, folding her against his body, the action making her tremble even more. His bare skin was warm against hers, his body hard where hers was soft. And her reaction to it was so startling she probably would have done something stupid like kiss him if he hadn't been rubbing his hands up and down her arms, obviously trying to warm her, although the trembles had nothing to do with the cool night air.

A boulder—it confirmed her suspicions. No matter what weird reactions she was having to this reunion—to his closeness, his body—he was feeling nothing for the woman trembling in his arms.

A rustle in the bushes broke them apart, and although it was only an inquisitive lyrebird, it was enough to remind them of where they were and the inherent danger of being caught there.

But red flags of warning of another kind waved in Caroline's head as they crept back to the beach. Her reaction to Keanu holding her had to be a rebound thing. Devastated by Steve's rejection and reunited with her childhood friend, she'd really only wanted comfort.

Right.

So why was her body throbbing with what felt very like desire, not to mention an even deeper regret that the kiss hadn't happened?

Ridiculous! A relationship between them just couldn't happen. Not only had her uncle Ian done all he could to blacken the Lockhart name among the islands' population but he'd—what?—assaulted Keanu's mother?

Although he'd said worse than assault…

Little wonder Keanu had broken off all contact with her—and probably distrusted anyone who bore the Lockhart name.

At which stage she fell over, making enough noise as she landed in a baby palm tree to awaken the ghosts of the dead.

'What is wrong with you?' Keanu growled, hauling her to her feet. 'You're blundering along as if you've got your eyes shut.'

She could hardly tell him the line her thoughts had been following so she got back onto the edge of the path and resumed walking quietly along it.

'Tomorrow night we could walk along the fence,' Keanu said, breaking a silence that had stretched a little tautly between them.

'I might be on duty. I haven't met Hettie yet, let alone get a roster from her.'

'Come to think of it, you probably will be on duty,' Keanu told her. 'Anahera does extra day shifts so she can be at home with Hana in the evenings. Besides which we probably wouldn't see much—the plantings are too thick.'

'On duty all night?' Caroline ignored his fence conversation because she was interested in the set-up at the short-staffed hospital, although she'd get back to him ordering her around some other time. They'd been a pair, a partnership, in all the right and wrong things they'd done, and now here he was, giving orders…

'No, three to midnight. We have a couple of local nurses' aides who share the night shifts between them.'

'And who supports them?'

Keanu sighed.

'It's a small hospital, Caro, and either Sam or whatever doctor is here is always on call. Hettie, too, for that matter. The staff quarters are just at the back of the hospital and it takes exactly two minutes to get from one of our apartments to the wards.'

'You've timed it?'

They'd reached the beach and paused beneath the palm

trees, talking quietly while they checked that no one else was taking a midnight stroll.

'I've done it,' Keanu told her. 'More than once. The aides are good, but they know what they can handle and what they can't. The system could be a lot better but it works.'

It didn't seem right to Caroline that Hettie was the nurse always on call, but until she knew more about the hospital, there was nothing she could do.

She was concentrating on hospital staffing issues because Keanu's use of her childhood name—his casual use of 'Caro'—had started up the disturbances the warming hug had caused.

'It seems quiet, let's go,' she said, and led the way across the sand to the shadow of the rockfall.

To Keanu's relief the tide had gone out far enough for them to wade around the rocks. Given the effect that holding her had had on his body, he didn't think he could handle seeing the wet shift again.

He had no idea why Caro had returned to the island, certain her coming to help because she'd heard it was in trouble wasn't the whole story.

What had happened to that sleazy-looking guy called Steve who was always with her in the society pictures?

Had he dumped her?

Keanu shook his head, angry with himself for even thinking about Caroline's private life, but angrier for feeling sorry for her. It was bad enough he'd become involved in tonight's escapade, but to have held Caro in his arms, felt her body pressed to his...

He must have been moonstruck!

They were scaling the rocky cliff path now and he paused to look around for a moon but failed to find one.

'Are you grunting?' Caro asked. 'I know it's steep but I thought you'd be fitter than that.'

'I was *not* grunting,' he told her, voice as cold as he could make it.

'Wild pigs, then,' Carol said cheerfully, although he knew she didn't for a minute believe it.

Though would she have believed he'd been grunting at his own stupid thoughts?

'Bright lights ahead,' the woman he shouldn't have held in his arms said cheerfully, and he locked away the past and moved himself swiftly into the present.

Bright lights indeed.

'The helicopter must have brought in a patient from an outer island,' he said, lengthening his stride so he passed Caro as he hurried towards the scene of the action.

Hettie had one end of the stretcher they were unloading, Jack, the pilot, holding the other end. He could see Manu, their one remaining hospital orderly, running towards the airstrip, Sam not far behind him.

'Tropical ulcer gone bad,' Hettie said as Manu took over her end of the stretcher and Sam and Keanu arrived. 'I'm actually dubious about it. I think it might be worse than that.'

'A Buruli ulcer?' Sam queried, and Hettie shrugged.

'We'll need to test it.'

She spoke quietly but Keanu knew they were all feeling tension from the words she'd spoken. Tropical ulcers were common enough and in many cases very difficult to treat, but the Buruli was a whole other species, and could lead to bone involvement and permanent disability.

'Is it common here?'

He'd forgotten about Caro but she was right behind him, so close that when he swung around to answer her his arm brushed against her breast.

And restarted all the thoughts he was sure he'd locked away.

'Not as common as in some islands in the west Pacific,'

he told her, then he caught up with Hettie, who was following the stretcher up the slight incline to the hospital.

'I've got a new recruit for you here,' he said. 'Sam's probably told you Maddie and the FIFO nurse weren't coming in today, but Caroline dropped from the skies yesterday and she tells us she's a nurse.'

He ignored the glower Caro shot at him as she stepped past him to introduce herself to Hettie.

'Caroline Lockhart,' she said, holding out her hand, while Keanu watched the meeting with some trepidation.

'Of the hilltop mansion Lockharts?' Hettie demanded, ignoring the proffered hand.

'Yes, and proud of it,' Caro said quietly but firmly. 'And I'd rather be judged by my work than the house I live in.'

Hettie pushed errant bits of hair off her forehead and sighed.

'Fair call,' she said softly, and this time, to Keanu's relief, *she* held out *her* hand. 'It's just been too long a day trying to work out how to replace a resident clinic nurse on Raiki Island.'

'What happened to her?' Caroline asked, and Keanu knew the answer was going to hurt her.

'Apparently she went off with your uncle Ian—she and all the drugs.'

'She what?' Caroline swung towards Keanu. 'Does my father know all that's been going on? Know his brother's stooped so low as to rob an island of their drugs, not to mention their nurse?'

'It was only discovered yesterday.' Hettie answered for him, and her voice was gentle. 'And as Ian's gone off in his yacht to who knows where, there's very little your father or anyone else can do about it.'

Keanu read the pain on Caro's face as she realised exactly why the Lockhart name was mud. The harm Ian had done reached out across all island life and all the islanders.

Following the little procession up to the hospital, Keanu felt deeply sorry for her, sorry for the pain the slights against her family must be causing her.

But the Caro he'd known would have pushed away any offer of comfort and tossed her head to deny any pain.

He glanced towards her and saw her chin rise.

This Caro wasn't so different. She'd take them all on and prove all Lockharts weren't tarred with the same brush.

And seeing that chin tilt—reading it—his heart cramped just a little at the sight of it. The woman she'd become wasn't so different from his Caro after all.

'A Buruli ulcer?'

Caroline had caught up with him so the question came from his right shoulder.

He glanced towards her and even in the poor light on the track he could see the remnants of her hurt.

He wanted to put his arm around her shoulders and pull her close. Comfort her as he had when she'd been a child, hurt or lonely or bewildered by her motherless, and usually fatherless, situation.

But with all the new disturbances she'd caused in his body, giving her a comforting hug was no longer an option.

Professional colleagues, that's all they were.

'It's not that common but it's a nasty thing if left untended, as this one may have been. Often it starts as a small nodule, hardly bigger than a mosquito bite, so the patient just ignores it, but the infection can lead to a bigger ulcer forming, destroying skin and tissue. If it's left too long there can be bone involvement, even loss of a limb.'

'Sounds like a similar infection to leprosy.' She was frowning now, no doubt thinking back to her years of study.

'Spot on,' he told her. 'The bacterium causing it is related to both the leprosy and tuberculosis bacteria.'

'Can you test for it here or do you have to send swabs to the mainland? Wouldn't that take days?'

Hettie answered for him.

'We're fortunate in that Sam is an avid bacteriologist in whatever spare time he has. Although the research station's closed at the moment, he still loves poking around in the little lab we have at the hospital and breeding who knows what in Petri dishes. If anyone can test it, he can.'

Caroline realised she'd have to rethink the laid-back, handsome doctor who ran the hospital. He obviously had hidden depths because even the simplest of biological tests was painstaking work.

They'd reached the hospital and, unsure of her part in whatever lay ahead, she followed the troop inside.

The patient was young, maybe just reaching teenage years, from French Island, so called, Caroline knew, because a French square-rigged sailing vessel had once foundered there, the sailors staying on, intermarrying with the locals, until rescued many years later.

Caroline concentrated on the now instead of on the past. The boy, Raoul—French names still being common—had been lifted onto an examination table, and Sam, assisted by one of the nurses' aides who had been waiting at the hospital, was carefully removing the light dressing Hettie had used to cover the wound.

Caroline swallowed a gasp. This was no small nodule like a mosquito bite but a full-blown leg ulcer, the edges a mess of tattered skin and deeper down, tender, infected flesh.

'I'm going to take a swab,' Sam was saying to the patient, 'but even before I test it, I'm going to start you on antibiotics.'

'It generally responds well to a combination of rifampicin and streptomycin,' Keanu explained quietly. 'If that doesn't work, there are other combinations of drugs we can use, usually with the rifampicin. The other combinations haven't been fully tested but the options are there.'

Tension she hadn't been aware she was feeling eased a little, but she hated the thought of the possibility of this young lad losing a leg.

'Okay, everyone out except Mina,' Sam said, using a shooing motion with his hand. 'She and I can handle it from here. Keanu, you might introduce our newest staff member to Jack. And Hettie, if you're not too tired, I've left Caroline's details on your desk, but you might want a chat with her yourself.'

Great, Caroline thought. A perfect end to a perfect day—an interview with a woman who obviously hated her entire family.

But Keanu had taken her elbow, and all thoughts but her reactions to his closeness fled from her mind.

'Come out and meet Jack Richards,' he said. 'There's a staffroom through here—we can have a coffee or a cold drink.'

A bit social for an introduction, Caroline thought, but apparently the pilot called Jack usually made for this staffroom when he returned from a flight. And, yes, he was sitting there, legs outstretched on a tilting lounge chair, draining the last dregs from a can of cola.

With his head tilted back, she could see a jutting jaw, and the breadth of his shoulders suggested muscle rather than fat. Here, in the light, she saw he was tall, but solid rather than rangy. His dark hair was cropped close to his scalp as if he ran an electric razor over it every now and then by way of hairdressing.

He had a strong face, a slightly skewed nose that suggested football in his youth, and smooth olive skin. But by far his most arresting feature was a pair of dark blue eyes, which, Caroline guessed, missed very little.

He set the empty can down on a small side table.

'God, I needed that,' he said. 'The day was a disaster from beginning to end. First the consequences of the disappearance of the drugs and the nurse from Raiki. You can imagine how angry the residents were. Then we headed over to Atangi because there are two nurses there and Hettie hoped one of them would cover Raiki until we got someone.'

'Did you get someone?' Caroline asked, intrigued by this idea of a helicopter flitting between the islands as casually as a city commute.

'Yes, I think so. Hett's still negotiating. Anyway, who do we find but a mum who'd mistaken clinic days and brought in a toddler for vaccination? A toddler who hated needles. Poor kid, who doesn't? He screamed like a banshee as Hettie gave him his triple antigen. Of course, the father came in and got stuck into Hettie and the scene developed into something like an old-time TV comedy, only it wasn't really funny because the poor kid was genuinely terrified.'

'Then French and the ulcer,' Keanu said, turning from the urn where he'd been making a coffee—holding out the cup to Caroline, who shook her head.

'Yeah, we had a call from the nurse there, whipped over and collected the lad, then to top it all off we were caught in a very nasty crosswind on the flight home. I know we have to expect that at this time of the year—it's the start of cyclone season—but heaven help us if there's an emergency call tonight.'

'You're the only pilot?' Caroline asked, sitting down on the couch across from Jack.

'Sorry, I'm supposed to make the introductions,' Keanu said. 'Jack, this is Caroline, new nurse. Caroline, this is Jack Richards and, yes, at the moment he's our only pilot. Although there's relief on the way Friday when the second flight for the week comes in. That's right, isn't it, Jack? A FIFO coming in to give you a break?'

'Yeah, young Matt Rogers is due to come in on Friday's flight.'

'You don't like him?' Caroline asked, unable to not hear the distaste in Jack's voice.

'Only because he's younger, and fitter and better looking than our Jack here,' Keanu teased, 'and they both share a very keen interest in the beautiful Anahera.'

'Who at least ignores us both equally,' Jack said with such gloom Caroline had to smile.

'I can't blame any man being attracted to her—she *is* beautiful,' Caroline said, now wondering if the nurse was ignoring these two suitors because she had her eye on someone else.

Someone like Keanu?

And if Vailea's daughter fancied Keanu and Vailea was thinking him a good match, maybe that's why she'd shown such animosity to Caroline. Everyone on the island would know the two of them had grown up together...

She must have sighed, for Keanu said, 'Come on, you're tired. I'll walk you up to the house.'

Jack straightened up in his chair.

'*The* house?' he said. 'Like the Lockhart mansion? Since when did our nurses get lucky enough to stay there while important blokes like me sleep in little better than prefabricated huts?'

'Since their surname is Lockhart,' Keanu said, enough ice in his voice to stop further speculation. 'And *all* the hospital buildings are prefabricated, as you well know. It makes it much easier to pack them into shipping containers and land them here, then it only needs a small team of men to put them together.'

He turned to Caroline.

'Prefab or not, the staff villas are really lovely so just ignore him.'

Jack was ignoring them both. He was still staring at Caroline.

'You're a Lockhart?' he said with such disbelief Caroline had to smile.

'Did you think we all had two heads?' she asked, but Jack continued to stare at her.

Maybe she *had* grown a second head.

But two heads would give her two brains and she only needed one—even a part of one—to know she didn't want Keanu walking her home. Her feelings towards him were in such turmoil she doubted she'd ever sort them out.

For years she'd hated him for his desertion. Hadn't he realised he'd been her only true friend? Even after they'd both gone to boarding school, he'd still been the person to whom she'd poured out her heart in letter after letter.

Her homesickness, the strange emptiness that came from being motherless, the pain of her time spent with Christopher, who couldn't respond to her words of love—writing to Keanu had been a way of getting it out of her system.

So he knew everything there was to know about her life, from her envy when other girls' parents came to special occasions to the realisation that, for her father, Christopher and the hospital on Wildfire were more important than she was.

She'd told Keanu things she'd never told anyone, before or since, then suddenly, he'd been gone.

Nothing.

Until now, and although the confusion of seeing him again had at first been confined to her head, since he'd held her—if only to warm her—it was in her heart as well.

Damn the man.

'I don't need you to walk me home,' she said when they'd left the staffroom. 'I *do* know the way.'

'And *I* know there are a lot of unhappy Lockhart employees—or ex-employees—on the island at the moment, and while I don't think for a minute they'd take out their frustration on you, I'd rather be sure than sorry.'

So he was walking her home to protect her. Looking after Caroline as his mother had always told him to when they'd been children.

She felt stupidly disappointed at this realisation then told herself she was just being ridiculous.

As if that kind of a hug meant anything. And anyway she didn't want Keanu hugging her.

That just added to her torment.

'What employees and ex-employees are upset?' she asked to take her mind off things she couldn't handle right now.

'Just about all of them,' Keanu replied. 'But mostly the miners, and although some of them are from other islands, a lot of them live in the village. They've had their hours cut and the ones who've been sacked haven't been paid back wages, let alone their superannuation.'

'But if Ian's gone, who's here to pay them or to cut hours? Who's running the mine?'

'Who knows? Ian's disappearance, as you may have gathered, is fairly recent. He was here last week, then suddenly he was either holed up in the house or gone.'

'Gone how?' Caroline asked as they reached the front steps of the house, where Bessie had left a welcoming light burning.

'Presumably on his yacht. It was a tidy size. One day it was in the mine harbour and the next it was gone.'

'But the mine's still operating?'

Keanu nodded.

'Then we should go down and check it out.'

'Go down to the mine?' Keanu demanded.

Caroline grinned at him.

'Not right now, you goose, but tomorrow or whenever we can get some time off together. That's if you want to come with me.'

'Well, I damn well wouldn't let you go alone, although why you want to go—'

'Because I need to know—*we* need to know. Without the mine there's no way we can keep the hospital going, not to mention the fact that the entire population, not just those here on Wildfire, will lose their medical facilities as well as their incomes.'

She was so excited her eyes gleamed in the moonlight, and it was all Keanu could to not take her in his arms again, only this time for a different reason.

But if holding her once had been a mistake, twice would be fatal.

And he was still married—or probably still married, even if he hadn't seen his wife for five years.

Did that matter?

Of course it did.

He could hardly start something that she might think would lead to marriage if he couldn't marry her.

So forget a hug.

'We can't run the mine,' he said, far too bluntly because now a different confusion was nagging at him.

She shook her head in irritation.

'Then we'll just have to think of something.'

He had to agree, if only silently. The continued survival of the hospital—in fact, of all the health care in the islands—depended on support from the mine.

'I imagine once we know what's happening we can find someone who can,' he said, reluctantly drawn in and now thinking aloud. 'Some of the local men have worked there since it opened, or if they're not still there we could find them. We want men who trained under Peter Blake or maybe beg Peter to come back.'

'And pay him how?' Caroline demanded.

Keanu held up his hands in surrender.

'Hey, you're the one who wanted to think of something. I'm just throwing out ideas here. You can take them or leave them.'

He saw the shadow cross her face and knew he'd somehow said the wrong thing.

'Is that how you felt about me back then? That you could take me or leave me? Yes, Ian obviously hurt your mother, but what did *I* do to *you* to make you cut me out of your life?'

She was angry—beautiful with anger—but he stood his ground, then he leaned forward and touched her very gently on the cheek.

'You were never right out of my life, Caro,' he said quietly, his hand sliding down to rest on her shoulder. Momentarily. He turned and walked swiftly back down the track, not wanting her to see the pain her words had caused written clearly on his face.

But she was right. He *had* come back to see what he could do to save the hospital, and saving the mine should have been the obvious starting place.

But joining forces in this crusade would mean seeing more of her, working with her outside hospital hours, feeling her body beside his, aware all the time of the effect she had on him, aware of her in a way he'd never been before, or imagined he ever would.

Physically aware of the one woman in the world who was beyond his grasp—the woman whose trust he'd betrayed when she'd been nothing more than a girl...

Caroline watched him stride down the path, long legs moving smoothly and deliberately over the rough track, stance upright, broad shoulders square...

Was it just the length of time since they'd seen each

other that was making things so awkward between them, or was Keanu still brooding over whatever had happened to make him stop writing to her? Even stop reading her letters…

'Bother the man,' she muttered to herself, climbing the steps and wandering through the house towards her bedroom.

Her bedroom. Still decorated with the posters of the idols of her teenage self.

Of course, with Ian gone, she could have the pick of any of the six bedrooms in the house, but her room felt like home, even if home was an empty and lonely place without Keanu in it. Helen *and* Keanu. Their rooms had been in the western annexe, but the whole house had been her and Keanu's playground—the whole island, in fact.

Stupid tears pricked behind her eyelids as memories of their youth together—their friendship and closeness— threatened to overwhelm her.

Pulling herself together, she ripped the posters off the walls. One day soon—when she'd done the things she *really* needed to do, like visit the mine, she'd find some paint and redo the room, maybe redecorate the whole house, removing all traces of the past.

Except in your head, a traitorous voice reminded her.

But she'd had enough of traitorous voices—hadn't one lived with her through most of her relationship with Steve?

She'd learned to ignore it and could do so again.

Although, with Steve, maybe she'd have been better off listening to it. Listening to the whisper that had questioned his protestations of love, listened to the niggling murmur that had questioned broken dates with facile excuses, listened to her friends…

Had she been so desperate for love, for someone to love her, that she'd ignored all the signs and warnings?

'Oh, for heaven's sake, get with it, girl!' she said out loud, hoping to jolt herself from the past to the present.

There was certainly enough to be done in the present to blot out any voices in her head.

Work was the answer. Nursing at the hospital, and during her time off finding out exactly what had been happening on the island.

CHAPTER FIVE

THE PREVIOUS EVENING Hettie had disappeared by the time Caroline had finished talking to Jack, so she wasn't sure if she was employed or not. Deciding she had to find out, she walked down to the hospital at seven-thirty the next morning.

It was already hot and the humidity was rising. Jack's mention of cyclones had reminded her that this wasn't the best time of the year to return to the island—although she'd spent many long summer holidays here and survived whatever the weather had thrown at her.

Hettie was in a side ward with the patient she'd brought in the previous evening, and it was, Caroline decided, almost inevitable that Keanu would be with her as she examined the wound.

'Will you have to cut away the ulcerated tissue?' she asked, walking to the other side of the bed and peering at the ulcer herself.

Hettie looked up, beautiful green eyes focussing on Caroline.

Focussing so intently Caroline found herself offering a shrug that wasn't exactly an apology for speaking but very nearly.

'I came down to see if you had work for me to do—a slot in the roster perhaps, or some use you could put me to?'

Hettie was still eyeing her warily, or maybe that was just her everyday look. She was neat—a slim figure, jeans and a white shirt, long dark hair controlled in a perfect roll at the back of her head—and attractive in a way that made Caroline think she'd be beautiful if she smiled.

'What do you know about Buruli ulcers?' Hettie asked, and, breathing silent thanks for the instinct that had made her look them up on the internet, Caroline rattled off what she'd learned.

Then, aware that the internet wasn't always right, she added, 'But that's just what Mr Google told me. I haven't had any experience of them.'

To her surprise, Hettie smiled and Caroline saw that she *was* beautiful—that quiet, unexpected kind of beauty that was rare enough to sometimes go unnoticed.

'You'll do,' Hettie said. 'Welcome aboard. It's hard to work to rosters here, but there's always work. Maddie, one of our FIFO doctors, usually does the checks on the miners but she didn't come in and the checks are due—or slightly overdue. You'd know the mine, wouldn't you? Perhaps you and Keanu could do that today?'

Excitement fizzed in Caroline's head—the perfect excuse to go down to the mine.

'What kind of checks do we do?' she asked Hettie, ignoring Keanu, who was arguing that she was too new in the job to be going down to the mine.

'Just general health. They tend to ignore cuts and scratches, although they know they can become infected or even ulcerated. And we've got a couple of workers—you'll see their notes on the cards—who we suspect have chest problems and aren't really suited to working underground. But you know men, they're a stubborn lot and will argue until they're blue in the face that they haven't any problems with their lungs.'

'Stubborn patients I do understand,' Carolyn said, smiling inwardly as she wondered if seemingly prim and proper Hettie had experienced many run-ins with stubborn men in her own life. She certainly seemed to have some strong opinions when it came to men in general.

'As a matter of course,' Hettie continued, 'we check the lung capacity of all the men and keep notes, and those two aren't so bad we can order them out of the mine. Yet. The hospital is, in part, funded by the Australian government, and the health checks at the mine are a Workplace Health and Safety requirement.'

'More paperwork for Sam,' Caroline said, and Hettie smiled again.

'He does hate it,' she agreed before turning to Keanu. 'You're not tied up, so you can take Caroline down there. You can show her where all the paperwork is kept, and the drugs cabinet we have down there.'

'If Ian didn't pinch it when he left,' Keanu muttered, but Caroline couldn't help feeling how lucky they were, to both have this excuse to visit the mine.

And although more time with Keanu was hardly ideal, this was work, and all she had to do was concentrate on that.

If she was gathering whatever impressions she could of what was happening at the mine she'd hardly be aware Keanu was there.

Hardly.

Stick to business!

'So, who do you think will be in charge of the mine now Ian's gone?' she asked Keanu as they took the path around the house that led to the steps down to the mine.

He stopped, turning around to take her hand to help her over a rough part of the track where the stone steps had broken away.

'Ian's never really been hands-on, leaving the shift bosses to run the teams. Reuben Alaki is one of the best,' he said, speaking so calmly she knew he couldn't possibly be feeling all the physical reactions to the touch that were surging through her.

'I remember Reuben,' she managed to say, hoping she sounded as calm as he had, although she was certain there'd been a quiver in her voice. 'His wife died and he had to bring his little boy to work and your mother looked after him. We treated him like a pet dog or cat and he followed us everywhere.'

Fortunately for her sanity the rough bit of track was behind them, and Keanu had released her hand.

'That's him, although that little boy is grown up and is over in Australia, getting paid obscene amounts of money to play football.'

Then of course Keanu smiled, which had much the same result on her nerve endings as his touch had.

'Good for him,' Caroline said cheerily. 'Maybe you should have gone that way instead of becoming a doctor.'

Then you wouldn't be here holding my hand and smiling at me and totally confusing me!

Lost in her own thoughts, she didn't realise Keanu had stopped. He turned back to face her, his face taut with emotion.

'We had an agreement,' he reminded her, and now a sudden sadness—nostalgia for their carefree past, their happy childhood—swept over her.

'What happened to us, Keanu?' she whispered, forgetting the present, remembering only the past.

'Ian happened,' he said bluntly, and continued down the path.

Guilt kept him moving, because he *could* have kept in touch with Caroline, but in his anger—an impotent rage at his mother's pain—he had himself cursed all Lockharts.

Of course it had had nothing to do with Caroline, but

at the time fury had made him blind and deaf, then, with his mother's death, it had been all he could do just to keep going. Getting back in touch with Caroline had been the last thing on his mind.

'All the files are in the site office,' he said, all business now as they reached the bottom of the steps.

He pointed to the rusty-looking shed sheltering under the overhang of the cave that led into the mine.

'That's Reuben there now. Let's go and see him.'

He knew Caroline was close behind him, aware of her in every fibre of his body, yet his mind was crowded with practical matters and he needed to concentrate on them—on the now, not the past...

The rumbling noise from deep inside the tunnel told him the mine was still being worked, but who was paying the men? And the crushing plant and extraction machine were standing idle, so they could hardly be taking home their wages in gold.

'Who's paying the men?' Caroline asked, as if she'd been following his train of thought as well as his footsteps.

'Reuben will tell us.'

Reuben stepped out of the shed to shake Keanu's hand, then turned to Caroline.

'New nurse?' he asked.

'But old friend, I hope, Reuben. It's Caroline Lockhart.'

Reuben beamed with delight and held out his arms to give Caroline a hug.

'You've grown up!' Reuben said, looking fondly at her. 'Grown up and beautiful!'

And from the look on Caroline's face, it was the first friendly greeting she'd received since her return.

'And your father? How is he?' Reuben asked.

'Working too hard. I hardly see him.'

'Working and caring for that poor brother of yours, too, I suppose. Same as always,' Reuben said. 'Me, I did that when my wife died but later I realised pain didn't go away with work. I have a new wife now and new family, and my big boy, he's rich and famous in Australia—sends money home to his old man even.'

'That's great, Reuben,' Caroline said, and Keanu knew she meant it. Her affinity for the islanders had always been as strong as his, and they had known that and loved her for it.

'So, what's happening here, Reuben?' he asked to get his mind back on track.

'Well...'

Reuben paused, scratched his head, shuffled his feet, and finally waved them both inside.

'The men working the bulldozer and crusher and extraction plant hadn't been paid for more than a month so they walked off the job maybe a month ago.'

He paused, looking out towards the harbour where machinery and sheds were rapidly disappearing under rampant rainforest regrowth.

'The miners are in the same boat, but they believe they'll eventually be paid. I think their team bosses sent a letter to your dad some weeks ago and they're waiting to hear back, hoping he'll come. They're happy to keep working until they hear because most of them—well, they, we— don't need the money for food or fancy clothes. It just puts the kids through school and university and pays for taking their wives on holidays.'

The words came out fluently enough but Keanu thought he could hear a lingering 'but' behind them.

'But?' Caroline said, and he had to smile that they could still be so much on the same wavelength.

'The miners—they mine. It was the crusher team that did the safety stuff. Your uncle's been putting off staff for months, and he started with the general labourers, saying the bulldozer boys and crusher and extraction operators could do the safety work when the crusher wasn't operating, but now they've gone.'

'Then the miners shouldn't be working,' Keanu said. 'You've got to pull them out of there.'

Reuben shook his head.

'They've got a plan. They're going to stockpile enough rock then come out and work the crusher themselves for a month and that way they can keep the mine going. The miners, they're all from these islands, they know the hospital needs the mine and they need the hospital and the clinics on the islands. Because they're younger, a lot of them have young families—kids. Kids have accidents—need a nurse or a doctor...'

Keanu sighed.

He understood that part of the situation—but nevertheless the mine would have to shut! Safety had to come first and their small hospital just wasn't equipped should a major catastrophe like a mine collapse happen.

Caroline's heart had shuddered at the thought of the miners working in tunnels that might not have been shored up properly, or in water that hadn't been pumped out of the tunnels, but the best way to find out was to talk to them.

'Well, if there are people working here, shouldn't we start the checks?' She turned to Keanu, and read the concern she was feeling mirrored in his eyes. 'How do you usually handle it?'

But it was Reuben who answered her.

'I'll ring through to the team and they send one man out at a time—we do it in alphabetical order so it's easier for you with the files. I'm a bit worried about Kalifa Lui—his cough seems much worse.'

'Should we see him first?' Caroline asked, but Keanu shook his head.

'He'll realise we've picked him out and probably cough

his lungs up on his way out of the mine so his chest's clear when he gets here. Better to keep to the order.'

Reuben had placed a well-labelled accident book in front of Caroline and a box of files on the table where Keanu sat.

Index card files?

Caroline looked around the office—no computer.

Ian's cost-cutting?

She didn't say anything, not wanting to confirm any more Lockhart inadequacies or bring up Ian's name unnecessarily.

Keanu was already flipping through the files, and Reuben was on the phone, organising the check-ups, so Caroline opened the book.

But she was easily distracted.

Looking at Keanu, engrossed in his work, making notes on a piece of paper, leafing back through the files to check on things, she sensed the power of this man—as a man—to attract any woman he wanted. It wasn't simply good looks and a stunning physique, but there was a suggestion of a strong sexuality—maybe more than a suggestion—woven about him like a spider's web.

And she was caught in it.

The memories of their childhood together were strong and bitter-sweet given how it had ended, but this was something different.

'Aaron Anapou, ma'am.'

Jerked out of her thoughts by the deep voice, she looked up to see a dust-smeared giant standing in front of her.

'Ah! Hi! Actually, Keanu's doing the checks. I'm Caroline—I'm the nurse.'

She stood up and held out her hand, which he took gingerly.

'You should have gloves on, ma'am,' he said quietly.

'But then I might miss a little gold dust sticking to my fingers.'

Aware that she'd already held up things for too long, she waved him along the table towards Keanu, who already had the first card in front of him.

Reuben had helpfully laid out the medical implements between the two of them—a stethoscope, ear thermometer and covers, and a lung capacity machine. So what did she do? Act as welcoming committee? Wait for orders?

Behind her desk Reuben had also opened the doors on what looked like a well-stocked medical cabinet.

Maybe she did the dressings.

But, in the meantime, there was the accident book to go through. She looked at the recent pages, then flipped back, interested to see if there were always so few accidents recorded.

It wasn't hard to work out when the crushing and extracting operations had closed down as most of the reported accidents had been caused by some chance contact with some piece of the machinery.

In the background she heard Keanu chiding men for working in flip-flops instead of their steel-capped boots, listened to explanations of water not being pumped out, and her heart ached for the days when the mine had been a well-run and productive place.

'If you're done, you can give me a hand.' Had Keanu guessed she'd been dreaming?

The next miner hadn't tried to hide the fact he'd been working in flip-flops—they were bright green and still on his feet. The skin between his big toe and the second one, where the strap of the sandal rubbed, was raw and inflamed, and a visible cut on his left arm was also infected.

Caroline worked with Keanu now; he cleaned and treated wounds, handing out antibiotics, while she did the lung capacity tests and temperatures.

'I'm surprised there are any antibiotics to give out,' she said when there was a gap between the miners.

'I keep the keys of the chest and no one but me can ever open it,' Reuben said firmly. 'I suppose it was too big for Mr Lockhart to take away and he couldn't break the bolt, although I think he tried.'

Caroline sighed.

Her uncle had left a poisonous legacy behind him on what had once been an island paradise.

And, given her name, she was part of the poison.

'We definitely have to close the mine.' Keanu's voice interrupted her dream of happier times, and she realised the parade of miners—a short parade—from the mine to the table had ceased. 'It would be irresponsible not to do it.'

'And *that* will damage the Lockhart name even more,' Caroline muttered as shame for the trouble her uncle had caused made her cringe.

He touched her quickly on the shoulder. 'We'll talk about it later,' he said, pulling the accident book from in front of her and checking the few notes she'd made.

'Given the state of the mine, there've been remarkably few accidents,' he said. 'Unless, of course...' he looked at Reuben '...you haven't been recording them.'

Reuben's indignant 'Of course I have,' was sincere enough to be believed, especially when he added, 'But remember, not all the men are working. Only this one team at the moment.'

'But even if there haven't been many accidents, that doesn't mean there won't be more in future,' Caroline said, seeing the sense in Keanu's determination that the mine should close.

So what could she do?

Find out whatever she could?

'Reuben, would you mind if I looked at the accounts and wages books?'

He looked taken aback—upset even.

'I'm not checking up on you, but it would help if I could

work out how much the miners are owed. I know Dad would want them all paid. Do you have the wages records on computer?'

'It's all in books, but I keep a copy on my laptop,' Reuben told her, disappearing into the back of the office and returning with the little laptop, handing it over to her with a degree of reluctance.

'We *do* have to close it down,' she admitted to Keanu as they climbed back up the steep steps to the top of the plateau. She was clutching the laptop to her chest.

'You're right,' he said, 'but do you think the men will stop working just because we say so? I'll phone your father—he's the one to do it, and if he can't come over, he can send someone from the Mines Department, someone who might carry some weight with the miners. They could come on Friday's flight.'

Keanu got no answer to his common-sense suggestion. *She's plotting something*, he realised as they climbed back up the steep steps to the top of the plateau.

He knew Caroline in this mood and more often than not whatever she was up to would be either rash or downright dangerous.

But he had worries enough of his own. The elders had placed their faith in him to save the livelihood of the island and the continuation of medical facilities.

'Do we have to go straight back to the hospital or can we sit down with a coffee and work out what to do? I can try to get in touch with Dad,' Caroline said as she led the way towards the house, as if assuming he would agree.

Keanu followed, but hesitated on the bottom step of the big house, his mind arguing with itself.

Of course he could go in—it was just a house, the place where he'd spent so much of his childhood.

Yet his feet were glued to the step.

Caro turned back.

'You're not coming? Do you think we should go back? Bessie would get us some lunch and we could have a talk.'

Then, as if they'd never been apart, she guessed what he was thinking, headed back down to where he stood, took his hand and gently eased him down onto the step, sitting close beside him, her arm around his shoulders.

'Tell me,' she said, and although she spoke softly, it was an order, and suddenly he needed to tell, as if talking about that day would help banish the memories.

He looked out over the island, down towards the sea surrounding it, green-blue and beautiful.

Peaceful…

'I came home on an earlier flight. One kid had measles just before the holidays so they closed a week early. I didn't tell Mum, wanting to surprise her.'

And hadn't he surprised her! The memory of that ugly, desperate scene lived on in his nightmares. He concentrated on the view to block it out of his mind even now…

'I walked up from the plane and into the house. I knew Mum would be in there—dusting or cleaning—she loved the house so much.'

Had Caro heard the break in his voice that her arm tightened around his shoulders?

'They were in the living room, on the floor, on one of your grandma's rugs, like animals.'

He turned to Caroline, needing to see her face, needing to see understanding there.

'I thought he was raping her. I dragged him off, yelling at him, trying to punch him, and…'

'Go on.'

The words were little more than a gentle whisper but now he'd gone this far he knew he had to finish.

'He laughed!' The words exploded out of him, his voice rising at remembered—and still lingering—anger. 'He stood there, pulling up his shorts, buttoning his shirt, and laughed at me. "Do you think she didn't want it?" he said. "Wasn't begging for it? Go on, Helen, tell him how desperate you were to keep what was nothing more than an occasional kindness shag going.'"

'Oh, Keanu! I can only imagine how you felt and your poor mother—'

'I lost it, Caro! I went at him, fists flying, while Mum was covering herself and gathering clothes and telling me to stop, not that I did much good. At fifteen I was a fair size, but nothing like Ian's weight. He eventually pushed me to the ground and told me to get out, both of us to get out. He'd ask the plane to wait so we could pack then be out of there.'

'But it was your home, Keanu. It always had been. Grandma had promised that before I was even born!' Caro hauled him to his feet and hugged him properly. 'Anyway, after I arrived Helen was employed by Dad, not Ian.'

Keanu put his hands on her shoulders and eased her far enough apart to look into her face.

'Ian's words destroyed Mum. She refused to talk about it except to say she'd always known she wasn't the only one. I realised then it had been going on for some time. But to humiliate her like that, in front of me—it was more than she could take! When we got back to the house in Cairns she phoned your father to say she wouldn't be there to look after you during the holidays and that she'd retired. No other explanation no matter how often he phoned, even when he visited. With the admiration she had for your father, there was no way she could have told him about it. She just shut herself away from life, then only a few years later she was gone.'

Caro drew him close again, wrapping her arms around him, holding him tightly.

'Oh, Keanu,' she whispered, the words soft and warm

against his neck. 'At least now I understand why you deserted me. How could you have had anything to do with any Lockhart after Ian's behaviour to your mother?'

Was it the release of telling her the story, of her finally knowing why he'd cut her off that made his arms move to enfold her?

He didn't know—he only knew that he held her, clung to her, breathing in the very essence that was Caroline— his Caro. And like a sigh—a breath of wind—something shifted between them…an awareness, tension—

Attraction?

You're married.

Probably.

He didn't actually leap away from her embrace, but the space between them grew.

They were friends, but whatever this new emotion was, it hadn't felt like friendship.

Had Caro felt it?

Were warning bells clanging in her head?

For once he had not the slightest idea of what she was thinking, but deep inside he knew that, whatever lay ahead, he couldn't do anything to hurt her, not again, which meant not getting too involved until he knew he was free.

Something had obviously happened between her and Steve because she was back on the island and he could see she was hurting.

Abandoned again by someone she loved?

Wouldn't he have to do that if his divorce didn't go through?

Get out of here and sort it out!

'You have lunch here,' he said, aiming for sounding calm and composed—sensible—although his whole body churned with emotion. 'I'll go back to the hospital and talk to Sam. He'll know the best way to close down the mine.'

Caroline nodded. 'Yes, good idea.'

Perhaps she hadn't felt what he'd felt when they'd hugged, because she'd never sounded more together—practical, professional—putting the past firmly behind her.

But then, she'd always been a superb actress, having grown adept at hiding her feelings.

Though usually not from him…

CHAPTER SIX

HAD THEY BEEN going to kiss?

Surely not!

But Caroline was very relieved he'd pulled away, and hopefully without seeing her suddenly breathless state.

And if he hadn't?

Would that surge of attraction have led to a kiss—right there on the front steps of the house?

Her heart ached for him after hearing the story of his return from school, his mother's humiliation, and imagining the pain the pair must have suffered, leaving the place that had been their only true home.

Her first reaction had been numbness. After Bessie's chance remark about no woman being safe around Ian, she'd imagined rape, but humiliating Helen as he had done had been emotionally so damaging. How impotent Keanu must have felt in the face of Ian's callousness.

Of course she'd had to hug him!

But hugging Keanu had never felt like that before!

Hugging Keanu had never produced that kind of mayhem in her body. Not even Steve, who'd never failed to boast about what a great lover he was, had ever managed to evoke something like that.

Or was that unfair to Steve?

He hadn't really boasted of his prowess, it was just the

impression she'd got from his confidence, and the fact that other women had envied her the man who had wooed her with flowers, and gifts and promises of undying love.

Actually, now the hurt was gone and she could look back rationally, it had been the undying love thing that had got her in the end; the fact that this person had come into her life, vowing to be there for ever—to never let her down or abandon her. That last had been the clincher.

How stupid had *she* been?

A practised lover, he'd sniffed out the silly issues she had with abandonment—with the loss of so many people in her life and the distraction of others—and had worked on it!

Jilly had been right, she was well out of that relationship, and as the days had turned into months Caroline had realised that as well, glad the man she'd thought she loved had turned out to have not only feet of clay but whole legs of it!

And Keanu?

She closed her eyes and breathed deeply then decided she wouldn't think about that right now. She had more important things to consider, the first being to find some way to pay the miners what they were owed.

She didn't think it would go all the way to restoring the Lockhart name but those people had worked for her family—they deserved to be paid.

And they would be.

She'd phone Dad, talk to him about the mine closure and the problems Ian had left behind him on the island—the damage he had done to the Lockhart name.

Although could she add that much more worry to his already over-burdened shoulders?

An image of her twin rose up in front of her—Christopher's crippled, twisted body, his lovely blue eyes gazing blankly towards her as she talked to him, the pigeon chest battling for every breath...

No, she couldn't pull Dad away from Christopher, especially right now when he had been hospitalised again...

So it was up to her.

Or was she fooling herself?

'Nurse Hettie phoned to say she expected you back at the hospital.' Bessie appeared at the front door. 'I told her you're having a late lunch and will be down soon.'

Bother!

'Thanks, Bessie, I'll go right now.'

'You'll do no such thing. You come into the kitchen and have lunch.'

'But Reuben gave Keanu and I fruit salad and cold juice. I don't need lunch.'

'You do need lunch!'

Realising it was futile to argue, she went into the kitchen to eat the gargantuan sandwich Bessie had prepared for her.

Footsteps on the veranda sent Bessie scurrying from the kitchen, and Caroline carefully wrapped the remainder of the sandwich and popped it into the fridge.

The deep voice she heard was definitely Keanu's.

Her heart made a squiggly feeling in her chest as she hurried to the front veranda.

'There was no need for you to come up, I just had to wash and put on a clean top—it was dusty down there.'

Keanu nodded, just that, a nod, the story he'd shared with her like a glass wall between them.

Or had it been the hug?

Whatever, he'd turned away and started back towards the hospital, pausing only to explain, 'Hettie's done two trips the last two days so she's taking a break, but the patient with the Buruli ulcer needs the skin around it debrided and the wound cleaned, and Anahera has her hands full with the other patients.'

Other patients?

Caroline realised with a start how little she knew about

the hospital and what was going on there. She was a nurse, and the patients should be her first concern, not worrying how to pay the money owed to the miners.

She followed Keanu down the path, ignoring the hitch in her breathing at the breadth of his shoulders and the way his hair curled against the nape of his neck, catching up with him to ask, 'Do we use the treatment room where I first saw him or the operating theatre?

'He doesn't need a full anaesthetic, just locals around the wound, but the theatre is more sterile so we'll do it there.'

Caught up in what lay ahead, Caroline set aside the disturbances Keanu's presence was causing and concentrated on the case.

'Are we using the theatre because the ulcer bacteria are easily transmitted?'

Keanu shook his head.

'We've no idea how it's transmitted, although the World Health Organization has teams of people in various places working on it. Using the theatre is a safeguard, nothing more.'

'And debriding tissue?'

He turned to look at her as they reached the hospital.

'Are you asking questions to prove your worth as a nurse or because you're genuinely interested?'

The deliberate dig took her breath away but before she could get into a fierce, and probably very loud, argument with him, he added, 'I'm sorry, that was unfair. I'm so damned mixed up right now.'

He sighed, dark eyes troubled, then touched her lightly on the shoulder.

'The thing about Buruli is that it produces a toxin called mycolactone that destroys tissue. We have the patient on antibiotics but they are taking time to work, so we're going to clean it up in the hope that we'll kill off any myolactone spores.'

Caroline's mind switched immediately to nurse mode. They'd need local anaesthesia, scalpels, dressings, dishes to take the affected skin to be disposed of in the incinerator.

And she had no idea where that was or, in fact, where any of the other things were kept. Instead of prowling around in the dark with Keanu last night, she should have been checking out the hospital.

She must have sighed, for Keanu said, 'It's okay, Mina will have everything set out for us.'

He *was* still reading her mind!

And, given some of the thoughts flashing through it, that could prove very dangerous—*and* downright embarrassing.

The ulcer was inflamed and looked incredibly painful, but the young man was stoic about it.

Keanu injected local anaesthetic into the tissue around the wound, then checked the equipment while he waited for it to take effect.

'I want to keep as much of the skin intact as I can,' Keanu said, speaking directly to her for the first time. 'I'll trim the edges and try to clean beneath it. I'll need you to swab and use tweezers to clear the damaged bits as I cut.'

Caroline picked up a pair of forceps. The wound was long but reasonably narrow, and she could see what Keanu hoped to do. If he could clean out the wound he might be able to stretch the healthy skin enough to stitch it together.

'If you stitch it up, would you leave a small drain in place?'

He glanced up from his delicate task of scraping and cutting and nodded. Seeing his eyes above the mask he was wearing made her heart jittery again.

This was ridiculous. She was a professional and any interaction between them, at least at the hospital, had to be just that—professional!

She selected another pair of forceps and lifted the skin towards which he was working.

He continued to cut, dropping some bits in one dish and some in a separate one.

Intrigued, she had to ask.

'Why the two dishes?'

He glanced up at her with smiling eyes and any last remnants of hope about professionalism flew out the window—well, there was no window, but they disappeared. That smile re-awoke all the manifestations of attraction that she'd felt earlier, teasing along her nerves and activating all her senses.

'I think I mentioned Sam's a keen bacteriologist,' Keanu was explaining while she told herself she was being ridiculous. 'He's never made Buruli a particular study but he'll be interested to look at it under a microscope. The more people around the world peering at it the better chance we have of developing a defence against it. It's not so bad here in the West Pacific but in some African and Asian nations when it's not treated early it attacks the bone and causes deformities or even loss of limbs.'

'I don't want to lose my leg,' their patient said firmly, and Keanu assured him that no such thing would happen.

'We've got you onto the drugs early enough and once we clean it up you should be fine.'

Keanu was being professional—purely professional.

Until he looked up, caught her eye, and winked.

'I think that's it,' he said, much to her relief. It had been an 'I'm finished' wink, nothing more.

Yet her reaction suggested that keeping things purely professional between herself and Keanu would prove impossible—from her side at least.

No way! She was stronger than that. And she had plenty to occupy her mind. The sooner she could get the back payments for the miners sorted out, and get the mine closed until it could be made safe, the better it would be for the hospital, and if she concentrated on that—

'Okay, I'll get Mina to do the dressing. I think we deserve a coffee.'

She glanced at the clock—they'd been standing over their patient for more than two hours and probably did deserve a coffee.

Well, she could do coffee...

Except he was smiling.

Possibly not.

'What I need more than coffee is a tour of the hospital so I know where everything is and what patient is where. I'll do the dressing then maybe Mina can show me around.'

Keanu could hardly argue, although he could alter the plan slightly.

'Let's stick with Mina doing the dressing and I'll show you around instead.'

Caroline's reaction wasn't what you'd call ecstatic.

More resigned, if anything, but after being distracted by the telling of his mother's distress and their departure from the island earlier, he was hoping to have a chat about the situation at the mine—to find out what she was thinking.

Because she *was* thinking of something she could do to help matters. He'd known her too long and too well not to have picked that up.

But he could hardly ask about it while touring the little hospital and introducing patients, so he'd have to find another time.

'There are four wards, if you can call small two-bed spaces *wards*. Three on this side, with sliding doors that can close each of them off, although most of the time we leave it open for the breezes.'

He led her into the first of these, which, at the moment, had two patients, young men from another island who had taken the tide too lightly and had been injured when the boat they'd been in had overturned on the reef. 'As you can see,' Keanu pointed out, 'one has a broken arm, the other an injured ankle, and both have quite bad coral grazes—'

'Which can easily become infected if not treated promptly and continually.'

Keanu nodded. Anyone who grew up in the islands knew about infections from coral so he wasn't going to give her any brownie points for that. But walking with her, talking with her—even professionally—was so distracting to his body he couldn't help but resent her presence.

If she wasn't here—

No, he was glad she was here.

She belonged here, just as he did. He just had to get over this physical attraction thing.

Be professional.

'The patient in the third bed, in what's technically another ward, you might recognise—Brenko, Bessie and Harold's grandson. The flying surgeon took out his spleen last week after he'd had an accident on his quad bike. More muscle than sense, haven't you?'

The young man grinned, and the patients, who had been quiet as Keanu had brought the stranger into the room, all began to talk at once.

Was she really Caroline Lockhart? How could any Lockhart show her face here? What was going to happen with the mine?

The questions, and the animosity behind some of them, must have hurt Caroline deeply because he heard her sigh with relief when he stopped the talk.

'Caroline is here as a nurse, so if you don't want her jabbing you with unnecessary needles, you'd better start treating her with respect. She's spent more time in these islands than some of you have been alive and is not to blame for anything her uncle did.'

The anger that underlined Keanu's words quietened the

young men, then Brenko said, 'I'm glad you're back, Caroline. I still have the ukulele you gave me when I was little.'

Caroline smiled at the memory, but Keanu guessed that one happy memory wouldn't make up for the animosity that had been thick in the air around her.

He led her through the next small room, this one closed off with the shutters. An elderly woman patient was sleeping soundly, although the young men's voices could be heard quite clearly.

'Unstable diabetic,' Keanu murmured.

'It's the curse of all the Pacific islands,' Caroline replied quietly, and he nodded, then, feeling the hurt he knew she would be nursing, he put his arm around her shoulders and gave her a quick squeeze.

She shot away as if he'd burned her, then must have realised her reaction had been a little extreme and moved close again.

But not close enough for hugs or squeezes, however sympathetic.

In the fourth room, a young woman was sitting up in bed, nursing her baby, Anahera standing by in case either of them needed a bit of help.

'We don't have a maternity ward because we transfer all pregnant women to the mainland at thirty-four to thirty-six weeks, depending on the advice of our flying obstetrician, but this little fellow arrived early,' Keanu explained, smiling at the sight of the mother and child.

'By rights he shouldn't be here. His mum was to be going out on today's flight,' he continued. 'But Hettie and the local midwife who delivered him suspect his dates were wrong. As you can see, he's a good size and he's feeding lustily.'

He turned to smile at Caroline.

'In all truth, we love having him here—we've all gone a bit soft. Because the women and their babies usually fly in and go straight to their homes, we don't get to see the babies except on clinic runs. Consequently, we're happy to keep these two here just in case anything goes wrong. We've got them isolated in this room to keep them clear of any infection.'

'Because you don't know how Buruli ulcers are transmitted?'

'Exactly.'

'The lad with the ulcer will be transferred to the ICU across the passage, beyond the theatre, once Mina has finished dressing the wound. It's next to the recovery room and ICU is probably a grand name for it but it's got a ventilator and monitoring equipment in it. The lad doesn't need it but it does keep him isolated.'

Caroline nodded her understanding.

'We're not finished, are we?' she asked. 'Don't you have linen cupboards and drug cabinets and instruments and sterilisers and a million other things that a hospital, even a small one, needs? Where's your radiography department, for a start?'

'Through here,' he said, moving into a separate wing. 'The theatre you've already seen and all the sterilising stuff is in an annexe off that. Cupboards for sterile clothing, etcetera are also in the annexe, and there's a shower and locker room next to that and beyond the theatre is Radiography.'

'It's well planned,' Caro commented.

'We've your father to thank for that,' he said. 'And him to thank for us having the best and latest in radiography machines. Money from the mine put in the basics—X-ray and ultrasound—and the Australian government donated a mammography machine, but he won a grant from one of the big casinos to put in a CT machine. He really does everything he can for the island and the hospital.'

'The hospital and Christopher,' Caro pointed out, and

Keanu heard the catch in her voice. Did she think her father cared more for the hospital and his son than he did for his daughter?

Keanu remembered that as a child Caro had felt guilty about her mother's death, and Christopher's cerebral palsy, blaming herself for both problems, but there was no way Max would feel that.

'That was bitchy!' she said suddenly. 'Both the hospital and Christopher need him far more than I do. And Dad has so much on his shoulders, the least I can do is understand that and do whatever I might be able to do to lift some of the burden.'

Keanu wanted to argue that she had every right to feel left out, but he wondered if Max's avoidance of the island whenever possible was entirely to do with work and his disabled son, or was it that he was still haunted by his young wife's death?

Would too many heartbreaking memories lay siege to him whenever he was here?

Caro was wandering around the equipment, checking it all.

'So, what do you think?' he asked, dragging his mind from the Lockhart family tragedies to the present.

'It's great equipment for a small hospital but, given the isolation, I'd say it's all necessary. And I can see why Dad's been working his butt off, not only for money to keep the place afloat but doing all the lobbying with business and government.'

The way she spoke told Keanu she saw little of her adored father, but as he watched she shrugged off whatever she was thinking and tugged at one of the curtains that screened off various sections of the room.

She poked her head out from behind the curtain and grinned cheekily, doing terrible things to Keanu's heart, lungs, not to mention his determination to keep things professional between them.

'We didn't think of all of this when we decided to become the doctor and the nurse on Wildfire, did we?'

'Didn't know "all this" existed,' Keanu reminded her, hoping he sounded more in control than he felt.

Trying to get her and the past out of his mind, he remembered the look on her face as they'd come back from the mine and his wanting to find out what she was up to.

'The laundry cupboards and other stuff are closer to the kitchen and even if you don't want a coffee, I do.'

She followed him obediently, said hello to the cook when he introduced them, then politely but adamantly refused to answer any questions.

'To tell you the truth, Keanu, I have no idea what I can do to sort out all that's happened at the mine, but I know I have to do something. The hospital needs a functioning mine, and the islands need the hospital, so we can't just let it all fizzle out. Besides, it was a Lockhart who caused all the problems, so it's up to me to at least try to do something to sort it out.'

But what?

The question bugged him, to the extent that he found himself, much later, when all was well in the hospital and Sam and Hettie both on call, walking up the hill, skirting the lagoon, to the house where he'd grown up.

They'd grown up.

He climbed the steps but once again hesitated on the veranda, reluctant to go in.

'Caro?'

His call was tentative—pathetic, really.

'If you want to see me you'll have to come in,' she yelled from somewhere inside, and he guessed from the direction of her voice that she'd be sitting at the big table in the dining room, pen and paper at hand, trawling through the information on the laptop.

Of course he could go in. It had been his home as much as hers, and although as a Lockhart she probably had more rights, his mother had run the place for years.

Until...

Then Caro was there, so much sympathy in her eyes he thought his heart might crack.

She put both arms around him and drew him close.

'I know it must be dreadful, having to walk through here again, but I'm in the dining room, and you have to do it some time. Standing out here isn't going to banish the memory, now, is it?'

Her hair touched his shoulder, soft as silk, and the woman smell of her filled his head with fantasy.

So much so, his arms returned her hug until it became more than a hug and they were kissing—gentle, exploratory kisses that nonetheless sent fire throughout his body and a throbbing need deep inside it.

Eventually—fortunately—she eased away.

'Well, that was weird,' she said lightly, before leading him firmly into the house.

But it was more than weird, it was dangerous. The attraction he was feeling was obviously mutual, but there were so many ifs and buts about it...

She'd led him into the dining room, and Keanu looked at the bits of paper scattered across the shining surface.

'What on earth are you doing?' he demanded.

'I'm trying to work out exactly how much the workers are owed, and once I know that I'd like to know how much it costs to run the mine on a weekly or monthly basis.'

'And then you'll know how much you need to win on Lotto to fix everything up,' Keanu finished for her.

She glared at him.

'You may mock, but while it might be hard to find

money for projects like this, it would be impossible if we don't know what we need. If I can work out a kind of ball-park figure, we can take it from there—get some investors, speak to banks, big businesses, whatever. It might be beyond us whatever we do, but at least we'd know we tried.'

Keanu understood what she was saying and a tiny spark of light flickered in his brain. The seed of an idea he couldn't yet grasp.

Kind of hard to grasp at glimmers of ideas in his head when most of it was occupied with telling his body that a sympathy kiss from Caroline meant nothing, and the fact that his body was attracted to hers was probably nothing more than their closeness in their childhood, and he was still married...

Probably.

Was she feeling the awkwardness too, that she suddenly bundled up all her bits of paper into a very rough pile and said, 'The moon's up, let's go for a walk. I haven't been down to the lagoon since I got back—there always seems to be something else to do.'

She made it sound like a peaceful stroll down to one of their favourite childhood places, but his body screamed at him to resist at all costs. The moon was not just up, it was full. The lagoon would be bathed in its soft glow, as would the woman with whom he was strolling.

But when had he ever been able to say no to Caro?

Once outside, in the light of the said moon, Caroline realised what a stupid idea it had been. Bad enough that she'd already been kissing Keanu, kissing him and wanting to keep kissing him. It was more than weird, it was scary.

But wonderful.

That thought filled her with a kind of awe...

And how was she going to cope with Keanu *and* moonlight, twin attractions, twin magic?

But she could hardly back off now, so she strode down the slightly overgrown path they'd used as children towards the end of the lagoon just above the small waterfall, where a large, flat rock only inches above the level of the water gave a wonderful view, not only of the entire lake but of the village beneath the plateau.

Keanu caught up with her as she reached the thicker rainforest that protected the waterhole, reaching out a hand to steady her as the track was rough. Roots and vines conspired to catch at their feet and they brushed against each other often.

Definitely not one of her better ideas.

The touch of his hand had been enough, but skin on skin contact, no matter how accidental, had made goose-bumps rise on her arms and neck as her nerve endings battled with the notion that this was Keanu—just a friend!

They reached the lagoon, and trod carefully around its rocky edge towards the small opening through which the water tumbled its way down a rocky path to the flat land below.

And there was their rock. Caroline hurried on, anxious to be there as if sitting in such a familiar place would protect her from all the unfamiliar reactions she was getting from being around her old friend.

But once he'd joined her she realised the rock had shrunk.

Ridiculous, they had grown, so now they sat, close together, feet flat, knees raised, hands looped around their legs.

Very close together!

And in spite of the moonlight, the lagoon looked dark and mysterious, the surface silvered, but with a sense of hidden depths lurking beneath that shining skin.

Hidden depths...

The man beside her would have those too, not deliberately hidden but ideas, emotions, even ethics and beliefs that developed with maturity so for all she thought she knew him, she really didn't.

'I have got one idea to get the money,' she said tentatively, as the side of her body closest to Keanu heated towards fever level. 'Do you remember Dad explaining to us—well, to me, I suppose, but I'm sure you were there—that my mother's parents had left their house in Sydney jointly to Christopher and me? They'd also left most of their money, which was apparently considerable, in trust for Christopher and the interest on that pays for his full-time carers and the housekeeper and upkeep on the house.'

She leant forward so a curtain of hair saved her from looking at Keanu's face. Studying it in the moonlight that picked out the strong bones of his cheeks and jaw, the straight line of his nose was just too distracting.

'I vaguely remember, but is this story going somewhere?' Keanu replied, moving slightly and tucking her protective curtain back behind her ears, presumably so he could see her face, for he'd turned to study her at the same time.

She felt the brush of his fingers as he moved her hair, could feel his eyes on her skin—soft eyes, gentle, understanding, like a caress…

'Well, it might be—it *could* be a solution,' she said, her voice wavering as her body reacted to his gaze, *and* realised just how stupid this was all going to sound. 'I thought if I could borrow enough money by mortgaging my half of the house, we might just be able to get the mine working again and eventually there'd be money over and above what it pays to the hospital for me to repay the loan.'

He hesitated for a moment, then slipped his arm around her shoulders, as if preparing her for a hug when he disappointed her with his reply.

'Caro…' His voice was deep and husky and his arm

tightened around her shoulders. 'I know you said it was your first idea, but if you don't mind my saying so, it isn't the best idea you've ever had. What if we can't get the mine going again, and the bank forecloses and Christopher loses his home?'

'But surely they'd...' Caroline protested, so flustered by Keanu's touch she'd forgotten what she'd meant to say.

'Only take half a house?' Keanu finished for her, showing just how ridiculous the idea had been.

Had she looked so disappointed that Keanu used the arm around her shoulders to pull her closer? A comforting hug, nothing more, but given where her comforting hug to him had led earlier, she really should pull away.

Except it *was* comforting.

Too comforting...

For Keanu too, as he suddenly let his arm slip and got back to practicalities?

'Now, as you were right about knowing a ballpark figure for the amount of money we need,' he said, 'let's go back to your notes and see what we can come up with.'

He stood up, reaching down to help her to her feet, then keeping her hand in his, not exactly imprisoned because she knew she could pull hers out but firmly, as if he wanted it there.

Here she went again, feeling things between her and Keanu when in reality it was nothing more than their old friendship.

Back in the house, she made tea, and put out biscuits Bessie had cooked that day, carrying them through to the dining room where Keanu was already going through her figures.

Or would have been if he hadn't been holding the old notebook she'd pulled out of her room to use the blank pages in it, running his fingers over the hearts and flowers she'd drawn on the cover—the hearts with the arrow running through them, linking her initials to his.

She snatched it out of his fingers.

'It's the first thing I could find to write on,' she muttered. 'But to get back to the mine, the closest I've got to a total is the wages owed and the full wages for running the mine—from figures back when Peter was here. I just need weekly or monthly running costs from Reuben and we'll have some idea of what's needed.

'We can get them later,' Keanu assured her, taking the book from her but flipping back to the cover of the book and smiling at her. The teasing warmth of that smile sent ripples of what felt very like desire downwards through her body.

'I was ten, just look at the figures!' she snapped, but he kept smiling.

Damn the man. It was just so much easier being near him when he wasn't smiling.

But they stood up together, the air between them dense with tension.

In the end it was he who broke the spell, stepping back, so they stood, a foot apart, still looking into each other's eyes.

Then Keanu smiled, and she regretted the foot of space between them, because right then there'd be nothing she'd have liked more than to be locked in his arms.

Locked in his arms?

As in romance?

'You loved me when you were ten,' he reminded her, before turning and walking quietly out of the room, down the hall, across the veranda and down the steps.

Gone...

CHAPTER SEVEN

AS HE'D MENTIONED, Keanu was off duty, and Anahera and an aide Caroline didn't know were working in the hospital when Caroline arrived the next morning.

'Sam's in his office,' Anahera told her. 'And Hettie says she's taking a day off, which she should, but I bet she's doing paperwork in her little villa—she finds it hard to stop, although she does love exploring the island, swimming in the lagoon and climbing around the waterfall. She has a true passion for this place.'

'And you?' Caroline asked, glad to have an opportunity to chat with Anahera even if they were only counting drugs in the dangerous drugs cabinet.

Anahera didn't answer for a moment, then, to Caroline's surprise, she said, 'Well, me, I'm just glad you've turned up. The island is my home and I'm happy here with Hana, but since Keanu's arrival, Mum's been trying to push us both together.'

'Not interested?' Caroline said as casually as she could.

'Once bitten, twice shy,' Anahera answered obliquely. 'Not that being interested in Keanu would do me any good. Even Mum's realised how he is around you.'

Caroline felt heat in her cheeks.

'It's just because we've always known each other,' she said, then realised how lame she'd sounded.

The drugs all counted and checked off on the list taped on the cabinet door, the pair of them walked through the hospital.

'Do you want to change the dressings on the coral cuts while I do some bloods?'

It was good to be doing routine nursing work and now they'd accepted her, the lads with the coral cuts were fun. She took off the old dressings, cleaned the wounds, which were looking good, applied antibiotic ointment and covered them again.

By the next day, she guessed, they'd be able to go home.

She and Anahera had a coffee in the kitchen with a slice of extremely good hummingbird cake, and were just finishing it when Keanu appeared.

'Can you come down to the airstrip?' he asked, by-passing any politeness. 'There's an emergency call-out to Atangi. Hettie's done two flights the last two days so Sam suggested you come along to see what we do.'

You'll be okay, just don't touch him more than necessary, the sane voice in her head said firmly, but the professional part of her mind was focussed firmly on what lay ahead.

'What kind of an emergency?' she asked.

Keanu was hurrying beside her now, long strides eating up the ground.

'Pregnant woman, thirty weeks, having severe cramps.'

He paused—both feet and words—and turned to look at Caroline.

'We'll see how she is when we get there, maybe just bring her back here. Atangi's a good clinic for you to see first, as it has a fairly well-equipped and stocked operating theatre. Before the hospital was built, the flying doctors used it for their emergency visits.'

'Thirty weeks, so we'll take a humidicrib and resus gear?'

'Already in the chopper.'

They'd reached the airstrip, where Sam was talking to Jack.

'You're okay to do this?' Sam asked, looking at Caroline.

'Very okay,' Caroline assured him, not adding that she was actually excited at the thought of going to Atangi after so long a time. You could hardly tell your boss you were excited that someone was ill.

The flight was short, but so beautiful it brought tears to Caroline's eyes. The translucent green water over the reefs, the deeper blue of the sea between the islands, then there was the harbour at Atangi.

'Did you remember Alkiri telling us about the harbour being blasted through the coral by the Americans during the Second World War?' Keanu asked as they dropped down to land on a marked circle next to a building Caroline recognised as the clinic.

As children, she and Keanu had been brought here for their immunisations, and occasionally treated by the resident nurse for minor injuries.

'It seems funny, being back,' she said as she followed Keanu out of the helicopter, feeling a now-familiar tension as his hand held her arm to steady her.

Keanu leaned back in to pull out a backpack, and Caroline knew it would contain all the emergency equipment they might need.

'The clinic is actually well stocked and we probably won't need anything apart from the mobile ultrasound unit that's in here, but it's just as easy to take the lot.'

He spoke to Jack, who'd shut down the engine and disembarked, carrying the portable humidicrib and another bag of equipment.

'You'll stand by?'

Jack shifted uneasily from one foot to the other.

'Actually, I'd like to take a look at the engine. It was missing a bit on the way over, which sounds as if a little moisture has got into the Avgas. Last night was cooler than we've had and the supply tank I used to refuel was close to empty so there could have been some condensation in it.'

'Which means?' Caroline asked, pleased she hadn't heard the missing beat of the engine.

'I'll drain the tank—get an empty drum from the store to put it into—and refill the chopper tank here. We keep a small tanker of Avgas here because we often need to re-fuel, and it's useful if we're doing search-and-rescue work, which is co-ordinated from here.'

'How long?' Keanu asked.

'Three hours tops,' Jack replied cheerfully.

Three hours! They wouldn't be rushing the pregnant woman back to Wildfire.

Keanu introduced the local nurse, Nori, the name re-minding Caroline they'd been at school together. They hugged and exchanged greetings, although Keanu broke up the very brief reunion with a reminder that they had a patient.

Their patient was standing in a corner of an examination room, bent over and clinging to the table. A large woman, it was hard to tell she was actually pregnant.

'Baby's coming,' she said as they came in. 'Soon.'

'Are you able to get up on the table so I can examine you?' Keanu asked in his deep, caring voice.

'No way! I'm not getting up there. The baby's com-ing now.'

Nori was plugging in the crib to warm the mattress in it, and fitting an oxygen tube to the inlet, so Caroline grabbed a small stool that seemed to have no apparent purpose and pulled it over so Keanu could squat on it while he felt the woman's stomach for the strength of the contractions.

Nori had laid out clean towels, gloves and various instruments on a trolley beside the table. Caroline put on gloves, took a towel, just in case the baby did come unexpectedly, and checked that suction tubes and scissors were among the instruments.

If the baby popped out limp, they would have to resuscitate it, but at least they had the humidicrib to keep it pink and warm on the way back to Wildfire.

Keanu was talking quietly to the woman in their own language, and Caroline knew enough of it to know it was mainly reassurance, although he slipped in a question from time to time. Apparently this was her sixth child, so she probably knew more about childbirth than either she or Keanu.

She was thinking this when the woman gave a loud cry and squatted lower, Caroline getting her hands down quickly enough as a watery mix of fluid rushed out.

The baby followed, straight into Caroline's waiting hands—sure and steady hands, although inside she was a mix of trepidation and elation.

The little one cried out, protesting her abrupt entry into the world but with her little fat hands clutching the umbilical cord as if she was ready to take on whatever it had to offer her.

Certainly not a thirty-week baby, more like thirty-six, perhaps even full term.

Keanu reached out a hand to help Caroline and her precious bundle up from the floor, then took the child and passed her to her mother.

The look of love and joy on the woman's face as the baby nuzzled at her breast brought tears to Caroline's eyes.

Keanu was clamping the cord, ready to cut it, but the woman took the scissors out of his hand.

'I do this for my babies,' she told him, cutting cleanly between the clamps.

She passed the baby back to Caroline, who put her down

gently on the table on a warm sheet Nori had taken from the crib. Carefully, she wiped the tiny baby clean, suctioned her nostrils and mouth, Keanu taking over for the Apgar score, then Nori produced another warm sheet and Caroline swaddled the little girl, whose rosebud lips were pursing and opening like a goldfish's, instinct telling her she should be attached to her mother's breast.

Yet Caroline's arms felt reluctant as she passed the baby back, which was ridiculous.

As if arms even knew what reluctance was...

Nori led the woman to a comfortable armchair and said she'd take care of things from now.

Caroline made to argue but Keanu shook his head, just slightly, and led her out of the clinic.

'The islanders have their own rituals for disposing of the placenta,' he explained as they stood in the sun, feeling it warm on their skin after the cool of the air-conditioning inside. 'Before the hospital the islanders had their own midwife—sometimes two—who cared for all the pregnant women. When you and Christopher were born, your father called for one of these women but it was beyond her ability to save either Christopher from injury, or your mother. Your father then decided that all women should have their babies on the mainland and when young women went to the mainland for training as nurses, the midwives stopped passing on their skills.'

'But now?' Caroline asked. 'Seems to me someone having their sixth baby wouldn't have got the dates wrong—and then there's the baby who was in hospital when I arrived.'

'Exactly,' Keanu replied with a grin that made her stupid heart race. 'Now they have the hospital and helicopter as back-up, I think they've decided with a little cheating they can have an island birth. In fact, one of the local nurses is over in Sydney, doing some advanced midwifery training.

It might not be traditional midwifery but at least, when she returns, the island women will have the option of staying here.'

'Which is wonderful,' Caroline declared, smiling herself at the remembered feel of the little baby dropping into her hands. 'So now?' she added, feeling that standing in the sun smiling inanely was probably making her look like an idiot. 'Can we go for a walk? It is so long since I was on Atangi, I need to get the feel and smell of the place back into my blood.'

Keanu swallowed a huge sigh.

He could hardly say no. The baby was fine and whatever was going on inside the clinic was islander business—and women's business at that.

The problem was that the look on Caro's face as she'd stared in wonder at the baby she'd caught had stirred all kinds of uncomfortable thoughts in his mind, and unease in his body.

He'd felt tension from Caro's closeness the whole time they had been in the room and although he was professional enough to not let it affect him, now he wasn't fully focussed on something else, the awareness had grown.

It was because of the notebook, and something to do with sitting on the rock and feeling her hurt when he'd pointed out the flaws in her idea—feeling her disappointment, although she was smart enough to know it would never have worked. Up until then, he'd been able to explain away his physical reactions to her by the fact she was an attractive woman—nothing more than normal physical reactions.

But this was Caro…

'I *can* go for a walk by myself,' she said, obviously sensing his hesitation.

Get over it, he told himself.

'No, it'll be an hour before Jack finishes his refuelling,' he said to her. 'Why don't you wander down to the harbour while I go and see a couple of the elders about Alkiri's funeral?'

She hesitated, and he wondered if she was feeling the same awkwardness that was humming through his nerves.

'Come with me or I'll come with you,' she said quietly. 'Let's be friends again.'

He heard the plea in her voice and a faint tremor in the words caused a pain in his chest.

'Can we just be friends?' he asked.

Fire sparked in her eyes.

'Oh, for heaven's sake, Keanu, I don't know that any more than you do. But there's stuff that needs to be done, things we can do to help the situation here, so surely we can get over all that's happened between us in the past and this inconvenient attraction business that's happening now and work together to make things better.'

She paused, then added in a quieter voice, 'Our friendship was special to me and, I think, to you. Maybe the reward for our efforts would be finding that again.'

He put his arm around her shoulders and drew her close although every functioning brain cell was yelling at him to keep his distance.

The lovely eyes he knew so well looked into his—wary and questioning.

'Our friendship was the most important thing in my life, Caro,' he admitted. 'That will never change.'

She half smiled and shifted so her body wasn't touching his—apart from his arm, which still rested on her shoulders.

'Thanks,' she said, and moved away completely, then in a tone that told him any emotional talk between them was done she added, 'Let's go and see the school first.'

But that was a mistake.

The first thing they noticed—everyone noticed—in the schoolyard was the huge old curtain fig tree, so called because air roots grew down from the branches, forming a thick curtain around the trunk.

And behind that curtain, like hundreds of children who'd attended the school over the years, they'd once shared a very chaste kiss. Her grandma had died and Caroline had known they'd both be off to mainland schools the following year, and for some reason—playing hide and seek most probably—they'd both ended up beneath the fig.

Not that an innocent kiss between a ten-year-old girl and a twelve-year-old boy meant much, but the memory sent a tingle up her spine.

'All the kids are in school,' Keanu murmured. 'Should we?'

Of course they shouldn't but she was ducking between the trailing roots right behind him, letting him take her in his arms, turn her towards him, and lift her head to his, to relive that first kiss.

In actual fact, it was nothing like that first kiss, more like a first kiss between two people attracted to each other and early on in the courtship.

Tentative, exploring, tasting and then tempting, Keanu felt heat rise in his body, and strained to keep things—well, not exactly casual, more noncommittal, if such a thing was possible.

When Caro began kissing him back as if her life depended on the joining of their lips, the contact of their tongues…

Or was it he who'd intensified things—he couldn't think straight, could barely think at all, except that there was no way he should be kissing Caro like this when his life was such a mess.

It was a silly, sentimental thing to do, but there was nothing silly or sentimental about the way their lips met, the teasing invasion of Keanu's tongue, her own tangling with it, the heat in his body as her hands pushed up his shirt to touch his skin, no doubt matched by the heat in hers as his hand slid down her neck towards her breast.

A hundred questions jumbled in her head. Was this just attraction? Or perhaps leftover love from their youth? And hadn't attraction led her into trouble with Steve? No, she could answer that one honestly—it had been his attention to her that had made her lose her head with Steve.

But this kiss—this kiss was different. This kiss was amazing—

So why was she so bamboozled?

'Damn it all!'

The explosive words broke the spell.

'I thought we were trying to be friends,' he muttered, taking her hand and almost dragging her out from under the tree. 'Do you realise I could have made love to you right there under the tree with half of Atangi walking by? Why on earth would you kiss me back like that?'

'Oh, so it's all my fault?' Caroline retorted. 'Anyway, we're both adults and if we feel like it, why shouldn't we kiss?'

She could feel the heat in her cheeks, the disappointment and relief battling for supremacy in her body.

Not that he'd know it because she was stalking away from him, throwing back over her shoulder, 'Anyway, it was your fault—you started it!'

But hearing the words they'd flung at each other so often in childhood fights, she felt a deep sorrow for all they'd lost...

Or had they?

What about the friendship they'd decided to rediscover?

'Nice walk?' Nori asked brightly when they returned to the clinic, any further exploration totally forgotten.

'It had its moments,' Caroline replied, then proceeded

to ask Nori about her family, marital status and children, a conversation that lasted until Jack returned to tell them they could head back to Wildfire.

Not interested in the brilliance Nori's three-year-olds were already showing, Keanu had moved into the theatre to check their patient. She was dozing in the big chair, the baby sleeping against her breast.

The sight brought unexpected emotion welling up inside him, bringing a thickness to his throat.

Time he was out of there…

'Coming back with us?' Keanu said to Caro, who was still deep in a conversation about Nori's children.

Which made him wonder as she said, 'Yes, sir!' and followed him out of the clinic, why she'd never married the Steve guy and had children of her own.

Apart from their medical ambitions, if he remembered rightly they had been going to get married and have ten children.

Ten?

'Did you know Nori has six children—three sets of twins?'

Keanu shook his head. She'd been talking to Nori— talking about children—so it was a fairly innocuous thing for Caro to have said. But coming right on top of the thick throat and his memory of the past, it shook him. There were far too many things going on his head that he didn't want her picking up on, although he wouldn't have minded having a few clues about her thoughts.

Fortunately, by the time they arrived back on Wildfire he had an excuse to escape. He had to concentrate on the arrangements for Alkiri's funeral and the first thing on the list was to try entry to the research station via the gate, and get permission from whoever was in charge.

Should he ask Caroline to accompany him?

She'd been anxious to know what was happening at the station but walking with her through the scented tropical dusk with her was too much to contemplate.

He went in to see Sam, inevitably battling paperwork in his office, to check he wasn't needed at the hospital.

'You're free to go, mate,' Sam told him, 'and I've already got their okay. In fact, the bloke who's the foreman down there actually contacted me to see if I'd like to come down and see the laboratories, and I asked him about the longhouse. But if you want to check it out, just explain who you are to the gate people. Sounded to me that, now they've finished, they're happy to have people see what they've achieved.'

Sam's eyes slid away from his, and Keanu turned to see Caroline standing there.

'You want to go with Keanu and see the renovations down the road?'

'We're allowed in?' She sounded so delighted Keanu could hardly say he didn't want her with him.

'As of today,' Sam was assuring her.

At least she wouldn't be wearing a wet shift, Keanu told himself, but somehow that wasn't comforting at all. She'd been in the same mid-calf pants and uniform shirt when they'd kissed under the tree...

The foreman's name was Bill and he was at the gate talking to the guard there when Keanu and Caroline arrived.

'Sorry about the fence, but the boss wanted the place secure—or as secure as anything can be with so much beach frontage. It was mainly to keep out adventurous kids during the building process, and the fences and guard will remain because the laboratories will have some evil chemicals in them. Not that they won't be locked as well, and I imagine there'd be more kids coming by boat than down from the hospital, but what he says goes.'

'Who is he?' Caroline asked, so excited to be 'invited' to the station that she was barely registering Keanu by her side.

Well, almost barely.

'Some fellow from the Middle East apparently. I get my orders from his—what do they call him?—Australasian manager. He's from the Middle East as well, but speaks English the same way the Queen does.'

Caroline smiled. Children from all over the world were educated in top English public schools so undoubtedly all of them spoke 'like the Queen does'.

Keanu was talking to Bill, so Caroline dawdled behind them, trying to identify all the different scents. She saw the jasmine creeping up the fence—soon it would be smothered—and the broad leaves of the ginger plant, their drooping white bulb-like flowers giving out what was probably her favourite perfume. Or did she prefer the frangipani that was dominant now—?

'You with us?' Keanu asked, and she realised how far she'd fallen back. He and Bill were at the door of the newly renovated and freshly painted laboratory block.

She caught up as Bill unlocked the door, and she gasped at the difference. Admittedly, it had been thirteen years since she'd been in the lab—back when she'd had her last holiday here with Keanu and Helen.

After they left it had never been the same and she'd used the excuse of spending more time with Christopher to avoid island holidays.

'It's been completely redone,' Keanu was saying. 'No wonder Sam's so excited about it. But do you know if there are people booking to come here to use it?'

Bill shook his head.

'Not my department, but we have been hurrying to finish everything and be out of the way because the boss—the big boss—is planning some kind of exclusive, very clever scientists' get-together some time soon.'

They went to check the longhouse next, and once again Caroline could only gape in amazement. Rebuilt in the style of the island meeting places, thatched roof—probably with something underneath the palm thatching to stop it leaking—and open on all sides, it was finished with the best of materials, with cedar benches polished to a glowing shine, weavings hanging from the rafters, mats and cushions strewn around the floor. It was an island longhouse for today and for the future.

'It's totally awesome,' she said, shaking her head because it was hard to take it all in.

'And we can use it for Alkiri's funeral feast?' Keanu asked, as if he already knew this had been agreed.

'Sure thing,' Bill said. 'It will be a good test of the fire pits.'

'It's even got fire pits?'

She sounded so incredulous both men smiled, but she followed them beyond the building where, sure enough, a deep pit had been dug with a more shallow one beside it, big stones, firewood and white sand stored neatly in the bottom of open wooden cupboard-like structures beside it.

'We've had some of the local community here, doing the mats and cushions, and they told us about the fire pits. A big one for the fire that heats the stones, then a shallower one for the stones to go into when they're hot, baskets for the food and bags and sand to cover it all up. Have we got it right?'

He was obviously anxious, but Keanu clapped him on the back and said, 'Fantastic, mate, it's just fantastic.'

Caroline had opened one of the top cupboards and found the baskets for the food stacked inside it. The next one held the sacks that would be wet and placed across the food before the lot was covered with sand to keep the heat in and help the meal steam-cook.

The thought that she'd actually be here and celebrating with a *hangi* made her turn to Keanu in delight.

'Won't it be great? It's so long since we've been to a *hangi*!'

'Great if we don't have to cook it,' Keanu reminded her, but Bill assured them both that local staff had already been employed for the station and they were bringing in more people for the celebration of Alkiri's life the following day.

'Apparently people will come from all the islands, and as we're leaving soon, it will be kind of a reward for our workers to be here for the party.'

Bill hesitated then added, 'Although that sounds a bit rough, partying when someone's dead.'

'Not here,' Keanu assured him. 'Here we celebrate a life that enriched all who knew him—or her if it's a woman's funeral.'

Bill seemed content, but Caroline considered what he'd said.

Had *she* enriched anyone's life?

She rather doubted it.

Christopher's maybe.

He'd certainly enriched hers, getting through each day of pain and illness with a smile always ready on his face for her or their father. During the 'Steve years' as she was starting to think of them, she'd seen less of her brother and really regretted it. Love, or what she'd thought was love, had made her selfish.

They were walking back up to the hospital while these thoughts coursed through her head.

'You okay?' Keanu asked, and she realised she'd dropped behind again, drifting through the past.

Which, considering the confusion she was feeling in *his* presence, might have been a safer place.

'Fine,' she lied, and hurried to catch up with him.

CHAPTER EIGHT

IT WAS A day without end, or so it seemed to Caroline when they returned to the hospital.

'Would you mind keeping an eye on things while Keanu, Hettie and I have some dinner?' Sam greeted her. 'Hettie's cooking because Vailea's already preparing for the funeral feast and there's stuff the three of us have to go over, including juggling the roster for the funeral tomorrow.'

'No worries,' Caroline assured him, 'though you'd better tell me what to do in an emergency. Do I go to the back door and yell?'

'Oh, you don't know the system? Of course not, you've barely arrived and we haven't stopped working you. See the panel by the door? It was an ingenious idea worked out by your father. You hit the blue button for me—it rings in my room—the green for Hettie—and the red that will clang all through the villas for all hands on deck.'

'No fire alarm?' Caroline teased, and Sam pointed to the regulation fire alarm box set beside the panel.

'Open that one and press the button and they'll hear you over on Atangi! And the village will have men here almost as fast as the staff can get here. The hospital's very important to all the islanders—and they've your father to thank for that.'

Caroline thought the conversation was over, until Sam

added, almost under his breath, 'Although we'd prefer to be thanking him in person.'

'My father loves the island. All M'Langi. I can hear it in his voice when he talks about it, asks questions. But my mother's death, and Christopher... It seems he blamed himself, and now he says both the hospital and Christopher need him more on the mainland. Over there he can keep a watch on Christopher's care and also make money and lobby for money to keep this place going.'

Sam sighed and departed, but the conversation had brought Caroline's mind back to the problems at the mine. Of course mortgaging half a house had been a stupid idea, but Keanu hadn't come up with anything better.

Keanu...

The kiss...

Setting the past and the future firmly out of her mind, she went into the big ward, where she discovered that the boys with the coral cuts had been released. The woman with unstable diabetes was sleeping once again, as was their patient with the Biruli ulcer. The woman with the baby had also gone, so all she had to do was hang around in case she was needed.

And use the time to try to sort out the mess inside her head.

Start with the mine—there had to be *some* way...

But how could she think when she was hungry? She headed for the kitchen, where she found several salads made up in the main refrigerator.

'Staff salads,' the note attached to the shelf said, so she took one, went back into the desk in the ward to keep an eye on her patients and ate it there.

Thinking, almost subconsciously, of the grandparents she'd barely known.

How terrible for them to have lost their daughter—their only child—so far away from home. Max had flown his wife's body back to Sydney to be buried there, and had taken first his babies, and later his toddlers—well, Christopher had never actually toddled—to visit their grandparents.

But both of them had been dead before Caroline was six so it was difficult for her to summon up more than an image of a defeated-looking old man and woman.

Defeated by grief, she'd realised, much later.

'Are you okay? You must be tired. I can take over here if you like.'

Keanu's arrival interrupted her unhappy thoughts.

'No way. I have a feeling if I handed over, or even had you standing by, it would reinforce everyone's opinion of the worthlessness of all Lockharts.'

Keanu smiled, something she wished he wouldn't do, at least when she was around.

'Hettie will be over soon and she'll stay until Mina comes on, but I can at least hang around and keep you company. I'm being Maddie this week and she was on call so I might as well be here.'

He pulled a chair over from beside the wall and sat beside her at the small desk, far too close.

Caroline managed to manoeuvre her chair a little farther away from him but he was still too close. She could feel the force-field of him, as if the very air around him had taken on his essence. It was because of the kiss—she knew that. It had done something to her nerves and spun threads of confusion through her head.

'I talked to your father,' he said, startling her out of thoughts of kisses and physical closeness. 'He can't get over at the moment but has asked me to make sure the mine is closed, at least temporarily until he gets a chance to look at things and maybe get it going again.'

'*You* talked to Dad?'

'I thought it might be easier, the mine closure, coming from me and not a Lockhart. I know how distressed you are about the damage Ian's done to the family name.'

Caroline turned so she could study him.

'And you think you telling them will make a difference? It's still the Lockhart mine, and with everyone connected to it now losing their incomes, of course the blame will come back on the Lockharts.'

She was so upset she had to stand up—to move—pacing up and down the silent ward while her mind churned.

It was the right thing to do—she knew that. It was far too dangerous for the miners to keep working without the tunnel being shored up.

'I'll do it,' she said, suddenly weary of the whole mess, and when Keanu started to argue she even found a tired smile.

'Best all the blame lands on us,' she told him. 'We don't want everyone hating you as well.'

Keanu shot up from his chair and took her hands.

'No one will ever blame you, Caroline,' he said, and the feel of her hands in his—the security of her slim fingers being held by his strong ones—fired all her senses once again.

She eased away from him.

'I have patients to check, and it's probably best if you go, because it's too easy to be distracted when you're around.'

'Really?'

He smiled as if she'd given him a very special gift, then leaned forward to peck her cheek before leaving the room.

Keanu went back to his quarters but was too restless to settle down. His phone call to Max, the closing of the mine and his still-vague idea of how to save it, his increasing

attraction to Caroline—all were drawing him further and
further into the web that was the Lockharts.

He couldn't help but think of his mother, so humili-
ated by Ian.

Probably already ill, she'd never really overcome their
banishment from the island. It was as if Ian's words had
left an enduring scar in her mind, and poison in her body.
In his mother's mind, the happy Lockhart days had gone,
and the stories of the Lockharts taking her in after her own
family had disowned her and her husband had died had
been long forgotten.

Almost without orders from his brain, his feet took him
back out of the villa that was currently his home and up
the hill to the grassy slope behind the big house to where
his father was buried among dead Lockharts and other islanders who'd lived and worked on Wildfire.

To the grassy slope where Alkiri would be laid to rest
tomorrow...

Keanu sat down by his father's grave, idly pulling a few
weeds that had recently appeared, trying desperately, as
he often did, to remember his father.

But memories of a two-year-old were dim and not particularly reliable so all he had were the stories his mother
had told over the years.

His father, bright star of the school on Atangi, had been
sent to the mainland for his high-school education, all the
costs met by the Lockhart family. From boarding school
he'd gone on to university, studying science, and returning, with the woman he'd met and fallen in love with, to
Wildfire to work at the research station and begin the first
investigation into the properties of M'Langi tea.

His mother's tales had told of their early adventures,
the two of them roaming the mountains on the uninhabited islands, in search of the special tree from whose bark
and leaves the tea was made.

He'd been two years old when his father, working with a local friend, had been killed by a rockfall on an outer island.

Two years old when his mother and he had moved into the comfortable, self-contained annexe off the big Lockhart house. It was only after Caroline and Christopher were born, and their mother died, that old Mrs Lockhart had offered his mother a job—helping with the baby and generally running the house.

'I thought I might find you here.'

Caroline's voice startled him out of his reverie.

'What are you doing? What about your patients?'

'Hettie sent me home. Sam's just checked our patients and decided Mina can manage them.'

She sank down beside him on the grass.

'When I came back to work at the hospital,' he told her, 'I brought my mother's ashes here and scattered them in the grass.'

'So she and your father could be together.'

Caroline spoke quietly, a statement, not a question.

She rested her hand gently on his shoulder, and his skin burned beneath the touch, his body warring with his mind, wanting her so badly, yet here, beside his mother—

He *had* to tell Caro.

Now, before anything went any further...

But she was so damned insecure, wouldn't his marriage—for all it was over now—seem like a further betrayal?

Hurt her as much as his deserting her had?

She slid her hand down his arm to grasp his fingers.

'Come on,' she said, 'let's visit my mother now.'

They'd done this so often as children, coming to the little cemetery, sitting among the graves, talking to her mother and his father, telling them what they'd been doing, laughing, and sometimes crying.

They reached Charlotte Lockhart's memorial—a simple stone with her name and the words 'wife and mother'—Max having given the initial of her name to both her children.

'Hold me,' Caroline whispered, and Keanu put his arms around her and drew her close, feeling her softness, her breasts against his chest, long silky hair tickling his neck, covering his hands that now held her to him.

She raised her head, and he caught the glisten of tears in her eyes.

Her eyes were shadowed with memories, and not happy ones. This was Caro, so he kissed them, first one and then the other, his lips sliding to her temple, teeth nibbling at her ear lobe, kisses along her jaw, although her mouth—that wide, sensual mouth—had always been his destination.

Or so it seemed as he tasted her, his tongue sliding around her lips, delving, probing.

Had her mouth opened to him?

Were her lips responding?

For a moment it seemed as if she might have been a statue, then, with a groan that started somewhere down near her toes, she kissed him back, her mouth moving on his, her hands exploring his shoulders, arms, neck, gripping at his hair, his head, holding his mouth to hers as if her life depended on it.

They were in a graveyard.

His parents were here…

Somehow his lips had slipped lower, kissing her neck, while she pressed hers against his head and murmured his name. His hand had slid beneath her shirt, found a breast, a full breast that felt heavy in his hand. His thumb strayed across the nipple, already peaked by the heat of the kiss.

She'd dragged his head back to kiss his lips, so he gave in and let her, matched the heat of her kisses, and the little moan she gave as his fingers teased the taut nipple was like honey in his mouth.

Had his legs given way that he was on his knees, still holding Caroline, their bodies pressed together? Moonlight cast shadows from the trees around the graveyard, picked out writing on the stone beside which they knelt.

Charlotte Lockhart.

Wife and mother...

Wife!

'This is crazy,' he whispered as he eased himself away from Caroline, his body throbbing with need, hers hot within his hands, which had settled on her shoulders. 'I'm sorry, there's something I should have said—told you—have to tell you.'

Blue-green eyes—dazed with desire?—stared at him and she shook her head, as if trying to take in his stumbling words.

She released the grip she'd had on his shirt, raised her hands to lift his off her shoulders, then bowed her head so the hair on the top of her head brushed against his chest.

He saw her shoulders move as she took a deep breath, then she lifted her head and looked at him, into his eyes, hers questioning now but so beautiful.

Too beautiful to hurt?

Perhaps he could contact his lawyer first, before he told her, find out the situation...

Coward!

He took her hands in his and eased her back down onto the ground.

'So tell,' she said quietly.

But words wouldn't come. *I'm married* seemed too blunt, far too hurtful.

'It's about attraction,' he finally began. 'About attraction and love and how there can be one without the other but how do you know at the beginning?'

'Are you talking about our attraction?' she asked, her head turned not to him but towards the distant sea, so all he could see was her profile—no emotion...

'Not really but in a way, yes, and I should have told you earlier. I should have told you when it happened—but we'd been apart so long and I really didn't know how to. And I certainly should have told you before I kissed you.'

Now she turned to him.

'It's something bad, isn't it? You're already married, or engaged? I should have guessed. Why wouldn't you be?'

She went to rise, but he caught her hand and kept her on the grass beside him.

'Married but separated for five years,' he finally admitted. 'It was attraction, nothing more, but we didn't discover that until after we were married. We weren't exactly virgins, but Mum's greatest pain, later when she did eventually talk about Ian, was that she'd lost her moral compass—the ethical code by which she'd always lived. And that was in my mind—some half-formed ethical code that said if we were having sex we should get married. We'd met at uni, as physio and medical students—our paths crossed often—and the attraction was definitely there. Marriage seemed a great idea, but something didn't gel. We didn't fight, we didn't hurt each other, we just kind of drifted in different directions and in the end sat down and talked about it and agreed it had been a mistake.'

He ran out of words and leaned back on his elbows, looking up at the silvery moon above them.

'Where is she?' Caro asked.

He shrugged.

'She went to Melbourne. We didn't keep in touch, nor did we get around to divorcing. I don't know why—perhaps because it seemed like admitting what a huge mistake we'd made. Anyway, a couple of months ago she contacted me, told me she wanted a divorce and sent the papers.

She'd met someone else, sounded so happy I was pleased for her, so I signed the papers. They'll go before a judge some time soon, then a month and a day later I won't be married any more.'

Caroline had sat, stunned into silence, as Keanu told his tale. Somehow, in all her thoughts of Keanu over the years, the fact that he might marry had never occurred to her.

Not that it should matter, but obviously it did, because her heart was hurting, and her throat was tight, and what she really wanted to do was hit out at him.

But why shouldn't he have married?

Wouldn't she have married Steve if he hadn't dumped her when the mine had gone bad?

'Did you think of me at all?'

She wasn't sure where the question had come from, but heard it make its way out of her dry mouth.

'Only every minute of the ceremony, which is when I realised how wrong it all was. But I put that aside, and gave the marriage all I had, Caro. Moral compass stuff again. We were friends as well as lovers and I didn't want to hurt her.'

Now Caroline was sorry she'd asked the question, sorry about so much, but the pain in her heart remained and she knew she had to get away—think about this, work out why now, when it was all over, it was hurting her.

Why his being married was so ridiculously hurtful, especially as he wasn't really married at all…

And shouldn't he have told her all this before they'd kissed—the first time, not the last time?

Even if he wasn't *married* married, shouldn't it have been mentioned in passing?

She touched his shoulder as she stood up, then made her way up to the house, her mind so full of conjecture it felt too heavy for her neck.

* * *

Vaguely recalling, through a foggy haze of lust and shock, that Keanu had mentioned something about her being on duty at six, Caroline got herself out of bed, dressed, ate a lamington Bessie had apparently baked the previous day, drank a glass of milk and headed down to the hospital.

This time of the year, it was light by five in the morning, but half an hour later than that the morning still had a pearly glow and the sound of the birds waking up, the calm sea beyond the rainforest, and a sense of the world coming alive with a fresh new morning filled her with unexpected happiness.

True, there were problems but right now nothing, but nothing, seemed insurmountable.

Inevitably, Hettie was already there, in spite of Caroline being twenty minutes early.

'Anahera's off duty today and will be helping her mother with preparations for Alkiri's funeral. In fact, the fire's already been started in the fire pit.'

Fire? Fire pit?

The words seemed hard to understand in a hospital, until Carolyn remembered where she was and what was happening today—a funeral and funeral feast.

'Keanu's also gone down to the research station to help set everything up,' Hettie added. 'I'll take a look at the young lad with the ulcer before I hand over. I don't think the medication is working. I'll talk to Sam about changing the combination, but watch him carefully and if there's any sign of fever get Sam or Keanu here immediately.'

The diabetic patient was up and dressed.

'Doesn't want to miss the funeral feast,' Hettie said dryly. 'I'll sign her out later.'

She turned to Caroline.

'Okay, so you'll only have one patient, but that's largely

because everyone knows we're short-staffed and puts off coming to see us, either here or at the island clinics. But our one patient needs all the care we can give him, never forget that, and if you don't get one or two coming up from the feast with burnt toes or cut fingers I'd be very surprised. Apparently, the festivities kick off at ten—well, the funeral part, anyway.'

She paused, then added, 'I understand Alkiri was a friend of yours and you'd really like to be there, but the foreman wants to show Sam and me the laboratories—showing off, I suppose—and Keanu's doing the oration so he has to be there. Our second aide will be here with you. Her shift doesn't begin until eight, but if there's any problem at all, phone me or Sam—our cell numbers are by the phone in the main office.'

Caroline took it all in, and much as her heart longed to be there to say goodbye to Alkiri, she knew being left here was a sign of her acceptance. Lockhart or not, Hettie was trusting her.

What Caroline hadn't realised was that the statement—'Anahera is helping her mother with the celebration feast'—meant Vailea was not in the kitchen. Apparently, nurses here made and served breakfast to their patients when called upon to do so.

Vailea—bless her heart, or perhaps her organisational skills—had a list of all meals up on a corkboard near the door. Not only were the meal menus there, but they had the requisite 'GF' for gluten free, and a little heart beside ones suggested for heart patients.

Back to her patients—checking their notes: no dietary restrictions for either of them.

According to—

'How are you doing?'

Keanu was there, right behind her.

'I thought you were busy with the *hangi*,' she said, needing to say something as an almost overwhelming rush of what could only be lust weakened her knees.

She was *still* feeling that lust thing?

He was married!

And he hadn't told her.

Anyway, might he not be right about the dangers of attraction, which was just a weaker word for lust?

And shouldn't she show *some* reaction to this information?

But what?

'Too many cooks,' he said lightly, and she had to grapple her way back through her thoughts to where the conversation had started. 'I'm not needed until a lot later. I'm doing the oration.'

The lightness vanished from his voice with the last sentence, and yet again Caroline's first instinct was to hug him.

But hugs led to—

Well, trouble.

Change the subject.

'You've been down to check? They've got the fire going?'

He nodded, so close now she could see the smooth golden skin of his face—the strong chin he must have shaved extra-carefully this morning.

And being that close, *he* must be able to see she was having difficulty breathing.

She ducked behind a table, and he stood opposite her.

'And?'

'The women are hanging flower leis and putting huge baskets of leaves all around the place. It's really beautiful, Caro.'

'Sounds lovely but I've got to get breakfasts,' she managed, although her mind was on the kiss they'd shared the previous evening, not bacon and eggs.

'I know,' he said, his voice husky, his eyes unreadable.

'I really wanted to tell you I went down to see Reuben this morning just to confirm the order to close the mine.'

The broad shoulders that had felt so solid beneath her hands lifted in a shrug.

'I said it was a health and safety issue and, as a doctor overseeing that, I had the authority to issue the shutdown notice.'

Caroline sighed.

'That was silly. You've put yourself into the firing line of the workers' anger now. They already hate the Lockhart name, so what harm could a little more hate do? And as it's Ian's fault that the mine's in the state it's in, it's a Lockhart issue anyway.'

Keanu's sigh was almost as deep as her own.

'We'll just have to wait and see,' he said quietly. 'Reuben's going to get someone in from Atangi to fence the site and he was going to tell the small crew still working as soon as I was out of sight.'

'So they wouldn't rend you limb from limb?' Caroline queried, although she couldn't find even the slightest of smiles to go with the suggestion.

'Probably,' Keanu agreed. 'But it's done now, so that's one less thing for you to worry about. Let's get started on these breakfasts.'

He'd done it so she could stop worrying about it?

'Weren't you talking about making breakfasts?'

One word, and a practical one at that, yet tingles still ran down her spine.

'Of course. I've only got two and shortly I'll be down to one patient, but would you mind asking them what they fancy for breakfast? Vailea's left a list—there's scrambled, boiled or fried eggs, bacon, baked beans, toast and jam, and I think there's cereal.'

'I might have to have the lot to wake me up,' he said before turning and walking out of the kitchen.

To wake him up?

It hadn't been *that* late when they'd parted.

So, had he, like she, lain awake long into the night, re-thinking the kiss?

Or had he been thinking about his marriage?

About his wife?

Though perhaps he'd been worried about the mine closure and his decision to be the one to tell Reuben? Kept awake by things that had nothing at all to do with the heated, almost desperate kiss and the discussion that had followed it.

CHAPTER NINE

FINDING THE RATHER large kitchen altogether too small to share with Caro, Keanu delivered the breakfast orders and departed, excusing himself by explaining he wanted to change the dressings on the Buruli ulcer, which was causing both him and Sam a lot of concern.

It wasn't responding to the medication, the young lad was in severe pain and the flesh was continuing to deteriorate, as was the lad's general condition.

'Are you sure nothing got into it before you came in here?' he asked as he deadened the area around the wound to clean it yet again.

'Could have.' A shrug strengthened the typical boy reply.

'Like what?' Keanu asked, but all he got that time was a shake of his head.

He put the new dressing on the wound, wrote up stronger painkillers and was departing when the young aide, having just started on duty, brought in the breakfast tray.

Time he was gone, yet his feet led him to the kitchen.

'Hettie tells me she'll be here just before ten so you can come down to the longhouse.'

All he got for a reply was a frown, although eventually she must have summoned up enough courage to speak.

'I—um—I'm not sure, Keanu. I really don't like funerals—even the island celebratory ones. I hate that people say all the nice things about someone after they're dead and can't hear them. Why don't people tell them that stuff before they die?'

Keanu moved across the kitchen towards her and put his arms around her.

'You did tell him, Caroline, when we sat with him before he died. He knew how much he meant to you and if you don't want to come down, of course you shouldn't. I guess Hettie just assumed you would want to.'

He felt her body rest against his and tension drain from it. He longed to kiss her, but now he knew where kisses led...

He shouldn't have come close enough to touch her, let alone give her a hug, at least until they'd had time to talk about last night's revelations. About how she felt, about whether it mattered at the moment that he was still married...

So he let his lips brush the soft, golden hair on the top of her head and eased away from her.

'I'll bring you some food later,' he said, and got out of the place before the regret that he *hadn't* kissed her overcame his common sense.

The longhouse was busier than he'd expected, and he could pick out people from every inhabited island in the group. The harbour down at the mine would be crowded with boats and the old truck would have been ferrying locals from there to the research station all morning.

Someone had put a row of chairs at one end of the building, and he and the elders took their places there. The crowd grew quiet when he spoke, talking with love of the man he'd known—the young, strong man who'd been a master boatman, often called upon to rescue people who had fool-ishly put out to sea when the weather was bad.

He reminded his people of some of the history of M'Langi that Alkiri had passed on to him, true tales and folklore, fascinating stories for two story-hungry young-sters.

And finally he asked for others to speak, and speak they did. A flood of reminiscences followed, first the el-ders, then ordinary people whose lives Alkiri had touched.

Swallowing a lump of emotion as he listened, he was almost glad Caro wasn't here. Always a softie, she'd have been in floods of tears by now.

Caro...

A disturbance of some kind at the back of the longhouse brought him out of his reverie—useless reverie, in fact.

There were raised voices, angry voices, then one of the men departed, maybe told to leave by someone senior to them.

But the bits and pieces of talk he'd heard suggested the man was going to the hospital. He could see Hettie and Sam sitting with the works foreman, Hettie having obvi-ously returned when Caroline had explained she wasn't coming down.

Caroline!

The man was a miner...

With a very hasty excuse to the nearest elder he de-parted, following the man up the hill, hurrying to catch up, to get in front of him.

He recognised him.

Definitely one of the miners he'd seen the other day.

He called to him but in spite of the early hour the man had probably been drinking and nothing could make him deviate from his determined path.

Keanu was close on the miner's heels when he reached

the gate near the airstrip and there Keanu diverted from the miner's path, taking the back way, which he knew was shorter, running now, his heart thudding in his chest, reaching the hospital and racing in, calling for Caro.

He must have looked and sounded like a madman because she reached out her hand and rested it on his arm.

'Calm down, Keanu, tell me what's up.'

'Go back to the house—no, he'll go there next. Go out the back. My villa is the lowest one. Go inside and lock the door.'

He could hear the man by now, ranting about the closure, and knew how close he must be.

'Go now,' he said to her, but she stood her ground, wanting an explanation.

The phone broke their stalemate and she answered it, turning back to him to say, 'That was Hettie to tell you Sam and some of the young men are on their way. On their way where? What's happening?'

But it was too late for explanations. The angry man was already on the hospital steps, his voice crying out for a Lockhart and, woman or not, any Lockhart would do.

'I can't have them coming in here—there are patients, well, one patient. I'll go out and see him.'

Keanu grabbed her shoulders as she started to move past him, pulling her back, thrusting her towards the kitchen.

'At least go in there and lock the door. *I'll* talk to him!'

He turned away, sure the man wouldn't hurt a woman, yet only half sure. Who knew what a man made brave by cava might do?

'She's not here,' he said, meeting the man on the veranda. 'And she's not up at the house so don't bother looking there. Anyway, I'm the one who closed the mine, and it was for the safety of all the miners. It's a temporary measure until we find some money to give everyone their back-pay and start things up again.'

'That's what you say, Keanu, but for all your closeness you're not a Lockhart and we all know what *they* can do.'

The man pushed forward, but Keanu blocked the doorway.

'This is a hospital, not a boxing ring,' he reminded them. 'Let's talk about this in the garden.'

No one moved—well, the man threw a punch, which missed Keanu's jaw by a whisker but still served to fire his anger.

He hit back, knocking the culprit down the steps.

It had been stupid. He knew that immediately, because now he'd made the man look foolish, and that had angered him even more. He righted himself and pressed forward again and this time the punch that was thrown connected, knocking Keanu sideways against the doorjamb. He'd barely straightened when he felt a shove from behind, and Caroline stood there, hands on her hips and fury in her eyes.

'That's enough!' she said. 'Keanu's right, this is a hospital. And you are right as well—it *was* a Lockhart who brought the troubles on you. But he was one bad apple. Do you think I'm not as upset as you all are?'

The answer was another roar of anger. Keanu spun Caroline behind him.

'Go and protect the patients—lock the ward doors if you can, or put furniture against them.'

Would she do it?

No time to find out but somehow he had to protect her.

'Caroline's right about the one bad apple,' he said to the man who still loomed on the steps. 'But he's gone now and I know the Lockharts are doing all they can to fix things, Caroline in particular.'

'The mine's closed—what can *she* do?'

'Find the money to get the mine started again, to pay the wages you're all owed. But in the meantime, think of the other things the Lockhart family has done for you—and will continue to do in the future. You've got kids. If you chase them off, and the hospital closes, where do you go when one of your kids is stung by a stonefish? And what job will you have if you don't allow us time to get the mine operating again?'

It had certainly quietened him down.

'Now move away, we don't want trouble here.'

The new voice made them turn. Sam was there and with him a group of elders and young men, very strong young men.

'Shame on you,' the senior of the elders said. 'You do something like this on a day when one of our most revered friends is being laid to rest. And now the feast is ready— let us celebrate his life.'

The fight seemed to ooze out of the man, although Keanu wondered if he might return.

Or worse, raid the house while Caroline slept inside it...

CHAPTER TEN

SAM RETURNED TO the celebration. As guest of the resort foreman he had to stay for the feast, but Hettie insisted on remaining at the hospital.

'You go down,' she said to Caroline, who shook her head.

'Go down there where people hate the very mention of my name? I know that lout was drunk, but he was probably expressing the sentiments of most of the community. I doubt if anything will ever restore our name, given the amount of damage Ian's done—and I only know little scraps of it.'

'Something will work out,' Hettie said, but with so little conviction Caroline knew she was only being kind.

She probably didn't think much of the Lockhart family herself.

And who could blame her?

'Then I'll just head up to the house,' she said to Hettie, thinking she'd phone her father just to talk to him, to ask about Christopher, then...

Get back to the books.

'You will not go up to the house,' Hettie said firmly. 'Not until Keanu, or Jack or Sam are here to go with you, and then only to get whatever you need, then you can come back down here and stay in one of the empty nurses' villas.'

It bothered Caroline that even Hettie was being protective. Surely there wasn't that much risk.

Well, she could forget the phone call, but she had to do something.

And surely all this fuss was overdone...

Hettie had disappeared so Caroline slipped out of the hospital, taking the back path up to the house in case the angry man was still lurking around. It took her only minutes to collect what she wanted, then she headed back down the track, not to one of the nurses' villas but to Keanu's place.

Somehow she knew she'd be safe in Keanu's place.

The door was unlocked and as she entered and looked around, she had to smile. Helen had insisted they both keep their rooms neat and tidy and it was obvious the rule had stuck with Keanu for longer than it had stuck with her.

The little place was neat and functional. The design offered a largish room with a sitting space, a dining space and beyond that the kitchen. Off that, to the right, was the bedroom, complete with double bed—did married couples often choose to work here?

She smiled to herself at the naivety of the thought. Of course there were likely to be relationships among staff working in such an isolated place. Wasn't Jack hoping to win over the beautiful Anahera?

But going into Keanu's bedroom and what was presumably a bathroom off it was a step too far, so she dumped the little notebook and laptop on the dining table.

And sat down to do some work.

She still didn't have the running costs of the mine but Reuben would know, or once she found Peter she could get a rough figure from him. Where they'd get the money she didn't have a clue, but somehow she had to do this. She made up neat lists. The back pay she could put a figure against but superannuation had a question mark, as had running costs. And she'd have to work out how much pay was owed to Bessie and Harold.

On top of that, if she was going to continue to live at the house, she should check what food was there. The next flight was Friday—she should order supplies…

As she paused, considering what to do next, she heard the music from the longhouse. It flowed through her blood and sent her fingers tapping until she stood up and began to move. She would never have the lithe grace of the islanders but she couldn't help swaying her hips to the rhythm of the music.

Keanu had teased her…

Had she summoned him up by thought wave that he appeared in the doorway? She stopped her movement immediately before he teased her again.

'Don't tell me you've actually done what you were told,' he said, then he looked at the book and laptop on the table. 'Well, not entirely, you obviously went up to the house to get those and I'll bet no one went with you.'

'Everyone's back at the party—I was quite safe,' she retorted, then sniffed the air and looked at the basket he carried in one hand.

'You've brought food? Oh, Keanu, thank you. It is so long since I tasted *hangi* meat and vegetables.'

She pushed the laptop to one end of the small table and hurried into the kitchen area, finding plates on her second foray into the cupboards and cutlery in the top drawer she expected it to be in.

Keanu had taken a cloth off the top of the delicacies in the basket and the aromas made Caroline's mouth water.

He divided the food onto the two plates, stopping when she protested it was too much. But the delicious, tender pork, the taro and potatoes disappeared from her plate in no time, conversation forgotten as the food took them back to happier times when they'd often attended island feasts.

'Were you dancing as I came in?' Keanu asked when she'd pushed her plate away unfinished, and he'd slowed down his eating enough to talk.

'Maybe moving just a little,' she admitted. 'As you've told me so many times, girls with European blood can't dance.'

He smiled, remembering, as she had been, and sadness for those lost days filled her soul.

Keanu read the sadness in her eyes and knew what she was thinking.

'Our childhood was truly blessed,' he said quietly.

He set down his knife and fork and pushed his plate away, but as Caroline stood up to take it, he reached out and took her hand, closing his fingers around hers.

Just that touch sent messages he didn't want to acknowledge streaming through his body, but he needed to say what he had to say.

'I want you to stay here tonight, Caro. The rabble-rousers—if it turns out to be more than one—will probably be too drunk to do anything other than sleep but in case they want more trouble, they certainly won't go door to door in the hospital quarters in search of you.'

She eased her hand out of his and stepped back.

'No way. They could attack the house,' she reminded him. 'Not find me there, and become angry, burn the place. I can't stay here, Keanu. I'll get Bessie and Harold to stay there with me if you really believe there's any danger.'

She hesitated, and he sensed she wanted to say more.

But she returned to gathering up the dishes, taking them to the kitchen, putting leftover food into the refrigerator—busywork while she avoided him in case he asked what was going on.

'Aren't you in charge over at the hospital?' she asked when she'd finished cleaning. 'If you don't mind, I'll stay here until the party is over, then track down Bessie and Harold to ask them about tonight.'

Bessie and Harold, both well into their sixties, would be fine protection. He supposed if she was insistent about staying in the house, he'd have to stay there too, which, in fact, would be preferable to both of them staying here, her in the bed—he'd insist on that—and him on the couch, aware in every fibre of his being that she was there, so close.

And how could he return to that bed when she'd departed?

Wouldn't he always feel her presence there? Smell the Caro scent of her on the sheets and pillowslip?

'I'll be over at the hospital,' he said, knowing he had to get away from her before he was completely tied in knots. 'Hettie's very worried about the ulcer—worrying if we've misdiagnosed it as it seems to be getting worse, not better. You call when you're going up to the house and I'll walk you up.'

For a moment he thought she'd argue, but instead she flipped him a snappy salute, said, 'Yes, sir!' and opened her notebook again.

She wasn't going to stop Keanu sleeping in the house— Caroline was only too aware of his stubbornness—but it would be better than having him sleeping in the big house somewhere far from her, rather than right next door, through partition walls that wouldn't hold back the essence of him that seemed to fill her whenever he was near.

Every time she closed her eyes she felt the kiss they'd shared in the graveyard—felt the longing in her body for them to have taken it further.

But wasn't it too soon?

Of course it was.

And he was married.

Her senseless mental meandering led nowhere so she

sighed, gathered up the books and was halfway up the hill before she remembered she was supposed to summon Keanu to guard her on her walk.

But Bessie and Harold were there, arguing on the track not far from her, so she was safe.

'We are staying at your place tonight and don't you argue, missy.'

She'd caught up with Bessie and Harold, and on this subject they were obviously united for Bessie spoke and Harold nodded his head very firmly.

Harold and Bessie she could handle in the house.

But Keanu?

He came at nine.

Bessie had made a salad to go with leftover pork from the feast, and she, Harold and Caroline had eaten it at the kitchen table, Bessie refusing to eat in the dining room.

'Makes me too sad to see that lovely chandelier and think of your grandma polishing each crystal,' she said, by way of explanation. And in truth Caroline felt much the same way—plus she still had papers spread across the table, and although it looked like a mess, she knew where to put her hand on every record there.

She was sitting on the swing seat on the front veranda, watching the last flights of the seabirds—dark whirling shadows against the early evening sky, returning to their roosts on the island.

They were a fairly good reflection of her thoughts at the moment—dark and whirling.

The cause of her distraction appeared on the track below the house, striding resolutely up from the hospital accommodation, clad now in linen shorts and a dark green T-shirt—a man at home in his environment.

And wasn't she at home in hers?

Of course she was and the shiver of whatever it was

that had coursed through her body was probably only relief at seeing him.

Except that she hadn't been frightened by the loud voice and accusations earlier and she was reasonably sure that man and all the others would have drunk themselves stupid and collapsed into bed by now.

'Evening,' he said, touching a forefinger to an imaginary hat.

'And good evening to you,' Caroline replied. She could do this—she really could. All she had to do was completely divorce herself from all the manifestations of attraction that the wretched man was causing in her body.

But when he sat down beside her on the swing, took her hand and began to push the swing gently back and forth with his foot, she lost what little resolve she'd managed to gather, rested her head on his shoulder and swung with him, just as they had so many times in the past.

The moon rose majestically from the water, the birds had quietened and a peace she hadn't felt for a long time spread through her veins.

So even when Keanu turned to press a light kiss on her shoulder she barely reacted.

That was if you could define a small electric shock as barely...

'Nice here, isn't it?' he said, and although she'd swear neither of them had moved, their bodies were now touching from shoulder to hip and their clasped hands were in Keanu's lap.

Worse was the cloud that had wrapped around them, some unseen yet almost tangible blanket of desire.

Or maybe he couldn't feel it.

Maybe it was just her.

Being silly.

Imagining things.

'Not going away, is it, this attraction?' he said quietly, and she knew it wasn't imagination.

'Not really,' she answered, although the truth would have been *not at all*.

He turned away from a fascination with the moon to look directly at her.

'So, how do we tell?'

'If it's love?' she asked, guessing his earlier experience of attraction had made it hard to use the word. 'I wonder…'

Although maybe she *knew*.

Didn't her heart beating faster when she caught a glimpse of him, or heard his voice or even thought of him suggest it had to be love?

Was lying sleepless in her bed, her body wired, wanting…?

Him!

Was that love?

Or was it old friendship mixed up with attraction?

For a long time he didn't speak, and she wondered if he'd been giving it the same thought she had but had come to a different conclusion.

'So much has happened between us,' he said quietly. 'I let you down once before, Caroline, and please believe me when I say that it hurt me too. Then marrying. Not telling you. I let you down again. But now—now I'd cut off my hand if it would help you to forgive me.'

Her heart was juddering in her chest, the beat every which way, while some kind of madness filled her mind— a madness begging her to take him to her bed, to rip off all his clothes and dispense with the agony that was attraction.

With Harold and Bessie here?

So lighten up!

'And what would I do with a bloody hand?' she teased, and though he laughed, she hadn't quite achieved her aim for he'd let go of her hand and wrapped his arm around her shoulders, drawing her closer, close enough to look into her eyes and probably see through them to the muddle in her head.

The kiss, when it inevitably came, was like nothing she'd experienced before. A barely there brush of lips on lips, then butterfly kisses across her cheeks, her eyelids and her temple.

With maddening deliberation, his mouth eventually returned to hers, but only to tease again, his teeth nibbling softly at her lips, tongue darting in to touch her tongue, withdrawing, darting, departing so her lips were hot then cool, and the pressure building within her was volcanic—a volcano about to blow.

He must have kicked with his foot, for the swing began to move again, and the movement lulled her senses, so when his tongue invaded her mouth and his hand brushed against her breast, she sighed and leaned into him, welcoming him, kissing him back, the intensity of the kiss growing until it blotted out her mind.

It was such a cliché, sitting on a porch swing, kissing like this.

Keanu was desperately trying to keep a grasp on reality, to keep his mind from going blank and letting his body take over all his actions.

They'd stop soon—well, they could hardly make love out here, especially not when there might be murderous miners wandering around.

But right now kissing Caroline was filling his soul with delight. His body wasn't quite so delighted, wanting more than fervid kisses.

Did he love her?

Her tongue was tangling with his, and he felt almost painfully aroused, but he couldn't break the kiss, couldn't pull his lips from hers, his arms from around her body.

She was his.

That was what the kiss was saying.

His kiss, and her response, making a statement.

About the future?

Or about attraction?

'Go to bed,' he whispered, his lips close to her ear. 'Maddie is back tomorrow, and a FIFO nurse is joining her, so we'll both have time off. We'll talk.'

'About?' she murmured back.

'About us, and our future, and attraction and love and all kinds of things.'

She smiled and kissed him gently on the lips, her eyes bright with unshed tears.

Tears of happiness this time, the brilliance of her smile told him that.

He stood up and pulled her upright, then turned her and nudged her towards the front door.

'I'll sleep on the couch out here. Reuben's got some sensible young men staked out around the veranda, and Harold's in a swag in the kitchen.'

He knew she was going to protest, so he kissed her again—swift and hard—then pulled back.

'Go,' he said.

CHAPTER ELEVEN

KEANU WAS DOWN at the hospital early—just the thought of Caroline asleep inside the house had been enough to keep him sleepless. Deciding to use the time productively, he stopped in at the office, realising it had been a couple of days since he'd dealt with his emails. He logged on to the computer and drummed his fingers as he waited for the screen to load.

And suddenly, there it was. An email from his solicitor in Cairns. So it was official—just like that, and without a word exchanged between him and his ex, his marriage was dissolved. He was a free man, although in truth he'd never been free. Not from the only person who'd ever held his heart. Just what did this mean for him and Caroline? In so many ways this wasn't the right time, but if not now, then when? If she could forgive him, then maybe, just maybe, she could love him.

But Keanu was roused from his musings by the sudden appearance of Sam in the office.

'Keanu, I'm glad you're here. I've just been looking at that ulcer again. The more I see it, the more convinced I am that we're dealing with something different here. I'd value a second opinion.'

Forcing his thoughts back to his work, Keanu nodded briskly. 'Of course. I agree that there's more to this than meets the eye. Has our patient said anything else about it to you?'

Sam shook his head as he pushed open the door to the ward, Keanu following right behind. They made their way to Raoul's bedside, where Keanu leant over to examine the uncovered wound.

'It's not looking good,' Keanu agreed, frowning in concentration.

'Not only that, but according to the limited testing I've been able to do, and our patient's response to the medication—or total lack of response—it just has to be something else, but I've no idea what eats away at the flesh so badly and just continues to degrade the wound.'

'Hydrofluoric acid.'

Keanu wasn't sure where the answer had come from, though apparently it had surfaced from some deep recess in his mind.

Which must have been working, for all he felt like a very confused zombie what with all that was happening in his personal life right now...

Sam turned to face him, grabbed his arm and steered him back out through the door.

'What did you say?'

'Hydrofluoric acid,' Keanu repeated, but with more certainty this time. 'Dreadful stuff. It just eats away at the skin and flesh and if you happen to drink it you're done for.'

'Well, I'm glad you kept that little bit of information to yourself until we were away from the patient. I don't think I've ever heard of it—though I probably did as a student—but I've never come across it as an acid burn. Except...' He paused in thought. 'Now I look at the wound as an acid burn it's starting to make sense. But this—what did you call it?'

'Hydrofluoric acid. It's the only acid that eats through glass so has to be kept in plastic containers. Years ago a very small concentration of it was used in a product for taking rust marks out of clothing but I think that's been banned now.'

'So why on earth would anyone have any of it on the fairly isolated islands of M'Langi? If it's as dangerous as you say, you can't just order a gallon or two off the internet.'

'I doubt a plane would carry it. But someone's brought it back here in hand luggage or by boat. Apparently there *are* places you can buy it. I imagine it has commercial uses of some kind or it wouldn't still be manufactured.'

Sam frowned at him.

'But why?'

Keanu heard the plane coming in, hopefully bringing relief staff, but Sam showed no desire to go rushing off to meet it.

'Keanu?'

Neither would he until he got an answer.

'It dissolves glass,' he repeated. 'And glass is made of sand, which is very degraded quartz, and gold comes in quartz veins. You pop a piece of gold-bearing quartz into a jar of hydrofluoric and, *voilà*, in a couple of days you have wee nuggets of gold.'

Sam was staring at him in disbelief.

'You're saying men steal gold-bearing quartz from the mine?'

He hadn't really been saying that—hadn't wanted to mention the matter at all—but they had a patient...

'Not all of them, and I'd say theft was rare back when the place was properly managed, but those who haven't been paid for a while probably feel they deserve it. Some of them might pinch it anyway—no one's perfect.'

He certainly had Sam's attention now.

'So, it's possible our patient had been fooling around with probably his father's acid and splashed some on his skin. Wouldn't he know?'

Keanu shook his head.

'Maybe not straight away, and when it started to hurt—
from all accounts it's extremely painful—he didn't want
to tell anyone about it because I'm sure he'd been forbid-
den to go near it, let alone open the lid of the container.
Sniffing the fumes in close quarters can do horrible things
to your lungs. No, he was hardly likely to tell his family
what he'd done.'

'Treatment?'

Again Keanu could only shake his head.

'I was a child when I heard about it and even if the treatment was discussed it would have gone over my head. Best
you get onto the internet or call the poisons centre back
in Oz.'

Sam sighed, but before he could say anything a gorgeous
and very pregnant young woman with short auburn curls,
startling green eyes and a smile that lit up the air around
her swept into the hospital.

'Maddie!' he and Sam cried in unison, holding out their
arms and somehow gathering her in a three-way hug.

Which was when Caroline walked in.

Now was not the time to fill Caro in on his divorce; instead, Keanu made the introductions.

'Maddie, this is Caroline Lockhart. She filled in for us
this week when the FIFO nurse didn't come.'

'And has been doing a great job,' Sam added.

He'd interrupted Keanu's, 'Caroline, this is Maddie Haddon, one of our favourite FIFO doctors.'

'Your only FIFO doctor now you've decided you'll be
permanent, Keanu,' Maddie corrected as she held out her
hand towards Caroline.

The introduction was interrupted as Bugsy, obviously
hearing his mistress's voice, came hurtling towards her.

Maddie crouched awkwardly to hug her ecstatic dog.

'So much for my walking him twice a day,' Sam complained, 'but now you're here, Maddie, do you know anything about hydrofluoric acid?'

Maddie looked a little startled but she accepted Sam's hand to help her upright again, and shrugged her shoulders.

'That's the stuff that melts glass so has to be kept in plastic containers,' she offered.

'I think we've already established that. Come through to the office and you can tell me all your news—check-up okay?—while I look up how to treat a hydrofluoric burn.'

They disappeared along the corridor, and Caroline followed Keanu into the young lad's room. He could feel her closeness—aware of her in a way he'd never been before.

'You think it's an acid burn?' she asked him, all business.

Keanu wasn't sure what to feel. Last night they'd sat together and talked of love and attraction, and his body clamoured to greet her with a kiss—at least a kiss...

But work was work.

Caroline was by the patient's bed, leaning forward to examine the wound, so Keanu joined her, pushing the swirl of emotions inside him out of his mind with the practicalities of work.

He bent over Raoul and spoke quietly to him.

'Did you spill something on your leg?'

The slightest of head movements, but definitely a very subdued yes.

'Can you tell me what it was?'

Another shake of the head, this one just as definitely negative.

'You're not going to get into trouble,' Keanu said gently, 'at least not from us, but we do need to know so we can treat it before it gets any worse.'

How he was enduring the pain now, Keanu didn't know, having heard horror stories of hydrofluoric burns.

'Calcium glucanate gel,' Sam announced, coming in to join them by the bed. 'We don't have it but I can make it up. In the meantime, Caroline, would you take a blood sample so can we check if it's affected his electrolytes and, Keanu, can you flush the wound again to remove the cream we've been using?'

He turned to Raoul.

'If you'd told us—' he began, but Keanu held up his hand.

'We've had that conversation and he's very sorry.'

Sam nodded and disappeared again, no doubt to mix the solution he needed.

Caroline tightened a ligature around Raoul's upper arm then tapped a vein inside his elbow. She was so aware of Keanu's presence she could feel her skin growing hot and tight.

While Keanu was doing nothing more than flush a wound?

Concentrating, remembering all her training, she slid the needle into the vein, released the ligature and drew out blood for testing, telling herself all the time that a strange conversation during one night on a swing didn't mean anything.

Or did it?

He said they'd talk.

She asked Raoul to hold the cotton-wool ball to the tiny wound while she set aside the phial and found some tape.

Professional, she could do it, for all her nerves were skittering with the…promise, maybe, that had been last night.

Pleased to escape Keanu's presence, she took the blood through to Sam.

'And?' Maddie prompted.

Caroline wondered if she looked as puzzled as she felt.

'And what?'

Maddie smiled at her.

'Just because I've been off the island doesn't mean I haven't been keeping up with the gossip. And that tells me that you and Keanu have renewed your old childhood friendship, though possibly the word *friendship* isn't quite enough to describe your relationship.'

'For heaven's sake, we've barely spent ten hours alone with each other and the gossip mill has us...'

She didn't have the words she needed.

'Practically married?' Maddie kindly put in.

Caroline sighed. Well, Keanu was married, just to somebody else, so no matter what island gossip suggested a real marriage between herself and Keanu wasn't even an outside possibility for the near future.

'Things haven't got quite that far,' she muttered, unwilling to share more with a virtual stranger.

'Well, there's still time,' Maddie said. 'Now, didn't Sam say you could take a break? Go home.'

Home.

The island *was* home to her and she'd been so happy here since her return. Disturbed by the problems, of course, and confused by her attraction to Keanu, but none of that had spoiled the feeling that she was back where she belonged.

Home.

Keanu.

What was *he* thinking?

Caroline sighed and headed up to the house, using the track past the lagoon, thinking a swim might clear her head.

But up at the house the bookwork beckoned. She hadn't got the maintenance and other day-to-day working figures of the mine from Reuben. Hoping he'd still be in the office there, organising the fencing off of the mine, she headed down the steep steps once again.

Keeping busy to keep her mind off Keanu.

But he was already there, sitting with Reuben in the shed.

Why wouldn't he be?

No reason, but something about the way the pair of them looked at her made her feel uneasy.

Keanu was the first to speak.

'We're just sorting out something here, Caro,' he said, and for some reason his voice sounded tight.

As if they'd been discussing her?

Of course they wouldn't have been...

'I'll see you later at the house,' he added, and knowing a dismissal when she heard it, she turned and headed back up the steps.

But halfway up she saw the faint marking of an old track, grassy now, and grown over with enthusiastic tropical vines and plants.

Had she been thinking of the grotto that she noticed it?

She certainly hadn't the last time she'd climbed the steps.

But her feet were already on the barely there track, picking their way through the tangled regrowth, quickening her pace where the track was clear but taking her time to find a way around where thorn bushes formed a barrier.

Hot and sticky, not to mention covered in burrs, she finally reached the pool where the water cascading down from the lagoon came to rest before trickling on past the village to the sea.

She breathed in the humid air, catching scents she couldn't quite identify, resting for a moment before turning towards the waterfall.

'You're being silly,' she told herself, speaking the words aloud in the hope they might stop this trek back into the past.

Didn't work, and she kept going, arriving eventually at the hidden space behind the waterfall, the water making music all around her, the thick fern growth giving the space a special magic.

He'd married someone else.

She told herself this was okay, only to be expected—of course he would have married, and it was only the small child she'd once been that was bleating *But he's mine* deep inside her head.

She sat on a rock, her clothes damp from spray, and tried to make sense of her life as it was—not as she'd once imagined it would be.

'Caro, are you in there?'

Keanu's voice.

How had he guessed?

And of course it wasn't anything to do with linked thoughts.

'Caro,' he called again, and this time she knew she'd have to answer.

'I'm in the grotto,' she called, and within minutes he was there beside her, sitting on what had always been 'his' rock.

'How did you know?' she asked.

'It was obvious that someone had been along the old track and as you were the only one stupid enough to be coming down here on your own, I just followed your trail.'

'Stupid enough?' she demanded, angry but not sure whether it was because her thinking time had been interrupted or because his presence always caused her tension.

'There could have been a landslip or a bit of the track washed away.'

'Well, there wasn't, and I'm quite safe, so you can go off and do whatever you were planning to do with Reuben.'

'Which was to come and see you,' Keanu told her, not as excited now as he'd been earlier, not quite as sure she was going to like the idea. And he'd already decided that now was not the time to mention his divorce. Other matters were more urgent after all.

'I was talking to Reuben about the mine. I talked to the elders about it yesterday, and spoke to your father this morning. Something you'd said about finding someone to invest in it—once we knew how much we needed—sparked a kind of shadow of an idea in my head, and it wasn't until yesterday at the funeral that I worked out what it was.'

He paused, waiting for a comment, perhaps a little excitement, or even a cool 'And?'

But there was no response so, feeling even more uncertain, he ploughed on.

'Reuben isn't the only islander with a son making good money on the mainland, so it seemed to me that the islanders themselves might like to invest in the mine, form a company of some sort, a co-op perhaps—and take it over.'

'Take it over?'

Caro's voice was scratchy.

'Completely?'

'That's why I had to talk to Max. I knew he'd know which way to go, the company or whatever, and of course he'd have to agree to the idea.'

'And he did? He's happy for the islanders to take over the mine?'

Keanu was worried now. He'd really expected excitement that he'd sorted out the problem, perhaps a little hesitation as Caro considered it. But not this flat, unemotional questioning.

Unable to work it out, he went with answering.

'Yes, of course. He was annoyed he hadn't thought of it himself. Of course, it can't happen overnight, but within maybe six months we could have the mine up and running again and money going into the hospital—that would still be part of the arrangement—with the shareholders benefiting as well.'

'And you never thought to talk to me about this?'

Not flat and unemotional now—no, now she was upset, although he couldn't fathom why.

'There's been no time,' he said, hoping to sooth whatever was bothering her. 'As you can imagine there's still so much to do. It's mainly been just contacting people.'

It was hard to see her expression in the gloom, but he saw the way she stood up, and knew from the way she held her body that she'd be glaring down at him.

'Contacting everyone but me!' she said. 'Do I not count? Wasn't I part of this save-the-mine project from the beginning? Wasn't I the one who got the books and put the figures together? Then suddenly it's all "Don't worry your little head about it, the men will fix it" and you don't even mention it to me?'

He stood too, and put a hand on her shoulder—a hand that was quickly shrugged off.

'Caro—' he began.

But she was already walking away, pausing only to say, 'You could have mentioned it as we sat on the swing, as we talked about love and what love was. I thought it was sharing, doing things together—not everything, that would be silly—but this was a joint project at the beginning, then suddenly it was all yours. I don't know how to feel, Keanu. I don't even know why I feel the way I do, when obviously it's the ideal solution for the mine, but right now I just have to get away by myself and try to work out what I really want from love.'

And with that she disappeared from the grotto, not going back along the track but climbing the rocks at the side of the waterfall.

She was as sure-footed as a cat, so he didn't worry about her going that way, and he knew it would be pointless trying to argue with her in the mood she was in, so he sat on his rock in the place where they'd practised getting married, and wondered just how things had gone so wrong.

She climbed the rocks to the top, skipped over the flat rocks where she'd sat with Keanu—had it been only a few days ago?

Keanu.

He'd sorted out the problem at the mine—or would eventually—and he'd spoken to her father.

But not to her.

Did he really know her so little he'd thought she wouldn't want to know?

After all the work she'd done on the figures, of course he had to know. Had to realise the responsibility—family responsibility—she felt towards it.

And didn't he even consider just how hard this might be—hearing that a chunk of her life, her heritage, had been taken from her without any discussion?

It wasn't that she wanted the blasted mine. As long as it continued to support the hospital, she couldn't have cared less what happened to it.

Somewhere deep inside she knew she was being silly, that it was just a mine. And she knew full well that without it the hospital couldn't keep going.

She made her way along the track to the house, still feeling wounded no matter how she tried to rationalise it.

Had Keanu talked to her about his idea, made her part of it right from the start, she knew she'd probably feel differently about it.

Probably even be as excited as he was about it.

She'd reached the hospital and was about to climb the hill to the house when Sam caught up with her, his face so serious she knew something was wrong.

Very wrong!

'You father phoned,' he said gently. 'Christopher has taken a turn for the worse. He'd like you home.'

Panic flooded her body. She'd always known this day would come. Known, too, that it was getting closer.

But now...

'He's sending a plane for you. You've got two hours. You father will send a car to meet the plane at Sydney airport.'

Caroline supposed she'd heard the words, but her total focus was on her brother, willing him to stay alive until she got there.

She'd been selfish, thinking only of her own unhappiness when she'd fled to the island, and now—

Shutting off *that* thought, she hurried up to the house.

Keanu left the grotto. He'd told Reuben he'd go over to Atangi to talk to the elders again—tell them he'd spoken to Max. Reuben was phoning them and they'd be waiting for him, no doubt filled with excitement and ideas about how they'd manage the mine.

He went down to the village where he kept a boat he'd bought from one of the locals almost as soon as he'd arrived back on Wildfire, half thinking he should have let Caro know where he was going, but he was already running late.

Plus, he needed to consider her reaction before he talked to her again. Out on the water he could think straight. Right now he felt there was a lot of thinking that needed straightening. Not only was the issue of the mine hanging between them but the knowledge that he had to tell Caroline that he was free, that his divorce was final worried at him too. Just how would she react to that news? Given the sour response to his plans for the mines and his ill thought-out decision to get the ball rolling without first consulting her, he imagined that trusting him with her heart was furthest from her mind right now…

He headed towards Atangi, easing the boat over the shallow part of the reef.

The little engine pushed them through the water and the tension he'd been feeling eased.

So *was* it love he felt for her?

Adult love?

Enough to build a future on? Now that he finally had a future?

It was hard to tell because he'd always loved her and even when he'd cut her out of his life rarely a day had gone by without something reminding him of her.

And now she was here, back on Wildfire where it had all begun, and he couldn't begin to work out...

What couldn't he work out?

Whether or not he loved her?

No, that part was settled, but there were so many different kinds of love.

No, he was playing with words.

He loved Caroline, and he was pretty sure that Caroline loved him. And if that was the case they could sort out the rest.

Hadn't they talked of love on the swing?

But had he *told* Caro that he loved her?

Had he actually said the words?

He tried to think but his mind went blank with shock at his own stupidity. That he, who knew Caro probably better than anyone else did, hadn't told her how he felt.

Her whole life had been filled with the uncertainty of love. Not that she spoke of it, or wallowed in self-pity. No, his Caro just got on with things. Like being left with her grandma for a start, then boarding school, and all the times her father hadn't come. Even Christopher kept his best smiles for his father.

So of course she'd be uncertain about his love, then taking the decisions about the mine away from her—that was how she'd have seen it—would have been the last straw.

He had to see her, tell her he loved her, that more importantly he was now free to love her. He'd start with that *then* sort out the mine business. He'd see the elders, go back to Wildfire.

Full of resolve, Keanu pulled into the harbour at Atangi, thinking not of the meeting but of the night ahead.

If only Keanu was here, Caroline thought as she flew over the Pacific. With him beside her she could face anything.

Was that what love was about?

Having someone to lean on, someone there to help you through the rough times as well as celebrate the good ones? She'd been stupid, reacting as she had to Keanu's suggestion about the mine co-op. She wasn't even sure why she'd reacted as she had.

And blaming Keanu...

Though if he really loved her, the way she now realised she loved him, wouldn't she be the first person to discuss it with?

Even before he knew it might actually work?

Of course not, that was a petty and stupid way to think.

She'd been unfair, but the calm way he'd announced *he'd* sorted out the mine problem, leaving her out completely, had temporarily blocked all rational thought and she'd struck out at him.

And now, heading further and further away from him, she couldn't tell him—couldn't say she was sorry and agree it was an ideal answer to the problem, even if she felt that a little bit of herself had been cut off.

In her head, the mine had been as much a part of Wildfire as the house she knew was home.

But stuff had gone from it and the house had still been home.

She'd phone Keanu as soon as she was in the car on the way to the hospital and tell him she was sorry.

Tell him she loved him.

Tell him she needed him?

Was it too soon for that?

CHAPTER TWELVE

RETURNING TO WILDFIRE, and heading straight to the house to tell Caro he loved her—this mission becoming more urgent by the moment—Keanu was disconcerted to hear she'd gone.

Because she was upset with him?

But Bessie was still explaining and he forced himself to listen.

Christopher…Sydney…charter flight…

He thanked Bessie and headed for his villa. Thankfully, he could get the regular flight out of here the next day. He sat at his computer, booking a flight from Cairns to Sydney, and arranging a hire car to be waiting at the airport.

Praying all the while—for Christopher, for Caro and for himself a little—hoping he hadn't left all he wanted to say until it was too late.

Mrs Phipps, the housekeeper, older now and somehow smaller, opened the front door of the Lockharts' Sydney house and squinted uncertainly up at him.

'Do I know you?'

'It's Keanu, Mrs Phipps. I used to come here sometimes during the holidays to play with Caroline and talk to Christopher.'

'Keanu?'

Her voice was slightly disbelieving.

'But you're much bigger now. You've grown. Of course you've grown! But welcome. You've come to be with Caroline, I suppose. They're up at the hospital—she and Dr Lockhart. Christopher's very poorly again.'

He didn't need to ask what hospital. There was an excellent private hospital just a few blocks away and the professional staff there all knew and loved Christopher, treating him with special care.

'Thank you, Mrs Phipps,' he said and turned away.

'But don't you want to leave your bag? You'll stay here surely?'

He looked down at the bag he was carrying, having decided a taxi was easier than a hire car in a city he didn't know well.

Would he stay here?

Would he be wanted?

He wished he were as certain as Mrs Phipps seemed to be.

'Best not,' he said, 'but thanks.'

And with that he headed down the ramp, out onto the street and up the road to where the hospital was built to look out over a part of Sydney's magnificent harbour.

With the money the twins' maternal grandparents had left in trust for Christopher, he would always have twenty-four-hour care, private hospitals and the best of doctors and specialists. So this hospital was a special place, and he would be getting the best possible treatment here.

But Keanu's heart quaked at the thought of Caro losing her brother. They might not have been physically close but there'd always been a special bond between them. Even as a child, if she woke with a nightmare in the night his mother would be sure to get a call the next morning to say Christopher wasn't well.

Poor Caro.

Would she let him comfort her? Take whatever support he could offer her?

Or had he hurt her too badly for that?

Once at the hospital, he asked a friendly receptionist if he could leave his bag behind her counter, then enquired about Christopher's whereabouts.

'He's in Room 22 on the second floor, but I think it might be family only. Dr Lockhart and his sister are in with him right now. He's very frail.'

The woman blinked back tears, and Keanu realised just how special Christopher was to all those who'd come in contact with him.

He tapped gently on the closed door of Room 22 then eased it open. Max was asleep in a big chair by the bed, while Caroline was sitting close to the bed, Christopher's hand clasped in hers, her head bent over it, possibly dozing as well.

He opened the door wider, and a slight squeak made her turn.

'Keanu?'

She mouthed his name, set Christopher's hand down on the bed and got up stiffly from the chair, easing out the door and closing it behind her.

'What are you doing here?' she demanded, but fairly weakly as her exhaustion clearly showed in the shadows under her eyes and the taut lines drawn in her skin.

'I hadn't said I loved you, really loved you—the now you not the past or anything else, just you,' he replied, and realised how lame it sounded when he saw the puzzled look on her face.

'I just wanted you to know. I know I don't deserve your love after the way I treated you, but somehow it seemed important to tell you anyway. We talked all around it at times, but on my way to Atangi it came to me that I'd never said the words. Not properly...

'There, I have more I need to talk to you about, much more, but that's the crux of it,' he added a little later, when the only reaction from the woman he loved had been a be-wildered stare.

'Now, how bad is Christopher? You look exhausted and I've never seen your father look so grey. Why don't you take him home for a proper sleep and I'll sit with Chris-topher? I'll call you the moment there's any change and don't bother about that stuff I said, just go home and rest for a while.'

'You'll sit with him?'

Teardrops sparkled on her eyelashes, and it was all he could do not to kiss them away.

'Of course I will. Don't you remember when he had measles at the island that time and I'd had them so I was okay and I sat with him every day? We like each other.'

Caro reached up and kissed his cheek.

'I'll get Dad,' she said, nothing more, but somehow Keanu felt it was enough.

For now...

Max and Caro left, Max shaking Keanu's hand in wel-come, and thanks and goodbye.

'We won't be long,' he promised, 'but don't hesitate to call if there's any change.'

'I won't,' Keanu promised, then he watched them walk away, Caro turning at the door to give him a puzzled look.

Keanu took his place in the chair Caro had been using and took Christopher's hand in his, holding what was little more than a bag of frail bones and skin very gently.

He massaged the skin, just rubbing it, and, remember-ing himself and Caro sitting with Alkiri, he began to talk, quietly but clearly.

'It's Keanu, mate. I've sent the others home to sleep. You're causing them a bit of worry at the moment. Any-way, I'm glad I've got this chance to sit with you because there's a lot I have to tell you. I love her, you see, your sister, though I'm not sure how she feels about me. For a while there, back on Wildfire, I thought she might love me back, but I've made a bit of a mess of things so it's hard to tell.'

He paused, then continued, this time gently rubbing Christopher's withered arm, spreading cream on it he'd found on the table by the bed.

'If she does love me, mate, I want to let you know that I'll never let her down. I did before because I didn't want to hurt my mum, and then again, recently, when I told her I'd married someone else. But you have to believe me, that part of my life is over, it's really over now that my divorce has finally come through. And I swear to you, Christopher, that I will never do anything to hurt her again. She's so special, your sister, that she deserves the very best, and although I know I'm not that, I'd do my darnedest to become it just for her.'

Was it his imagination or had Christopher's eyes fluttered open, just momentarily?

Keanu kept talking, moving to the other side of the bed to put cream on the hand and arm over there. He talked of the island, of how well the hospital was doing and how much his family had done for the people of M'Langi.

He talked about the day outside, cool but cloudless so the sun sent sparkly diamonds of light dancing across the waters of the harbour.

'I guess you've seen it like this before if they always put you in this room, but it's magic to me. I'd like to buy her a diamond, but then I think of her eyes and wonder about sapphires. I don't suppose you have any idea of her stone preferences? Not that she's likely to want anything from me. I kind of did something that upset her.'

And this time the eyelids definitely fluttered, and Keanu could have sworn he'd felt a tiny bit of pressure from the claw-like hand clasped in his.

'But I guess if she doesn't love me, there's not much I can do.'

Definite pressure this time. Keanu looked up at the nurse who'd remained in the room to do the regular obs and update Christopher's chart.

'Did he move his fingers?' the young man asked. 'I'm sure he did, and his eyelids fluttered as well.'

'I'd better get the family back,' the nurse said.

'They won't have had much sleep.'

The nurse was obviously torn.

'I'll give them another ten minutes and phone the house. The housekeeper will know whether to wake them.'

'Maybe suggest she wake Caroline. I'm sure Dr Lockhart has been more sleep deprived than she has.'

The nurse did his checks, agreed that all the signs were that Christopher might be improving, then left the room.

'Of course you're improving,' Keanu said. 'I'll want you around for the wedding, you know. That's if she'll have me.'

He took a deep breath and put all thoughts of love and weddings out of his mind.

'Do you remember,' he said, letting go of his hand and moving down to massage Christopher's toes now, 'how we took you swimming in the lagoon that time you were visiting? Mum put you in a life jacket and we all lay on our backs in the water and looked up at the sky through the canopy of the rainforest.'

Christopher's eyes, so like Caroline's, opened slightly and Keanu could swear he was actually looking at him.

Christopher's smile might be but a shadow, but Keanu's answer was a broad grin.

'And what about when we took you down to Sunset Beach in your wheelchair but the path was too steep and we tipped you out, and when we got you back in, we had to spend ages wiping red sand off you so your nurse and Mum wouldn't know?'

Open eyes *and* a smile!

Keanu's hand surged with joy.

'Oh, Christopher, we had such fun!'

'Didn't we?' a quiet voice said, and Keanu looked up to see Caro on the other side of the bed.

'Where did you come from? I thought the nurse was going to let you sleep for ten minutes before she rang the house.'

Caroline came into the room and sat down in the chair she'd been in earlier. She took Christopher's other hand in hers, leaned forward to kiss his cheek, then finally looked at Keanu.

'I never left,' she said. 'I went as far as the lift with Dad then thought of something.'

She hesitated, heart pounding, knowing what she wanted so much to say, but still held back by uncertainties she couldn't name.

'Thought of something?' Keanu prompted.

She nodded, saw Christopher's eyes open, looking at her, urging her on, it seemed.

'I hadn't told you I loved you either. I'd wanted to but I hadn't. I was upset about the mine business—stupid really when it's a good idea—then Dad phoned to say he'd sent the plane to bring me home and all I could think about was Christopher. Then, when I came back just now, I heard you talking to him—I stood and eavesdropped and put my finger to my lips so the nurse wouldn't betray me and now I want to tell Christopher something too.'

She lifted his hand and pressed her lips to it.

'I love this man Keanu, Christopher, and I do hope you approve because without him I don't think I could go on. He is part of me, part of my heart and soul, and always has been, and now that I understand why he broke away, well,

I love him even more, because that was done from love—love for his mother.'

She reached across the bed and took Keanu's hand in hers.

'And in case Christopher didn't tell you, I like sapphires.'

Max, alerted by the nurse, came in to a surprising tableau. His son, who'd been lingering close to death for days, was not quite alert, but definitely had his eyes open and a lopsided smile on his face, while his daughter shone with luminous radiance, sitting with her hand linked in Keanu's across the bottom of the bed.

And Keanu's face wasn't exactly doleful either.

'You two got something to tell me?' he asked.

'I'd like to marry your daughter,' Keanu said.

'But not right away, Dad,' Caroline assured him. 'There's a lot of stuff to sort out at the island and when we're married there, I want it to be the perfect, happy, heavenly place it used to be.'

'I presume you'll let me know a date,' Max said, smiling at the pair. 'Now, I'm sure you've got plenty to say to each other so leave me with my son, and go make your plans.'

* * * * *

LET'S TALK
Romance

For exclusive extracts, competitions
and special offers, find us online:

facebook.com/millsandboon

@MillsandBoon

@MillsandBoonUK

Get in touch on 01413 063232

For all the latest titles coming soon, visit
millsandboon.co.uk/nextmonth

MILLS & BOON

THE HEART OF ROMANCE

A ROMANCE FOR EVERY READER

MODERN

Prepare to be swept off your feet by sophisticated, sexy and seductive heroes, in some of the world's most glamourous and romantic locations, where power and passion collide.

HISTORICAL

Escape with historical heroes from time gone by. Whether your passion is for wicked Regency Rakes, muscled Vikings or rugged Highlanders, awaken the romance of the past.

MEDICAL

Set your pulse racing with dedicated, delectable doctors in the high-pressure world of medicine, where emotions run high and passion, comfort and love are the best medicine.

True Love

Celebrate true love with tender stories of heartfelt romance, from the rush of falling in love to the joy a new baby can bring, and a focus on the emotional heart of a relationship.

Desire

Indulge in secrets and scandal, intense drama and plenty of sizzling hot action with powerful and passionate heroes who have it all: wealth, status, good looks…everything but the right woman.

HEROES

Experience all the excitement of a gripping thriller, with an intense romance at its heart. Resourceful, true-to-life women and strong, fearless men face danger and desire - a killer combination!

To see which titles are coming soon, please visit

millsandboon.co.uk/nextmonth

JOIN US ON SOCIAL MEDIA!

Stay up to date with our latest releases, author news and gossip, special offers and discounts, and all the behind-the-scenes action from Mills & Boon...

 @millsandboon

 @millsandboonuk

 facebook.com/millsandboon

 @millsandboonuk

It might just be true love...

GET YOUR ROMANCE FIX!

Get the latest romance news, exclusive author interviews, story extracts and much more!

blog.millsandboon.co.uk